PRAISE FOR THE FIRST RIVETING THRILLER STARRING MANHATTAN ASSISTANT D.A. SUSAN GIVEN

GIVEN THE CRIME

"Immensely amusing debut suspenser. . . . This kick-off in a series barrels along on a gift for witty dialogue that already sounds like a top TV crime show. Great entertainment."

—*Kirkus Reviews*

"A first novel that is both amusing and deadly."

—*Rocky Mountain News* (CO)

"Great debut in what I hope is a new crime series. . . . Refreshing tongue-in-cheek approach. . . . A welcome addition to the legal procedural sub-genre."

—*Painted Rock Reviews*

"Reminiscent of the hard-boiled novels of Raymond Chandler. . . . A thoroughly enjoyable read with a satisfying ending."

—*Library Journal*

GIVEN THE EVIDENCE

GIVEN THE EVIDENCE

MARGARET BARRETT
and
CHARLES DENNIS

POCKET STAR BOOKS
New York London Toronto Sydney Tokyo Singapore

A Pocket Star Book published by
POCKET BOOKS, a division of Simon & Schuster Inc.
1230 Avenue of the Americas, New York, NY 10020

Copyright © 1998 by Rangeloff-Century, Inc.

Originally published in hardcover in 1998 by Pocket Books

ISBN: 0-671-00154-X

First Pocket Books paperback printing March 1999

10 9 8 7 6 5 4 3 2 1

POCKET STAR BOOKS and colophon are registered trademarks of Simon & Schuster Inc.

Cover design and illustration by Matt Galemmo

Printed in the U.S.A.

For Kim Eveleth

Acknowledgments

Thanks to my lifelong friend Lorne Weil for use of his house in Montauk, where much of this book was written; to Berry Perkins, who runs the bar down the beach from Ascension's; to Emile Riley Abdelnour and Geoffrey Holder for their special insights into island life; to Georg Stanford Brown for inspiring Desmond Wilmot; to the late Eric Donkin, who will cross the Henry Morgan lobby throughout eternity; to Sid Ganis, who is breathing life into Susan Given off the printed page; to Paula Prentiss and Richard Benjamin, Myra and Earl Pomerantz, Robin Dearden and Bryan Cranston, Luisa and George Bloomfield, Betty and Peter Langs, Ruth and Lou Jacobi, Sol and Rita Dennis, Donna and Dan Aykroyd, Barbara and Ed Astrin, Susan and Fred Milstein, Joan and Augie Schellenberg, Audrey Mills Hall and Alan Bleviss, Rebecca and Steven Dennis, Cynthia and Bob Sherwood, Ken Welsh, Nuala Boylan, Josh Mostel, Kate Rudman, Osgood Perkins, Amanda Mettler, Michael Marsh, Emily Rudman, Elvis Perkins, Michele Scarabelli, Brian Cox, Tracey Washington, Harvey Korman,

ACKNOWLEDGMENTS

Margot Kidder, Mark Hammond, Kathy Wenning, John Banks, Janice Fischer, Larry Dobkin, Andora Hodgin, and Dabney Coleman for their continued support.

Long overdue thanks to Bill Gross, who originally commissioned this series of books, and to Amy Pierpont, who has edited them so ably and enthusiastically. A special nod to Michael Dennis and Macey Dennis, who with our mother Sade continue to be cheerleaders nonpareil.

Finally, thanks to Peggy Barrett, without whom I could never write these books (and vice versa).

Charles Dennis
New York City
April 1998

"You must not tell us what the soldier, or any other man said, sir," interposed the judge, "it's not evidence."

—DICKENS

GIVEN THE EVIDENCE

1

SHE STOOD ALONE on the terrace. The ferocity of the wind blowing from the East River froze her hand, numbing it. She desperately needed that hand to fire the gun that could save her life.

"You're not gonna shoot me," he said, advancing on her menacingly.

"Why not?" asked the pretty blonde, clasping her left hand over her right to warm it up and get a better grasp on the weapon.

"Cuz your kinda people don't do things like that. You haven't got the killer instinct."

"Don't come any closer," she warned, pushing long strands of hair away from her face. "This is self-defense."

"Hit me with your best shot," he sang tauntingly. "Come on and hit me with your best shot. Let's go, Susan. You better shoot or I'm gonna snap your neck like a twig."

He lumbered toward her, the Incredible Hulk stalking his prey. She shut her eyes and pulled the trigger. Again and again and again.

She opened her eyes and gasped. He was still standing. Blood was pouring from the multiple entry wounds in his powerful torso but he didn't seem to mind.

"My turn," grinned the Hulk, placing his powerful hands on her neck and squeezing the life out of her. "Say bye-bye, Ms. D.A."

Susan screamed. Long and shrilly, which amazed her since the Hulk had effectively cut off any air to her windpipe.

"Mom! Mom! Wake up!"

Susan Given opened her eyes and saw her fourteen-year-old adopted Salvadoran daughter, Polly, standing over her bed.

"What's wrong, Polly? Are you all right?"

"Like, I'm not the one who was screaming, Mom."

"Screaming?" Susan glanced over at the illuminated digital clock on her bedside table. 4:30 A.M. "Jeepers! What are you doing up at this hour, Polly?"

"You woke me, Mom. It was that dream again, wasn't it?"

"What dream?"

"The one where that man's trying to kill you."

"How do you know about that?"

"The dream or the real thing?"

"I'm sorry I woke you, Polly. Please, go back to sleep."

"I wish Michael was here."

"What does Michael have to—"

"Why did you break up with him?"

"We weren't going together—"

"Duh! You were sleeping with him, Mom."

"I was not!"

"Mom, I'm not a fool. His agent phoned from Los Angeles one night and when I went to his room to wake him he wasn't there. Where was he? Hmm? Then I heard the noises coming from this room."

"You didn't!! What sort of noises?"

"Smoochy noises. You know."

"Oh, jeepers! You weren't supposed to know about us. I wanted to keep it a secret. Well, not a secret secret but separate. Until . . ."

"When? After your death?"

"You have a wonderful sense of humor, Polly. Does your father know about us?"

"I didn't tell him. Ivy's the snitch in this family."

"Ivy knows!?" Susan was horrified that her younger daughter—also adopted, also Salvadoran—had knowledge of her affair with writer Michael Roth.

"Ivy only knows what time *Xena: Warrior Princess* comes on. And what time the candy store on Lex closes."

"Where is she now?" asked Susan, looking around for her ten-year-old daughter in the semidarkness.

"Fast asleep. Nothing wakes her. So why'd you break up with him?"

"I didn't," replied Susan stubbornly. "Michael and I are just on a break from each other."

"You're weird, Mom."

"Thank you for your loyalty."

"Oh, God!" groaned Polly. "You're so New England! You need help. If you broke your arm, you'd go to a doctor. You're having a breakdown."

"I am *not* having a breakdown."

"Even Dad thinks—"

"I don't care what your father thinks, Polly. He and I are not—"

"He *is* a shrink, Mom, and he feels, after what you've been through, you could use a little help."

"I . . . don't . . . need . . . any . . . help!"

3

2

PASSING BY THE PRETTY BLONDE attempting in vain to light up her cigarette, one might think her hand was trembling from the nip in the air that early March morning. But, on closer examination, it was apparent that Susan Given was more visibly annoyed than cold as she stood outside the building on Fifth Avenue staring in defiance at the brass plate that read "Imogen Blythe, M.D."

Susan held all psychiatrists in contempt; she had been forced to socialize with far too many of them during the course of her almost twenty-year marriage to Hugh Carver (a man she considered an absolute nut job and with whom she had been locked for three years in a Promethean struggle to obtain a divorce). But when Manhattan District Attorney William Archibald finally made the "polite request" that his chief of the Asset Forfeiture Unit pay Dr. Blythe a visit, Susan was forced to acquiesce to her boss's thinly disguised order.

"I'm glad you finally came," said Imogen Blythe, a willowy, fortyish brunette with a perfectly oval face and a smoky voice that seemed better suited for women's perfume commercials than plumbing the depths of the psyche. "Bill was very concerned about you."

4

Susan resented what she considered the unnecessary use of the word "finally" and was even more put off by the woman's overly familiar "Bill." Mr. Archibald was old enough to be this woman's father. What was her relationship to the legendary, handsome District Attorney? But the Chief of the Asset Forfeiture Unit merely flashed her patented polite Greenwich, Connecticut, smile, pushed her tumbling hair off her forehead—she'd have to get it cut one of these days—and said: "I have a very busy schedule."

"Too busy, perhaps?"

"Crime never sleeps," said Susan, reciting her mantra.

"What about you? How are you sleeping these days?"

Is this a trick question? wondered Susan. Do I say "alone" because I banished my lover to California? Or "not well" because of the recurring nightmare for the past ten weeks? How much does this woman know?

"How much do you know?" asked Susan. "About me?"

"Only what I read in the newspapers and what I saw on TV. You're an assistant district attorney and you were involved in a pretty harrowing situation around Christmas."

"Harrowing was hardly the word," said Susan. "You're remarkably diplomatic for a psychiatrist."

"You can smoke if you want to," said Imogen.

"Psychic, too," said Susan, reaching into her red leather briefcase for a cigarette. "My husband positively forbade his patients to smoke in his presence. Felt that was coddling them."

"Your husband is a shrink?"

"Was my husband. Is a shrink."

"Given. Given. I don't think I know—"

"Given's my name. His name is Hugh Carver."

"Oh, I *am* sorry." When Susan burst out laughing, Imogen added hastily: "I didn't mean it to sound like that."

"Do you know Hugh?"

"Yes."

"Then you meant it. I understand. I think we'll get along fine, Dr. Blythe."

"Why are you here?"

"Mr. Archibald insisted. He wanted me to take a leave of absence following the 'harrowing' incident at Christmas. I preferred to bury myself in my work."

"Perhaps the work is burying you."

"Did Mr. Archibald say that?"

"No. He just thinks you're stressed. You *did* kill a man."

"It was self-defense!"

"I didn't say murder, Ms. Given. What happened?"

"Don't you read the tabloids? Ray Murphy chronicled everything."

"Tell me about it."

"I run the Asset Forfeiture Unit. We seize criminals' ill-gotten gains and use the confiscated money to combat crime. Mostly drug money and prostitution. Then last year we went after the private garbage companies. Mob controlled. Nicolo Tesla is the head of the cartel and his son Junior—well, Junior was stalking me and my children. Did you ever know Abner Rosenthal?"

"The psychiatrist? The one who vanished?"

"Yes. He was Junior's therapist. Not the safest person to have as a patient. What's wrong, Doctor?"

"This all happened?" asked a stunned Imogen. Then hastily: "Not that I don't believe you, Ms. Given."

"Call me Susan."

"And please call me Imogen. I just don't hear stories like this every day. When we spoke on the phone, you mentioned not sleeping."

"I have this recurring dream. Junior Tesla is still trying to kill me. I shoot him and shoot him and shoot him and he still keeps coming. It's very disturbing, Imogen."

"Crime never sleeps."

"I beg your pardon?"

"That's what you said when you first came in here. It's relentless. It never stops. Neither do you, Susan. Junior's just a symbol of your work. You've got to stop for a while. You've got to give yourself a break."

"I can't! The office will fall apart without me. I'm the only one who—"

"How are your children?"

"Oh, they're wonderful!"

"Do you spend much time with them?" asked Imogen.

"As much as I can. They're with Hugh Tuesday and Thursday nights and alternate weekends. Well, not exactly alternate. Being Hugh, he worked out a bizarre schedule that only an insurance actuary could appreciate or understand."

"Do you have someone in your life?"

"Yes. But I've put him on hold."

"How does he feel about that?"

"Not great."

"I'll bet. How do you feel about it?"

"I haven't got time to feel anything, Imogen. I am dedicated to my work. I'm a Virgo."

"Have you always been like this?"

"A Virgo?"

Imogen laughed, then asked: "Do you think you might be a touch obsessive?"

"I believe in a work ethic. When I take on a job, I see it through."

"No matter what the price?"

"I don't follow."

"Susan, you just lived through something that most people only see at the movies. But it wasn't a movie. It really happened. To you. And your family. You can't ignore it. There's psychic damage here whether you want to accept it or not. You need to take a break. A rest. A vacation."

"This summer. I've got the girls this summer."

"Sooner, Susan. Do it sooner."

3

WAS IT REALLY fifty years ago? Longer. On the eve of his induction into the Navy, Archie paid a visit to his father in Washington. Jack Archibald ushered his son into the library and introduced him to his new assistant. The younger Archibald stared up at the tall, blond, blue-eyed Adonis standing by the bay window, leafing through the latest issue of *Esquire*.

"Dwight? This is my son Bill. But we all call him Archie. Son, this is Dwight Pelham. Remember that name. Years from now, you'll tell his biographer how you first met him here ogling a scantily clad Varga girl."

"I was reading an article on General Patton," protested Pelham, snapping the magazine shut and holding his large hand out to Archie. "Your dad's told me a lot about you, Bill. Helluva student, he says. Helluva piano player, too."

"I want you boys to be friends," said Jack Archibald, oblivious to the fact that his son was nine-teen and his assistant was thirty-two.

The "boys" became more than friends. Dwight Pelham was the big brother William "Archie" Archibald never had. He took the younger man under his wing and introduced him to the best and most discreet brothels wartime Washington had to offer. He showed Archie how to get around the tyranny of ration books so that the young man's Studebaker was always brim-filled with gasoline. He taught him what cologne made the ladies purr most and how to mix the best martinis in the District of Columbia. And when Jack Archibald's only son finally shipped out to the Pacific, Dwight Pelham hosted a farewell dinner of such bacchanalian legend that it remained the measure for future generations of party animals in the nation's capital.

"Mr. Archibald? . . . Sir?"

The Manhattan District Attorney came out of his reverie and stared at Ned Jordan standing across the desk from him in his Hogan Place office. How long had the Federal Prosecutor been trying to get his attention?

"I'm sorry, Ned," said the District Attorney. "This brings back so many memories. I've known Dwight Pelham for over half a century. I'm loath to believe the charges against him."

"Mr. Archibald, I can assure you we wouldn't be proceeding in this matter if we didn't have sufficient proof of—"

"Ned, please understand. I am not trying to defend the man. Far from it. I've read hundreds of pages of evidence. You have a solid case. The Overseas International Credit Bank under the stewardship of Nassim Narouz is nothing less than an abomination. OICB's banking practices in Europe have flagrantly abused international laws as we know them. Their direct links with drug lords and terrorists

10

are an insult to the financial community. I don't understand how Dwight could have been drawn into business with these people."

"He always wanted to run a bank." Ned Jordan shrugged. "Narouz gave him American Patriot to play with."

"And Dwight, in exchange, gave Narouz his soul," sighed Archibald. "How do you want to proceed?"

"My boss is afraid if we take American Patriot to court first and lose, Pelham and Levenstein will get away scot-free. Under the Constitution's double jeopardy principle, we wouldn't be able to prosecute them again. So we thought—we hoped—you might go after them first here in Manhattan. If you win, great. If not, we will have learned by your mistakes."

"Asset forfeiture?"

"Makes sense to me," said Jordan. "Susan would be the perfect person to prosecute."

"I'm not sure if Ms. Given could handle this case at the present time."

"Susan? Come on, sir. You know she's the best—"

"I don't know anything until I see the psychiatric evaluation." Then Archibald shook his head sadly. "Susan isn't Susan anymore."

4

SUSAN GIVEN WAS AWARE of the fact that Alvin Gasmer's lips were moving but she couldn't explain her inability to hear a single word he was saying. The usual, constant drone of traffic and construction floated up from Centre Street but not enough to drown out the nasal whine of the pop-eyed, toucan-beaked lawyer who represented the Tesla family.

"Well?" Gasmer finally asked.

Susan heard this last word and heaved a mental sigh of relief in knowing she had not gone deaf. She had merely drifted off again in the middle of a conversation, a recent and unfortunate habit she would definitely have to get under control.

"I'm sorry, Mr. Gasmer. Could you repeat that again?"

"Is this a joke, Ms. Given? What part of the last twenty minutes did you miss?"

"I'm glad you've kept a sense of humor about this."

"When is the judge going to appoint a permanent receiver, Ms. Given? I find it humiliating for both myself and my client that I must appear in your office every week begging for the subsistence money to keep him and his family alive."

"You must be joking," said Susan, whose unit had

been acting as temporary receivers for the mob-controlled garbage companies since the forfeiture proceedings began against them in early March. "Subsistence? We're not talking about welfare recipients, Mr. Gasmer. These are not people living in some hellhole in Washington Heights." Her eyes glanced down in disbelief to the formal petition typed on the lawyer's firm's embossed letterhead. "Twenty-five thousand a week? Surely you mean a month."

"The request is not unreasonable," replied Gasmer without blinking. "The mortgage payments on Mr. Tesla's Glen Cove property, his vacation home in Florida, payments on his vehicles . . ."

"Why does he need eight automobiles?"

"Not to mention the round-the-clock nurses attending his wife, his daughter, and himself since the recent tragedy . . . which you are only too aware of."

"What the hell does that mean?" asked Susan, losing her cool in a most uncharacteristic fashion. "They must pay you an awful lot of money to abandon all sense of morality, honor, and decency."

"I resent that remark."

"A woman was killed. An innocent, unsuspecting woman, Mr. Gasmer, and I was tortured by your client's son. I still have nightmares about it. So don't you dare come into this office and try to do a number about responsibility and tragedy."

"Perhaps I should come back another time." Gasmer began to rise from his chair, realizing he had, indeed, gone too far in attempting to bait the Assistant District Attorney.

"Why doesn't your client just dip into his Swiss

bank account? Why doesn't he sell some of his wife's jewelry? Has his restaurant become a charitable institution?" Susan was now backing a retreating Gasmer toward the door.

"They need money for the week," bleated the lawyer. "The other carters have all received—"

"Go and see my assistant," Susan said, curtly nodding in the direction of Alan Becker's door down the hall. When the lawyer had left, she slammed her office door shut, walked over to her briefcase, delved into it, pulled out a fresh pack of Salem Lights, opened it, and murmured to herself: "Next week I'll quit."

There was a knock at the door.

"What?" It was more of a bark than a question.

The door opened and Gretchen, her slender, even-tempered African-American secretary, entered warily.

"Is it safe to come in?" asked Gretchen.

"No," replied Susan, sucking the smoke deep into her lungs. "What's wrong?"

"Alvin Gasmer is making ugly noises about going to see Lydia. He says you're being unprofessional."

"Let him dare."

"Did you give him any money?"

"No."

"Susan, you have to give him money. You're the receiver. If he goes to the judge—"

"I'll give him his money. But I'm not giving him twenty-five thousand a week. That's ridiculous. How much did we give DeFillipo or Gerussi or—"

The telephone rang and Susan nodded at Gretchen, who picked up the phone and said: "Susan

14

Given's office . . . Oh, hello . . . I'm not sure."
Gretchen covered the mouthpiece and told her boss:
"It's Michael Roth."

"Not here," whispered Susan, shaking her head.

"I'm not going to tell him that. He's phoned every
day this week."

"I can't talk to him now," said Susan.

"He's your boyfriend," hissed Gretchen.

"He is not," mouthed Susan. Then aloud: "How
does everyone know about Michael? Is there no concept of privacy anymore?"

Gretchen held the receiver out to Susan, who
finally took it from her with great reluctance. Then
her secretary left the office discreetly.

"Hello, Michael," said Susan frostily.

"I'm not trying to sell you insurance."

"What are you talking about?"

"The tone in your voice. Eskimos would have trouble dealing with that chill."

"This isn't a good day."

"It hasn't been a good week or a good month,
Susan."

"How have you been, Michael? How's L.A.?"

"Do you care?"

"Did you call me long distance to pick a fight? I
have Hugh to fight with. That's more than enough."

"What's happening with the divorce?"

"What's happening in North Korea? Some things
never change."

"Susan, I'm worried about you."

"Thank you very much, Michael. But I'm doing
just fine."

"I'd like to see you."

"Not right now. I'm very busy."

"What's wrong? What happened? We had a wonderful relationship, I thought."

"I just can't handle it right now. Remember what I said in Israel when we first met? 'Thank God, you don't live in New York.' It's true. I can't handle work and a relationship and raise my daughters."

"You need to take a break."

"Why does everyone keep telling me that?" asked Susan irritably.

"Because it's obvious to everyone except you. Take a leave of absence. Go away somewhere. Far away from crime. I'd love to take you somewhere."

"Michael, please, don't!"

"Let me finish, Susan. I know you won't go with me. I don't expect you to. But go somewhere. Soon. Okay?"

Susan hung up the phone and for a moment allowed herself to think of those nights in Michael's arms. Making love until they both collapsed with exhaustion. No! She wouldn't think of that anymore. There was far too much work to do. Crime does not sleep.

The telephone rang on her desk and she answered it with her trademark: "Given."

"Where the hell are you?" The voice belonged to Lydia Culberg, the deputy district attorney and Susan's mortal enemy.

"I'm in my office, Lydia. Where would you like me to be?"

"Where would I like you to be, sweetie? How 'bout in court?"

"What are you talking about?" asked Susan nervously.

"The Matador. Remember? You were due in court ten minutes ago. Judge Halloran is not a happy camper."

"That's impossible! The Matador case isn't until . . ." Susan stared down at her desk diary and saw that it was open to the wrong week. "Jeepers! I'll be right there."

Susan felt dizzy for a moment as she rose from her desk and grabbed her briefcase. Maybe I *should* take a vacation, she thought.

5

THE ANCIENT AND RICKETY elevator came to rest on the ground floor of the Lefkowitz Building and Susan thanked Delbert, the harelipped operator, for getting her there safely.

"It was nothing," said Delbert, anticipating the door's opening and Susan's departure. But the door did not open.

"What's wrong?" asked Susan.

"It must be stuck," said Delbert, in the mangled tones that required years of careful listening to comprehend.

"I beg your pardon?"

"The door won't open."

"Please, open the door, Delbert! I have to get over to Thomas Street. I'm very late."

"Not my fault."

This last statement emerged as "Fot fy fall" and Susan became more unwound.

"Isn't there an emergency bell you should ring? Someone to notify? I can't just stand here like this." Susan began pounding on the elevator door with her fists.

On the third pound the doors opened, as if by

magic, and Susan found herself staring up at her old friend, Ned Jordan, the federal prosecutor.

"Hey, Delbert! You been putting the moves on Ms. Given?"

"The door was stuck!" bellowed an outraged Delbert.

"C'mon, Del," teased Jordan, "everyone's known your reputation for years. You run this elevator like your private boudoir."

"This never happened before," said Delbert, not quite sure how he felt about his new Casanova image.

"Please, excuse me, Ned," said Susan, whose path was blocked by the handsome black prosecutor. Jordan's not-so-secret crush on Susan dated back to his days in the District Attorney's Office.

"Were your ears burning, Susan? Mr. Archibald and I were just talking about you."

"Can't talk now, Ned! Late, late."

Rushing across the dimly lit, tiled lobby of the classic Art Deco building, Susan ran smack into a petite brunette with a look of grim determination on her face.

Susan muttered something and kept moving until the woman called after her in a hoarse voice.

"Hey, Greenwich! You ever heard of 'Excuse me'?"

Susan turned around and recognized Janie Moore, her best friend and an assistant district attorney in the homicide unit. The buxom, violet-eyed Ms. Moore normally possessed the mouth of a stevedore and mercilessly ragged Susan's sex life, upbringing, and ladylike manner. But this morning something was clearly bothering the homicide A.D.A.

"Excuse me, Janie. It's just that I'm late for court

and Lydia's on the rampage. What's wrong? You look awful."

"Homicide never agrees with me right after breakfast. You know how delicate I am, Greenwich. Plus our old friend Lisa Mercado turned up with her news truck demanding an exclusive like I owed her . . ."

"What happened to your voice?"

"I tore my vocal chords shouting at some misogynist cops this morning. I have become inured to garden variety murders but then a sick fuck like this asshole rapist rears his head and I just smell Rice Krispies."

"Rice Krispies?"

"Stella made the name up." Stella was Janie's daughter and a classmate of Ivy's at Balmoral School. "Kevin and I were trying to explain the concept of a serial murderer to her when she was smaller and that was the best her mental Cuisinart could come up with."

"Who was murdered? When? Where?"

"Central Park. Early this morning. Around 110th Street. Female jogger. Blond. Twenty-three years old. Surprised you didn't hear me chewing out those cops when you were on your run."

"I haven't run in ages." Susan glanced nervously at her watch. "I'm really late, Janie. Maybe we'll have lunch next week."

"You aren't running? That's like the Postal Service calling it quits. What's wrong, Greenwich?"

"Nothing is wrong," snapped Susan, rushing away from Janie. "Why does everyone think something's wrong?"

6

TWO YEARS EARLIER, Dick Rashley, another A.D.A., had innocently asked Susan to do him "a little favor." Rashley was forsaking the District Attorney's Office to accept a lucrative job in the private sector and was speedily clearing his desk before he left. There remained only one final case that needed someone's attention, and perhaps Susan could lift that last load off Dick's shoulders and transfer it to hers.

Being the responsible Virgo she was, and already carrying the weight of the entire world on her shoulders, what would one more legal load matter to Susan? Ha! So Miss Soft Touch took on *Archibald* vs. *Eduardo San Juan*, aka The Matador. Over the next twenty-four months San Juan's already bulging file multiplied until the case spread like an oil spill occupying two entire filing cabinets with no court date in sight. In Susan's mind The Matador and her husband, Hugh Carver, had become one: a mythic, superhuman creature who would elude Judgment Day forever.

The Matador case encompassed all the frustration inherent in the criminal justice system. The Matador controlled the numbers rackets around the city that generated $400,000 a week in business through nickel and dime bets: $20 million a year in gambling money that could easily be funneled through Asset Forfeiture to aid the war against crime. Not to mention the millions in assets that San Juan had accrued through his brilliant 'banking' career.

Now, as if by magic or, perhaps, sheer exhaustion, San Juan's lawyers were ready to make a deal. The Matador had no fear of jail time, it seemed, so long as he could keep as much of his money as possible. Susan had been fascinated by the notion of a man giving up his freedom in exchange for money until the first day the Puerto Rican "financier" had turned up in court accompanied by his wife (named as a codefendant) and *three* mistresses (two of whom were also listed as codefendants). A few years in prison would probably be a well-earned vacation to the amorous Matador.

A breathless Susan was fifty yards away from the entrance to the Thomas Street courthouse when she spotted the Channel 8 news truck parked outside. She prayed that her nemesis, Lisa Mercado, was not covering the trial.

"Girlfriend!"

Susan froze in terror as newscaster Lisa Mercado wiggled her way across the sidewalk in a skintight miniskirt, with a microphone thrust out in front of her like an old-fashioned Geiger counter hunting for radioactive news.

"Sorry, Lisa. Can't stop to chat. I'm late for—"

"So what do you think of the plea bargain?"

"What plea bargain?" Susan's blood turned to ice.

"The one Roger Rappaport just made for the San

Juans. I'm surprised you weren't there. Wasn't that your case?"

Red was the only color in Susan Given's universe as she pushed past a startled Lisa Mercado and took the steps two at a time inside the Thomas Street courthouse until she reached the third floor.

Inside the courtroom, she looked up at the bench and saw that Judge Halloran was nowhere in sight. Over at the defense table, the fabled Eduardo San Juan was nodding affirmatively as his high-priced lawyer, Roger Rappaport, shoved papers into his battered briefcase and whispered intently to his client. Hovering nearby were four females (Señora San Juan and the three infamous mistresses) looking like a tableau from the second act curtain of a García Lorca play. Then, as one, the women turned their scornful gaze on a visibly shaken Susan, who, in turn, looked at her watch in despair.

"Nice of you to finally turn up, sweetie."

Susan turned around and found herself staring up at the tall, volcanic redhead who made her life a daily commute to Hell.

Lydia Culberg (nee Slaney) had fought her way out of Hell's Kitchen and, via NYU Law School and some gravity-defying moves that would have made the authors of the Kama Sutra blush, had maneuvered her way up the ladder on Centre Street until she had become the deputy district attorney. Blessed with a showgirl's body more suited to a Vegas runway than a courtroom, she employed it and the capacity to outdrink any man she came in contact with to gain patronage both official and unofficial.

Lydia was determined to become Manhattan's district attorney someday, and the only person who stood in her path was Susan Given (whom the paranoid redhead was convinced coveted the same prize). But all Susan wanted was to continue bringing bad guys to justice via the Asset Forfeiture Unit. This simple tenet, however, did not deter Lydia from her tireless efforts to either discredit and sabotage Susan at every opportunity or take credit for all of Susan's media-attracting victories. In fact, behind her back Lydia was referred to by all the A.D.A.s, as The Human Faucet because she constantly leaked self-aggrandizing stories to the press.

"What happened?" asked Susan, dreading the worst.

"*You* didn't," replied Lydia. "Judge Halloran was royally pissed. I wouldn't suggest coming up before him for a while, sweetie. He was about to throw the whole case out of court until I finally stepped in and rescued the situation."

Amazing, thought Susan. She doesn't even blink. In addition to her reputation as a man-eater and two-fisted drinker, Lydia Culberg was known up and down Centre Street as a compulsive liar, whose blatant ambition was exceeded only by her incompetence.

"What did you do?" Susan's mind was spinning. When was the last time Lydia had actually argued a case? She'd only turned up in the courtroom that morning because of her egomaniacal obsession with having her image published in the tabloids and/or beamed into every living room in the Tri-State area.

"I brokered a deal."

"You what?"

"This case has been dragging on for two years, Ms. Given. At considerable expense to the taxpayer and countless work hours for our already overburdened and understaffed—"

"Shouldn't you be making this speech outside?" asked Susan. "Lisa Mercado is desperate for an exclusive."

"Get off your high horse, Susan."

"I want to know what kind of deal you made."

"Judge Halloran approved heartily."

He approved of your cleavage, thought Susan. But aloud, she merely repeated: "Tell me about the deal."

"San Juan forfeits a million dollars and does ninety days jail time with probation."

"What!? You're joking! Tell me you're joking."

"We took a million dollars, Susan."

"And The Matador walks away in three months. Probably thirty days by the time Rappaport finishes his song and dance."

"A million dollars, Susan."

"I would have put him away for three years, Lydia! Thanks to you, he'll be out on the street in a month and back to business as usual. A million dollars is nothing to him. I would have—"

"But you weren't here. Were you, sweetie? Where were you this morning? And where the hell have you been for the past three months?"

"I have been in my office every day. Except for my court appearances."

"Your body has been in the office. I don't know where your mind has been, sweetie."

"Please, don't call me that."

"Ooooh! Is Susan upset? You should be. You've been fucking up left, right, and center and I've been covering your ass."

"You've been covering for me? Why do I have trouble with that concept? Who got you out of jail six months ago when you were arrested for assaulting a police officer?"

"Oh, I knew you'd bring that up. One little aberration in an unblemished career."

"Are you wearing a wire? For whose benefit are you making these self-serving speeches?"

"Believe it or not, sweetie, I'm the best friend you've got right now. I've seen the psychiatric evaluation on you. Mr. Archibald is not happy with your performance these days."

"What was the doctor's name?" asked Susan, determined to call Lydia's bluff.

"Imogen Blythe. Okay? She says you're in denial. That it's only a matter of time before they find you wandering down Madison Avenue in your bathrobe begging for Lassie to come home."

"I don't have a dog," whispered Susan, the wind having been taken completely out of her sails.

"You won't have a job either if you fuck up once more. Now, get it together, girl. Or else."

Lydia swept out of the courtroom sufficiently pumped up for her encounter with the waiting media. Susan collapsed at the defense table feeling all the world like Cinderella after her wicked step-mother had gone off to the ball. And where was a fairy godmother to rescue the Chief of the Asset Forfeiture Unit from this world of pain?

"Hello, dear."

Susan looked up and saw a thin, perfectly coifed, white-haired woman in a stylish Hanae Mori suit, beaming down at her. The only thing Marian Given was missing was a magic wand.

7

"HOW EVER DID YOU find me?" asked Susan, dipping the porcelain spoon into her hot-and-sour soup as she stared at Marian Given, her still pretty, widowed, seventy-year-old mother, seated opposite her inside the crowded Chinatown restaurant.

"I went to your office," said Marian. "Just as we agreed."

"I'm so sorry, Mother. I mixed this week up with next week."

"Oh, I do that all the time, dear. It's probably a good thing that you're doing it now at your age. It won't seem so startling later on."

"Mother, do you think I'm having a breakdown?"

"That's a crazy thing to say," said Marian Given, searching the Szechuan menu for a dish she recognized. "They don't have any sweet-and-sour here."

"That's Cantonese, Mother. I know it's crazy. That's why I'm asking. People have been saying that I'm behaving oddly. That I've been under a lot of strain."

"I think you should take up golf again. You were a wonderful golfer, Susan. Much better than Linda ever was. Although she's quite brilliant now." Linda was Susan's younger sister, who had moved to Chattanooga years before and transformed herself into a

Southern belle. "Do you think they have shrimp in pineapple here?"

"No. How *is* Linda?"

"The dogs had puppies."

"Both dogs?" Susan had meant her question as a joke. But somehow it had triggered her mind back to the image of Lydia standing in the courtroom reading her the riot act. How much of what Lydia had said was true? Was Mr. Archibald truly not happy with Susan's work?

"No, dear. The bitch."

"What bitch? Mother! I've never heard you talk like that before."

"Like what?"

"Who did you just call a bitch?"

"Linda's dog. The dam. Wherever is your mind, Susan?"

"That's what I'm talking about, Mother. Something's wrong with my concentration. I haven't admitted it to anyone till now. I have nightmares."

"About Hugh?"

"Nooo!"

"Well, I couldn't blame you. I think he's behaved appallingly. Especially since the incident. Did he really try to take the girls away from you?"

"Neil put a stop to that."

"Your boyfriend?"

"My lawyer."

"What's your boyfriend's name again? The man from California?"

"He's not my boyfriend."

"Oh? Ivy told me he was—"

"Ivy romanticizes things. Michael and I are just friends."

"Michael! That's his name. The one with all the wives."

"He didn't have them all at once, Mother."

"I should hope not. How would it look, you both being bigamists? Didn't he invite you out to California right after the incident? You should have gone. The change would have done wonders for you."

"Why do you keep calling it 'the incident'? I killed a man."

"But it was self-defense."

"Of course it was, Mother. Do you think I might do it again? Maybe I'm a serial killer." What did Stella Moore call them? Rice Krispies?

"Sometimes I think it's all my fault," said Marian.

"What?"

"Ever since that lunch with Henry at the Stuyvesant Club. The afternoon that man held you hostage. I remember it so vividly. How I kept hoping you'd get a murder case so I'd have something to brag about at the club. I've learned my lesson now. You should see the looks they all give me at Cedarhurst! And the ones who squeeze my hand and whisper: 'How *is* she?'"

"So it's all *your* fault?" laughed Susan. "Thank goodness. Maybe I'll sleep better now."

"*I* almost killed a man once."

"You're joking!"

"No," replied Marian, continuing to peruse the menu. "It was a long time ago. Before I married your father. Before I met your father. When I was a secretary in Washington. I guess they'd call it 'date rape' now."

"Mother!" Susan stared in amazement at her mother as if she were looking at a stranger.

"Oh, he didn't succeed. But I cracked him over the head with a flashlight to stop him. He still has the scar. I've noticed it through the years in newspapers and magazines."

"Who was it?" asked a fascinated Susan. "Who is it?"

"Do you know anything about Kung Pao shrimp?" asked Marian, deftly avoiding her daughter's question. "Do you think it has pineapple? Oh! Did I tell you about Andrea Grant?" Andrea had been Susan's best friend in kindergarten and they had gone right through high school together.

"No," said Susan, realizing her mother had dropped her astonishing reminiscence for the time being. "How is Andee? How are her kids?"

"They're living with David."

"Of course they are. David's their father. Andrea's husband. What detail have I missed out on?" asked Susan.

"Andrea left David. She fell in love with the children's gym teacher."

"Andrea!? You're joking! Straitlaced Andrea. What does he look like?"

"It's not a he."

"Mother, you're making this up. Andee's gone gay? When? How?"

"Don't ask me, dear. I only know poor Ellen Grant is beside herself. Wondering where she went wrong.

Gay! I remember when a woman's biggest worry was going *gray!*"

"But when did all this happen? We had lunch with Andee, David, and the kids at Cedarhurst last Mother's Day."

"Apparently it was right after that."

"Jeepers! What did she eat?"

"It's not funny, Susan." Then Marian began to giggle. "Poor David's beside himself. He went 'round to the gym teacher's house in Cos Cobb the other night to plead with Andrea to come home and found the two of them . . ."

"What? No! He didn't walk in on them . . . ?"

"They were in the garage."

"The garage?!"

"Taking Andrea's Mustang apart!" Marian finally burst into uncontrollable laughter. "I'm just glad I grew up when I did. I don't know anything about cars. Oh, isn't that child adorable!" Marian turned her head to stare at a little Asian boy in shorts and a striped crew shirt bouncing a soccer ball along the floor of the restaurant. "I suppose his parents are the owners. Isn't it amazing how the world has gone soccer mad?"

"It always was, Mother. It's just that we finally caught up with everyone else. . . . Oh, my God! Soccer!"

"What's wrong, dear?"

"Davis Kumba! What time is it? I *am* losing my mind, Mother! Forgive me. I'll make it up to you. I'm so sorry. Please, excuse me!" And Susan dashed out of the restaurant in a state of complete panic.

8

A FRANTIC ALAN BECKER was waiting outside the courtroom on Centre Street, clutching his battered brown briefcase to his chest as a visibly harried Susan dashed toward him.

"I wish you'd break down and get a beeper," said the short, stocky Becker, as he rocked back and forth and ran a hand through his receding hairline. In his thick Bensonhurst accent, the word had come out "beepah."

"I don't need a beeper, Alan. I'm here, aren't I?"

"Yeah," replied her assistant warily, as Susan led the way into the courtroom, "but you're sure cutting it close. I don't mean to sound like some kind of Jewish mother—"

"Then don't!"

"—but I could do my job a lot more efficiently if I knew where you were a lot of the time."

"Am I late?" asked Susan pointedly.

"Look, Susan. I'm not trying to give you a hard time. Okay? You're a private person and I respect that. But we work together and I don't want to get an ulcer not knowing if you're going to turn up on time or not."

"You're so melodramatic, Alan. When have I not turned up in court?"

"This morning. Lydia spread the word up and down Centre Street that you'd finally lost it."

"Goddamn her! I opened my diary to the wrong week, that's all. You know how meticulous I am. Nothing gets past me. Nothing! And she's only besmirching me because she made the world's worst deal with Roger Rappaport. What is that in your hand?"

"What?" asked Becker, making a futile attempt to shove a piece of thermal paper into his back pocket.

"That piece of paper you're trying to hide from me."

"It's a fax," murmured Becker. "From him." Dr. Hugh Carver's abusive and imperious faxes to Susan were the stuff of legend on the eighth floor of the Lefkowitz Building where the Asset Forfeiture Unit was housed. The faxes were also in direct violation of a court order forbidding him to harass his estranged wife at work.

"Give it to me." She held her hand out to Becker like a schoolteacher demanding that a naughty pupil surrender his water pistol.

"May I suggest you don't look at it until we're finished here?"

"Have you read it?" asked Susan accusingly.

"Of course not! But I know how upset you get whenever he sends them. Upset? You're like something rescued from a burning stable."

"Give it to me, Alan."

"Don't read it now," begged Becker.

"Don't worry. I won't."

Becker relinquished the folded fax, then he and

Susan sat down at the prosecution table. She stared over at the defense table but neither Kumba nor his attorney, Bart Sugarman, was anywhere in sight. Then she began to toy with the folded fax.

"Don't!" whispered Becker.

"Don't worry. I won't," said Susan, setting a glass of water on top of the fax. "I am not going to let myself get upset any further today. As far as I'm concerned, this case is a slam dunk. We would have had it wrapped up six months ago if Judge Silverberg hadn't short-circuited."

"You're such a nice woman, Susan. The way you put things. 'Short-circuited.' Leo Silverberg went *meshuga*. He lost his marbles."

"The man was once a brilliant jurist, Alan."

"Yes. When Lindbergh landed in Paris. He's suffering from Alzheimer's now. Everybody knows it. He thought you were Mrs. Logan, whoever that is."

"That only happened once. Where is your compassion?"

"Hey! I was raised on the Old Testament. The how-much-do-you-love-me God? 'Yo, Abraham! Doing anything special today? How 'bout killing your only son to show how much you love me? Whoa, whoa, whoa! Put the knife down, Abie. I'm just kidding. It was a little test.' Your guy doesn't test, Susan. He just loves. Or so Nancy says."

"How *is* Nancy? Have you told your mother about her yet?" Nancy Gerhardt was the widow of the trucker Junior Tesla had slain in a fit of rage and whose death had been the linchpin in the criminal case to bring down the garbage cartel. Becker had fallen for the pretty little *shiksa* like a ton of bricks at Susan's Thanksgiving dinner and had kept the romance a secret from his very Jewish mother ever since.

"Did you read anything in the *Post* this morning about an elderly Jewish women in Bensonhurst throwing herself in front of a speeding subway train? C'mon, Susan. She wants me married but not outside the tribe."

"Can't Nancy get dipped?"

"Is that the way people refer to it in Greenwich? How quaint."

"You know what I mean. The ritual bath."

"Is that what you did when you married Dr. Carver?"

"Hugh is only Jewish when it serves his purposes. Or when he's on the losing end of an argument. Then he cries 'anti-Semitism' and his opponent backs off." She glanced at the defense table again and asked: "Where is Bart Sugarman? Where's Kumba?"

Becker shrugged. "I don't know. Maybe we've got the wrong date."

"That's not funny," snapped Susan. "I intend to teach Lydia Culberg a lesson this afternoon and put those ugly rumors of hers to bed once and for all. We are walking out of this courtroom with three hundred thousand dollars. And we have Sooky Lavelle to thank for that."

Sooky Lavelle was the mistress of the defendant, Davis Kumba, an outrageous con man charged with grand larceny. In addition to bilking 150 soccer-mad expatriate Ugandans who had paid him $2,000 each for a phony World Cup package tour, Kumba was also involved in welfare fraud and had a thirty-year rap sheet that crisscrossed the length and breadth of the United States.

Fortunately for Susan, the nineteen-year-old Ms. Lavelle (a former *Penthouse* centerfold) had become a cooperative witness and her testimony would have ensured a successful prosecution.

That *was* the intended scenario six months earlier before Judge Silverberg fell apart in court and was forced to continue the case at a later date.

Now, that day had arrived and Susan looked forward to a speedy resolution.

"Good afternoon, Ms. Given."

Susan recognized the thick African accent and stared up at the huge six-foot six-inch Davis Kumba staring down at her and flashing a toothy smile.

"I love your pearls," added Kumba, and took his seat at the defense table just as the door from the judge's chambers opened and his lawyer, Bart Sugarman, appeared with a shit-eating grin on his bearded face.

"What was Sugarman doing in there?" asked Becker. "He's not supposed to be in the judge's—"

Susan gestured for her assistant to be silent. Then the familiar roly-poly shape of court officer Mario DeStefano waddled into the room and announced: "Order in the court. All persons having business before this court, please rise."

Seconds later Leo Silverberg emerged from his

When Susan had last set eyes on the judge, he was a bald, stooped-over, pasty-faced man struggling to keep a hold on reality. The man who walked through the door now was tall, erect, deeply tanned, and wearing a black toupee.

"What happened to Leo?" asked Becker. "He looks twenty years younger. How can we be sure it's him?"

Susan shrugged. The day was spinning completely out of her control. Every instinct in her body was warning her of impending doom. No! That was just residue left over from her confrontation with Lydia. She, Susan Given, was in charge. Sooky Lavelle's deposition put the Kumba case back in the arena of the slam dunk. But what the hell had Bart Sugarman been doing in the judge's chambers a moment ago?

Susan rose to address the bench: "Your Honor, I trust that you have now read Ms. Lavelle's testimony and will rule swiftly on—"

"Miss Given, I have read what I have read. And I have reread. Thoroughly. I have examined every aspect of this case. I don't need you to instruct me as to the speed with which I should—"

"Your Honor, I didn't mean—"

"You inferred."

"I requested."

"Request denied."

"You can't deny my request for judgment!"

"I'm sick of your attitude, Ms. Given. I realize you took advantage of me during my illness—"

"I wasn't aware of any illness, Your Honor."

"Don't bullshit me, Ms. Given. Everyone knows I was sick. But I'm better now. And I know who my friends are and who they aren't." And Silverberg nodded appreciatively in Sugarman's direction.

"He's crazier than ever," whispered Becker.

"You! Second Chair. What is your name?"

"Becker, Your Honor."

"Pecker?"

"Becker. Alan Becker."

"You want to be barred from this court, Becker?"

"No, Your Honor."

"Then keep your remarks to yourself. Now then, Ms. Given, I have read the deposition of Ms. Lavelle." Judge Silverberg looked up from the document in question and gazed about the courtroom. "Where is she, by the way?"

"There was a death in Ms. Lavelle's family, Your Honor. She's originally from Louisiana and she went back there to attend the funeral—"

"That sounds like as big a crock of shit as her testimony," said Silverberg. "This woman is no better than a prostitute. Why should we take her word for anything that occurred? She's a slut."

"Your Honor, I object to your language and to your defamation of the witness who is not here to—"

"What is it? You got a thing for prostitutes, Ms. Given? Huh? You going to report me to the Mayor and the Governor because I'm standing in the way of free enterprise? Tell those goddamn politicians to keep their noses out of my courtroom. The only mistress I've ever had is the law. No tabloid tribunal is going to force Leo Silverberg into a popular verdict. Is that understood?"

Bart Sugarman leapt to his feet and chirped: "I move at the present time for a dismissal of all charges against the defendant."

"On what grounds?" demanded Susan. "What kind of a deal did you cook up with him in his chambers?"

"Your Honor," bleated an offended Sugarman, "I resent the aspersions Ms. Given is casting on me and the bench."

"You're out of order," thundered Silverberg.

"I move for a mistrial," said Susan. "This is a travesty of justice."

"Sit down, Ms. Given," growled Silverberg.

Becker tugged anxiously on Susan's arm. She yanked herself free from her assistant's hold and announced: "I will *not* sit down! I believe in the law. I believe in the American justice system—" Susan began to cough and reached for the water glass on the defense table.

"Ms. Given, if you do not sit down and keep quiet at once, I will hold you in contempt of court."

"This is outrageous!" Susan's coughing spell grew worse.

"I'm warning you, Ms. Given."

"Siddown!" hissed Becker.

"Alan, let go!"

Susan reached for the glass of water on the table and the fax underneath it floated away onto the floor. Susan knelt down to pick it up. She knew she shouldn't read the contents but she couldn't help herself.

TO: SGC
FROM: HC

Ivy informs me that you are suffering from recurrent nightmares. This comes as no surprise to me.

As ever, you are in denial about everything that you cannot control. Including your subconscious. You thwarted me once in my attempt to rescue the girls from your negligent and irresponsible supervision. I will not roll over this time. When I return from Aspen, I intend to petition the court for full custody of my daughters. You have no one to blame but yourself for my present course of action.

"The son of a bitch!" roared Susan, her hands trembling after she'd speed read the fax.

"What did she call me?" asked Silverberg in disbelief. Then he turned to DeStefano. "Mario? Did you hear that?"

"I'm not quite sure, Judge," said the roly-poly court officer, who had a soft spot in his heart for Susan.

"Then get a hearing aid," thundered Silverberg. "You've gone too far this time, Ms. Given."

"I didn't mean you, Your Honor."

"No? What other son of a bitch would you be shouting at then? I order you to pay a thousand-dollar fine."

"That's outrageous!"

"So's your behavior!"

"I was not addressing the bench, Your Honor."

"I don't give a shit! I won't have that language in my courtroom."

"May I approach the bench?"

"No!"

"Please?"

"Make it quick."

Five minutes later a visibly shaken Susan walked down the steps of the courthouse on Centre Street, having finally persuaded a reluctant Leo Silverberg to continue the case until the following week.

At the bottom step, she lit a Salem Light and was about to walk down the street to her office when a tall, swarthy man with a black mustache barred her path.

"Miss Given?" The voice was Brooklyn and Susan took him to be a Mafia foot soldier.

"Yes?"

"Could you come wit' me, please?"

"I'm sorry but I really have to . . ."

"Just over here," said the man, taking her elbow firmly but gently and steering her toward a Lincoln Town Car with dark tinted windows, parked by the curb.

Not again, thought Susan, fearing this had something to do with the Tesla family. She wanted to cry out for the police but it all seemed too much like her nightmare. Perhaps she was still home asleep. No. The street noises were too real. Her escort's sweet cologne was too overpowering. This *was* happening. Susan took a deep breath and was about to scream when a familiar voice in the backseat said: "Wow! He wasn't kidding. You *are* in bad shape."

9

SUSAN STARED WITH immense relief into Barry Praeger's twinkling Tony Curtis eyes as the Lincoln pulled away from the curb.

"You scared the hell out of me, Barry."

"Why?"

"Where did you get this driver?" she whispered.

"Dominic? He's worked for me for years."

"He *has*? Oh, I'm so embarrassed."

"Susan, you've been watching too many old movies."

"Barry, I don't watch old movies. Remember? I deal with Dominic's relatives all day."

"Oh, yeah," laughed Barry. "I forgot. So how are you?"

"A little curious about your behavior."

"I got a call from Michael." Hotelier Barry Praeger was Michael Roth's best friend. The two had grown up in Toronto together and had shared many adventures in far-flung places around the world. It was while attending Barry's son's bar mitzvah in Jerusalem the previous year that Susan and Michael had begun their ill-fated love affair.

"Please, don't get caught in the middle of this," said Susan anxiously. "Where are we going?"

43

"Around the block. And I'm not in the middle of anything. Michael phoned me an hour ago. He's worried about you. Says you're not yourself."

"Who am I?"

"Well, you're a nice woman, who's always been straight and gracious with me and my kids. Also, for reasons I've never been able to fathom other than innate Christian charity, you've befriended and tolerated my lunatic wife."

"How is Cynthia?"

"Please, I just had lunch."

"Are you two still separated? Living together? I can't keep track."

"Neither can I. Thank God I'm in the hotel business. I've got lots of places to sleep. Which makes a pretty good segue into what I have to say to you. And it has nothing to do with Michael. So just relax." The car phone rang at that moment and Barry excused himself while he talked to the manager of his hotel in Bangkok.

Susan stared out the window and tried to avoid looking at Barry. He reminded her too much of Michael. People had often mistaken them for brothers. They had even posed as siblings at a fake Sicilian funeral to assist her during the investigation of the garbage cartel. (This was a once-only masquerade: lady-killer Barry had almost blown his and Michael's cover completely while coming on to the late Junior Tesla's sister, Toni.)

"Sorry," said Barry, hanging up the phone and turning his attention back to Susan. "Where were we?"

44

"We weren't anywhere. You've abducted me for reasons that are completely beyond my—"

"Oh, yeah. I remember. You ever been to St. Stephen's?"

"Is that an Episcopal church?"

"No," laughed Barry. "It's an island. In the Caribbean. Belonged to England once upon a time. Beautiful, isolated. Lot of pirates hung out there. Lot of buried treasure. Too bad they didn't have asset forfeiture then."

"I'm lost."

"Not really. We just built a new hotel there. And you're this year's recipient of the Barry Praeger Grant. Which entitles you to be my guest for a week, a month, however long you want to stay."

"Stay where?" asked Susan, fishing in her briefcase for another cigarette. "Do you mind if I smoke?"

"Yes. I quit ten years ago. I've never seen you like this before, Susan. You're a nervous wreck. You need to go somewhere and chill out."

"Did Michael put you up to this?"

"No. I get ideas of my own once in a while. Haven't you got vacation time coming to you? Do you ever leave your office?"

"Yes. Now. And I've got to get back there. Thank you very much, Barry. It was a very kind offer but I have to say no."

10

THE TELEPHONE MESSAGES were littered all over Susan's desk when she finally returned to her office. Phone Ray Murphy. Phone Lydia Culberg. Phone your sister Linda in Chattanooga. Phone Lydia Culberg. Phone your brother at home. Phone Lydia Culberg. Phone Neil Stern. Phone Lydia Culberg.

"What the hell does Lydia want?" asked an exasperated Susan as she let the pink memo pages float down onto her desk. "Gretchen! What is going on? I've got four different messages from her."

"I don't know," her assistant called back from the outer office area. "Maybe she thinks you're here and just playing hard to get." The telephone rang at that moment. "That's probably her again."

Susan seized the phone and snapped, "Given!"

"Mom?"

"Ivy, my sweet. My darling child."

"Mom, are you okay?"

"Of course, I'm okay. I'm talking to you, aren't I? Which means everything's okay."

"Then why did you growl when you answered?"

"Because I thought you were someone I didn't want to speak to. Where are you?"

"Home."

"Alone?"

"No. Cordelia's here."

"And what's Cordelia doing?"

"Watching her TV shows."

"Why isn't she watching you?" Susan groaned audibly at the image of Cordelia Brown, her dreadlocked St. Kitts housekeeper, glued to the television and pronouncing judgment on the endless parade of fin-de-siècle freaks recounting their dysfunctional stories to Maury, Sally, Montel, and the like.

"Mom, can I ask you something?"

"What is it, darling Ivy?"

"Do you think I'm a dyke?"

"What! Where did you get such an idea? Where did you learn a word like that?"

"Mom, please! I'm ten years old. I've known about them since I was eight."

"You have? Well, then you should know the proper word is 'lesbian.' " Susan flashed abruptly on the image of her old friend Andrea Grant exchanging spark plugs and heated kisses with a faceless, muscular woman over the exposed motor of a Mustang. "Who called you a lesbian?"

"Gwillim Griffiths." The aforementioned Griffiths was the heartthrob of Ivy's fourth-grade class and the much younger half brother of Toby Griffiths, the star of a mindless but hugely popular Generation-X TV sitcom. "I hate him, Mom."

"I think that's a bit extreme, Ivy. Why did he call you . . . what he did?"

"Because of my warrior women drawings. And cuz I don't kiss his butt like all the other girls."

"Ivy, please, don't use language like that."

"He's an a——hole, Mom! A major a——hole."

The second line rang on Susan's phone and she called out for Gretchen to answer it. But the line continued to ring incessantly. Susan put her younger daughter on hold, and pressed the second button.

"Given!" There was no reply except for a racking nicotine cough, which Susan recognized instantly. "Ray?"

"Gimme a second, Suzy," rasped veteran crime reporter Ray Murphy on the other end of the line. "Christ on a crutch! I got to give up these goddamn cigarettes."

"Ray, may I please phone you back? I've got my daughter on the other line and she's going through a bit of a—"

"Only be a second, Suzy. I need your help."

"Please, Ray . . ." Susan looked down and saw the other light had gone off on the telephone. She heaved a sigh of resignation, silently vowed to phone Ivy right back, and asked Murphy: "What is it?"

"Janie Moore. She's holdin' out on me."

"I don't follow."

"I've known that little harp since she was in diapers. I knew her old man and her grandfather. We go way back."

"What is it, Ray?"

"The jogger this morning."

"Jogger?"

"Mary Ellen Chernin. The Central Park murder."

"Ohhh! Rice Krispies."

"What? What did you call it, Suzy?" Murphy was all

48

but drooling on the other end of the line and Susan could hear the reporter's pencil scribbling fiendishly on a scrap of paper—probably a bar coaster. "Whaddaya mean by Rice Krispies? Is that what they're callin' it?"

"It's not official, Ray," said Susan, wishing she'd never opened her mouth at all. "It's just a joke."

"Some joke, Suzy. A poor girl was raped and murdered by a—Ohhh! I get it. A serial murderer."

"I never said that, Ray. Don't you dare quote me. It was Janie's daughter Stella."

"Thanks, Suzy. I can run with this."

"Ray, please!"

"Relax. Deep background. I owe you, Suzy."

Susan listened in shock to the sound of the dial tone, then slowly replaced the receiver on its cradle. What had she done? What madness had prompted her to blurt out "Rice Krispies" to the veteran tabloid reporter? She could just see the front page the next morning. And Janie would never speak to her again. Lydia would have her head for sure. Lydia! There was no putting the volcanic redhead off any longer.

Susan picked up the phone once again to dial when she heard someone say "hello" on the other end. A simple enough word but she recognized the voice and it made her blood run cold.

"What do you want?"

"I didn't hear the phone ring," said Hugh Carver, in his carefully studied, Gregory Peck wannabe tones.

"You are not supposed to phone me here," she hissed at her estranged husband.

"You didn't reply to my fax," said Carver, ignoring

the reference to the court order barring him from phoning his soon-to-be ex-wife at work.

"I do not reply to veiled threats."

"It was neither veiled, Susan, nor a threat. It is a course of action you have forced me to take. Believe it or not, it's very painful for me to have to do this. To wrench children away from their mother is a primal—"

"Have Ralph Kregar phone Neil Stern." The two men were Hugh's and Susan's respective divorce lawyers.

"You brought this on yourself."

"Get off the phone, Hugh! I don't want to talk to you. We have nothing to say to each other. We never did!" The second line rang and Susan all but bellowed: "Gretchen! Would you please answer these phones? Where the hell are you?" She almost broke her finger attacking the button on the telephone. "Who is this?"

"It's your boss," purred Lydia Culberg. "Is that how we're answering the phone these days? Hmm? And why haven't you called me back? I've left several messages for you. Or didn't you get them? Is your staff suffering from 'overwork' as well?"

"I'm sorry, Lydia. I saw your messages. I was just about to call you. It's only that I'm a little—"

"You're more than a little, Ms. Given. You're a lot. I've had Judge Silverberg and Bart Sugarman on the phone to me complaining about your—"

"When did they become a team?"

"No, no, no, Susan. Spare me your witticisms. You're not wriggling out of this one. Your behavior is completely out of control."

"According to whom? A slimy ambulance chaser

and an octogenarian jurist, whose hold on reality is tenuous at best."

"I wouldn't be so quick to criticize other people's mental states."

"Take off the gloves, Lydia."

"They're off, Susan. Believe me. I'm just warming up, that's all. I've waited a long time for this."

Gretchen entered the office at that moment. Susan clasped her hand over the mouthpiece and whispered: "Where on earth have you been?"

Her assistant said nothing but held out a registered letter.

"What is this?" asked Susan.

"The Bar Association," replied Gretchen, who rushed out of the office as soon as Susan had taken the letter.

"Susan? Susan, are you there? Susan?"

She ignored Lydia's voice as she undid the letter from the New York State Bar Association and read the contents. No! Susan couldn't believe her eyes. How was it possible? This was exactly what she needed to rescue her from the slings and arrows of outrageous whatever. She began to laugh uncontrollably. Then she quoted aloud her all-time favorite movie line: " 'Thanks, God. I really mean it.' "

"Susan, what the hell is going on there? Who are you talking to?"

"Did you ever see *San Francisco*, Lydia? One of my favorite childhood movies. Right after the earthquake when Clark Gable is wading through the rubble. He turns to Spencer Tracy and says: 'I want to thank God. What do I say?' "

"What does this have to do with—?"

"And Father Tim—that's Tracy—says: 'Just say what's in your heart, Blackie. He'll listen.' And it's true, Lydia. It's really true. He *does* listen."

"You've finally lost it, Susan. That shrink was right."

"I'm sorry, Lydia. I just received a letter from the—"

"You don't know what sorry is, sweetie. You're not going into court tomorrow. Or the next day. Or even—"

"How did you know?" laughed Susan. "Are you psychic?"

"What the hell are you talking about?"

"It seems . . ." Susan had to take a deep breath before continuing. Then: "It seems I haven't paid my dues to the State Bar Association for the past two years. So they're suspending me until I do. You can't stop me from lawyering, Lydia, if I'm not a lawyer."

"What?!"

"Let me get back to you, Lydia. There's something I have to take care of."

Susan began humming to herself for the first time in months as she searched her Rolodex for a phone number. Then she dialed, and when the man answered on the other end, she said: "Barry? It's Susan. I've reconsidered your offer. . . . Is tomorrow morning too soon?"

11

THE AMERICAN AIRLINES JET dipped down through the clouds to reveal a breathtaking turquoise and azure sea below. The island of St. Stephen's came into view with its peculiar shape and myriad unexpected inlets where pirates of old had steered their galleons laden with booty.

It had been freezing that morning when Susan arrived at JFK after a tearful good-bye with the girls, who left for Aspen with their father later in the day. Stepping off the airplane after a needlessly air-conditioned three-and-a-half-hour flight, Susan was overwhelmed by the combination of intense heat and sultry breezes. The island's tiny airport was deserted except for a few porters and local customs officials, who waved Susan and the other passengers through with no apparent concern for security, which made Susan wonder where St. Stephen's stood on the list of world drug-smuggling centers. She'd check with her DEA contacts as soon as she got back to New York. Stop it! she said to herself. You're supposed to be on vacation. Don't even think about work.

Susan made a quick visit to the ladies' room, where she was shocked to discover the semiprimitive condition of the island's public toilets. She prayed the hotel facilities would be more modern. By the time she managed to turn the arthritic faucets off and emerged once more into the arrivals area, her fellow passengers had all vanished and there were no more taxis, minivans, or airport limousines in sight.

Finally, Susan approached a sleepy-eyed native policeman in a khaki shirt, shorts, and knee socks, standing in front of the terminal and staring dreamily at the verdant hills in the distance. When she asked him how she could get to the Henry Morgan, Barry's new hotel, the policeman asked with surprise: "Dey don' come pick you up?"

"I'm sure they must have but they clearly didn't wait for me."

"Wait for you?"

"I made a detour."

The policeman stared at Susan as if she were speaking in tongues. She chewed at her lower lip, then stared up and down the badly paved road that ran in front of the tiny terminal. There wasn't a car in sight.

"Is it a holiday?"

"Where?"

"Here. The place is deserted. Where is everyone?"

"At de beach." The policeman shrugged.

"I'd like to get to the hotel."

The policeman nodded appreciatively but offered no suggestion as to how the problem might be solved.

"No ideas?" asked Susan, when it finally dawned on her that the policeman might not utter another word for the rest of the day.

"Me tinkin' about it," replied the policeman.

Susan's first instinct was to curse Barry Praeger for ever talking her into this adventure. Then she took a deep breath and realized there was nothing she could do about her present predicament. Besides, the policeman might turn out to be one of the island's great original thinkers.

It was at that moment a dilapidated pickup truck came rattling along the road. The policeman stepped cranelike into its path to flag it down.

The pickup barely screeched to a halt with what drops of brake fluid remained at its disposal and the policeman began an earnest conversation with the driver that lasted about ten minutes. By this time, a dehydrated and sticky Susan was seated on one of her upended suitcases, wondering when this particular dream would end and she would wake up cool and comfortable in her Upper East Side duplex. Finally the policeman turned his attention back to her and waved enthusiastically.

"Him gon' take you," announced the policeman proudly.

"In that?" asked Susan, staring in disbelief at the dilapidated truck. "I don't think so."

"Is it your wish to arrive at the Henry Morgan before nightfall, madam?" asked the driver, after he emerged from the truck. He was a tiny, dapper black man with a pencil-thin mustache and was wearing a striped shirt, pink bow tie, and seersucker trousers. "There won't be another aeroplane arriving before this evening so there won't be another bus from the hotel."

Susan couldn't decide if it was the tiny man's pink

bow tie, his courtliness, or his use of the word *aeroplane* (her grandfather was the last person she had heard use the word) that finally persuaded her to get into the truck, but get in she did. The policeman acted as porter and hoisted her luggage up onto the back between several cases of whiskey.

"How far is the hotel?" asked Susan, as the truck lurched away from the terminal.

"Perhaps half an hour."

"Jeepers! I wouldn't have thought the island was that big."

"It's not. But the roads are appalling. Are you an actress, madam?"

"Hardly. What made you think that?"

"You are very pretty. You carry yourself very well. And they are making a movie at the hotel."

"No, I'm just here on a vacation."

"Ascension."

Susan stared out the window trying to locate the peak the climbers might be scaling.

"I'm sorry," she said, "but I don't see anyone—"

"My name is Ascension."

"Oh, I'm sorry. I didn't understand."

"What is your name?"

"Susan."

"Where did you come from, Susan? Besides Heaven."

Susan laughed. "New York City." She liked this little man.

"Ah! Perhaps you know my sister. Conception. She lives in New York as well."

"It's a pretty big city, Ascension."

"Do you know a village called Harlem?"

"I've been there a few times. On business."

"What sort of business, Susan?"

"I work for the District Attorney's Office."

"Is that like a crown prosecutor?"

"Exactly."

"My, oh my! A pretty woman like you. Who would have thought? Do you have a husband?"

"I had one."

"A widow?"

"No such luck."

"Ahhh! You like riddles, Susan. My youngest boy would like you very much. He makes riddles all the time."

"How many children do you have, Ascension?"

"Eleven."

"Is your wife still alive?"

"Of course." Then Ascension thought about this and laughed. "That's very good, Susan. I will use that one at the bar."

"You're a lawyer, as well?"

Ascension turned sideways to Susan and grinned. For the next half hour he regaled her with tales of the island's history, gossip about some of its more notorious visitors, and bargaining tips for dealing with the local merchants.

For the first time in months, Susan felt the weight of the world finally beginning to leave her shoulders. She had no idea that this chance encounter would lead her into all too familiar territory and even greater tragedy.

12

DIRK ANGELUS, the manager of the Henry Morgan Hotel, was less than thrilled to see the dusty and disheveled woman with the wind-blown hair enter his lobby like the tragic heroine of some early Tennessee Williams play.

Angelus, blonde, baby-faced, plump, in his midfifties, traversed the vast lobby determined to stop the poor demented creature from proceeding any further.

"Excuse me," said Susan, pushing the long strands of hair from her face. "I have a—"

"I'm sorry, madam, but the hotel is full up at the present time. Perhaps the concierge could recommend a bed-and-breakfast in the town—"

"I have a reservation," said Susan, barely able to release the words from her parched throat. "Barry Praeger assured me that everything was taken care of."

"Mr. Praeger? The CEO?"

"I believe that's his title. My name is Susan Given and he told me that everything—"

"Ohhhh, Mrs. Given! We wondered what had happened to you. I'm Dirk Angelus, the hotel manager. Our limousine went to fetch you and you weren't there."

"I made a detour."

58

"A detour? Ohhh, a detour. How continental! But how did you get here from the airport? The taxi drivers are having their biweekly strike. The natives are such characters. How ever did you get here, clever girl?"

"This gentleman kindly drove me." Susan pointed to the dilapidated pickup parked so incongruously beneath the hotel's majestic porte cochere.

"Ahhh! You've met Ascension. Talk about local color. You must be ready for a stiff one if you came all the way up here in that old heap."

"I beg your pardon?"

"A drink. Two drinks. All the drinks you want. *Anything* you want. You're Mr. Praeger's very special guest."

Susan wasn't sure if she liked the innuendo the hotel manager had attached to the phrase "very special guest," but maybe that was just his camp manner. He certainly had the staff under control. With his fingers snapping furiously like castanets, Susan's bags were zipped in from the bed of the pickup and she was being escorted by Angelus toward the elevators.

"I'm sorry the golf cart isn't available this afternoon," drawled Angelus.

"It is a trifle large," replied Susan taking in the vastness of the alabaster lobby.

"I think they overdid it myself," whispered Angelus. "But, hey! I just work here. Want to see the casino now or wait till later?"

"Casino?"

"That is the big attraction on the island. And, for blondes like us, that sun is a definite no-no. Nothing less than thirty-five, Mrs. Given."

"It's Ms. Given. Thirty-five what?"

"Sunblock. Don't let the trade winds deceive you. Or those passing clouds. The big C is out there."

"What kind of gambling goes on here, Mr. Angelus?"

"Anything you want: blackjack, craps, chemin de fer, roulette. You look like the roulette type to me."

"This is legalized gambling, correct, Mr. Angelus?"

"My dear, someone might think you were a cop."

"I'm an assistant district attorney." Then she added hastily: "But I *am* on vacation."

"Good for you!"

Susan's sunblock must have stopped somewhere short of 30 for she felt like a lobster after a half hour by the pool.

By dinnertime she *looked* like a lobster and was having difficulty finding a comfortable position to sit in. But she was famished. So she pulled on a simple white cotton dress and headed downstairs.

The sumptuous dining room was divided into two distinct camps: the red-faced high rollers, who had come from Kansas, Nebraska, Iowa, wherever, on junkets to part with their hard-earned dollars; and a group of what appeared to be survivors of some sixties commune, who laughed too loudly, drank too much, and continually touched and kissed each other between mouthfuls of food (the maître d' informed Susan that this was the film crew Ascension had mentioned earlier that morning).

Susan opted for a table by herself but no sooner had she perused the menu than a large bleached blonde in a Technicolor muumuu, wearing red lipstick and huge tortoiseshell glasses plopped herself down in the next chair.

"Mind if I join you? You look so forlorn, honey. My name's Bonnie Blue Waffington. From Tulsa. My goodness, honey! You must have just arrived. Does that burn hurt? I'll bet it does. You gotta ease into the sun. Ease into it. Bud never goes in the sun anymore. He lives in that casino. I love the sun. But I mustn't get it on my face. I don't believe I caught your name. Oh, there he is! Buuuud! Over here, honey. You gotta talk loud to Bud. He's a little deaf. What is he doin' now? Stoppin' to chat with those movie people. He just wants to check out Colette Cooke's boobs. But she never comes into the dining room. Just sits up in her room like the Queen of Sheba. Bud, get over here and meet—what was your name again, honey?"

"Susan."

A man who looked like a grizzly bear in a madras sports jacket sat down next to Bonnie Blue. He reeked of nicotine and whiskey and his crisscrossed face reminded Susan of an old leather camera case she had neglected to keep oiled.

"How ya doin' tonight, Bud?" shouted his wife. "Up or down?"

"Down two thousand," growled Bud Waffington. "Who's this?" He nodded in Susan's direction as if she were an autograph hound invading his sacred sphere of celebrity.

"This is Suzy. She's new. And awful cute. Don't you think Harry'd like her?

"Harry's wife is dead."

"I know she's dead," shouted Bonnie Blue. "That ain't what I'm talkin' about. I wish you'd plug your hearing aid in once in a while. Oh! There's Harry. You're gonna love him, Suzy. He's a real practical joker."

Turning her head, Susan saw an ancient man with dyed orange hair, who looked like Strom Thurmond's stand-in, hobbling toward the table with a huge grin plastered across his badly peeling face.

"Park it here, you old hoot owl," growled Bud. "Bonnie went and got you a date for this evening."

"Please excuse me," said Susan, rising from the table. "I'm expecting a long-distance call in my room and I don't want to miss it."

"If yer not back in twenty minutes," cackled Harry, "I'll start without ya."

Susan hurried out of the dining room, then raced toward the huge double doors leading out to the swimming pool and the beach beyond.

At the water's edge she removed her sandals and walked barefoot. She thought she might burst into tears at any moment. This trip was an unmitigated disaster. What was she doing here in this gambling den with these dreadful people? What had Barry been thinking of? She'd pack her bags and leave first thing in the morning. Perhaps she could sneak back into her apartment without anyone knowing and just sit there quietly until the girls returned from Aspen.

"Good evening, madam. Can I get you something to drink?"

Susan looked up and saw a tiny man in a striped

shirt standing behind a bamboo- and palm-covered bar at the edge of the sea.

"Ascension? Is that you?"

"Susan? I did not recognize you in the moonlight. What are you doing out here alone?"

"I've escaped from the hotel! Does that sound too dramatic?"

"Would you like a drink? You look like you need one."

"I'm starving, Ascension. Do you have any peanuts or pretzels back there? Is this your bar?"

"You didn't eat your dinner?"

"I couldn't eat with those people, Ascension. I go up against some of the most hardened criminals in New York and none of them has ever frightened me as much as my fellow diners. I don't mean to sound like a snob. Do I sound like a snob? I don't sound like my mother, do I? Isn't that ridiculous? You don't even know my mother."

"Susan, when was the last time you ate?"

"Ate? Eight? Long before eight. I ate my All-Bran just before I ran this morning. Around a quarter to seven."

"You run?"

"Oh, yes. Every morning. Rain or shine. Though I have slacked off a bit in the last few months. I run around Central Park. You see, my mother's very thin. Doesn't have to work at it. But my sister and I take after our father. Our late father. Big man. Big-boned."

"Susan, you have not eaten for fourteen hours. You better come home with me right now and eat something."

"Oh, I couldn't dream of imposing—"

"You are starving to death, girl."

"Don't be ridiculous!"

"You are babbling, Susan. And you got a bad sunburn on top of it. Come home with me and Betty will take care of you."

"Betty?"

Ascension turned the light off inside the bar and stepped out from behind it. Then he gestured for Susan to follow him over to his pickup parked on a nearby rise.

"Aren't you going to lock up?" asked Susan, pointing toward the unguarded bar and its plenitude of liquor.

"No one will steal from me."

"You're very trusting, Ascension."

"I have protection."

Susan grimaced at the irritation her legs felt as they rubbed against the truck's crusty old leather seat.

"This is very kind of you, Ascension."

"Nonsense. This way you get to eat real island cooking. And Betty is one of the best cooks on St. Stephen's. Oh, my! You really done yourself in bad, girl. Stay out of the sun tomorrow."

Ascension turned the key in the ignition and the motor made a spluttering sound before it finally kicked in. Soon they were rattling along the dirt road away from the posh hotels toward the ramshackle village where the locals lived.

Ascension beeped his horn as he turned the truck onto a cul-de-sac and half a dozen screaming children emerged from a small stucco, thatch-roofed house.

"Daddy mon! Daddy mon!"

The children were crawling all over their father as if they hadn't seen him for years.

"Have you been away?" asked Susan innocently.

"Since this morning," replied Ascension with a huge grin on his face. "I am a blessed man. My children love me very much."

"Be dat Princess Di?" asked the smallest of the girls, clinging to her father's neck and pointing at Susan.

"No, Clarissa. Princess Di is in heaven. This is our new friend Susan. She's come for dinner."

"Who come for dinner?" boomed a voice from inside the house.

Seconds later a huge black woman—easily two heads taller and a hundred pounds heavier than Ascension—waddled out of the house with a ladle in her hand and a scowl on her face.

"Susan," said Ascension, swelling up with pride, "here is the love of my life and the mother of my children. Betty, put down that threatening ladle and say hello to Susan."

"Why you bring she here wit'out tellin' me, you wicked man? My, her be pretty! My, my, my. You got de bad burn, gal. Orestes, you and Priam go pick some aloe. Cool de lady down. Come inside, pretty lady. Tell Betty what lies dis wicked man been tellin' you?"

"She has not eaten anything since this morning, Betty. Don't be making her say anything until her stomach's full."

"Don't him talk posh!" Betty shrieked with laughter and wrapped an arm around Susan's shoulder. "Dat what come of goin' to school. Come on, gal. Me be pinchin' you too hard?"

"I am a little sore," replied Susan, who had been trying not to wince under Betty's powerful grip.

"Me little boys bring de aloe soon and me make you a nice cream to cool you down. You like pigeon peas wit' rice?"

Susan felt like one of the orphans in the national tour of *Oliver* as she shoveled spoon after spoon of the spicy chicken dish down her throat.

"Her be hungry," observed Betty approvingly.

"This is delicious," said Susan. "Very unusual. I'd never eat this in New York, you know."

"You don't find dat nowhere," said Betty.

"Conception would know how to cook it," said Ascension.

Betty snorted and said: "Me tink you little sister ain't done no cookin' since she left de island. When her wit' Crimson her don't need no—"

"Hush, woman. Our guest doesn't need to know all the family secrets."

"Is this your sister, who lives in Harlem?"

Before Ascension could reply, his children swarmed into the house and began climbing all over him until he had all but vanished from sight.

"Daddy mon, play a song!"

"Oh, please, Daddy mon!"

"I can't play without arms," laughed Ascension, as he lovingly shook the children off him. "Someone go fetch my guitar."

Seconds later a battered guitar rested across his

chest and Ascension began to strum the strings.

"What shall I sing about?" asked the tiny man, staring down at his adoring children seated at his feet.

"Princess Di!" chirped Clarissa.

"What is wrong with you, girl? Her name is Susan. Do you have a second name, Susan?"

"Given."

"Ahhh! That is good. Very good. Let me see." The tiny man began to play a few chords and slap the instrument in a distinct calypso rhythm.

> "There was a lady from New York
> Her given name was Susan
> Turned into a lobster quick
> That's what comes from snoozin'
> Oh woe! What a pity!
> Sunburned gal from the city."

And the children chimed in:

> "Oh woe! What a pity!
> Sunburned gal from the city."

Ascension continued to sing the song and his sons, Orestes and Priam, thirteen and twelve, dragged Susan to her feet and began dancing with her.

"Her dance good, Daddy mon!" announced Priam.

"Me tink she can do cockatrice wit' dem legs," said Orestes.

"What's cockatrice?" asked Susan.

"Foot fighting. All us boys on St. Stephen's learn to do it."

Before Susan knew it, she was learning the fundamentals of the island's peculiar form of kickboxing.

"You done did dis before," said Orestes, as Susan quickly assumed the basic stance.

"I took a self-defense course at work a few years ago," said Susan. "But this is very different."

Her martial arts lesson was interrupted by a loud knocking at the front door. Betty looked nervously at her husband but he merely gestured for her to relax as he went to answer the door.

The door was still ajar as Ascension stepped outside into the tropical moonlight. From her vantage point, Susan was able to see the caller's shoes. They were very large and two-tone: black and red leather.

An argument was ensuing and Ascension was trying to calm his visitor down. Susan could not make out what the two men were saying but she could distinguish the contrast between her host's mellifluous tones and the animal-like growls of his visitor. Then the conversation ended abruptly and smacking sounds were heard.

A few seconds later a visibly shaken Ascension came back inside the house and resumed strumming his guitar.

"Is everything all right?" asked Susan.

"Of course. Of course."

But Susan did not believe him. She could see the fear in his children's eyes, the tears running down Betty's face, and the stinging marks on Ascension's cheeks where his mysterious visitor with the two-tone shoes had clearly slapped him around.

13

IT WAS ALMOST 11 P.M. when Susan crossed the Henry Morgan lobby in her bare feet carrying her sandals in her hand.

"Gone native already?"

Susan spun around and saw Dirk Angelus leaning against a pillar, lighting up a cigarette.

"The alabaster feels so cool on my feet."

"Somebody didn't take my advice this afternoon," said the hotel manager, drawing the smoke deep into his lungs and pointing to Susan's red skin.

"I learned my lesson."

"Where did you have dinner?"

"Am I under investigation, Mr. Angelus?"

"Just doing my job, Ms. Given. Mr. Praeger phoned from New York to see if you were all right. I have to keep my eye out for you. We *do* want to keep my mother happy, don't we?"

"What does your mother have to do with this?"

"Let me put it this way: If you're happy, Mr. Praeger's happy. If Mr. Praeger's happy, Dirk's happy. And if little Dirk is happy, Mrs. Angelus sleeps soundly. So what happened? The maître d' told me you fled from the dining room."

"I didn't flee the dining room. Just my fellow diners."

"Wait, wait. No hints. Were they from Oklahoma?"

"Do you know everything that goes on in this hotel, Mr. Angelus?"

"A good manager always does. Pleasant dreams."

Susan rode up in the elevator to the eighteenth floor, then emerged and drifted down the corridor toward her room.

The evening with Ascension and his family had been enjoyable and reminded her of Christmases she had spent in Harlem visiting with her housekeeper Cordelia Brown's brood. The hours had sped by and managed to erase the overpowering sense of loneliness Susan had been feeling since her initial arrival on the island. Betty was the epitome of the great earth mother and her seemingly endless number of children were a constant delight. Particularly little Clarissa, who, by night's end, still refused to call Susan anything but Princess Di. So much love! So much laughter! But, try as she might, Susan could not banish the memory of the mysterious visitor at the door and the temporary pall his appearance had caused on the household. What had that been about?

Sliding her plastic security card inside the door slot, Susan heard the bolt release and stepped inside the room. Barry had given her a vast suite befitting an empress (no wonder Dirk's innuendo quotient was so high), and Susan realized the sitting room alone was larger than the square footage of Ascension's house.

She stepped out onto the balcony, luxuriating in the warm breeze blowing in off the magical Caribbean. Feeling a sense of calm enveloping her,

Susan stared up at the starlit sky and wished she had someone to share the moment with.

The calm was shattered by a strident female voice: "What is your fucking problem? Get over it, buddy!"

Susan looked across to the adjoining balcony and saw a stunning brunette in a black lace teddy pacing back and forth with a telephone in her hand, snarling into the receiver: "I am sick and tired of your jealousy, Mitch. Take it out on your shrink—not me!"

The brunette slammed the receiver down, screamed in frustration, then turned her head toward Susan's balcony and, without any introduction, asked: "Do you understand men at all? Or is it just me? You don't have to answer. What is their problem? Do you think it's breast-feeding? Or lack of it? Get over it, buddy! Know what I mean? I'm on my fucking feet all day long in this . . . this dehydration. How much water are you drinking? That's the secret, you know. Eat all you want. Anything you want. Just drink a gallon of water a day. He phones me long-distance to find out who I'm having an affair with. *Who?* Who am I going to have an affair with on this shoot? Every time he sees one of my old movies, he's convinced I fucked my leading man. Half of them were gay! More than half!! Get over it, buddy! God! You're so easy to talk to. How come we haven't met before? You've got a terrible burn, kid. What are you taking for it? I've got just the answer. No, no, no. No problem. I'll be right there. What's your room number? Ha! That's a good one. You're right next door."

Before Susan could register the stunning brunette's

invitation to drop over, there was a knock at the door.

"Who is it?"

"Me."

"Oh." Susan felt foolish. She didn't even know the woman's name. Why was she letting her into the suite? "Hello," said Susan, opening the door for her uninvited visitor, who was now wearing a black silk dressing gown over her teddy. "I'm Susan Given." She thrust her hand out.

The stunning brunette plopped a tube of aloe into Susan's palm and, without offering her own name in return, strode into the room and asked: "How's your AC? It's like an icebox over in my place. Ohhh! Whose kids are these?" She scooped up the framed photos of Polly and Ivy displayed on the sideboard.

"Mine," replied Susan proudly.

"They're gorgeous! Adopted, huh? I didn't want to say anything in case they were your housekeeper's. I'm sensitive that way. I've been debating adoption. I could still have kids, you know. I mean I'm only thirty-five. I'm not bullshitting you. Everyone thinks I'm younger. Want me to go get my driver's license? Water. That's what does it. And wheat grass enemas. Plus I'm one-eighth Cherokee, which gives me these great cheekbones. They're all mine. Nobody pulled any molars. Mitch freaked when he found out I was Cherokee. I think he thought I was Jewish. He told his mother I was Jewish. She still doesn't know. Thirty-five's not too late, right? It's just Mitch. My husband. The one on the phone. Travels all over the world. Never has time to do it for recreation let alone pro-creation. He'd have to leave his sperm in an ice cube for me. With my luck, I'd mix it in with my power shake in the morning. Got anything to drink?"

The brunette kneeled down beside the minibar and checked out the supply of booze.

"And what's *your* name?" asked Susan pointedly.

"Colette. Cooke. I'm Colette Cooke." Susan stared blankly at the brunette. "You never heard of me?"

"Is there a warrant outstanding for your arrest?"

"What is that, a joke?"

"Yes. The only famous people I know are criminals."

"Why is that?" asked Colette, still smarting from Susan's not recognizing her.

"I'm an assistant district attorney in Manhattan. Asset Forfeiture."

"Wow! Do you carry a gun?"

"No."

"I knew it! I told that asshole producer D.A.s don't carry guns. Wouldn't listen to me. Another man who knows everything. Goddamn pilot would have sold if I hadn't been running around waving a gun with my tits hanging out."

"You're an actress?"

"The verdict's not in on that yet. Hey! That's funny, isn't it. 'Verdict's not in.' I like you, Helen. You're so easy to talk to—"

"My name is Susan and I'm really tired so—"

"Here," said Colette, holding up two miniature bottles of brandy. "This'll wake you up."

"It's a little late for—"

"You due in court in the morning?"

"No."

"I've got to shoot tomorrow and you don't see me popping under the covers. Come on. Loosen up. You're the first girlfriend I've had since I left the States. Were you ever an actress?" Colette broke the label on the first miniature brandy and passed it over to Susan.

"Only in college. I played Mary Haines in *The Women* and got the bug for a while. Actually thought I might give it a whirl. But I just didn't—"

"I was the Playmate of the Year. That's how I got into movies. Down in Florida. I had a one-day bit. Sitting on Burt Reynolds' lap. I didn't have a line of dialogue. Just wiggled around a lot. Burt's toupee kept sliding off all the time. He got very uptight. Not like Sean Connery. He doesn't care about his rug. Hell! He doesn't wear it anymore. I met him at a party once. Sooo sexy. These are still my own tits, you know. I haven't touched them yet. Nobody believes me. Wanna feel them?"

"Not really."

"Hey, I'm not making a pass, Susan. Not my scene. I'd probably have a bigger career now if I'd done my share of rug munching. There was this one tiny dyke mystery writer had the biggest crush on me. Flowers dumped on my bed every morning. Hyacinths! I finally grabbed the love-crazed bitch by her teeny-weeny double-breasted lapels and said: 'Get over it, buddy!' Didja ever have any liposuction?"

"No!"

"Smart. Complete waste of time. Actually you're in pretty good shape. What are you? Forty?"

"Forty-five."

"You're in *very* good shape. Married?"

"Estranged. Separated. Trying to get a divorce."

"How long?"

"Three years."

"Oh, honey! That's terrible. Yuck! What's the problem? You're a lawyer. Hell, you're a D.A. Can't you cut through all that red tape?"

When it became clear that Colette might actually listen to her, Susan unfolded the story of her nightmare union with psychiatrist Hugh Carver and how he and his lawyer had been making life a living hell for her. She recounted the endless list of girlfriends her estranged husband had gone through right up until the most recent one.

"We all thought she was a Swedish salesgirl. I mean she *was* a salesgirl at Barney's and she *was* supposed to be Swedish. Then it turned out she was a former hooker from Los Angeles named Annabel—"

"Dwyer!" shrieked Colette. "My God! I don't believe this. And we don't have to cut Kevin Bacon in on it. Zero degrees of separation. Annabel Dwyer was my stand-in!"

"Stand-in?"

"In the movies? You know, whenever they want to light a shot and they don't want you standing around melting under the . . ."

Susan knew exactly what a stand-in was. That wasn't why she had reacted to the word. What made her stop was the fact that she already knew Annabel/Sigrid had been Colette's stand-in. And it wasn't via some psychic revelation. No, it was something Michael Roth had told her months before in the kitchen. Not about Annabel either. What was it? Something about this Colette Cooke.

Of course. They had been lovers. She'd wanted to marry Michael. Susan stared at the gorgeous, buxom, one-eighth Cherokee brunette, who had wanted her to squeeze her breasts and insisted that she was her girlfriend after knowing her less than half an hour. People in Greenwich never behaved like that. That was California. That was Michael and all the reasons she ultimately couldn't have had a relationship with him. And what did it matter anyhow, thought Susan. The affair with Michael was over. She was certain of that now. How could she have had a relationship with a man who was cheating on her with—? No, it was Colette's husband who'd been cheating. Wait a minute! She didn't even know Colette's husband. It must have been Hugh. Oh! Enough of all these men.

"Colette, I'm sorry. I have to go to sleep. I cannot keep my eyes open another second."

"No problema, kid. Come visit me on the set tomorrow. We'll have fun."

"I look forward to it. Thanks again for the aloe."

It was after midnight by the time Susan finally shut her eyes atop the king-sized bed but she went into a deep sleep immediately. And dreams. Wild, erotic dreams where she was in bed once more with Michael. Legs entwined with Michael's. Then another pair of legs. Long, gorgeous legs. Colette's. What was she doing in the bed? And all the while Ascension leaned against a wall strumming his guitar and the ubiquitous Dirk Angelus chuckled away while snapping Polaroids to fax overnight to Hugh Carver.

14

TWO WEEKS LATER Susan sat under Colette's sun tent on the beach, sipping an icy fruit-juice cocktail and staring out at the tranquil waters of the Caribbean. "Whose boat is that?"

"Hmmm? Wha'd you say, kid?" Colette's face was buried in her script trying to learn the new "pink" pages that she had just received twenty minutes earlier. "I don't get this. These lines make no sense. Anthony! What is this shit?"

Anthony, an angular assistant director in his late twenties with a hopeless crush on Colette, buzzed over to the tent and dropped to his knees as if he were a different Anthony bringing a message to Cleopatra herself. "They're rewrites the network asked for. The earlier draft was politically incorrect."

"Gimme a break, buddy! Who could possibly take offense at anything in this moronic piece of soft porn."

"Anthony?"

"Yes, Miss Given?"

"Do you know whose boat that is out there? The three-masted sailboat? There's something very ominous about it."

"That's Crimson's boat," said Anthony, lowering his voice. "The local drug lord."

Susan's brow wrinkled upon hearing the name. Hadn't Betty made some cryptic remark about him that first night in her kitchen?

"Take it easy, Susan," said Colette, peering over the top of her sunglasses. "You're on vacation."

"I didn't say anything."

"No, but I could hear your heart pounding when you heard the phrase 'drug lord.' Leave that guy alone or you'll have the entire crew after you. Mr. Crimson's probably their dealer."

"We'll need you in about ten minutes, Miss Cooke."

"Better write these new lines out on cards for me, Anthony, or draw them in the sand. I'm a slow study."

"I'm not telling Jean-Yves that."

"Oh, please! Is our poor Québecois director going to have another grand mal seizure? How the hell's he going to know if I'm saying the right lines anyhow? Did you hear what that Frog said to me yesterday? 'Speak closer when you speak English.' Hello-ooo? Anybody home?"

Susan laughed (after two weeks she had finally plugged into Colette's humor), stood up, and set off for a stroll down the beach.

"Where are you going?" shouted Colette when she finally noticed Susan disappearing toward the horizon.

"Visit my other friend."

This had been the pattern of Susan's days on St. Stephen's. Get up early. Run on the beach. Have breakfast. Swim in the pool. Catch up on her reading. Visit with Colette on the set. Hang out farther down the beach at Ascension's bar. Evenings visiting Betty and the kids. Not to mention more cockatrice classes with Orestes and Priam.

When she reached the palm-and-bamboo establishment, Susan discovered Ascension staring mournfully at a framed photograph of a little girl wearing a white communion dress standing in front of an island church.

"Are you okay?" she asked.

"This is my little sister," replied Ascension, holding the photo out for her to examine.

"The one in New York?"

"Yes. Conception. I raised her. She was the child of my mother's old age. My son Achilles is older than she."

"When did you last hear from her?"

"Not since she went to New York. Five years ago."

"I could help locate her when I get back. If you'd like."

"She does not want to be found, Susan. She is a bird who flew too far from the nest. She has lost her sense of direction. I mourn her absence every day."

"I'm so sorry, Ascension."

"Don't worry your pretty head about it, Susan. What news of the movie people? Will they finish soon?"

"I think so."

"You will miss Colette when she leaves."

"I'll have to leave soon myself."

"Why?"

"Crime never sleeps, Ascension. I've been resting and building my strength up again. Soon I'll be ready to go home and do what I do best."

A tall, handsome boy in his late teens jogged up

from the beach toward the bar at that moment and greeted Susan like a long-lost relative.

"This must be the famous Susan. I've heard so much about you, girl."

"I wish I could say the same about you."

"This is Ulysses, my second oldest son. The family entrepreneur."

"Want to take a virtual-reality tour of the island? The only one of its kind in the entire Caribbean. Only twenty dollars. Normally thirty. You get the special family rate."

"What does this virtual-reality tour involve?" asked Susan, fearing the young man wanted to sell her some drugs.

"You got strong arms?" asked Ulysses, who abruptly squeezed Susan's biceps. "Not bad. Not bad. You can hang on wit' no trouble at all."

"Hang on to what? What does this tour consist of?"

"Parasailing," replied Ulysses, staring deeply into Susan's eyes. "Nothin' like it in the world, girl. The ultimate high. Hiiiigh."

"I don't think so."

"Why not?"

"Because I've never done it before."

"Did Edison invent the lightbulb before he invented it? Dat's no excuse," replied Ulysses, taking her hand and pulling her off the bar stool. "Nothing bad will happen to you. You have a safety harness and a life preserver. And I will be in the boat wit' Randall. What more could you ask for?"

"To sit peacefully in the shade and sip my fruit juice cocktail."

"Why don't you go with the boy?" coaxed Ascension. "I have to do some shopping in town anyhow. This way we can all keep an eye on you."

"How can you do that?"

"Up above the world so high," smiled Ascension, saucily pointing his long black finger toward a puffy white cloud drifting by.

"I feel like the understudy for the Goodyear blimp."

Susan begrudgingly followed Ulysses down to the water's edge where a small speedboat lay at anchor bobbing up and down. Asleep in the boat was an obese teenage boy with dyed blond hair.

"Wake up, Randall. We got a customer."

Randall opened his eyes and focused on a wary Susan staring down at him. Then, with an agility belying his girth, Randall leaped to his feet and began gathering up the parasailing equipment.

Seconds later Susan was standing on the beach in her blue one-piece bathing suit with a harness strapped across her chest and shoulders, feeling the tug of a huge red kite sail floating about in the sky. A nylon cord connected the harness to the boat.

"It's pulling me!" squealed Susan, digging her toes into the sand and attempting to remain earthbound.

"It's just a little breeze," replied Ulysses. "When we take the boat farther out, you really gonna fly, girl."

"What do I do with these?" asked Susan as the boy hung a cheap pair of binoculars around her neck.

"That's the virtual reality." Ulysses dashed back into the surf and climbed into the boat next to Randall. He signaled to his friend to gun the motor, then turned around to Susan and called out: "Don't resist! Just let it carry you up like a feather."

"What if something goes wrong?" shouted Susan. "What if we have to abort?"

"You're not an astronaut, girl. When you come down in the water, release the clasp on the harness."

"What clasp?"

But Ulysses did not hear her question over the revving of the motor. Susan, in turn, felt her body rudely defying gravity. Shutting her eyes for a second, she gasped at the curious sensation she was experiencing. Then she opened her lids, stared down, and saw her feet leaving the ground. Moments later she was airborne.

"Jeepers!" crowed Susan, feeling a rush of excitement surge through her body. Ulysses was right. This *was* the ultimate high. She felt like a goddess in the *Iliad* gazing down at the pathetic combatants fighting the Trojan War. How small and insignificant such ancient and modern battles were! Susan was as far from Centre Street and Lydia's interminable machinations as was imaginable. And this suited the blond prosecutor to a tee. All that mattered now, from her Olympian vantage point, were the sea and the sky and the point on the horizon where they melded together.

Fishing boats were bobbing about on the water, bringing in the catch of the day. Birds would occasionally dive down from the heavens in pursuit of their own daily bill of fare. Closer to the shoreline, motorboats were dragging skiers along the water's surface. The luxury hotels were now coming into view. There was the Henry Morgan. Susan wondered if she could possibly recognize anyone from this height. Ah! The binoculars. But how was she supposed to hold on to the parasail and focus the glasses? What was the trick? Look, Ma! One hand. Wait, wait, Susan. Don't make this any more complicated than necessary. Rest your elbows on the bar. You're strapped in. The wind does all the work. There. Now, focus the lens. Sharper, sharper.

Wow! There was the swimming pool with the waiters threading through the cots and chairs dispensing mai-tais, daiquiris, and similar libations calculated to blur the senses. She could see (but mercifully not hear) Bonnie Blue Waffington in her Technicolor muumuu chattering away to a gaggle of gambling widows while their husbands shunned the sun in favor of the permanent shade of the casino. (The dreaded Bud bellowed at Susan, on those occasions when she encountered him in the lobby, that Harry was still available and "a damned good catch" in the bargain.)

Now Ulysses's boat was shifting direction radically and going past the stretch of beach where Colette and the crew were filming. Where was Colette? Sometime, before they parted company, Susan was determined to ask the actress the details of her affair with Michael Roth.

Where were they going now? Floating over a deserted stretch of the island. One of the myriad little coves where pirates and buccaneers of old had stolen ashore to bury their treasure.

The wind was beginning to shift and Susan felt the sail begin to dip. The island was drawing closer and closer. What was wrong? Then she looked up and saw the tear in the sail. Did Ulysses see it as well? Shouldn't they pull her in?

"Ulysses! Ulysses!"

She looked down at the boat through the binoculars and saw the two boys lying on their backs listening to the deafening sounds of a boom box and sharing a joint. Oh, perfect! In their present condition, the two entrepreneurs had probably forgotten she was even attached to the sail.

The hole in the sail was now growing larger and she was losing altitude at an alarming rate. If she went down in the water, Susan would be all right. But there was too much line on the sail and it was now considerably inland.

She felt panic beginning to set in. This was not the way she wanted to die. Dragged senseless across some rugged terrain until her skull caved in. This was not the way she wanted to be remembered: ASSISTANT DISTRICT ATTORNEY DIES IN FREAK PARASAILING ACCIDENT.

No! What had Ulysses said about hitting the water and unfastening a clasp? Where was it? She groped the circumference of the harness like a blind person speed-reading in Braille. This must be it! How had she suddenly acquired ten thumbs? Relax, relax. Don't panic. She fumbled with the metal catch securing the nylon line to the harness. It was a crazy gamble but she'd rather take her chances this way. Polly and Ivy's faces flashed in front of her.

Then she was free of the nylon line and the tug of the boat. Sailing through the sky. Free as a bird. A bird with a broken wing.

15

MITCHELL LEVENSTEIN sat contemplatively behind his priceless Louis Quatorze desk (purchased two years earlier at a heart-stopping Sotheby's auction) in his imported Turnbull & Asser striped shirtsleeves, staring blankly out the window onto Fifth Avenue. The lawyer-banker aspired to a state of serenity assisted by a CD of Tibetan wind chimes piping through the speakers of his office sound system.

In just a few minutes, his devoted secretary, Viebeka, would place a long-distance phone call to the swami on Maui and the holy man would remind a grateful Levenstein, yet again, of the god that dwelt within him.

"Mr. Levenstein?"

"What is it, Viebeka? Is my watch wrong? It's not time for the swami already?" Levenstein hoped his secretary had not noticed the level of anxiety in his voice. That was one of the myriad issues he was desperate to discuss with the swami. At four o'clock. His Raymond Weil de Genève wrist watch read 3:50 and it kept perfect time.

"No, sir. It's Draycott Simms. The Third."

"Third what?"

"That's his name, Mr. Levenstein. Draycott Simms the Third. From the *New York Times.*"

"Tell him I already have a subscription," replied Levenstein, hoping to emulate the lofty patrician tones his employer and mentor used so frequently and, thus, bring the conversation to a speedy conclusion. He mustn't keep the swami waiting.

"He's writing an article on the bank, sir. About the investigation."

"Can't he speak to what's-his-name? You know. The public relations person. What the hell is his name?"

"Tim Eisinger."

"Tim Eisinger. Exactly. Isn't that what we pay Eisinger for?"

"Mr. Eisinger suggested he speak to you."

"He did?"

"Yes, Mr. Levenstein."

"Well, I sure as hell want a word with Eisinger. I don't speak to just anyone."

"I tried to explain that to Mr. Simms. But the story is running tomorrow, apparently, and he wanted you to have the opportunity to comment and/or correct any of the—"

"All right, Viebeka." Levenstein sighed, rose from behind his desk, and put on his suit jacket as if he were actually going to receive this Mr. Simms III in his princely Fifth Avenue office. Instead, Levenstein lifted the well-manicured forefinger of his right hand and pressed the speaker button on his telephone.

"Mr. Simms?"

"Mr. Levenstein?" A sophisticated, prep-school-and-Ivy-League-educated voice filled the room with tremendous self-confidence. "Thank you so much for taking my call."

"Pleasure. I hope we can make this swift. I have a four o'clock conference call that I cannot—"

"Shouldn't take long. Just a few questions."

"Proceed."

"You're forty-six years old?"

"Correct."

"And you've worked for Dwight Pelham for the past eighteen years?"

"More like twenty. I went straight from law school into Mr. Pelham's Washington office. But surely these facts are all a matter of public record, Mr. Simms. You don't need me to corroborate them."

"And when exactly did you two take over the American Patriot Bank?"

"We didn't 'take it over,' Mr. Simms. Mr. Pelham was on the board of the bank when it was still Great Northern Fidelity—"

"Before OICB bought it?"

"The Overseas International Credit Bank is an investor along with a great many other investors."

"Yes. Well, this is where I and a lot of other people get a little confused, Mr. Levenstein. You and Mr. Pelham have been running the bank since 1991."

"That is correct."

"But your law firm still acts as counsel for the bank."

"Do you find that unusual, Mr. Simms?"

"A little. Especially since you and Mr. Pelham also act for OICB, the bank's parent company."

"OICB has no authority or influence whatsoever over American Patriot."

"Can I quote you?"

"Why not?"

"So neither you nor Mr. Pelham are answerable to Nassim Narouz, the founder of OICB?"

"Mr. Narouz is an investor in our bank. He neither dictates policy nor—"

"Didn't he instruct you to rent offices directly across the street from OICB?"

"Absolutely not."

"So you're just coincidental neighbors of his on Fifth Avenue?"

"As are the Disney Store and Trump Tower, Mr. Simms. I really don't see where these questions are—"

"Did you not tell a Senate subcommittee four years ago in Washington that OICB was merely a passive investor in American Patriot?"

"Possibly."

"Possibly you said it? Or possibly passive?"

"You've run out of time, Mr. Simms. I can't imagine what further use I can be to your article."

"District Attorney William Archibald seems to think—"

"Good-bye, Mr. Simms." Four o'clock. Time for the swami.

"One last question?"

"What is it?" Swami, swami, swami.

"Your wife is forty. Correct?"

"What!?! She's thirty-five! And what does her age have to do with the bank or anything?"

"She was Playmate of the Year twenty years ago. Are you saying she was only fifteen when she posed for *Playboy*?"

"Good-bye, Mr. Simms."

Mitch Levenstein hung up the telephone and felt a wave of nausea overtaking him. Who the hell was this

Draycott Simms III anyhow? Levenstein removed his jacket and discovered his shirt drenched in perspiration. He stumbled toward the Queen Anne armoire on the other side of the office, opened the reversed doors, and found another shirt still under plastic from the cleaners. He popped two buttons whipping the wet shirt off his back, then took a deep breath and waited for his body to cool down before putting on the clean shirt.

Forty! She *was* forty, as he'd always suspected. She'd lied about her age as she'd obviously lied about everything else. Particularly the men. Why had he ever married her? She was a savage. A Cherokee, for God's sake. Insatiable with a couple of drinks in her. She'd ruin him yet. That's what he really had to fear. Not Archibald's investigation or the feds. No, Mitchell Levenstein's fate rested solely in the hands, legs, and other body parts of Mrs. Levenstein, aka Colette Cooke, who, unlike Caesar's wife, was everywhere near reproach. And where was his forty-year-old Calpurnia now? Probably arching her back on some beach sharing her favors with the entire crew of that TV movie. Oh! Help! He felt a migraine coming on.

Moving swiftly to his desk, he buzzed the devoted Viebeka.

"Yes, sir?"

"Where's Mr. Pelham?"

"In his office. But he has someone with him."

"I need to see him right away."

"But it's four o'clock, Mr. Levenstein. We have to call the swami."

"Fuck the swami! We'll call him later. This is more important."

16

SUSAN FELT EXTREMELY foolish. She also felt extremely grateful that she was still alive. Even if she was presently hanging upside down from the limb of a pepper tree in the middle of nowhere. Susan certainly had no intention of paying Ulysses a penny for his virtual-reality tour.

When Susan had released the metal catch securing the nylon line to the boat, the wind shifted course yet again and the sail carried her off in an entirely different direction. At the same time, the tear in the sail grew larger, bringing her closer and closer toward the ground.

Then she saw the pepper tree holding out its limbs to catch her. What was that old Disney cartoon she had seen as a child? Black and white. Dancing trees. Holding hands in a circle. At the time, being a nononsense child of Greenwich, she had pooh-poohed the idea of trees having hands and arms. Now she was grateful for the notion. Catch me! Catch me! Break my fall. But please, don't break my neck!

The torn red sail collided with the highest tree limb, arresting her descent. But the old and twisted limb snapped under the unexpected weight, leaving Susan and her rigging entangled and defying gravity as she hung upside down, gazing at the ground ten feet below.

Now what? Fiercely competitive at school, Susan had excelled more at volleyball than gymnastics. The parallel bars and vaulting horses were not sources of triumph for her. Always practical, she couldn't imagine a time in her life when she would ever need to roll her body into a ball or twist her limbs into some grotesque posture. Ha! The hubris of youth.

She was going to have to right herself somehow. There was no way she could possibly unfasten the harness and drop ten feet to the ground. Not upside down. And not at forty-five. She was a marathon runner, not an escape artist.

And where were Ulysses and Randall while she was paying her unintentional tribute to Harry Houdini? Had the two teenagers finally realized their client was no longer "up above the world so high" as Ascension had so merrily suggested? Would they already be organizing a search party to comb the island for her? Or notifying the Coast Guard to dispatch a boat to sea? And what Coast Guard would they notify? If the policeman at the airport was any indication of the speed and efficiency of St. Stephen's law enforcement agencies—What on earth was that?

Twisting her head around uncomfortably, Susan squinted at a huge crow perched above her, energetically pecking away at the remnants of the red sail. What was it doing? What possible nutritional value could the tattered sail offer? Perhaps it wasn't the food content but the color that held the black bird in its thrall? Was red as great an irritant to crows as to

91

bulls? Maybe that was the answer. Whatever it was, the crow was now attacking the sail with a fury and Susan could feel her body starting to sway as the sail began to tear once again.

"Go 'way! Go 'way!"

Susan gesticulated vainly with her arms in the crow's direction. The black bird insolently cawed back at her and continued to attack the sail.

"Oh, jeepers!" cried Susan, as she saw the earth rushing up toward her.

Thrusting her palms down in a hopeful effort to break her fall, she blinked in amazement as her hands stopped two inches short of the ground.

The crow cawed in triumph and flew away.

Shaking her head in amazement, Susan hastily undid the harness and allowed herself to slip to the ground.

Free at last! But where exactly was she? Where was the sun? Up in the sky where she'd left it. No longer a resident of Olympus but just another mere tax-paying mortal with a lousy sense of direction, she'd have no clue as to where she was until the sun finally set in the west. Except it would be pitch black then and, sure as hell, she didn't want to be out here in the middle of nowhere after dark. Should she try to find a road while it was still daylight or look for the ocean? Or should she stay put and wait for a rescue party to find her? Assuming there was a rescue party. Shading her eyes with her hand, she blinked up at the sky. The sun had already moved considerably. How long had she been out there? Was it now closer to five o'clock or six? For the past two evenings, she and Colette had

sat out on the balcony watching the red fireball liter-
ally drop into the sea. What time was that? Six-thirty.
It would be dark by six-thirty. Dark and frightening.
Ulysses *must* have gone for help by now. Or were he
and Randall planning on being their own rescue
party?

Here comes the crow again. No. It's a white bird. A
seagull. Which way is it flying? It must be going
toward the ocean. Follow that bird!

She tried to keep her eyes fixed on the seagull's
flight path but the bird seemed to be on an aimless
pleasure trip, dipping its wings purposelessly this way
and that. Where was the sea? Didn't it care? Weren't
there loved ones to provide for? Dinner to be served?

Susan paused when she realized she had uttered
the last three questions aloud. She'd been in the sun
far too long. She had become delirious. And thirsty.
How long had it been since she'd first snapped the
harness on and left the earth behind? Surely not
more than an hour. How could she have dehydrated
already? Dehydration. Colette's obsession. Not hers.
She'd be fine.

Was she still talking out loud? No. Then whose
voices was she hearing? Those weren't voices. Well,
not human. Gulls. Lots of gulls. Crying out to each
other. Susan moved in the direction of the cries and,
as she drew closer, was thrilled to hear the sound of
waves washing against the shore. The seagull had led
her in the right direction.

Soon she came to a rise and peered down, taking
in the familiar turquoise and azure of the Caribbean.
The island wasn't that big. If she walked along the

shore, she would eventually end up somewhere. The airport. The hotel. The town. Somewhere. Eventually.

Fifteen minutes later she saw a huge sailboat moored fifty yards offshore. A rowboat was making its way toward land and a huge black man with a shaved head leaped out of the bow once it had swept up onto the sandy beach. The man stared up and down the beach, looked at his watch, then cursed Cecil and Percy, two muscular men in their twenties who had rowed him ashore.

Susan debated whether or not to make her presence known to this landing party. Internal radar told her the man with the shaved head wasn't the likeliest candidate to ask for a lift home. He had "bad guy" written all over him. But Susan had always been a sucker for a good crime. Real or potential. And there was something familiar about this man that made her want to take a closer look.

This was one of the legendary coves that the smugglers and pirates had sailed in and out of for centuries, so Susan had no trouble scrambling unseen over the rocks that hugged the shoreline for a better look and listen.

"Where him be?" growled the man with the shaved head, checking his watch once again.

Susan was close enough now to clearly hear his native dialect and see that his watch was a gold Rolex. Then her eyes panned down to his shoes and her heart stopped cold. Nothing wrong with her radar. The shoes were two-tone leather, red and black. It was the same man who had slapped Ascension around her first night on the island.

"Dere him be!" Percy pointed a long finger down the beach.

The man with the two-tone shoes turned his head at the same moment Susan did. A familiar-looking dilapidated truck was bumping along the sand toward them until it finally came to a halt.

"Where the hell you was, little man?"

"I had errands to run," replied Ascension, climbing down from his truck.

"You got de shit?"

"In the back of the truck. Have you got my money, Crimson?"

Crimson! If Susan's heart had gone cold when she'd remembered Crimson's two-tone shoes, it was now positively frozen as she realized her beloved Ascension was in cahoots with the island's drug lord.

"You get de money when me give you de money."

"You said that the last time."

"Ain' me good to you, little man? Don' me take good care of you? Don' me watch out for you sister? Don' me make sure nobody dare steal from you bar when you ain' dere?"

"I will not do any more work for you until our accounts are up to date, Crimson."

"Are you threatening Crimson, little man? Don' you wanna live no more? You wanna make you big fat Betty a widow and leave all dem kids orphans?"

"I want what is due to me," said Ascension with seeming fearlessness.

Behind the safety of the rocks, Susan shook her head in despair. Either her dapper little friend was a brilliant bluffer or the biggest fool in the world. How had Ascension ever become involved with an obvious scumbag like this Crimson? Was the answer as simple as eleven mouths to feed? She would speak to Ascension later. She had to make him understand that no matter how lucrative the pay was he was contributing to the world epidemic of crime that—Oh, shit! Susan's foot had slipped on the wet rock, causing a smaller rock to go tumbling down toward the beach.

"What dat?" asked Crimson, whipping around in the direction of the rocks. Then he barked an order to one of his men: "Cecil, go look!"

Cecil started toward the rocks and Susan prayed she wouldn't be discovered.

"Here she am!" shouted Cecil.

Seconds later Susan felt her heels pounding along the wet sand with Cecil hard on her heels.

Crimson's voice shouted: "Get de bitch!"

You'll have to catch the bitch first, thought Susan as she took powerful strides along the beach. I run every morning, Mr. Crimson. Which is more than your hired thug can say for all his huffing and puffing—What the hell was that?

A bullet whizzed by over her head.

Now, thought Susan, that isn't playing fair.

17

"GET OVER IT, buddy! I'm not going up in that thing!"

"What are you? Crazy?"

"No, you're crazy if you think I'm going up in it!"

"I'll have you fired."

"On the last day of shooting? I don't think so, Jean-Yves. It's bad bookkeeping. You'd have to start the whole picture over again. I don't think the network would go for it."

"You are being purposely sabotogical, Colette."

"The only thing 'sabotogical' here, Jean-Yves, is your abuse of the English language. I don't like helicopters. All the script said was 'Kelly gets in helicopter.' *Period.*"

"I don't understand. You take your clothes off without the slightest hesitational—"

"Hesitation, honey. And that was for Hef. Twenty years ago." Then Colette hastily corrected herself. "Fifteen."

Star and director stood staring at each other on the beach in front of the Henry Morgan Hotel. Quite a crowd had gathered to watch this little contretemps/temper tantrum as the sun began to sink rapidly in the west.

"I've got an idea," said Anthony, the second assistant director.

"What is it?" asked Jean-Yves Corbeau, as he nibbled on his all too thin upper lip.

"Break it up into two shots. Show Colette getting into the chopper. Then cut and have her stand-in do the actual flight."

"No!" replied Jean-Yves emphatically. "That is not the way I designed it. I want one smooth shot."

"The Steven Spielberg of Quebec," laughed Colette.

"You would not behave like this if your husband was not a millionaire," snarled Jean-Yves.

"Leave my husband out of this, Frenchie, unless you want to get my Cherokee up."

"Don't threaten me with your Cherokee. I am part Iroquois."

"Since when?"

Before the director could reply, Dirk Angelus rushed onto the set, followed by Ulysses, Randall, and a local police sergeant.

"We need this helicopter," said Angelus.

"Are you crazy?" asked Jean-Yves, pointing toward the sun. "We are losing the light."

"And we've lost a guest," countered the hotel manager. "A very important guest." Then he turned to the crowd of familiar faces and added hastily: "Not that you aren't all important to us. It's just that Ms. Given—"

"Susan?" asked Colette. "Something's happened to Susan?"

"These boys took her parasailing and something happened to the sail."

"Her cut herself loose!" protested Randall, determined to stick to the story he had already told the police sergeant.

"Where is she?" asked Colette.

"The north side of the island," said Angelus. "But we need to find her while it's still light."

"Let's go!" said Colette, marching toward the helicopter.

"Where do you think you are going?" asked a dumbfounded Jean-Yves.

"Going to rescue my girlfriend. Okay?"

"Do you think you can just march in here and commandate my helicopter?"

"It's not your helicopter, Frenchie," said Colette as she climbed into the chopper behind Angelus and the police sergeant.

"But I rented it!"

"And kindly loaned it to the police to assist in their search," said Angelus. "Isn't that correct, Sergeant Roberts?"

"Thank you very much." Roberts nodded.

"Where do you all think you're going?" asked the pilot, who had been silent until now. "This isn't a Greyhound bus, folks."

"We're on a rescue mission," said Colette breathlessly.

"How many are we rescuing?" asked the pilot.

"One," replied Angelus.

"So that leaves one spotter and everyone else off. Otherwise they'll be sending a rescue party for us."

Sergeant Roberts climbed into the chopper but Colette was adamant about squeezing in as well. Ulysses gave the pilot a vague idea of where he had lost sight of Susan, then ducked out of the way of the whirring blades.

Jean-Yves watched in shock as the helicopter whisked the star of his movie away from the set.

"What am I going to tell the network?" wailed the director. "I was on schedule. Under budget."

"Don't worry," said Anthony, tapping his frantic boss on the shoulder. "I got the shot for you."

"What?" The director spun around and stared in amazement at his grinning second assistant.

"I had the camera rolling the whole time."

"Who authorized you to—?"

"Did you want the shot or not?"

"Did you pan left or right?" asked Jean-Yves.

"Left."

"Good boy, Anthony. Just like I planned it. Remind me to buy you a drink later."

The helicopter made a few passes over the coves without any luck. There were only a few brief minutes of daylight left. Then Colette shrieked with delight.

"I think I see her."

"Where?" asked the pilot.

"Down on the beach. I don't believe it. Here we are worried to death over her and she's down there jogging."

"I don't think so. Take a look behind her. Those guys don't look like personal trainers. Shit! Did you hear that?"

"What?"

"Sounds like gunshots. What are you laughing at, Colette?"

"This is better than anything Jean-Yves has in his lousy movie and there isn't a camera in sight to film it."

"Hold on tight!"

"What are you doing?" asked a terrified Sergeant Roberts.

"Giving those guys a haircut."

Susan's heart was pounding. Percy and Cecil were still behind her somewhere and continuing to fire their gun. Guns? How many were there and did it really matter? It only took one bullet to get the job done. What irony! Just when she had finally managed to relax and forget about Junior Tesla and work, somebody else was trying to kill her. Why? What had she seen? Or what did Crimson think she'd seen?

Damn! The sun had just gone down. Someone had thrown the celestial light switch and everything was dark. Did they ever have blind people running in the marathon? Susan couldn't remember.

Oh, no! Where had that rock come from? Or whatever it was that had sprung up from the darkness and sent her flying through the air and sprawling onto the sand. She struggled to get back up on her feet. No luck. Pain! Lots of pain. What had she done to her ankle? Susan couldn't get up. No matter how hard she tried. Through the darkness she could hear the men breathing and cursing as they drew closer to her. It wasn't going to be pleasant when they caught up with her. Not one bit.

Could the men hear her heart pounding through her chest as loudly as she could? This was all Michael's fault. If the man had only minded his business and not phoned Barry, she would not be in this predicament now.

Then she heard the deafening sound directly overhead. She looked up and saw a searchlight combing the beach and nearby rocks. Who could this be? Good guys or bad? Should she wave her arms to signal them or lie low? One good thing about the helicopter: it was drowning out the sound of her own heartbeats.

Cecil and Percy scurried along the beach, fearful of their boss's wrath.

"Us in deep shit, Percy. Crimson ain't gonna like dis."

"What us s'pose to do, Cecil? Dat damn helicopter almost cut me head off. Where you at, man? I can't see you."

"Me be worried, Percy. Dat gal seen us."

"Her don' see shit, man. Her run for she life."

"Damn but her a good runner! Did you see dem legs, Percy?"

"What for you tink about de sex now, Cecil? Me thought you worried 'bout Crimson."

"Mebbe Ascension got de right idea. Stand up to Crimson. Him not used to dat."

"And mebbe you a bigger fool than me ever tink, Cecil. Is you so tired of life dat you gonna cross Crimson?"

"But de little man!"

By this time Cecil and Percy had reached the spot where the rowboat was moored. The tide had come in and Crimson was struggling to keep the boat from drifting out to sea.

"Dere were a chopper!" blurted Percy, hoping to circumvent his boss's wrath. "It come and took de gal away."

"Me seen it," growled Crimson. "C'mon. Us got to get out of here." Percy and Cecil started to climb into the rowboat but Crimson stopped Cecil with a powerful hand in his chest. "Here." He dangled a set of keys in front of Cecil's face. "Get rid of de little man's truck."

"Where be Ascension?" asked Cecil, searching about in the darkness.

"Him gone."

18

SUSAN SAT ON the edge of the bathtub holding a large daiquiri in one hand and staring in disbelief at her swollen ankle. Putting her drink down, she replaced the Ace bandage and reached for the brightly colored, hand-carved walking stick Angelus had given her following the hotel doctor's examination.

Two weeks. She'd be walking with a cane for two weeks. *If* she felt compelled to walk at all.

There was a knock at the door. Susan looked at her travel clock. Almost ten. Time for bed. Only one more day in "paradise," then she could return to the comparative safety of New York. The knocking continued. Susan limped across the room to answer the door. Anthony, the assistant director, stood there with a silly grin on his face. He'd been drinking.

"Hi."

"Hello, Anthony."

"Colette—Miss Cooke—sent me up to fetch you."

"What for?"

"The wrap party. We finished shooting tonight and we leave tomorrow. Everyone's having a helluva time. There's a steel drum band and dancing—"

"I don't think I'm quite up to dancing, do you?"

"Miss Cooke gave me strict instructions not to come back without you."

Susan finally gave in and rode down in the elevator with the slightly inebriated assistant director, who boasted about the shot he'd managed to sneak in that afternoon. But Susan wasn't really listening. Her mind was on Ascension and why he had not interceded on her behalf when her life was in danger. How could he have ignored her plight? How serious was his involvement with Crimson? How could she have been so mistaken about a person's character?

Throughout the helicopter ride back Susan gave Sergeant Roberts a professional report of what had transpired at the pirate's cove. But the sergeant seemed more concerned with the state of Susan's health following hours of exposure and dehydration (there was that word again!) than any criminal activity that might have occurred. Might have occurred! What about the men who'd been shooting at her? The sergeant assured her that all those "minor details" could be dealt with the next day if she cared to come around to the police station.

The movie people had taken over the hotel terrace for their farewell party and Colette was posing for photographs with various members of the crew. When the former Playmate of the Year saw Susan limping out onto the patio, she forsook her admirers, rushed toward her new best friend, and grabbed her in an embrace.

"Are you okay, kid?"

"I'm fine. Really. That hotel doctor's a bit of an

alarmist. Two weeks? I don't think so. I just twisted my ankle, that's all."

"I meant those guys chasing you down the beach. The pilot was certain they were firing at you. Were they?"

"It's curious, Colette. I managed to get through the first forty-five years of my life without anyone ever pulling a gun on me—let alone actually shooting. Somehow, in the last six months, I've become everyone's favorite target."

"Bad karma."

"Do Episcopalians have karma?"

"I don't know, kid. It must be life imitating TV. God knows there's no art left. Maybe you *should* be carrying a gun. Just a little one. Does Tiffany's make guns? What are you drinking?"

"I had a daiquiri upstairs."

"Then you can have one down here, too. Come and sit down. How's your ankle? I can't believe I'm leaving tomorrow. Will we see each other in New York or was it just another location romance? Just kidding! You have no idea the grilling my husband is going to put me through when I get back. 'Who did you sleep with? How many times? Don't lie to me.' Mr. Spirituality. Do you know he phones a swami in Maui once a week for spiritual advice? Gimme a break! You've been with me all week. Did I sleep with anyone?"

Susan stared at Colette and realized this was the last opportunity she would ever have to broach the subject that had been gnawing away at her since the first evening they met.

"That Annabel Dwyer person. The one my husband was involved with?"

"What about her?" asked Colette.

"She once mentioned a screenwriter to Hugh. I was wondering if you knew him or his reputation. Drat! I'm no good at names. Michael something. Canadian, I think."

"Not Michael Roth?"

"Yes," said Susan, wondering why she was bothering with all this subterfuge. "I think that was the name."

"My God! Michael Roth. If my husband could have one man on this planet bumped off, it would be Michael."

"Why?"

"Cuz my husband's insane, that's why. I hadn't even met Mitch when Michael and I were involved. Well, we weren't involved. Not publicly. We were acting in a movie he wrote. Up in Toronto. People thought we actually hated each other. But it was all a front. He had this nutty girlfriend and I had just broken up with—I can't tell you his name but he finally won an Oscar a couple of years ago. So Michael and I were getting it on incognito or whatever the word is. He was amazing! I lost it completely in that hotel room. Would have made a Marseilles sailor blush.

"Anyhow, flash forward. I'm married to Mitch. I think it was our honeymoon. It was. His boss gave us his place in East Hampton. Very romantic. That night I dreamt I was with Michael in that hotel room again. Did my blushing sailor routine. In my sleep! The next morning when I came down to breakfast, Mitch wouldn't say a word to me for half an hour. Finally he asked 'Who's Michael?' and went into a ten-million-dollar hissy fit. I had to take the Little Prince back upstairs and play the jade flute for an hour till he swore he wouldn't file for an annulment. Ohhh! I'm unnerved just thinking about it. How do you know Michael?"

"It must be a different Michael Roth," lied Susan.

"How many can there be? Oh! I'm getting flushed just thinking about it. Hey! Want to go to the casino? I haven't set foot in the place the whole shoot."

"I don't think so. I'm not much of a gambler—"

"Susan, it's research. How can you prosecute people without understanding the fever? You were an actress, kid. What did you do for motivation when you played Mary Haines? C'mon. I'll carry you piggyback."

"You're a wild woman, Colette."

"I'm part Cherokee. Remember? C'mon."

The casino was packed as it was every night. Susan watched in fascination as her fellow guests so eagerly and obligingly parted with their money. She and her assistant Alan Becker had argued for hours over the morality of people living on welfare risking what little income they had in gambling parlors run by the likes of The Matador. But, ultimately, they agreed on the bottom line: it was against the law in New York State and it was their job to prosecute offenders. How strange it now felt for her to stand in an opulent room far from home watching affluent people wager their money legally.

"Where do you want to start?" asked Colette.

"I'll just watch."

"No way, kid. C'mon. Let's try roulette."

Colette put twenty dollars down on red and Susan bet five on black. Within minutes Susan was up a hundred dollars and feeling the first symptoms of "the fever."

"This is very dangerous," whispered Susan, staring in disbelief at the pile of chips she had accumulated.

"Your bet, madam?" asked the croupier.

"Can I bet it all?" asked Susan.

"Save some of it," said Colette. "For tipping."

"But I feel lucky."

"And what if you lose it? You'll be bummed out all night."

"You bitches gonna bet or not?" rumbled the large black man in the plaid dinner jacket standing on Susan's left. "Me ain't got all night."

Colette was about to vent her Cherokee on the sexist with the shaved head when Susan's eyes panned down from his shaved head to his shoes. They were two-tone leather: red and black. Susan did not dare bring her eyes to meet his.

"What is your bet, madam?" repeated the croupier.

"Let it ride," said Susan, certain she could feel Crimson's gaze burning into her.

"What's wrong?" whispered Colette, picking up her companion's vibe.

Before Susan could reply, the gamblers in the casino flooded out of the room en masse.

"What's going on?" asked Susan.

"Let's see," said Colette, moving swiftly toward the lobby.

The two women moved through the glass doors and out onto the beach where cries and shouts were heard from the crowd now assembled.

"What's wrong, Jean-Yves?" asked Colette, as she

joined her director and the rest of the crew amidst the crush of people who had congregated as if by magic at the water's edge.

"A drowned man," replied Jean-Yves. "His body washed up on the beach."

A piercing female shriek was heard.

Then another voice cried out: "Oh, my God! Look at his neck. Think it was sharks?"

The drowned man's head had been all but severed from the rest of his body.

The next thing Susan recalled was Dirk Angelus's hands gripping her shoulders and urging her not to look at the corpse.

"You don't want to remember him that way," whispered the hotel manager.

"But who is it?" asked Susan, despite the fact she instinctively knew the answer.

"Poor little man," intoned Crimson, staring down at Ascension's mutilated body.

Susan looked up at the drug lord in the plaid dinner jacket and tried her best to stifle the emotions welling up inside her. How would she react, she kept repeating to herself, if she was back in New York? But she wasn't back in New York and the "poor little man" had befriended her.

"You killed him!"

Crimson stared down at Susan contemptuously and asked: "What you said, lady?"

"You heard me, Mr. Crimson. You killed Ascension and you tried to have me killed as well."

"Me tink you been in the sun too long. You not used to de heat."

"You're the one who better get used to the heat, Mr. Crimson." And, to her amazement, Susan found herself assuming the basic cockatrice defense stance that Orestes and Priam had taught her. Not easy to do while holding on to a cane.

"You gon' fight Crimson?" The drug lord burst out laughing. "What me supposed to do? Tie one hand behind me back? Look at de crazy white woman tryin' to do cockatrice."

"Please, Miss Given." Angelus put an arm around Susan's shoulder and attempted to steer her away from the drug lord.

"Isn't anyone going to do anything?" asked Susan. "Where are the police? Isn't anyone going to file charges?"

"Come on upstairs, kid." Colette now had her arms around a dazed and shaken Susan. "There's nothing you can do here. Leave it to the police."

"But where are the police?" asked a bewildered Susan.

Turning to the voyeuristic crowd, Angelus urged them all to return to the hotel, resume their evening recreations, and leave the authorities to deal with the unfortunate accident.

The concierge was hovering on the terrace waiting for Susan as Colette continued to lead her toward the lobby.

He placed two hundred dollars' worth of chips into a stunned Susan's hand.

"What's this?" murmured Susan.

"Your winnings, Miss Given."

19

THE ANCIENT YELLOW TAXICAB wound its way through the ramshackle village where the locals lived and turned into a familiar cul-de-sac. Susan struggled to emerge from the backseat and asked the driver to wait for her.

A few scrawny chickens were pecking desperately for food on the parched front lawn as Susan limped toward the front door, leaning on her cane. What would she say to Betty and her orphaned children? What words of comfort could she possibly offer them? Susan reached into her bag for the envelope containing her previous night's casino winnings plus an extra hundred dollars of her own. But what was three hundred dollars compared to the loss of a husband and father? She knocked once, then knocked again. There was no answer.

The door was slightly ajar. Susan pushed it open with her cane and stepped across the threshold into the tiny house.

"Betty? Are you there? It's Susan Given."

There was no reply. Only an eerie silence. Where could everyone be? And why was her leg starting to bother her again?

The pain seemed to increase as she moved slowly

around the house checking out the bedrooms. Were there any signs of violence? No. Nothing to indicate there had been any further reprisal by Crimson. Steady, Susan. This is not an official investigation. There is no physical evidence in sight. There is nothing. Except a little man who befriended you. A little man who is now dead and whose family has, seemingly, disappeared.

Pushing the doors open with her cane, Susan wondered: How could so many people live in such a tiny space? And still love each other? The wall of one bedroom was covered in orange, yellow, and red crayon drawings depicting island life—all with the bold signature "Clarissa" in the bottom right-hand corner. Dear little Clarissa. "Princess Di's" favorite. Susan smiled at the memory then opened the rough-hewn chest of drawers in the children's bedroom. Empty.

Walking through the kitchen where she had spent so many happy evenings during the previous two weeks, Susan could still see Ascension strumming his guitar and hear his lilting voice:

> "Oh woe! What a pity!
> Sunburned gal from the city."

The trade winds created a cool breeze as Susan gingerly stepped outside into the sun-bleached front yard. She limped around to the back of the house, hoping to discover some sign of life. Nothing.

Confused and disappointed by her visit, Susan was about to get back into the waiting taxi when she saw a local woman crossing the street, humming aloud and balancing a basket of laundry on her head.

Susan called out to her: "Excuse me!"

The woman stopped humming, then turned around and stared suspiciously at the white woman limping toward her.

"I'm looking for Betty." Susan felt foolish and ashamed for never having bothered to learn Ascension's family name.

"What you want wit' she?" asked the woman, removing the laundry basket from her head and setting it down on the ground next to her.

"I'm a friend of the family. I came to pay my condolences."

"Dey be gone."

"Gone? Where?"

"Las' night. Her gone wit' de childrens."

"But why?"

"Dey don' need no mo' trouble. Her ain't got a man no mo'. Why for her need to lose de childrens, too?"

"Was it Crimson? Were they afraid of Crimson?"

Abruptly picking up her laundry basket, the local woman betrayed no emotion as she balanced the load atop her head and continued on her way. Susan knew there would not be any further information from this woman or any of the other neighbors for that matter. She might as well be back in New York trying to get sworn statements from any terrorized witness. What incentive did law enforcement offer in exchange for cooperation? Was civic responsibility a reasonable reward compared to the bigger carrot of a longer life just for keeping your mouth shut?

Finally settled painfully in the backseat of the taxi,

Susan asked the driver to take her into town. Slowly. No bumps.

The local constabulary shared space with the library and tax office in a pink, picturesque, but highly dilapidated colonial structure in the town center.

Walking with extreme discomfort up the front steps of the historic building, Susan entered a musty foyer where the teak wood blades of the ceiling fan squeaked irritatingly as they revolved around and around overhead.

A short, pudgy policeman leaned against a pillar wearing a Walkman with his eyes glued shut, bobbing his head in all directions as he listened to unheard music.

"I'm looking for Sergeant Roberts," said Susan loudly as she approached him.

The pudgy policeman was grooving to the sounds of an entirely different planet as Susan tapped him sharply on the shoulder. He opened his eyes, removed his earphones, and glared in annoyance at Susan leaning on her cane.

"What you want?"

"I'm looking for Sergeant Roberts."

"Him gone to de beach."

"I see. Is there anyone else in authority I might speak to?"

"Captain Wilmot. Him de head man."

"Ah! And where might I find this head man?"

"Dere." And the pudgy policeman proudly pointed out a tall, handsome, black man in his late forties walking across the foyer, wearing a crisp, well-tailored white uniform.

Susan hobbled after him, calling out his name and waving her cane needlessly to get his attention.

"Oh, my!" said the handsome police captain, in a deep mellifluous voice as he halted halfway down the steps and pointed sympathetically toward her injured leg. "Waterskiing?"

"Parasailing."

"Is it painful? I'd always been told it was a harmless recreation."

"It's not as bad as it looks, Captain Wilmot."

"Ahh! You have the advantage of me, Miss . . ."

"Given. Susan Given."

"What a charming name. Very English for an American. But then you were colonized as well, weren't you? How can I be of service, Miss Given?" Captain Wilmot flashed her a rakish, engaging smile.

"I'm a guest at the Henry Morgan."

"The latest jewel in our island's inestimable crown. Aside from your regrettable accident, I trust you've been enjoying your stay with us, Miss Given."

"I was until last night."

"Ah, yes! The drowning on the beach. A most unfortunate episode."

"It was not a drowning, Captain Wilmot. A man was murdered. Executed."

"Executed? Aren't we being a bit melodramatic?"

"It was a drug-style execution. Commonly referred to as a 'Colombian necklace.' "

"Are you an aficionado of your country's tabloids, Miss Given?"

"I'm an assistant district attorney in New York City and I've seen more than my fair share of these things."

"Your specialty being homicide?"

"Asset Forfeiture actually. Mostly drug related."

"Fascinating. I'd love to have lunch with you some time and discuss your work but I have a previous engagement." The Captain's eyes drifted toward a Rolls-Royce convertible parked out on the street. A pretty young woman wearing a sun hat and a sleeveless polka dot dress sat behind the wheel beaming in his direction. "My niece."

"Your niece is blonde?" asked Susan, staring at the young woman, whose ancestors had clearly not come from Africa.

Wilmot stared at the Rolls for a heartbeat, then turned back to Susan and muttered a deadpan: "Perhaps she's not my niece."

"Look, Captain, someone attempted to kill me yesterday afternoon. The same person responsible for Ascension's murder."

"And who might that be?" Wilmot's grin was now a curious blend of fascination and indulgence.

"I don't know his real name. Everyone refers to him as Crimson."

"Ah, yes! That would be Edward John Claxton. A most notorious rogue."

"Is that how you refer to drug dealers and cold-blooded killers on your sleepy little island? 'Notorious rogues'? The man tried to have me killed yesterday."

"Did you swear out a complaint? An attempted murder of so important a guest would certainly have come to my attention. Even on this sleepy little island."

"No. I did not. Your Sergeant Roberts didn't seem the least bit interested last night. He suggested I drop around this morning."

"And here you are."

"Yes, but Sergeant Roberts has apparently gone to the beach. The national pastime of St. Stephen's, from what I've seen. How does anyone make a living here, Captain? Anyhow, that's why I'm standing here now keeping you from your 'previous engagement.' " And Susan nodded toward the young woman now waiting most impatiently behind the wheel of the Rolls.

"I'm at a loss for words," purred Wilmot.

"Well, I'm not. If you're not prepared to properly investigate this murder, I'd like to know who is. Who do I have to see? Who's above you?"

"Are you referring to a Higher Power? Or just my superior? If so, I am 'the man,' as you are so fond of saying in your country. And I appreciate both your passion and concern."

"So what do you plan to do?"

Wilmot chuckled, then asked: "Why do I suspect you're very good at your job, Miss Given? And how much longer does one have the pleasure of your company on St. Stephen's?"

Susan couldn't tell if Wilmot was gently mocking her or genuinely interested. His manner was very unsettling. "I'm supposed to take the six o'clock flight back to New York this evening."

"Are you still planning to do that?"

"At the moment, yes."

"Barring what, if I may ask? Were you thinking of staying on and assisting us in our investigation?"

There it was again. Mocking or genuine? He was really getting under her skin. She shifted the weight on her cane, cleared her throat, and asked: "Will there actually be an investigation, Captain Wilmot?" Damn! She tried to copy his blend of sarcasm and legitimate concern but was certain she'd only come off sounding, at best, whiny and, at worst, bitchy. And why was she bothering anyhow?

"I'll have to review all the evidence first," replied Wilmot, "then talk to various witnesses."

"The usual suspects? Don't bother trying to question Ascension's wife or family, Captain. I went around there this morning. They're gone. Vanished. Hopefully, they're still alive."

Wilmot stared deeply into Susan's eyes, then shook his head and said: "I'm curious, Miss Given. Did you come down here for a vacation?"

"Yes."

"Mmm. Has the weather been glorious?"

"Yes."

"And your accommodation luxurious?"

"Yes, but—"

"Then what, pray tell, would cause you to forsake all this pleasure in order to obsess on the inevitable fate of a notorious beach character, who has been walking the thin line of respectability and villainy as long as one can remember? Ascension Westerfield was a charming little man, Miss Given. He sat behind me in school many years ago. A first-class mind but far from an innocent. I warned him many times that his fingers were too close to the fire. As did his darling Betty. But he would not listen to us. There are entire chapters of this book you have never read, my dear Miss Given. I suggest you take the six o'clock plane back to New York blissful in your ignorance. Now, shall my niece and I give you a lift back to the Henry Morgan?"

"No, thank you, Captain. I can manage quite well on my own, thank you. I'm planning to buy a few souvenirs in the market before I leave."

"Do mention my name. It's usually good for a minimal discount from most of the merchants."

Wilmot saluted Susan jauntily and walked toward the waiting Rolls. Susan limped down the steps, muttering unquotable opinions of the Captain and his niece under her breath. Neither she nor Wilmot had noticed the Rover parked nearby with Percy and Cecil seated inside watching their every move and itching to make their report to Crimson.

20

IT WAS HALF PAST ONE in the morning when Susan Given finally emerged from the airport limousine and limped across the foyer of her building at Eightieth and Madison. Exhausted and monumentally hungover, all she wanted from life was to crawl into her own bed and collapse.

She'd arrived at the airport at five only to be told of hurricane conditions off the coast of Florida. Her flight would be delayed. How long? No one knew. She remembered the primitive ladies' room on the premises and debated whether or not to return to the Henry Morgan. What if the weather broke? She'd miss her flight.

While debating her course of action, Captain Wilmot turned up on the scene and, having learned of her plight, made the decision for her. She couldn't possibly sit around the sweltering airport waiting for hurricane reports. No, no, no. He would whisk her away for a farewell drink. At St. Stephen's fashionable, old country club nestled into the highest peak on the island with a breathtaking view of the bay below. It turned out to be several drinks. Very powerful ones. His family's own rum. Special reserve. Rum had been the family business. His older brother still

ran the company. Champion cricketer. Knighted by
Queen Elizabeth. A framed photo of HRH touring
the factory in 1967. The rest was a bit fuzzy. Susan
vaguely recalled Captain Wilmot driving her back to
the airport. Later. How much later, she couldn't say.
With positively no idea how she'd actually gotten
onto the plane, she did remember a stewardess shaking her awake from a deep sleep, helping her fasten
her seat belt, and advising her that they'd be landing
in New York in ten minutes.

Susan was bending down to retrieve her bag and
cane from the floor when she noticed that her Ace
bandage was no longer wrapped around her ankle.
She groped around beneath her seat. How could the
bandage have come undone?

Isn't that bandage a bit too tight?

It's fine, Captain.

Call me Desmond.

Desmond?! Had she really called him Desmond?
Desmond Wilmot. What had he put in those drinks?
How long had she stayed at the country club? Where
was her bandage?

The night doorman carried Susan's suitcase out of
the elevator and dropped it off in her hallway. She
thanked him, then entered the living room. It was so
good to be home again! She limped over to the window and stared out at the gold dome of the Carlyle
Hotel. I'm never leaving this apartment again, she
swore to herself. Except to go to work.

I'm thirsty, she thought to herself. Dehydrated.
She grinned. Colette's legacy. They'd hugged each
other good-bye and exchanged phone numbers,

promising to call each other soon. But Susan wondered if she'd ever really see the actress again.

Entering the darkened kitchen, Susan saw light from the refrigerator. The door was open. Then she saw the man's body bent over examining the contents. A burglar! He must have come up the fire escape and through the window. Oh, why hadn't she listened to her brother Henry and installed those bars? She just couldn't imagine a burglar bothering to climb up to the twelfth floor. But here he was now. A burglar who obviously belonged to a health club. Susan tightened the grip on her cane. What would her next move be? Whack him with the cane or sneak off and buzz the doorman?

That was when she noticed the burglar was barefoot. In March?!

Then the burglar hollered out: "Hey, babe! Wanna brewski?"

"Sure!"

Susan recognized the tones of the monosyllabic response that had sailed down from the floor above. Female, enthusiastic, and Southern. She opened her mouth and bellowed: "Brandy!"

"Jesus Christ!" The barefoot burglar gasped with surprise and dropped the bottle of Heineken he'd been holding in his hand. It shattered on the marble floor. "You scared the shit out of me."

Susan flicked on the wall switch and discovered the "burglar" was not only barefoot but nude. She switched the light off immediately (but not before she'd noticed the man she'd scared the shit out of was a hunk in his mid-twenties with three tiny hoop earrings in his right earlobe).

A second later, Brandy Prescott, twenty years old and an awesome six feet of honey blond Southern pulchritude, appeared next to Susan in a transparent Victoria's Secret ensemble and crushed her in an affectionate bear hug.

"Aunt Susan! What a surprise!"

"The surprise is entirely mine, Brandy. What are you doing here?"

"Didn't Mom tell you I was coming?" Mom was Susan's younger sister Linda, who lived in Chattanooga.

"No. She mentioned you might be coming at Easter."

"Well, it's almost Easter. How was Jamaica?"

"St. Stephen's."

"Did you get a tan? Lemme see."

Brandy flicked on the light switch and Susan took in the state of the kitchen: dishes piled up in the sink; food out everywhere; empty beer bottles; cigarette butts crushed out in the dessert plates. And, of course, the naked burglar.

"Could you please put some clothes on?" asked Susan.

"This is my friend Russ. Russ, I want you to meet my Aunt Susan. This is her place."

"Hi, Aunt Susan," said Russ, slipping past Susan's studiously averted gaze of his manhood. "Sorry about the broken glass. You really scared the shit outta me."

"Yes, yes, I know," said Susan, mentally counting to a thousand. Once Russ was gone she turned her attention back to her barely clad niece and asked: "Who is that man?"

"Isn't he awesome!" gushed Brandy in her best retro Scarlett O'Hara tones. "I'm just crazy about him. Did you see how tight his ass is?"

"How long have you been staying here, Brandy?" asked Susan, ignoring her niece's question.

" 'Bout a week. What happened to your leg, Aunt Susan? Wow! Cool cane. Native art?"

"And Russ has been here all that time?" Susan dreaded what the state of her bedroom would be. She'd give the soiled linen away to the Spence-Chapin Thrift Shop.

"Of course not. I only met him tonight."

"You said he was your friend."

"Well, he is. Sort of."

"Brandy, friendship is something one cultivates over weeks, months, years. Not *hours!*"

"Oh, lighten up, Aunt Susan. You sound like Mom. Haven't you ever met a man and had a couple of drinks with him and felt as if . . ."

Call me Desmond.

No, no, no. This was not the same scenario at all. What had occurred on St. Stephen's—and what exactly *did* take place?—was nothing like the present situation. Not by any stretch of the imagination. Still, there was the inexplicable disappearance of the Ace bandage to contend with.

Russ bounced back into the kitchen zipping up his jeans and tucking in his T-shirt. "Great pad, Aunt Susan. You rich or what?"

Susan stared into his eyes and said: "I'd like you to leave, Russ. Now."

"What!?" Russ seemed legitimately shocked.

"Aunt Susan!"

"This is my home, Brandy. You are my niece and you are welcome to stay here. But my hospitality does not extend to men you pick up in bars—"

"Hey, babe! Get one thing straight. I picked *her* up. Nobody picks me up."

"Do you need taxi fare, Russ?"

Russ snorted contemptuously at Susan's inquiry, then pointed his index finger at Brandy and said: "Later."

No sooner had the elevator whisked the swaggering Russ away then Brandy burst into tears: "I loved him! I loved him so much!"

"Don't be ridiculous," said Susan, struggling valiantly with a broom in one hand and her cane in the other in an attempt to clean up the shards of broken beer bottle. "You didn't even know him. Could you please help me with this?"

"He was the nicest guy all week," said Brandy, now squatting down, picking up the bigger pieces of green glass, and dropping them in the nearby garbage can.

Susan stared at her niece in disbelief before echoing the words: "All week? How many others have there been?"

"Just two."

"In my bed?"

"Of course not. We slept in Ivy's room."

"Jeepers, Brandy. Have you got a death wish? This is New York City, not Chattanooga. Didn't you ever read *Looking for Mr. Goodbar*?"

"What's that?" asked Brandy, wiping the tears from her face.

Susan stared at her niece and realized the kid wasn't even born when Diane Keaton had starred in the *movie* of the book. Wow, indeed! Where *did* the time disappear to? Probably into the same mysterious vortex that had swallowed up her Ace bandage.

"Grandmother's been calling every day," said Brandy as she helped Susan climb the stairs to the second floor. "Wants the three of us to have lunch together."

"We'll see," grunted Susan, who now regretted ever moving to a duplex. "I've got a lot of work to catch up on."

"When do the girls get back?"

"Tomorrow evening."

"Are you mad at me, Aunt Susan?"

"No, Brandy. Just tired and feeling a little old."

"Old? You? The marathon runner?"

"I won't be running in any marathons for a while."

"I'm sorry the place is such a mess, Aunt Susan. I've been so busy looking for a job and I didn't think you were coming back till tomorrow."

"Brandy, you're old enough and I'm still young enough that you can finally call me Susan. Okay?"

"Okay . . . Susan."

"Good. See you in the morning."

Susan lay in bed wondering what sort of employment her niece hoped to find in New York. What had Brandy's major been in college? Before Susan realized, she was tumbling down the rabbit hole of sleep and eventually landed once more on St. Stephen's.

This time, however, the island was not bathed in sunshine. Ominous black clouds gave the landscape a

sinister cast as she found herself running for her life.
With Cecil and Percy in deadly pursuit. In and out of
the pirates' coves. Then along the beach. Every time
she thought she saw the Henry Morgan, the safety of
the hotel receded farther and farther toward the
horizon.

She was exhausted. Her ankle was killing her. Why
couldn't she stop? Why didn't someone come to her
rescue? Then she saw the Rolls convertible bearing
down on her. She waved for the car to stop. Wait a
minute! Crimson and Desmond Wilmot were seated
in the front seat wearing team sweaters and cheering
her on. What were they doing together? And in the
backseat waving an Ace bandage back and forth like a
banner was poor Ascension—holding his head in his
lap.

21

SUSAN'S ALARM WENT OFF at 6:30 A.M. Normally she'd leap out of bed, put on sweats, and get ready for her circuit round the Park. But there'd be no running for a while. What about a walk instead? Nothing too strenuous. Just a little walk. Anything to banish the memory of her dreams. Nightmares.

Susan swung her long legs out of bed and tried sitting up. Bad idea. She felt awful and promptly collapsed back onto the pillow. Her head was throbbing. Not enough sleep? Definitely. With the possibility of alcohol poisoning. Coffee. She needed coffee. Ideally, dripping down into her arm from an IV. Special reserve, he'd said. His family's own rum. Knighted by HRH the Queen. Ha! Oh, that laugh hurt. Yecch. Had someone been making mud pies in her mouth? Crippled and terminally hungover. What a fabulous vacation! She could hardly wait to thank Barry Praeger.

The fire alarm rang next to her bed. No, it was just the telephone impersonating a fire alarm. Who could be calling at this hour?

"Hello?" She hoped there was a frog on the other end of the line. No one else could possibly understand the croaking sound she had just made.

"Hello, dear. It's Mother."

"Mother?" Susan's reply made it sound like an alien concept.

"Did you get home all right?" asked Marian Given.

"My body is here, Mother. I'm still taking inventory of the rest of my—"

"Shall we have lunch today? Henry made a reservation for the four of us at the Stuyvesant Club."

"The four of us?"

"I invited little Brandy as well. She's planning to live in New York and I want her to feel she's a part of the family."

"She *is* a part of the family. We can't do anything about it. What sort of work is she looking for?"

"Weather."

"Whether what?"

"Not whether. Weather. As in rain, snow, or sleet."

"She wants to be a meteorologist? Was that her major?"

"I don't think so. She wants to do the weather on television. She's quite keen on it. It's not anything I'd want to do but I'm grateful she knows what she wants. So many young girls her age are positively adrift. So I think we should be as supportive of little Brandy as we can. This is a huge step she's taken coming up here from the South. New York can be such a lonely city. Not the easiest place for a stranger to make friends. And little Brandy always struck me as being such a shy child."

"I think she managed to get over it, Mother." Susan flashed on Russ's triple hoop earrings as well as other more intimate parts of his anatomy.

"Oh, I do hope so. Little Brandy has so much to offer."

"Mother, would you stop calling her little Brandy? She doesn't sell matches on street corners and she's at least six feet tall."

"Well, someone certainly got up on the wrong side of the bed this morning."

"I'm not entirely up yet."

"When do the girls get home?"

"Sometime this evening."

"Did they have a nice time?"

"I'm not psychic, Mother."

"*You* obviously didn't."

"Didn't what?"

"Have a nice time on your vacation. You remind me of your father. He could be such a grouchy old bear, too."

"The girls and I have not communicated for two weeks. But for the record, Mother, I had a wonderful time." Susan decided it was best not to tell her about the murder or her accident. Marian would see the cane soon enough. "I played roulette and went parasailing."

"Good for you! How much did you lose?"

"I won, Mother. Two hundred dollars."

"Well, you can buy us lunch then."

"But I gave it away." Susan hastily caught herself in an unintentional lie. She had intended to give her winnings to Betty. The envelope containing the cash was still in her bag. What had happened to Betty and the children? Had they been sucked into the same vortex as her Ace bandage? Stop it, Susan. Crime never sleeps. But it was someone else's case. Captain Wilmot's. Call me Desmond. Enough! This island is called Manhattan. Not St. Stephen's.

"You gave the money away? Charity begins at home, dear."

"I have the money, Mother. I was thinking of something else."

"See you at one? I'm taking the eleven o'clock train from Greenwich. There's a dress I saw on sale at Bergdorf's that just might . . ."

Standing under a shower for the first time in twenty-four hours, Susan felt she might actually be ready to start life again. And her ankle didn't hurt as much as the previous day.

She toweled herself down, put on her robe, then walked across the hall to Ivy's room to see how "little" Brandy was faring. She opened the door a crack to peek at her sleeping niece and was shocked to discover the girl wasn't there. Where could she be at seven in the morning? Had the wannabe weather lady slipped out after Susan had fallen asleep? Was she lying in that awful Russ's arms? Or worse?

"Susan! Susan!"

"Brandy, where are you?"

"Downstairs."

Susan hobbled down the stairs—her ankle was not as improved as she'd hoped—and discovered her niece breathing heavily in a tight-fitting velour track suit and earmuffs.

"You've been jogging?" asked an amazed Susan.

"Every morning," replied Brandy, crossing her

heart. "You're my inspiration. But I only do the reservoir."

"I envy you. I wish I was out there."

"No, you don't," said Brandy, briskly shaking her head for emphasis. "There's a dead woman in the park."

"What?!"

"She was raped and murdered. It was just awful."

"You saw this?"

"No. Your friend told me all about it. She's coming over here now."

"What friend, Brandy? Who are you talking about?"

"I was running around the reservoir when I saw all these police cars and barricades. Up around 100th Street. Then I saw this TV truck and . . . Did I tell you about wanting to be a news reporter?"

"I thought you wanted to do the weather."

"That's just a way in, Susan. Only bimbos do the weather. I want to be Diane Sawyer. Do you know how much that woman's worth? Anyway, you never know what kind of connections you can make around a TV truck. Networking, right? So I squeezed my way through the police barricade and there she was. New York's highest-rated six o'clock anchor person. We got to talking and I told her my aunt was the chief of Asset Forfeiture and she just shrieked with joy. Said she was on her way over to talk to you. Exclusive!"

"Lisa Mercado?"

"That's right. Lisa. She just loves you, Susan."

"Oh, Brandy! How could you?"

MARGARET BARRETT and CHARLES DENNIS

"Did I do something wrong? She seemed real nice."

"This isn't my case, Brandy. I don't do homicides. Lisa knows that. Why on earth would she want to talk to me?"

"Because you named the killer."

"What? What is she talking about?"

"You're the one who called him Rice Krispies."

134

22

THE MAYOR'S PRESS OFFICE had been boasting for months about the reduction of the city's crime rate in general and particularly how murder was at its lowest level since 1951. So when the second dead jogger in two weeks turned up in Central Park, the shit hit the fan and the D.A.'s Homicide Division began to resemble the American Embassy preparing for the fall of Saigon. A.D.A.s and their assistants rushed about in panic mode with bulging suspect files, shouting at each other, hollering into telephones, sending faxes, etcetera.

Susan limped through this chaotic scene in search of Janie Moore. She knocked at her friend's office door and received a blend of canine bark and human growl in response. It did not bode well for their reunion.

"Ohhh, Greenwich!" said Janie with mock enthusiasm as she saw her colleague's head tentatively peek around the door. "What perfect timing! Come to see how the other half lives? Nice tan. Have you had breakfast yet? How 'bout some Rice Krispies?"

"That's what I came to talk to you about, Janie."

"Funny. Everyone else wants to talk to me about it, too."

"Oh, be kind, Janie, for old times' sake. Lisa Mercado just accosted me in the lobby of my building."

"Fuck her and the night school she went to! You wanna file charges? Might take some of the heat off me."

"Please, Janie. It's my first day back on the job. I'd like to pretend I know what's going on."

"Why should you get preferential treatment, Greenwich? Come wander through the fun house on Centre Street with the rest of us. Bottom line: we got another dead person. Natalie Margolis. Female jogger. Nineteen. Blonde. Lived on the West Side with her boyfriend. Both students at Columbia. She'd have been twenty next month. He was planning a surprise birthday for her. Surprise is on him now."

"What's wrong? Why are you carrying on like this?"

"You mean why aren't I taking this in stride? It's just another stiff? I get tired, Greenwich. Okay? I don't like examining dead girls at six in the morning."

"Okay. Okay. But what does it have to do with me? Why does Lisa think I'm responsible for all this Rice Krispies business? I thought Stella made it up."

"She did. She did. But I made the mistake of telling you that little anecdote in confidence. Never dreaming you'd blab to Ray Murphy."

"What!? I never—"

"Careful, my dear. Did you or did you not speak to Ray Murphy before you flew off to Suntanland? And, by the way, I hope that leg was damaged falling out of some divine man's bed."

"I had an accident parasailing. And, yes, I vaguely recall speaking to Ray."

"Mmmm. Vaguely. Well, our favorite leprechaun wrote a column during your absence deploring the fact the NYPD had failed to make an arrest after the first victim was discovered. He sincerely hoped that the city was not about to face the specter of yet another 'Rice Krispies Killer,' as Assistant District Attorney Susan Given had suggested."

"He didn't!"

"He did."

"I will never speak to Ray Murphy again. He swore to me it was deep background."

"No, no, no. You have to tell *him* it's deep background. You know the rules, Greenwich."

"I was under a lot of stress at the time, as you well recall. I don't think it's fair to hold this against me."

"My God, Greenwich! Are you copping a plea? Are you asking for special consideration?"

"This isn't just the Rice Krispies business, is it, Janie? There's something else you aren't telling me."

"Can I trust you, Greenwich?"

"Now *I'm* insulted."

"C'mere." She gestured for Susan to come around behind her desk. Janie unlocked the top drawer, removed a file folder, laid it flat on the desk, and gestured for her colleague to open it.

Susan pushed her hair back and thumbed through half a dozen fuzzy eight by tens revealing what appeared to be a space capsule photographed at a great distance from earth.

"What is it?" asked a mystified Susan.

"It's what I am trying to keep Señorita Mercado and the rest of her cohorts from finding out about."

"Does Mr. Archibald know about this? Since when do we do reports on UFOs?"

"Are you wearing your contacts?" groaned Janie.

"Yes."

"Well, take another look, will ya? We're on Planet Earth. Okay?" Janie kneaded her forehead with her fingers to drive back an encroaching migraine and sighed deeply. "I hate this fuckin' job. Five generations of cops, you know. I had to be the first woman in the family. So? What do you think?"

"I give up. What is this thing?"

"A thimble," whispered Janie.

"Why are we whispering about a thimble?"

"Because we found one on the dead girl's finger two weeks ago. Then another one this morning. Cute, huh?"

"Sleeping Beauty."

"What?"

"In the fairy tale, the princess pricked her finger on a spindle and went into a deep sleep. All because she didn't have a thimble."

"So you think we have a Sleeping Beauty Murderer?"

"I don't know, Janie. That's just what came into my mind. Did you get any prints off the thimble?"

"Of course not. And we didn't get the tops of the fingers either."

"What do you mean?"

"The sick fuck cut the tops off the victims' ring fingers and capped them with these thimbles. Trophies.

Rice Krispies keep body parts of their victims—nipples, toes, earlobes—as trophies. This one's probably got his at home somewhere in the freezer or in a cigar box."

"Who else knows about these thimbles?"

"Couple of cops in homicide. And some spin doctors in the Mayor's office. Maybe ten people."

"And you've managed to keep this a secret?"

"We're going for our pensions, Susan. The Mayor hates Rice Krispies. Feels they're bad for tourism. Everyone thinks the Big Apple is part of the Magic Kingdom now. Don't want to get visitors upset, do we?"

"But what about Archie? What about Lydia?"

"Please! All we'd need is The Human Faucet obsessing on this case. She'd wanna be on the front page of the *News* and the *Post* every day. DEPUTY D.A. CULBERG VOWS TO CATCH THE SLEEPING BEAUTY MURDERER. Hey, it does have a certain ring to it!"

"You can't keep this a secret, Janie. It's insane."

"That's what Kevin says. I just figured half the cops on the force are related to me so I wouldn't have to worry about them. Oh, Jesus, Susan! What the hell should I do? The Mayor's office wants the thimble angle kept under wraps. They want it kept out of internal reports. This isn't some Stalinist puppet state. We can't do things like that. It's evidence!"

"And you're suppressing it . . . comrade. You're looking at serious jail time if you do, Janie. Don't do it! Get the story out there. Give it to Lisa."

"No way!"

"Lisa will do it from the woman's angle. She'll make it sympathetic. And she'll take all the credit. Lydia need never know the source."

"When did you become La Mercado's agent? And why should I throw her a bone?"

"Because we owe her."

"For what? Tesla's restaurant? She had no business being there."

"Junior almost killed her."

"Which I'm sure she reminded you of this morning, you guilt-ridden Episcopalian. What else did the Puerto Rican spitfire say?"

"What a field day the tabloids will have with Natalie's death. How they'll dig up pictures of her in a bikini. Maybe nude Polaroids her boyfriend took once when they were both a little high. Shame her grieving parents. Make her death meaningless."

"Lisa sure did a number on you, Greenwich. You bought the whole enchilada. They'll probably run that segment during Sweeps Week."

"Then forget Lisa. Give it to Ray."

"Murphy? I thought you weren't speaking to him again."

"This has nothing to do with me, Janie. It's your case. And why do you have to go the tabloid route anyhow? Give it to the *Times*. Draycott Simms."

"The Third," grinned Janie. "Only if he promises to take his shirt off and bark like a dog. I have fantasies about Dray-Three. Whoo! That could be dangerous. Maybe I will give Lisa a break on this one. Is she still balling Haskell Abrams?"

"I don't know." As ambitious as he was mendacious, the NYPD's Lt. Haskell Abrams had been the lover of the equally ambitious and mendacious Lydia Culberg for several years until the Deputy D.A. opted out for more expensive sheets to thrash about in (belonging to wealthy developer Nathan Marshak). Abrams, in turn, found solace and a bountiful source of media exposure with luscious Lisa, no stranger herself to the main chance. "But I do know you can't keep something like this under wraps much longer."

"Keep what under wraps?" asked Lydia Culberg, whose sense of timing bordered on the supernatural as she swept unannounced into Janie's office.

"Hello, Lydia." Susan's smile was a rictus of false bonhomie. "How nice to see you again."

"Ms. Given! Don't you look tanned and arrested. Oh! That was a Freudian slip. Did you have a nice vacation? Where'd you get that cane? Tijuana?"

"Hardly. I went to—"

"Am I to understand you'll be practicing law again?"

"What do you mean, Lydia?"

"Last time I saw you, you hadn't paid your dues to the Bar Association. Remember?"

"I mailed them a check this morning."

"Good girl. Don't want anyone breaking the law around here. Do we, Janie?"

"Business would be slow if they didn't, Lydia." Janie feigned nonchalance as she closed and locked the top drawer where she had just stashed the photos.

"Oh, Susan, seeing as you're back on the job, you'd better get over to Hogan Place right away. Mr.

Archibald's been looking for you all morning. No one seemed to know if you were coming back to work or not. Better hurry up, sweetie. Janie and I have business to talk about, don't we?"

"Do we?"

"Yes, we do," said Lydia, once Susan had limped out of the office. "How's your daughter?" The Deputy D.A. lifted the framed photograph of Stella Moore snuggled in her father's lap.

"She's fine." Janie was nervous. Lydia had never asked about her daughter before. Ever.

"And hubby Kevin? When an Irishman is gorgeous, you've got to admit he's the most gorgeous man in the world. Right?"

"He's fine, too. Thank you very much."

"You're a lucky girl to have a family like this. It hasn't been easy for me raising Ethan alone. I'm thinking of sending him to diet camp this summer. He weighs close to two hundred pounds, you know. Takes after his poor dead father. But enough of my sorrow. Where are the pictures?"

"I beg your pardon?"

"I want to see those pictures, Janie, and I want to see them now."

"What pictures?"

"The thimbles, Janie Moore. The thimbles. And don't you dare glare at me like that, you devious little harp. There's only one team to bet on in this game: the one that wins. And I'm the fucking captain. So you better play ball with me, darlin', or you're going to jail."

142

23

MARC MEET BARRETT and CHARLIE DENNIS

ALL THREE MEN in the District Attorney's office rose as one when they saw Susan Given limp into the room. The trio—William Archibald, Ned Jordan, and undercover policeman Tucker Maxwell—were all great fans of Susan's and were greatly distressed seeing her reduced to this temporary state of lameness.

"What can I get you?" asked Bill Archibald. "Want a pillow for your leg? Shall I have Audrey bring you some herbal tea? Want to stretch out on the sofa?"

"I'm all right, Mr. Archibald. Truly. Please, don't fuss." Susan was secretly flattered by her idol's attention as he carried a chair over to her. "It's not as serious as it looks."

"Indulge me in a bit of forties chivalry, Susan. There's so little of it left in these last dwindling days of the century. Waterskiing?"

"Please, sir. I'd rather not talk about it."

"Fine, fine," said Archibald, holding his hands up in mock surrender. "How much longer do you think you'll need the cane?"

"Not sure, sir. Why?"

"It'd certainly be an impediment to gliding around a dance floor."

"I hadn't really planned on any serious dancing in the near future, Mr. Archibald."

"One never knows, Ms. Given. One never knows. Well, welcome back. I'd love to say that, in your absence, crime in the city had ground to a complete halt. Unfortunately, that will never be the case. But I am pleased to inform you that yesterday a New York County grand jury announced the return of two indictments for criminal conduct arising out of the operation of the Overseas International Credit Bank."

"I thought your office was handling that, Ned."

"We're going to see how it flies in New York first," said Archibald. "Dan Grover is hard at work on the criminal side. You, Susan, will handle the asset forfeiture against Dwight Pelham."

"Isn't he one of your oldest friends?" asked Susan.

"Read the indictment," said Archibald, ignoring her question. "Nassim Narouz and his three associates set up the OICB as a criminal enterprise fifteen years ago. The bank has operated as a corrupt criminal organization throughout its history. It systematically falsified its records. It knowingly allowed itself to be used to launder the illegal income of drug dealers and other criminals. And it paid bribes and kickbacks to public officials.

"Dwight Pelham was one of those officials. He was Narouz's lawyer and he assisted OICB in secretly gaining control of American Patriot, which he and Levenstein, his partner, now run. They lied to the state bank regulators when they said there was no connection between American Patriot and OICB.

They borrowed money from OICB to buy American Patriot, then defaulted on the loan so that OICB would have to take over the bank. And all the while they continued to be the lawyers for both banks, charging annual million-dollar fees. Those days are over. We're closing him down. Freezing his assets. Here. So you'll recognize him."

"I know what Mr. Pelham looks like."

But Archibald paid no attention to what Susan said as he passed her a file folder showing the eagle-proud, still tall, octogenarian lawyer-statesman-banker photographed against backdrops of the Supreme Court, the White House, and the United Nations.

"He's still a very attractive man," said Susan, not knowing what Archibald expected her to say.

"I daresay you'll fall under his spell, Susan. I've never known a woman who didn't. Watch out. He is the most ruthless and shameless manipulator I've ever known."

"Who's this?" asked Susan, pointing to a photograph of Pelham staring adoringly at an intense, smartly dressed man in his mid-forties. "His son?"

"No. His partner and heir apparent. That's Mitchell Levenstein. He does all the real work."

Susan stared in shock at the next photograph showing Levenstein in formal wear standing outside the Kennedy Center with a scantily clad woman on his arm. "Isn't this Colette Cooke?"

"Hey, Susan," grinned Jordan, coming around to peruse the photograph as well. "I had no idea you read *Playboy.*"

"I don't," said Susan, not wishing to reveal her connection to Colette. "Isn't she an actress or something?"

"Yes," replied Archibald. "I believe she is. But she's also married to Mitchell Levenstein."

Mitch. All that time on St. Stephen's Colette never referred to her husband as anything but Mitch. And she certainly never discussed what he did for a living. Just how he traveled all over the world. And how jealous and paranoid he was. Particularly when it came to Michael Roth.

"How much money are we talking about?" asked Susan, trying to get her mind off her personal life and back to the matter at hand.

"In between bribes and legal fees," said Archibald. "Perhaps forty million."

Susan emitted a low whistle, then asked: "Why? Why would a man with his power and prestige get involved in such a shady enterprise at this stage of his life?"

"More power and more prestige. I don't know, Susan. Who knows what our own private tempters will be? Dwight always envied bankers. Thought they got preferential treatment at all the best restaurants and country clubs. How much higher can a mere mortal rise than Olympus? I always thought he was omnipotent. Who knows what he thought?"

"And what about you, Tuck?" asked Susan, turning to address the whippet-thin, black undercover policeman with whom she had worked on so many cases before. "Where do you figure in all this?"

"I'm a badass drug dealer from Philly," grinned

146

Tuck. "And I'm expandin' my operation into New York."

"We want to make a direct link between American Patriot and the drug world," explained Archibald. "Specifically a notorious dealer, whom we know does all his business with American Patriot. We're hoping Tuck is going to step on Mr. Claxton's toes enough to make contact with him."

"Claxton?" asked Susan.

Archibald picked up a confidential report on his desk and read off the name: "Edward John Claxton. Also known as—"

"Crimson."

"Susan," grinned the District Attorney. "You never cease to amaze me. How could you possibly know who this man Claxton is?"

"He's the reason I need this cane," replied Susan grimly.

And the three men stared in rapt fascination at Susan, who proceeded to tell them how she had spent spring break.

24

"CAN YOU FEEL the light within you? Can you?"

"Yes."

"Don't lie to me."

"I'm not lying."

"Of course you are. What is a lie but the cloak a man puts on his soul for protection? Take off the cloak. Toss it into the wind. Now what do you feel?"

"Scared."

"Good!"

"It's good to be scared?" Mitch Levenstein looked at his watch. He paid the swami five hundred dollars an hour for these long-distance phone sessions. For that kind of money, he didn't need to hear that feeling scared was good. "I don't think I understand, swami."

"The boat does not always sail on calm waters. Tempest tossed and tempus fugit."

"Yes?"

"Both are lessons to be learned."

"Swami, do you know what a grand jury is?"

"Of course."

"Well, a grand jury has just indicted me. I'm having considerable difficulty dealing with concepts like prison and poverty."

"These are not things to be frightened of, Mitchell."

Maybe not in a five-thousand-square-foot house on Maui, thought Levenstein, but a few years in Sing Sing will not do wonders for my soul or my anal sphincter. That much I am sure of.

"Hi, baby!"

Levenstein stared in disbelief as his drop-dead gorgeous wife breezed into his office unannounced. Clapping a hand over the telephone receiver, he hissed at her: "I'm talking to the swami."

"Give him my love," said Colette Cooke Levenstein, who sank down onto the sofa, crossed her shapely legs, and buried her face in the British *Vogue* she had brought with her from the reception area. "I'll read till you're done."

"Colette, pleeease! This is private."

"We need to talk, Mitch."

"How did you get past reception?"

"I'm your wife. Remember? The woman you shrieked at hysterically until two o'clock this morning?"

"I told you I was sorry. You know how lonely I am when you're away. I get a little nuts sometimes. Please, just let me finish with the swami."

"Did you tell him about your tantrum?"

"I don't discuss petty things with him."

"Petty? It wasn't petty to half the residents of Trump Tower. Do you know how many phone calls we got? They're threatening a tenants' meeting just to discuss you."

Levenstein looked at his watch and groaned. The

hour was up and the swami was no longer available. He pounded on his priceless desk with his fists, then raced toward her as if she were next on his list of things to pummel.

"He's gone now. For a whole week. Are you happy? Does it please you to know I'll be fucked up for the rest of the day?"

"Get over it, buddy! Why don't you just take Prozac?"

"I will not introduce chemicals into my body that could have an adverse affect on my mind. Dwight needs me—"

"Why don't you and Dwight just move in together? He *is* the only satisfying relationship you've ever had."

"I owe everything to Dwight Pelham. I would gladly fall on my sword for him."

"What size sword do you take? I never know what to get you for your birthday anymore."

"What do you want, Colette?"

"My agent phoned this morning."

"You're not going away again, are you?"

"Relax. We're stuck with each other for a while yet. Scott just wanted to know if there was any truth to this grand jury story he read about in the *Post.*"

"What does he care?"

"Oh, don't get jealous of Scott. I thought it was sweet he even noticed."

"Why shouldn't he notice? My picture was on page three of the *Post* and the front page of the *Times.*"

"You're kidding! Me, too?"

"No."

"Since when do they run a picture of you without me?"

"You weren't indicted," roared Levenstein. "When you go to jail, Colette, you'll get your picture in the paper, too."

"How serious is this, Mitch?"

Levenstein's telephone rang but he ignored it to answer his wife's question: "How serious? What about the pillars of our existence tumbling down around us? How 'bout ten years of hard time? How 'bout millions of dollars in legal fees?"

"Gee. I'd have to get a whole new wardrobe for my *Court TV* appearances. The loyal and devoted wife."

"You bitch!"

"Get over it, buddy! None of this is going to happen."

"How do you know that, Colette? This isn't one of your stupid TV movies where everything is neatly wrapped up by eleven o'clock. This is the law, Colette. These are murky and uncharted waters. Tempest tossed and tempus fugit."

"What the hell does that mean?"

Before Levenstein could reply, the tall and imposing figure of Dwight Pelham loomed in the doorway. "Why don't you answer your phone?"

"I'm sorry, Dwight. I was in the middle of—"

"Hello, Dwight." Colette flashed her brightest smile at the founder of the feast and he, in turn, beamed his blue eyes at her.

"La belle Colette. No one told me you were here." The still vigorous former statesman took her hands in his and kissed her fingertips. "Most fortuitous."

"How so?" asked Colette, struggling to extricate her fingers from the amorous octogenarian's clutches. Pelham was the most relentless lecher the former Playmate of the Year had ever known. She'd never forget the first weekend Mitch brought her down to East Hampton to meet his surrogate father. Colette had gone into the poolside cabana to change into her bathing suit when Pelham burst in unannounced, wearing a thick white terry cloth robe, opened the flap, and presented her with an even thicker erection. He then dictated explicit instructions on how he wished the actress to kiss it. Not wishing to cause a scene or jeopardize her boyfriend's job, Colette managed to eject Pelham from the cabana without offending him. He, in turn, continued to treat the actress as if she were merely playing hard to get. Needless to say, Colette never mentioned this bizarre episode to her husband.

Pelham finally released Colette's hand and told her: "You may be of service to us. This bit of bother Mitchell and I are experiencing."

"The grand jury?"

Pelham waved Colette's question away as if it were a tiresome fruit fly buzzing about the dining table.

"Far from grand, Colette. Far from grand. I don't think anything will come of it. But one never knows. We live in peculiar times. One must be prepared for all contingencies. Which is where you come in, ma belle Colette."

"You should have been an actor, Dwight. The way you keep an audience hanging."

"Your new chum."

"Who?"

"From St. Stephen's."

"So there *was* a man!" exploded Levenstein.

"Would you please relax, Mitchell?" Pelham waved his junior partner away as he had done the invisible fruit fly. "This is strictly business." Then he pushed a white curl off his forehead—exposing the ancient and mysterious scar that began just below his hairline and disappeared into his scalp—and trained his blue eyes back on Colette: "I am speaking of Ms. Susan Given. From the District Attorney's Office. I want to know everything you know about this Ms. Given. Everything."

25

THE STUYVESANT CLUB sat on the north side of
Gramercy Park directly across from the National Arts
Club and the Players Club. Memberships were handed
down like family heirlooms from generation to generation, which suited the Givens of Greenwich to a
tee. Most of the people they'd run into at the Stuyvesant were the same faces they'd see on weekends in
Connecticut at the Cedarhurst.

So Susan was not the least surprised when she saw
David Carstairs, the husband of her childhood friend
Andrea Grant, astride a stool at the oak-lined bar on
the club's ground floor. What she *was* shocked by was
the forlorn, almost defeated look on David's normally ebullient, boyish face. How had the stockbro-
ker aged so since she had seen him last? Then Susan
remembered her mother's story of how Andrea had
been seduced by the kids' gym teacher. The female
gym teacher, with whom Andrea was now living. In
Cos Cobb.

"Hello, David."

Carstairs turned around and stared dully at Susan.
Then he forced a smile, got up from his stool, and
pecked her on the cheek. "Hello, Susan. Nice to see
you. Always nice to see you."

"How have you been?" asked Susan, wondering how many drinks Carstairs had partaken of that day and all the other days since Andrea had so abruptly changed her lifestyle.

"Not great."

"And the kids?"

"Confused—on a good day. Mostly suppressed anger. Principal suggests they see a shrink. They don't need a shrink. They need their mother."

"Do you speak to Andrea?"

"I try to speak. I end up shouting."

"I'm sorry."

"Yeah. Me, too. Can I buy you a drink, Susan?"

"No, thank you, David. I'm just waiting for my mother and my niece to turn up. Henry was supposed to join us but—"

"I like Henry."

"We all like Henry."

"Good old Henry. Captain of the softball team. Great pitching arm." Carstairs abruptly shifted conversational gears and asked: "You've known Andee since kindergarten, Sue. Did you ever have any inkling back then that she was . . . you know? Something less than girly?"

"Not really. When we did *Peter Pan* in third grade, I was the one who played Peter and she was Wendy."

"I remember. I think I fell in love with her then. Sure you won't have a drink?"

"Positive."

"How are *your* kids?" Carstairs polished off the last of his whiskey, then wiggled the glass in front of the bartender to refill it. "They're so exotic. Always got a big kick out of them running around Cedarhurst. Little exotics amidst the endless fields of wheat."

"They're fine. I hope. They went skiing in Aspen with Hugh. They're coming home this evening."

"What the hell did you do to yourself?" Carstairs took in Susan's cane for the first time. "Somebody run you over?"

"Recreational mishap."

"Oh? Fall out of bed? Anyone I know?"

"David!"

"Sorry. Sorry. I'm not myself lately, Susan. Not myself at all. Scuse me." And a sorrowful Carstairs wandered away from the bar.

Susan was ashamed of herself. If it weren't for the damned cane, she'd have run after David and apologized for being such a prig. For being *too* Greenwich. Maybe even given him a hug. A brief one, of course. Let him know that she understood his pain. That, under the circumstances, it was all right to make smutty jokes. These were extraordinary times they were all living through. After all, hadn't she lost her Ace bandage to Captain Wilmot under similar clouded—? Stop it! There was no evidence whatsoever to prove she had even—

"Hello, Susan. I was thinking about you this morning."

Who now? Susan turned around and saw Imogen Blythe's perfectly oval face smiling warmly at her.

"Oh, Dr. Blythe. Imogen. How are you? Are you a member here?"

"Please. I was practically born upstairs in the library on Christmas Day. My mother went into labor with me on her third cup of eggnog. I won't tell you what year. Three cups of eggnog! It's a miracle I didn't have fetal brain damage. So, I see you have a lovely tan. You obviously got away. But not without some damage. I wonder why Bill didn't mention your injury to me."

"Bill?"

"Archibald. I spoke with him this morning. He said you were back in top form." The psychiatrist nodded toward the brightly colored, hand-carved cane and asked: "How did it happen?"

Bill? Nobody called Mr. Archibald Bill. What *was* the relationship between the handsome, widowed, seventy-something district attorney and this forty-something shrink? And why did it bother Susan so much?

"I think I'm going to have some of those little cards printed. You know: 'I am deaf and dumb. Please help me.' Except mine will be a stern warning against the dangers of parasailing."

"Weren't you brave!" said Imogen. "At least it wasn't jogging. Right after our session, I bought myself a new pair of Nikes. Been running around the reservoir ever since."

"How are you enjoying it?"

"Very much. I wondered why I didn't see you out there this morning. Now I know. Did you hear about the poor young student they found murdered?"

"Yes."

"Do they think there's any connection between her and the girl two weeks ago?"

"I'm in Asset Forfeiture," replied Susan, hoping to

avoid lying to her former therapist. "Murder is not my specialty."

"Of course. But do you think it's safe for a neophyte to run in the park? Under the circumstances?"

"I wouldn't suggest running after dark. I never do myself."

Imogen nodded appreciatively, then asked: "So, you're feeling better now? Well rested?"

"Other than this stupid ankle? Fabulous."

"The tan suits you."

"Thank you," said Susan.

"Then I won't be seeing you in the near future?"

"I don't think so, Imogen. My kids get back today. Mr. Archibald has just handed me a huge new case. I'm way behind on my taxes. I'm desperate to start running again."

"Still a touch obsessive?" Imogen laughed hastily: "I know. I know. It's your work ethic."

Susan was about to defend herself when, out of the corner of her eye, she spotted a slightly unsteady David Carstairs weaving toward the front door of the club. An idea flashed through her mind. "Imogen? Are you seeing anyone?"

"I beg your pardon?"

"Are you dating? Or whatever people do these days."

"Why do you ask?"

"I have a friend. Actually my friend's husband. He's very nice. Just a little troubled at the moment."

"You're trying to set me up with your friend's husband? There are some who might think it inappropriate, to say the least."

"I was only trying to help him. He's such a nice guy and he's going through such a bad patch."

"Susan, I know you're a Virgo but you cannot micromanage the entire world." Imogen took Susan's hands and squeezed them: "You were the most entertaining patient I ever had. Brief as it was. Perhaps we could become friends."

"Is that allowed?"

"As long as I'm not treating you. Ah! There's my lunch date. Call me."

Imogen disappeared from the bar into the dining room and Susan realized she still hadn't discovered if the psychiatrist was seeing someone or not. Better brush up on your interrogative skills if you're hoping to convict the elusive Dwight Pelham, Ms. D.A.

"Who was that, dear?" Marian Given and Brandy had arrived while Susan was saying good-bye to Imogen.

"A friend," said Susan, desperate to avoid giving her mother the kind of ammo that could lead to a marathon grilling through lunch and beyond.

"Hmmm." Marian knew she was being lied to. "How's your ankle?"

"Mother, I'm sorry I didn't tell you about my accident on the phone. I just didn't want to worry you."

"Why don't we go and eat?" asked Marian, taking her daughter by the elbow and steering her toward the dining room. "Does it hurt? Why don't you have an Ace bandage?"

"She's a psychiatrist!" blurted Susan. "She consults with our office."

"That's nice, dear. But what does it have to do with an Ace bandage?"

That's what I'd like to know, thought Susan as the club hostess showed them to their table. She had recited to Mr. Archibald and the others the story of meeting Ascension and how she'd first seen Crimson's notorious shoes that night at dinner. She told them about her parasailing misadventure and how she had stumbled onto the secret meeting with Ascension and Crimson. How Betty and the children had vanished and how no one seemed to care. She even told them about Conception, the little sister, who had emigrated to New York five years before. What she didn't tell them about was Captain Wilmot and the Ace bandage. How could she when she herself didn't know what happened?

"Look what Grandma gave me," said Brandy, leaning forward and displaying the antique string of pearls hanging around her neck. "Aren't they gorgeous?"

"That was very generous of you, Mother." Then Susan muttered to her niece: "Don't lose them."

"I won't. I'll never take them off."

"A young woman in New York needs a pair of sensible shoes, a black dress, and a good set of pearls," said Marian, studying the menu as if the mysteries of the universe might be revealed therein. "What about an apartment, dear?"

"I gotta get a job first, Grandma."

"Yes, but you can't stay with your aunt Susan forever. Aren't the girls coming home today? There'll be no room. You come back out to Greenwich with me."

"And how'll I get into town?"

"Commute like everyone else. Your grandfather took the train back and forth every day for forty years."

"But I'll just die in Greenwich, Grandma! It's deader than Chattanooga."

The argument between grandmother and granddaughter came to a screeching halt when Vance Holland, the epitome of the Arrow Shirt man and a chum of Henry Given's, hovered over the table, barely able to disguise his interest in Brandy.

"Hello, Ms. D.A. How goes the battle against crime? I see you're beating them off with a stick these days. And who is this delightful young woman?" Holland's eyes were riveted on Brandy's skin-tight knit dress and the incredible body underneath it.

"Hello, Vance. Have you met my mother? Mrs. Donald Given. Oh, and this is my niece Brandy Prescott . . . a gifted young broadcaster from Chattanooga."

"Huh? Oww!" Brandy's cry of pain was in response to her aunt's sharply kicking her in the shin under the table.

"Actually," said Susan, staring at her slow-on-the-uptake niece and enunciating every word for the girl to take heed of, "Brandy did the weather down there but was hoping to graduate to hard news. Weren't you, dear?"

"Uh-huh," said Brandy, massaging her injured shin under the table.

"Well," said Holland, drawing up a chair and sitting next to the six-foot Diane Sawyer wannabe.

"Why don't you drop by the station tomorrow? We're always on the lookout for new talent."

"Station?"

"Mr. Holland is the news director of Channel 8," said Susan. "Here in the city."

"Oh. Ohhhh!" Brandy switched into full Southern mode and was oozing charm from every pore. "Why wait till tomorrow? I could drop by your little old station this afternoon."

Holland and Brandy were heavily on the make for each other and paid no attention as Susan struggled to get up from the table.

"Where are you going, dear?" asked Marian.

"I've got to change the rubber tip on my cane." When Marian didn't get it, Susan whispered her destination in her mother's ear.

"Why didn't you just say so?"

"You didn't raise me that way, Mother."

Susan limped inside the ladies' room and was greeted by a voice booming out: "Hello, stranger."

Susan looked into the mirror over the sink and saw Cynthia Praeger putting on her lipstick. The attractive, strong-jawed, streaky-blonde ad exec had been one of Susan's closest friends until her marriage to Barry Praeger started to founder and Cynthia's behavior grew progressively more bizarre. Susan had made a conscious decision to distance herself from Cynthia until . . . when?

"Hello, Cynthia."

"Have a nice time in St. Stephen's?"

"How did you know——?"

"Oh, you cut quite the figure down there from

what I'm told. Hobnobbing with movie stars. Hanging out in the native quarter. No wonder you don't phone me anymore."

"What are you talking about?"

"You're really into this double-life thing, aren't you? Miss Goody Two-shoes in New York. But once you leave the country . . . wow! First there was Michael in Israel and now this black policeman in St. Stephen's. What's your next port of call?"

Isn't your bandage a bit too tight?

It's fine, Captain.

Call me Desmond.

Susan hurried out of the powder room as quickly as her cane would allow and struggled back up the stairs into the dining room. Where was she? Where was she?

Finally Susan found her, seated opposite a tweedy old man in his early sixties.

"What's wrong, Susan?"

"We've got to put our friendship on hold for a while, Imogen. I've got to see you right away. Professionally."

26

RAYMOND CORDELL NORTHRIDGE was not used to the word *no*. His very name was a threat in legal circles and, more often than not, opposing lawyers would advise their clients to settle out of court sooner than risk going to trial against the silver-tongued orator, who had rarely lost a case. Curiously, the old-world behavior he affected before a jury was in direct contrast to his coarse, salty dialogue in private.

Northridge had ample opportunity to dust off some of his favorite four-letter words when he went to visit his old pal William Archibald in Hogan Place.

"Can the bullshit," said the bulky Northridge, undoing the bottom two buttons on the waistcoat of his tweed suit. "Your office isn't seriously going to proceed against Dwight."

"I *am* my office, Ray. The indictment reads '*Archibald* vs. *Dwight Pelham and Mitchell Levenstein.*' I take a personal interest in this case."

"But why the fuck do you want to prosecute Dwight? He's one of your closest friends. He was your father's goddamn protégé."

"Perhaps that's why. My father thought the world of this man. Worshiped the ground he walked upon."

"As did half a dozen U.S. presidents."

"That's what makes his ignominy unpardonable."

"Ignominy! Jesus Christ, Archie! Hang up your toga. This isn't ancient Rome. We live in a different goddamn world than the one we were raised in. People don't give a shit today. They're immune to scandal."

"Really? I guess I never got around to getting my shots. I still believe in honor and public service, Ray, and all the things I once thought Dwight believed in as well. And would you please not swear in my office? My secretary is a Mormon."

"Who the fuck is swearing? Jesus Christ, you were in the Navy too. I'm just talking. Listen to me, Archie. Dwight's very hurt. He can't understand why you're going after him like this."

"The man has broken the law, Ray. He's abused his reputation for reasons I will never understand."

Northridge heaved his bulk up from his chair, cursing under his breath, and walked over to the wall where a mix of awards and framed photographs were on display. Pausing in front of a picture taken at a White House function in 1962, he shook his head in amusement.

"I weighed one hundred and eighty pounds then. That's my fucking elbow," said Northridge. "I can't believe that asshole photographer managed to get you, Dwight, and Jack Kennedy in one frame and all that survives of me for posterity is my fucking elbow. No one'd ever believe I was a skinny fucking kid once."

"That was a very special evening," said the District

Attorney. "My wife was pregnant and the President was convinced she was going to have the child right there in the Ballroom. Dwight was hoping she'd give birth in the Rose Garden under the stars. He was always perversely romantic."

"He'll never survive the trial, Archie."

"Why not?"

"His health is too goddamn precarious."

"Oh, please, Ray! Dwight Pelham will outlive both of us. And he's twelve years our senior."

"You haven't seen him lately, Archie. It's finally catching up with him. He's a sick old man."

"Are you suggesting I dismiss the charges?"

"You could get away with that."

"No, I couldn't, Ray. A crime has been committed by a man who should have known better." Archibald stared at the White House photo, took a deep breath, and said: "Tell you what I'll do. For the sake of good bookkeeping, let him plead guilty to a misdemeanor and—"

"Dwight's not going to plead guilty to a goddamn thing, Archie. He's an innocent man."

"We're going around in circles. See you in court."

"Don't bet the fucking farm on it, Archie."

27

POLLY AND IVY CARVER raced out of the elevator and into the arms of their delighted mother.

"Oh, no!" groaned Polly, spotting her mother's cane. "I can't believe both my parents are cripples."

"What happened to your father?"

"He broke his leg skiing," said Polly. "Fifth day there. He's on crutches with a cast on his leg."

"Why didn't he come home early?"

"His girlfriend wouldn't let him," said Ivy, dashing inside the apartment and galloping up the stairs to ensure that all her treasures were still untouched in her bedroom where she had hidden them. "She was too busy nursing him."

"What girlfriend? I thought he'd sworn off women."

"Her name is Taylor," said Polly. "He met her on the slopes."

"Sounds familiar," said Susan, flashing back twenty years to her own first encounter with Hugh Carver, on a snow-covered Vermont mountaintop.

"I think you'd like her. I don't know. She's smart and she speaks English."

"What could she possibly see in your father?"

"Please, Mom. I'm trying to remain neutral. How's the divorce going anyhow?"

"Why ask me? Your father has been the sole impediment to the dissolution of our marriage for over—"

"He says you want too much."

"Polly, don't get caught in the middle of this. Okay? How serious *is* he about this woman?"

"You're not jealous, are you?"

"No. I was just hoping if he's really fallen in love, he might make an honest woman of her. Which means he'll finally have to go through with the divorce."

"I don't think she's a crook, Mom."

"No, Polly. I didn't mean that. It's an old-fashioned expression. When a man drags his feet about marrying a woman, you say it's about time he makes an—"

"What happens when a woman drags her feet? Dad said he chased you for years."

"Hardly. Although, I must admit, he was persistent."

"Do you think, if you hadn't married Dad, you'd ever have gotten married?"

"Are you writing my biography?"

"No. You just don't seem as man-oriented as other women. I mean, you were so hot and heavy with Michael, then you dropped him as if—"

"Polly, why are we having this discussion? Tell me about your vacation. Did you ski a lot? Did you meet any other children?"

"Like, I'm fourteen, Mom. I'm not interested in children. . . . . She wants to make him a star."

"Who?"

"Taylor. She's a TV producer and she wants to make Dad a star. She says he's a natural."

"Are you serious? Is *she* serious? They'll have to wait for those wide-screen TVs to hit the market before they can fit him on—"

"Dad's lost a lot of weight, you know."

"Strange. He never mentions weight loss in his faxes."

"Taylor thinks he sounds like Gregory Peck. That's one of the hooks for the show."

"Hooks?"

"Show biz talk, Mom. She wants him to be a TV shrink. Like *Home Improvement* but for nut jobs. Dad would give tips on mental health."

"And who'd give *him* the tips? Sorry. I should be more charitable to your father. This Taylor woman might be a good influence on him."

"Ivy doesn't like her," whispered Polly.

"Why not?"

"Cuz she's on to Ivy's tricks. Always busts her when she does her little-girl things."

"Ivy *is* a little girl."

"You know what I mean. She does that itty-bitty voice sometimes when she wants to get out of doing the dishes or cleaning the hamster's cage."

"I thought she liked cleaning the hamster's cage."

"Please, Mom, you're the only person with a 'Born to Clean' tattoo on her left breast."

"Polly!"

"Oh, chill out, Mom. Sometimes you sound just like Grandmother."

"And what's wrong with that?"

"Nothing. If you're presiding at the Salem witch trials."

Ivy's patented shriek of horror came sailing down the stairs.

"It can't be a hamster," gasped Susan. "I haven't bought her a new one since Angela bit the—"

"What is this?" demanded Ivy, appearing on the stairs and holding something objectionable between the nails of her thumb and forefinger. "What . . . is . . . it?"

"Let me see," said Susan. Then she grimaced when she realized her youngest daughter was transporting a used condom.

"Oh, gross!" said Polly. "Where did you find that?"

"In my bed," shrieked Ivy. "What is it?"

"Throw it in the garbage," said Susan.

"Nooo!" Ivy dropped the condom on the steps, shifted emotional gears, and ran off to the library to lose herself in one of her favorite cartoon shows.

Susan scooped up the condom and hobbled toward the kitchen to dispose of it with Polly hard on her heels.

"What have you been up to, Mom?" asked Polly as she watched her mother drop the birth control device in the garbage can.

"It wasn't me. Brandy's been staying here."

"Oh, no! I pray that slut only used Ivy's room."

"Polly! How can you talk about your cousin like that?"

"Duh! What did you just throw out, Mom? I'll bet it wasn't from a science experiment."

Susan wasn't sure how much to tell Polly—if anything. Her oldest daughter was bright and precocious, but Susan didn't think it appropriate—even in the In Your Face nineties—to discuss Brandy's good-old-girl promiscuity.

"She brought a friend home," said Susan, hoping it would put an end to the conversation.

"Did she know his name? Or did she just pick a number?"

"Polly, who writes your dialogue?"

"I'm a New Yorker, Mom. Remember? We grow up faster here than in Greenwich."

"Just don't grow up too fast. I want to enjoy you a little bit longer."

"Mommmm!" Ivy was shouting from the library.

"Does she have to shout like that all the time?" asked Susan. Then Susan shouted back in kind: "What is it?"

"Your boss is on TV!"

Susan hurried into the library where a disgruntled Ivy was curled up on the green brocade sofa, pouting at the images on the television screen.

"I was in the middle of *Gargoyles,*" said Ivy, "then this dumb news thing interrupted it."

Susan sat on the edge of the sofa and held Ivy's hand. The broadcast was live from the steps of the Lefkowitz Building with video trucks double-parked along Centre Street. A sea of reporters were crushed together, hanging on Deputy D.A. Culberg's every word. Lydia was in her tough Susan Hayward mode, mink coat, teardrop emerald earrings, breathless from leaving her hairdresser minutes earlier. What was this impromptu press conference all about? Was

Lydia resigning? As if! as Polly would say. And, if so, why would the media bother with all this hoopla when a simple press release would have sufficed?

"Wassup?" asked Polly, wandering into the library nibbling on a piece of string cheese. "When's Cordelia coming back? There's nothing to eat in this house."

"Shh!" said Susan. "This might be important."

"Yeah. Maybe Ethan's been kidnapped." Polly's eyes lit up at the prospect. Lydia's rotund son, Ethan, attended the same school as Polly and he was not one of her favorite people. "Maybe he's been arrested. Hey! Maybe he's that Rice Krispies guy. He's weird enough."

". . . and we are now certain," said Lydia Culberg, tossing her mane of red hair in the brisk winter air, "that the man who killed Natalie Margolis in the early hours of this morning is the same man who killed Mary Ellen Chernin two weeks ago."

"So he's definitely a Rice Krispies?" Ray Murphy's sandpaper-and-nicotine growl was unmistakable.

"Is he a serial murderer, Ray? Yes."

"How do you know he's not just a copycat killer?"

"Because of the trophies he took from the dead women."

Susan let go of Ivy's hand and moved closer to the TV. How did Lydia find out? What had transpired in Janie's office after Susan had left?

"Trophies?" asked a reporter from ABC News.

"We are dealing with a very dangerous and twisted mind. Not content to have raped and murdered his victims, this monster dismembers them as well. He cuts off the top two joints of their fourth finger as a souvenir, then caps the remaining digit with a thimble. For this reason, we refer to him as The Sleeping Beauty Murderer. Women throughout the city should be warned to avoid contact with any strange men. Female joggers should run in daylight hours only and always with a companion or two."

The Sleeping Beauty Murderer. Where did Lydia get that name from? Susan had coined it that morning. And only in Janie's presence. And what about the thimbles? Only a handful of people knew about them. Sure as hell Janie wasn't going to share that info with her archenemy. The homicide A.D.A. despised Lydia. The Human Faucet was the butt of all her jokes. She'd spent hours dishing the volcanic redhead's every foible.

Susan did a double take. There on the steps of the Lefkowitz Building standing directly behind Deputy District Attorney Culberg was Assistant District Attorney Janie Moore. What the hell was going on?

28

"WHAT'S THE MATTER, Lisa?"

"I just don't feel like it. Okay?"

"But we haven't been together for a week."

"So? Fuck your wife once in a while."

"Lisa, please. I'd rather you didn't talk about Arlene that way. In fact, I'd rather you didn't talk about her at all."

"Haskell, you're a wuss. You know that?"

Lieutenant Haskell Abrams gave Lisa Mercado one of his patented enigmatic Wheaton terrier stares. With a head of fluffy golden curls and the glassy blue eyes of a plush toy, the forty-five-year-old policeman had discovered as a child in the Bronx that his vacant, dead-ahead gaze worked wonders in rescuing him from situations on those rare occasions when his extraordinary penchant for lying failed him.

"And don't give me that puppy-staring-at-his-toy-for-eternity routine," snarled Lisa, rolling off the bed in her newly purchased one-bedroom condo across the road from Lincoln Center. "It's wearing a bit thin with me." The beautiful Puerto Rican newscaster hooked up her bra and slipped on her matching black lace panties.

"I don't know what you mean," lied Abrams. Damn! Not only did this Latina have an incredible body and a tongue like a Swiss watch but she was smart, too. He'd been married to his wife for seventeen years and she still hadn't figured out the deal with the stare. Arlene Abrams just assumed her husband was thinking about crime—something that had terrified her from the age of seventeen when her father was shot dead in his candy store—and steered well clear of him, instead of realizing the master buck passer was full of shit and not really thinking about anything.

"There's got to be some quid pro quo here, Haskell." Lisa, clad only in her Donna Karan underwear and black high-heeled shoes, stood with her hands on her hips, gazing down with ill-disguised fury at the naked police lieutenant.

"Is this about my wife?" asked Abrams, walking across the bedroom floor on his knees until his mouth was level with her navel. "You know I can't leave her. She has a preternatural fear of crime. That's why she clings to me. Her father was shot dead—"

"What do I care about your wife?"

"Didn't I ask you not to talk about her?" Abrams's tongue began to circle the circumference of her navel.

"Hey!" said Lisa, violently shoving the cop onto his back. "I'm not going to play Mind Fuck with you tonight. I'm not going to play anything. So you might as well put your clothes back on."

"Don't you want me to be your burro tonight?"

"No, baby. I'm putting you out to pasture."

"Why are you treating me like this? What did I do?"

"It's what you didn't do, Lieutenant. Okay? This has been a real shitty day for me. First, your old pal Susan Given gave me the runaround this morning. Then this afternoon I got caught with my DK's down around my ankles while Miss Lydia Culberg was going public with this goddamn Sleeping Beauty Murderer. I should have had the fucking exclusive on that. Not Big Chuck Sturges. I was the first reporter on those crime scenes every time. Where was Chuck? I cried on camera, for Chrissake! So what happens? Do I get to cover the goddamn press conference? No, Miss Taylor Parkhurst sends Chuckie in. What is that bitch's problem? Hmm? What's Dierdre up to hiring a thin-lipped anorexic like that? It's a WASP thing, isn't it? They keep me out there for the demographics but they stick together. You know what I mean, don't you, Haskell? It's not easy being a Jew on the force. Right?"

"It's been okay," shrugged Abrams, who appreciated playing golf on the High Holidays. "Everything isn't racism, you know."

"Know what's wrong with you? You've assimilated."

"You're just getting yourself upset, honey bunch."

"Don't give me that honey bunch shit, Haskell. What the hell is the use of sleeping with a top cop if he don't tip you off about nothing? Somebody should have told me about those fucking thimbles, Haskell."

"That was really hush-hush, Lisa. I couldn't tell you."

"You knew? About the thimbles?"

"Of course," lied Abrams. In fact, the lieutenant learned about the thimbles when the rest of the city did—at Lydia's press conference.

"How did you know? You balling that redhead again? Is that where you've been all week? Does your wife know?"

"You've got to try meditation or something, Lisa. You can't keep erupting like this."

"Try me, Haskell."

"Lydia and I are colleagues. We're both crime fighters. Our relationship is strictly platonic. I give her advice once in a while for old time's sake. That's all." Another lie. The callous Lydia hadn't spoken to Abrams since she had taken up with millionaire developer Nathan Marshak. But the mendacious cop needed to keep Lisa off guard at all times for fear she'd dump him for someone more influential.

"And did you advise her on this?"

"I'm not at liberty to discuss this with you, Lisa. It tears me apart not to. But my orders come right from the top these days. Way up there."

"Archibald?"

"And the Mayor," lied Abrams. "It's something big."

Lisa's eyes began to sparkle again. "How big?"

"Big big."

"As big as this?" asked Lisa, grabbing hold of him between his legs. "As big as my burro?"

"Bigger," gasped Abrams, always amazed at how quickly she could get him hard.

"Nothing is bigger than my burro," purred Lisa. "You gonna give me this exclusive?"

"You have it." Abrams grinned.

"Not your cock. I know I got that exclusive. I'm talking about your big secret with the Mayor."

"As soon as I can." Abrams was on the verge of swooning.

"Promise?"

"Have I ever lied to you?" asked Abrams, wondering all the while just how big a lie he was going to have to come up with to satisfy the scoop-happy Lisa.

29

THE WAITER BROUGHT the bottle of wine over to Nassim Narouz's table and displayed it for the swarthy, hawk-nosed man's approval. Narouz, in turn, deferred to Mitchell Levenstein, seated opposite him in Molnar's, that most elegant of Fifth Avenue restaurants.

"Does this meet with your approval?" asked Narouz. "I know how fussy you are about your wine."

"It's fine. It's fine," replied Levenstein.

"What's wrong, Mitchell?" asked the Arab banker after the waiter had decanted the wine and left the two men to their conversation.

"This grand jury business is making me very nervous, Nassim. I can't seem to concentrate on anything these days."

"I learned to deal with fear when I was very young, Mitchell. I had to choose between the possibility of my family never knowing a moment's peace or killing the man who threatened them. I was afraid of what would happen if I didn't succeed, if the man didn't die or if I was caught. I succeeded; the man died; I was never caught. I have never been afraid since. You are shocked. I can tell. Why? You are a lawyer. Surely you have heard worse confessions from your clients. This was many years ago in a small village in what was once Sumeria. I tell you this, my friend, so that you might better understand the challenges that life offers us."

"You're like my swami," said Levenstein, shaking his head ironically. "You tell me these stories and assume I will learn great lessons from them."

"The lessons need not be great, Mitch, so long as you recognize them as lessons."

"That's what I'm talking about, Nassim. You live on a spiritual plane I could never dream of accessing."

"Surely the fact that you know the plane exists, Mitch, should give you hope of attainment. Is the life you lead so miserable?"

"I didn't think so until this grand jury business."

"Curious. You use the word 'business.' You are an excellent businessman. Dwight and I would not have put all our trust in you otherwise. This should all be familiar territory. Business as usual. There is nothing here you can't overcome once you overcome your fear. Fear, my friend. That is the only enemy you have. How is your beautiful wife? I'm sorry you didn't bring her with you this evening."

"I needed to talk to you, Nassim. Colette is too much of a distraction."

"Did I tell you the sheik wanted to buy her?"

"What!?"

"He was quite keen," laughed Narouz. "You should be flattered. Please, have some wine. You need to relax."

"I'm worried about Dwight."

"Is he not well?"

"He's fine. He's fine. Still playing tennis at eighty-four. He's not worried about anything. Thinks of himself as invincible. That's what worries me. What if he leaves me holding the bag?"

"You think Dwight would betray you?"

"I don't know anymore. Ray Northridge went to see the District Attorney this afternoon. What for? He didn't consult me. Maybe he's cutting a separate deal for Dwight."

"If you could hear yourself, Mitchell, you would be ashamed. Dwight has been a father to you. Better than a father."

"And I've been a good son, Nassim. I've worked my ass off and made lots of money for everyone. So how come I'm the guy the *Times* zeroes in on? Did you read the piece that Draycott Simms guy wrote about me? What the hell is all that?"

"Are you having trouble with your wife?"

"What!? What kind of a question is that? I have a wonderful marriage. Colette and I are very much in love. What have you heard?"

"Nothing. I'm trying to help you, Mitchell. Ah! Here are my other guests." Narouz rose to greet the couple approaching the table.

"Other guests?" Levenstein sounded alarmed.

"Yes. That's why I wanted you to bring Colette along. Ah! Here they are. Mitchell Levenstein, I don't believe you've met Edward Claxton."

Levenstein rose and extended his hand to a huge black man with a shaved head, wearing a purple suit and two-tone shoes. Clinging to the man's arm, wearing a sculpted dress of scarlet voile, was one of the most exquisitely striking women the lawyer had ever seen. Levenstein had always thought his wife the most beautiful woman in the world but the enchanting café au lait creature standing in front of him now easily bumped Colette off her pedestal.

Narouz drew his guest aside and whispered something in his ear. The huge black man studied Levenstein's face carefully as the banker spoke. Then he nodded and removed the woman's hand from his powerful arm.

"Me go talk business with Nassim." The man nodded toward Levenstein. "Be nice to he." And with that the drug lord of St. Stephen's and the head of the notorious Overseas International Credit Bank left the beautiful woman alone with an astonished Mitch Levenstein.

"Please, sit down," said Levenstein, lost in the girl's eyes. "I'm Mitch."

"Hello," she whispered.

"Don't you have a name?"

"Yes."

"And it is . . . ?"

"Conception."

30

VANCE HOLLAND SAT alone in his Ninth Avenue office, deliriously succumbing to the last vestiges of the girl's scent lingering on his lapels. She had only meant it as a hug of gratitude but the embrace had lasted long enough for the fifty-year-old news director to feel how firm the girl's twenty-year-old body was—she was so tall!—and to fantasize how grateful Brandy might be if Holland gave her the job she so desperately wanted. Clearly the six-foot-tall Southern belle had a thing about her father; she'd mentioned him at least seven times during the course of the interview. "My daddy says this, my daddy says that." Why couldn't Holland be a daddy to her? He was the right age. And height. Those legs! He could feel them wrapped around his neck. Choking the life out of him.

God! What was he getting himself into? Lisa Mercado all over again. But Lisa, not he, had been the instigator that autumn afternoon three years earlier.

Channel 8's news director felt familiar stirrings as he reconstructed moment by delicious moment how the ambitious temp from Payroll had materialized in his office and asked him if he had a minute. When

Holland said yes, the girl from Washington Heights promptly locked the door. Then, serenading herself all the while, she danced around the office, piling her hair up like Rita Hayworth in *Gilda*, putting the blame on Mame and anyone else she could think of. Holland was about to call security when she executed a few impressive bumps and grinds, pulled her Filene's Basement dress over her head, and exposed her incredible body. (Where had she left her underwear? Bunched up under her calculator? Holland had always meant to ask Lisa about that.) No need for security after all, he decided as he watched her pull her tangled dress up into her crotch, gliding it back and forth between her legs, then offering it up to his nostrils like an overzealous Bloomingdale's salesgirl hoping a new scent would please a passing customer.

Holland reached out for her hungrily but Lisa was clearly in charge, unfastening his trousers, straddling him, and entreating him all the while for a chance to go on camera. Just once! The rest was television history.

So how would this child of Chattanooga show her gratitude to the star maker? Would she dance for him, too? Oh, no. Miss Prescott was no Esmerelda dancing barefoot on cobblestones. Her anima evolved more from Spelling than Hugo. And the *Sports Illustrated* swimsuit video. Oh! Holland was hard as a rock now just thinking about Brandy striding along the beach on those extra long legs. But how was he supposed to slip this towering young sex goddess past the independent station's already overextended budget? And how would he ever get the girl past his wife (whose father, Harry Mallard, just happened to own Channel 8)?

Dierdre Mallard Holland returned from her favorite substance abuse spa in New Mexico just after New Year's in a new high-energy persona: off the sauce, twenty pounds lighter, her blonde hair buzzed down to the scalp line, and determined to finally make something of her life. So impressed was her father by Dierdre's heartfelt conversion—she was jogging twice a day now—that he agreed to let his forty-five-year-old daughter become a more active participant in the family business. This involved her stealing a hot news producer from a Boston station, hiring an Israeli decorator to give the Ninth Avenue studio a face-lift, and keeping an eagle eye on her notoriously philandering husband.

"Please, God!" prayed Holland. "Let her fall off the wagon again soon. Sober, she is such a high-energy pain in the ass!" Ah! The erection was still brushing against his new Paul Stuart suit. Ohhh! Wouldn't it be wonderful to have Lisa pop in and reprise their amorous idyll? But those days were long gone. La Mercado was a star now and, if rumors were true, danced only for Haskell Abrams of the NYPD.

The telephone rang on Holland's desk.

"Vance? I have to see you. Can I come down now?"

"You must be psychic, Lisa," said Holland, praying his rigidity would sustain the two-minute journey between her office and his.

Holland thanked his long-neglected Higher Power, then sniffed his lapels to see if any telltale traces of Brandy Prescott were lingering there. More important, does the lock still work on the office door? Don't need Dierdre barging in with her Israeli decorator.

He put his hand out to try the knob just as the door was pushed open. Vance found himself face to face with Taylor Parkhurst, the painfully thin, painfully pushy type-A producer whom Dierdre had imported from Boston to revamp the evening news.

"Can I talk to you?" asked the thirty-year-old Taylor, making it clear by her tone that "no" was not an option.

"Not right now. I'm going into a meeting."

"Where?"

"Here."

"But there's no one else here, Vance."

"Someone's coming."

"When can we speak?"

"Later."

"When?"

"What is so urgent, Taylor?"

"I want to hire someone else."

"For what?

"Just a five-minute spot twice a week to begin with."

"Five-minute spot where?"

"The evening news, of course."

"Is this a new movie critic?"

"Why? Has Marbella quit?" asked Taylor, barely able to conceal the hope in her voice. Marbella Morgan was obese, paranoid, and incapable of giving a coherent summary of any film she reviewed. She also couldn't get any actors' names straight.

"Not that I know of," replied Holland. "We're still the only news station on either coast with an angry fat woman who consistently pans any movie starring Harriman Ford or Mike Gibson. Curiously, she gets more fan mail than any one besides Lisa."

"For a man who supposedly had no time to talk," said Taylor, "you've managed to filibuster remarkably. Perhaps I should just speak to Dierdre."

"Why don't you?" asked Holland, peeking over the news producer's head and out the open door, where he saw Lisa marching aggressively down the hall in his direction.

"Because you're the news director. I believe in a chain of command. And I'm no ball buster."

"Good for you. Now, if you'll—"

"I met the most amazing man in Aspen. When I went to the TV conference."

"Congratulations." Lisa was drawing closer and Vance Holland's erection was still intact. "Are we talking wedding bells?"

"He's married. Separated. A psychiatrist. Brilliant. Forceful personality. Sounds just like Gregory Peck."

"Really!"

"Looks a little like him, too. He's TV, Vance. Trust me. He could have his own show in no time. I'm talking network, self-help books on tape, his own chat room on the Internet. We'd be fools not to sign him. Oh, hello, Lisa."

Lisa ignored Taylor and gave Holland a fierce what's-she-doing-here look. Followed by: "I thought this was just going to be us."

"*She* is your meeting?" asked Taylor. There was

clearly no love lost between the two women.

"You know what?" asked Lisa. "Why don't we get this out on the table right now? Just the three of us."

"No, no, no," said Holland, who felt his erection ebbing. "I want to talk to you alone, Lisa."

"Why did you send Chuck to that Rice Krispies press conference yesterday?" Lisa's face was less than an inch away from Taylor's.

"Chuck Sturges is senior anchor," replied Taylor.

"What the hell is this senior anchor bullshit?" asked Lisa. "We're coanchors. Between you and me, I do a helluva better job than Chuck ever did. With his padded shoulders and his hairpiece. You're just scared of not having an Anglo out there. Maybe that's how it works in Boston, Ms. Parkhurst, but this is the Big Apple, baby. I got a huge following. I had my own morning show before you ever came along. Ask Vance. I'm no prima donna. I don't even have an assistant, for Chrissake. Name me one other female anchor in this town who doesn't have a personal assistant."

"Are you finished?" asked Taylor.

"No! I discovered the first two Sleeping Beauties. I'm the one who broke the stories both times. I cried on the air, for Chrissake. The only time Smilin' Chuck cries is when they announce the winning lottery number and it ain't his. I have resources. I have highly placed friends in the District Attorney's Office."

"And no assistant," said Taylor, shaking her head. "I'm very impressed."

"What the hell is that supposed to mean?"

"Ladies, ladies," said Holland, who had by now given up any hope of dalliance with the fuming Lisa. "Can't we settle this in a more amicable and professional fashion?"

"I am behaving professionally," said Taylor. "I'm not ranting and raving—"

"Bitch!"

"Or using vile language."

Holland's eyes zipped over to his desk, praying there was no letter opener or similarly sharp object in sight. If so, he was certain Lisa would grab it in an instant and plunge it into Taylor Parkhust's heart.

The potential homicide scenario was also alleviated by the appearance of five-foot-nothing Dierdre Holland, complete with her new Demi Moore G.I. Jane buzz cut and designer-chic track suit, carrying fistfuls of swatches in both hands.

"Should I be jealous?" Dierdre asked facetiously, as she stared with amusement at the two incensed women. Then she abruptly thrust the swatches in her husband's face. "Pick one."

"Are you doing magic tricks now, Dierdre?"

"Nooo, silly. Aviva. The woman is brilliant. Who in their right mind would ever think of putting these fabrics on a wall? Think oasis. Think Bedouin tents. Oh! Did Taylor tell you about the new shrink spot on the news?"

Holland stared at Taylor but the painfully thin, painfully pushy news producer didn't dare meet his gaze. Some chain of command. No ball buster, indeed.

"It's exciting as hell," babbled Dierdre. "I figure

MARGARET BARRETT and CHARLES DENNIS

we'll give him a shot for a week or two. Just like we did with you, Lisa. Look how well that turned out. Oh, Vance! Did Taylor tell you who he was? The shrink? Henry Given's ex-brother-in-law-to-be. Hugh Carver. Small world, huh?"

"Growing smaller ever day," nodded Holland, who thanked his Higher Power once again for finding the solution to his problem. "I just hired Henry Given's niece to be Lisa's personal assistant. Did you realize she is the only female anchor in town who doesn't have one?"

31

"HOW HAVE YOU BEEN?" asked Delbert, holding the gate for Susan as she moved slowly but unassisted across the lobby of the Lefkowitz Building toward his elevator. "See you got rid of the cane."

"Yes, yes," nodded Susan, pretending to understand every word the harelipped elevator operator was saying.

"Ankle all healed?"

That last sentence sounded remarkably like "Handcuffs appealed" and Susan wondered what specific case Delbert was referring to.

"When was this?" asked Susan, hoping she'd guessed what he'd said correctly.

Delbert went into the pouting mode he always affected when people couldn't understand him. Then he answered the call on the third floor and Elaine Morton stepped inside. The overweight Ms. Morton, aka "Miss Piggy," was another A.D.A. and suspected of being her patron Lydia Culberg's biggest snitch.

"Hello, Susan."

"Hello, Elaine."

"Did you get my message?"

"No. What is it? Not again, I hope?" Susan and

191

Miss Piggy worked on the same floor and Morton was forever wailing about the Asset Forfeiture staff hogging precious space in their shared supply cupboard. "I've warned them not to go over the demarcation line. I know how important those eighteen inches are to you."

"No, no, no, no." Then Miss Piggy whispered: "Lydia's surprise birthday party next month. The big four-oh."

"She turned forty last year."

"I don't think so."

"I'm certain of it, Elaine." Susan was positive because Lydia was so traumatized by the milestone that she stayed drunk for a week.

"Whatever." Miss Piggy shrugged. "The thing is, Janie and I are planning a surprise party at Rain. You know, that fabulous Thai restaurant on the West Side."

"Janie Moore?"

"Yes."

"You and Janie Moore are planing a surprise birthday party for Lydia?" Susan was in shock. Much as Janie hated Lydia, she despised Miss Piggy.

"Not so loud," whispered Miss Piggy, nodding her head toward the elevator operator.

"I won't tell anyone!" said an affronted Delbert, stopping the elevator on the fifth floor.

The door opened and Janie Moore got in.

"Speak of the devil," said Miss Piggy. "I was just telling Susan about the party for you-know-who."

"Great," said Janie. "Are you coming?"

"I . . . I don't know the date," said Susan, staring in

disbelief at Janie, with whom she hadn't spoken for over a week.

"Should be a lot of fun," said Janie. "I hope you can make it, Susan."

The elevator stopped on the sixth floor and Janie got out. Delbert was about to close the door when Susan stopped him and tried to catch up with her best friend.

"Janie! Wait a second."

"What is it?"

"I've been phoning you. Your office and at home. You haven't called me back."

"I've been really busy, Susan. This case is—"

"Why are you calling me Susan?"

"Isn't that your name?"

"Janie, it's me. Greenwich. What's going on? What's with you and Miss Piggy? What is this surprise party?"

"Please call her Elaine. That's her name."

Susan stared up and down the corridor, then drew Janie to one side. "Am I dreaming this? It's like *Invasion of the Body Snatchers.* Am I talking to Janie Moore or her pod?"

"Susan, I don't know about you but I haven't got time to waste. There's a murderer out there stalking the city."

"How's the investigation going? Any leads?"

"I can't talk about it."

"Why not? Talk to me, Janie. I miss you. What's happening? Have you made some unholy alliance with Lydia?"

"I don't know what you're talking about. Lydia's my boss."

"Yes. And you've hated her for years. Now suddenly you've become her handmaiden. Giving her surprise parties. You and Miss Piggy. I find it all very disturbing."

"Why don't you tell your shrink about it? I've got work to do."

"I just want to understand what's going on, Janie. Why you've gone over to Lydia's side."

"There are no sides, Susan."

"Oh, yes, there are. Lydia's in law enforcement for totally different reasons than I am. To say the least. She has the mind of a criminal. You know that. I believe in the system. It may not be perfect but the alternative is anarchy and chaos. Lydia's in this for power. She told me so last year. In the powder room at the Plaza. She said she was a realist, which made her perfect for her job. And I was an idealist, which made me a liability. You're a cynic, Janie. You grew up in Hell's Kitchen just like Lydia. But you've always believed in your work—our work. I'd hate to think that Lydia has managed to corrupt you."

"Nice speech. But I've got work to do."

Susan was near tears as she watched the woman who used to be her best friend walk briskly down the hall.

32

CONCEPTION WAS THE envy of all the other girls as she stood on the steps of the church in her white communion dress.

"Ain't her all stuck up!" said Margaret Carter, a full head taller and over twenty pounds heavier than Conception. "Talkin' like some rich white woman."

"I'm not the least bit stuck up," said Conception, ever proud of the books her brother had given her to read when she was only four years old.

"Listen to how she talk," said Margaret. "Why her got to use dem big words and shame de rest of we? Dere be no place on dis island for no stuck-up gal like you."

"Then I won't live on this island, Margaret Carter. I won't live anywhere I'm not welcome and where people aren't nice to me."

"Where you gwine go? England? Dere be nuttin' dere for you. You ain' so light-skinned dat de Englishman gwine take you to him bed."

"Get your mind out of the gutter, Margaret. We're standing in front of God's house."

"Her gwine take tea wit' God, don't you know,"

said Margaret, putting a hand on her hip and sashaying about to the amusement of the other girls.

"Foolish girl," said Conception, playing Alice to this insufferable Red Queen of St. Stephen's.

"Me ain't such a fool as you," said the Red Queen, striding toward Conception and shoving her so hard she fell down into the dirt. "Or such a whore."

"Me be no whore," said Conception, reverting to patois. "Me be as good as anyone."

"You just a orphan whore," chanted another girl, who picked up a stone and hurled it at Conception.

"Me be a good girl! Why t'row de stone at me?"

Instead of answering, the other girls began throwing stones at Conception until her face was a dartboard of open wounds and her communion dress was dyed blood red. The nuns rushed out of the church and Conception begged them to make the girls stop hurting her. But these brides of Christ only ushered Margaret and the others girls inside the church and locked the massive wooden door, leaving Conception all alone, sobbing on the steps.

Conception was wakened from this nightmare by a man's voice. "Colette? What's wrong?" Conception opened her eyes and gazed at the man lying next to her talking in his sleep.

"Go back to sleep, honey," he muttered, then sank back into a deep sleep himself.

Conception stared at the man, momentarily in confusion. Who was he? Oh, yes. The banker.

Snoring now. She got out of bed. Damn! It was cold. Why was it always so cold? She was starting to get the shakes. Soon she would go into a dive, crash and burn. Burn in the flames of Hell.

She heard voices coming from the sitting room. Where was her dress? There. On the chair.

Opening the door, she walked into the sitting room high up in the clouds with a breathtaking view of the city. Where were the voices coming from? Television. Someone had left the TV on. She stumbled toward the large screen and groped about beneath it in search of a power switch.

"What you tink you doin', gal?"

Conception gasped and whipped around: "You scared me to death, Crimson."

"You done wit' dat white man?"

"I don't feel well, Crimson. I'm cold."

"Me no be cold. Dis hotel got good central heating."

"What hotel?"

"You don' remember?"

"Why did you make me sleep with that man?"

"Me no make you do nothin', gal. Dis America. Everybody free to do what dey wants."

"I'm so cold, Crimson."

"Look at de thermostat, gal. Seventy-two degrees. Why you don' put on a sweater?"

"Help me, Crimson."

"How me gwine do dat, gal?"

"Please!"

"Me tink you don' like me no more, baby."

"I love you, Crimson. You know I love you."

"Den why you give me attitude? Sayin' me make you sleep wit' men. Dat ain't so, is it?"

"No. No, it's not. Please, Crimson, help me."

"Is you me gal?"

"You know I am." Conception was on her knees now, clinging to the drug lord's legs and sobbing pitifully.

"You gonna be good?"

"Yes, yes."

Crimson put his thick fingers underneath her chin and lifted her head up. "Lemme see you eyes. Hmmm. Me tink you tell de truth dis time. Mebbe me give you some candy?"

"Please, please, please."

He reached for a snakeskin pouch on the coffee table and withdrew a hypodermic needle, a Zippo lighter, a rubber tube, a package of white powder, and a spoon. Within minutes Conception had succumbed to her fix and was stretched out on the sofa with her head in Crimson's lap while the drug lord stroked her hair.

"Your brother send you lots of love," said Crimson.

"Yes?" Her voice was dreamy and disconnected.

"Him want to know when you gwine come and visit he and Betty. Dey miss you so much."

"I miss them, too. It's too bad they can't get visas to come here."

"Me keep tryin', baby. Dat man in de bedroom, him try too. Him important man. You done good, gal."

"Crimson?"

"Yes, gal?"

"Perhaps we could go back to St. Stephen's some-day and visit Ascension."

"Of course. Maybe Christmas."

"Oh, yes, please! Christmas with my family." Staring up at him with fervid, drugged adoration she exclaimed: "You're so good to me, Crimson!"

33

SUSAN CLICKED OFF the remote and flopped back against the pillow in frustration. She had hoped the TV would lull her off to sleep. Instead the relentless junk on all the stations merely outraged and irritated her. She groaned and switched off the bedside lamp. Sleep. All she wanted to do was sleep. Half past midnight and she'd have to be up again in less than six hours. Back to the old routine. Just lie still. Allow your body to relax. Sleep is waiting there. All you have to do is reach out to it.

There was a knock at the bedroom door. A woebegone Ivy walked in and asked: "Are you asleep?"

"No. But why aren't you? You've got school tomorrow."

"I know. Why aren't *you*?" countered Ivy, crawling up on the bed beside her mother.

"I've got things on my mind."

"Me, too."

"Want to tell me about them?"

Ivy fiddled with her mother's fingers until she finally murmured: "Stella's not my friend anymore."

"Stella Moore?"

"Uh-huh."

"When did this happen?" Susan couldn't believe that the rift now involved two generations.

"Last week. She and the other girls blackballed me."

"Why?"

"Because of that a——hole Gwillim Griffiths."

"What did he do?"

"It's what I did to him. I told him he was a jerk. The girls hate me for it."

"What did Gwillim do?"

"Tried to kiss me. The girls were pissed cuz he didn't want to kiss *them*. I just want to barf when he comes near me."

"Ivy, please! Your language."

"You asked!"

"Yes. Yes, I did. You're right. Did you tell your teacher?"

"No! That'd be worse. Besides, Gwillim's such a liar. He gets out of everything. Just cuz his half brother Toby's a big TV star."

"What are you going to do?" asked Susan. "Do you want me to speak to Gwillim?"

"Nooo! Stay out of this, Mom. I've got ways of dealing with that a——hole. He'll regret it." Then a rejuvenated Ivy pecked her mother's cheek, leaped off the bed, and skipped out of the room.

Susan suddenly felt very lonely. The episode in the elevator with Janie had shaken her more than she'd admitted. How could Janie have gone over to the enemy? Worse, how could she have stopped being her friend? They'd been so close for so many years. Now she felt alone. Isolated. No one to talk to.

She closed her eyes again. Was it possible? Yes. Out of this despair sleep was slowly, slowly overtaking her body.

The telephone rang beside the bed. She was awake again. Who could be calling at a quarter to one in the morning?

Susan grabbed the receiver and announced: "Given."

"Did you just phone here?"

"Hardly," said Susan, snapping into combat mode the instant she recognized her estranged husband's Gregory Peck wannabe tones. "Why would I want to phone you?"

"Somebody just phoned and hung up, Susan. I pressed star sixty-nine and you answered the phone."

"Maybe it was one of the girls."

"I doubt they'd be up at this hour."

"Why? Ivy just left here."

"She's gone out? You let her leave the apartment at this hour?"

"No, Hugh, she just left my bedroom. Relax, will you? She was having trouble sleeping and came in to see me. She just went back to her room." Susan heard a peculiar noise on the phone line. "Do you hear that scratching sound?"

"Does she have insomnia?" asked Hugh, ignoring the question.

"She has . . . problems."

"Like what? I'm her father, Susan. You have to share this information with me."

"In a better world, I could. In a world where people part amicably and in a civilized fashion when things don't work out. In a world where fax machines aren't modern instruments of torture. You really don't hear that scratching sound on the line?"

"Have I sent you any faxes in the past three weeks?"

"Only because you were on vacation. With the girls. There was no need to harass me. How's your leg, by the way?"

"Still in a cast," said Hugh. "And yours?"

"I threw my cane away."

"Now what is Ivy's problem?"

"She's having boy trouble. She came in to talk to me about it. Maybe she called you afterward and changed her mind."

"Maybe."

"How's the new girlfriend?"

"I beg your pardon?"

"Oh, come on, Hugh. I know all about her. Is she really going to make you a TV star?"

"It's just a medical spot on the Channel 8 'News at Six.' Are you still in therapy?"

"Who told you that?"

"Ivy."

Susan shook her head in disbelief. Was her youngest daughter incapable of keeping anything to herself? Or was this just the deal with divorce? "I only went once. Twice, actually."

"Anyone I know?"

"Imogen Blythe."

"She's very attractive."

"You're such a sexist!"

"Why?"

"She's a fellow therapist. Not some babe in a bar. Can't you, at least, comment on her professional abilities?"

"I'm not qualified. Never having been analyzed by the woman. She certainly hasn't made you any less combative."

"Good night, Hugh."

"Prickly as ever."

"It's late and I need to sleep."

"What's wrong, Susan? Why are you seeing a therapist?"

"Hugh, I don't really think this is something I should be discussing with you."

"I'm a therapist, too. Sometimes a second opinion isn't a bad thing."

"Please, Hugh. I can't talk to you about this."

"I'm speaking as someone who was once your friend."

It was madness to trust him. He'd been her enemy for three years. But he *had* been her husband for years before that. Something in his voice now reminded her of long ago when they were young. She had to talk to someone. She was about to tell him about her blackout on St. Stephen's when she heard a high-pitched whistling sound on the line.

"Damn!" said Hugh. "Can you hold on a second?"

"What's wrong?"

"Nothing, I just have to—"

"What?" The lightbulb went on in Susan's brain. The scratching sound. The high-pitched whistle. He was recording their conversation. She had almost hanged herself with the story of her rum-soaked evening with Captain Wilmot. "You son of a bitch!"

"What's wrong, Susan?"

"Why don't you just buy a new tape recorder? That one's been giving you trouble for years, you deceitful, slimy, disgusting—"

"I don't know what you're talking about, Susan."

"Hello, Ralph! How are you? How's Joyce? And anyone else who may be listening to this tape recording."

"You're paranoid, Susan."

"I don't think so, Hugh. Nice try. Good night."

Susan slammed down the phone, shaking with rage. The man was incorrigible. He'd do anything to get the girls away from her. How could she have been so stupid to even think of trusting him? She wanted a drink. No! A cigarette? No! How 'bout a friend? Yes! That would be wonderful. Someone to talk to. But there wasn't anyone. Wait a minute! She grabbed her bag and began poring through her address book. Why hadn't she thought of her sooner? Where was that number? Probably on the memo page waiting in limbo for a chance to become a permanent entry. There it was! Susan dialed the number and prayed she wasn't waking anyone else up.

The phone was answered on one ring.

"Honey, are you okay? I'm sorry about before. Please, come home!"

"Colette?"

"Who's this?"

"Susan Given. I'm sorry if I'm disturbing you."

"Oh, Susan! I'm so glad to hear from you. I was hoping you were my husband. Mitch went out to a dinner meeting hours ago and never came back." Then, to Susan's amazement and embarrassment, Colette Cooke Levenstein began to cry. "I'm so scared, Susan. Can you come over now?"

34

ONE WEEK LATER Draycott Simms III watched in amusement as Susan Given removed a bottle of Windex from the bottom drawer of her desk and attacked her office window.

"Now, please, don't mention this in your article," said Susan, as she sprayed the detergent on the glass and wiped it briskly with a paper towel. "I don't want people to get the wrong idea about me. There. Now you can see the Statue of Justice."

"And what might the wrong idea be?" asked the handsome, preppy, thirty-something reporter from the *New York Times*.

"Where were we?" asked Susan, deliberately ignoring his question as she sat down behind her desk once more.

"American Patriot Bank. There are some people who are calling the case a personal vendetta of William Archibald's against Dwight Pelham."

"That's not true," said Susan. "American Patriot is a front for OICB, a bank with blood on its hands. A bank that bilked millions of customers around the world for billions of dollars. Pelham and Levenstein took forty million in bribes from OICB and lied to federal bank regulators."

"They claim they were duped," said Simms.

"Then why was Mitch Levenstein seen having dinner with Nassim Narouz at Molnar's last week?"

"Who saw them?"

"I have my sources, Mr. Simms." Susan was certainly not prepared to discuss her relationship with Colette Cooke and how she spent close to an hour on the phone with the sobbing actress the previous week until her missing husband finally wandered in at two in the morning from his meeting with the notorious Arab banker.

"Are you confident of a conviction?"

"I'm always confident of a conviction. Now, are we, by any chance, finished? I've got a lot of work to do."

"I guess that's it for now," said Simms, as he rose from his chair and walked over to the rack where his camel-and-cashmere-blend overcoat was hanging. "Thank you for your time. I've been a big fan of yours for quite a while."

"Really?" Susan stepped back, put on her glasses, and took a good look at the well-dressed young reporter. "How old are you, Mr. Simms?"

"Please call me Dray. Thirty-three."

"Are you married, Dray?"

"No."

"Engaged?"

"No."

"Involved?"

"Would you like my shirt size?"

"Why?"

"You're doing a helluva job interviewing *me.*"

"That's very funny, Dray," said Susan. "She appreciates a good sense of humor."

"She?" Simms had been charmed by the prosecutor's eccentricity but thought referring to herself in the third person a trifle pretentious.

"My niece. You'd be perfect for her."

"Is this how you disarm all reporters?"

"You'd never have passed through the metal detectors downstairs with any kind of weapon."

"Except my wit." Simms shrugged. "Tell me about this niece of yours."

"She's tall, blonde, Southern."

"How tall?"

"Tall. And she works for Channel 8 news. So? Have I piqued your interest?"

"I think I'd rather date her aunt."

"I'm far too young for you," said Susan ironically. "You're much better off with Brandy."

"Well, I'm a little disappointed but I'm willing and available."

"Good. I'll get back to you."

Simms left and Tucker Maxwell stuck his head in the door: "Busy?"

"Always. Come on in."

Tuck entered the office wearing jeans and a nylon ski jacket. He nodded admiringly at the large window overlooking Centre Street.

"Hmm. Y'all been doin' them windows again, Ms. Gee. Wish you'd come out to Brooklyn sometime and give my missus a few pointers. You are the cleanest woman I ever met."

"Hardly. It's a fetish. Believe me, Tuck. The last thing you want is a woman like me. So, what have you heard from Nip?" Nip was the nickname for Paul

Regan, Tuck's partner, who had taken a much-needed leave of absence following his undercover work on the Tesla garbage case.

"Nothing, Ms. Gee. Nobody knows where Nip is." Tuck yawned audibly, then excused himself. "Sorry, Ms. Gee. I've got to get some sleep. Your old pal Crimson is the last of the party animals."

"Have you made contact?"

"Oh, yeah. We been hanging out at the same clubs up in Harlem. We shoot a little crap once in a while."

"Have you met Conception?"

"Once or twice. Real sad about her."

"What do you mean?"

"She's a beautiful girl, Ms. Gee. Stunning. But she's got a real bad jones."

"Heroin?"

"Mr. Aitch himself"—Tuck nodded—"and that son-bitch Crimson runs her like a bitch in heat."

"How does he run her?"

"She tricks for him."

"Poor Ascension." All Susan could think of was the framed picture of the little girl in the communion dress so proudly displayed in the outdoor bar on St. Stephen's.

"That's the other thing, Ms. Gee. That girl don't know her brother's dead. No idea. Crimson just keeps stringing her along how they're all gonna have some big reunion on the island at Christmas."

"I want to meet her."

"That's impossible, Ms. Gee. The only time she gets loose from Crimson is when—"

Gretchen opened the door at that moment, nodded to Tuck, then told Susan: "It's your brother on the phone. Says it's very important."

"Excuse me a second, Tuck." Susan picked up the phone on her desk and asked: "What's wrong?"

"We have a problem," said Henry Given. "I'm at your place."

"I'll be right there."

35

SUSAN DASHED IN from the elevator and found
Cordelia Brown sitting on a wooden stool in the
kitchen, gazing out the window into space and humming "Just a Closer Walk with Thee."

"What's wrong?" asked Susan breathlessly.

"You home early," said the squat housekeeper
from St. Kitts, looking up at the clock on the wall. It
was ten to five. Susan rarely got home before six-
thirty. "What be wrong wit' you?"

"There's nothing wrong with me. Henry phoned
and told me—"

"Him be upstairs." Cordelia returned fervently to
her hymn and gazing out the window.

Susan went upstairs and entered the library, where
she discovered Ivy and her twelve-year-old cousin
Donald Given sitting together on the sofa like two
hardened cons waiting for their parole hearing.
(Neither dared look up at Susan.) The warden in
this case was Henry Given, Susan's brother and two
years her senior. A historian of considerable repute
(his specialty being the City of New York), Henry
lived directly across the park from his sister on
Central Park West, where he spent most of his time
writing and raising his two sons while his wife, Sheila,

continually circled the globe in the employ of an international hotel chain.

"You certainly got here in record time," said a duly impressed Henry.

"I took a taxi."

"Good heavens!" said Henry, who was even thriftier than his sister. "I didn't mean for you to go to such extremes."

"Frankly, from your tone, I expected to find a body or two littered about the place."

"Give them time," said Henry, adjusting his bow tie and nodding toward the two children on the sofa.

"What's going on?" asked Susan, walking toward her daughter and nephew. "Ivy?"

Ivy tried to speak but her lower lip merely trembled.

"Donald?"

The gangly blonde boy, his father in miniature, looked up at his aunt with a curious mixture of fear and pride and declared: "I'm not ashamed of what I did!"

"Well, that's a start," said Susan. "What specifically aren't you ashamed of?"

"That little snot," said Donald. "Molesting my cousin."

"He never molested me," squealed Ivy.

"You know what I mean," said Donald. "He bothered you. He was tormenting you."

Susan turned in confusion to her brother but Henry merely gestured for her to let the boy continue.

"Go on, son. Tell Aunt Susan what happened."

"I phoned him the other night—"

"Who?" asked Susan, hoping to set the record straight.

"Gwillim Griffiths. I called him and warned him, if he didn't lay off Ivy, my gang would do a knee jcb on him and toss him off the George Washington Bridge."

"What gang?" asked Susan. "You're in a gang?"

"Nooo!" said Donald. "That was just to scare the little snot. To make him back off. I really scared him, too. He started crying."

"Did you tell him who you were?"

"Of course not. But his mom dialed star sixty-nine afterward and she found out who I was. She said she was going to call the police and have me arrested. I told her to go ahead and try cuz my aunt was the district attorney."

"You didn't! Oh, Donald! You can't use my name to threaten people."

"The woman was quite distraught," said Henry, "and somewhat of an hysteric. I tried to reason with her but she's intent on filing charges."

"Charges?! Her son has been harassing Ivy."

"Mrs. Griffiths says it's a lie." Henry shrugged. "Her Gwillim's an angel and she's struggling from day to day as a single mother."

"Welcome to the club. What's this woman's phone number?"

"Shouldn't we form a strategy first?" asked Henry.

"What do you suggest, Henry? Have your gang do a knee job on her and toss her off the George Washington Bridge? By the way, Donald, what *is* a knee job?"

"You take a big spike," her nephew replied keenly, "and a sledgehammer and you drive it through the kneecap right into the floor."

"If they're stuck to the floor," said Ivy, "how can you toss them off the bridge?"

"That'll be enough of that, you two," said Susan, once her brother had given her Gwillim's mother's phone number. "I don't want to hear a peep out of either one of you." She dialed the number, then turned back to her brother and asked: "What is this woman's first name?"

"Jewel."

"You're joking! . . . Hello? Is this Jewel? . . . My name is Susan Given. Our children are in the same class at Balmoral School. . . . Please, Jewel, I am not threatening you. I'm calling you to try and straighten out this misunderstanding before—" Clapping a hand over the receiver, she whispered to her brother: "The woman's mad as a hatter."

"Didn't I tell you?" asked Henry. "We should have mapped out a strategy first."

"Jewel? Jewel? Please, calm down and listen to me. Donald is not an urban thug. He was merely defending his cousin's honor in an overzealous manner and I'm sure if you allowed him to apologize to you for—"

"No way!" shouted Donald.

Susan waved for her nephew to be silent, then spoke gently into the receiver: "Jewel, I think you might be overreacting to the situation. . . . Yes, I'm sure Gwillim is an angel but his behavior is inappropriate, to say the least. He's been making unwelcome

advances to my daughter and threatening her—
What?! I don't think so. I can assure you, Mrs.
Griffiths, that my daughter has never . . . I think your
son needs help. Fine. Go ahead. . . . Mrs. Griffiths,
this is the second time you used that phrase. I did
not in any manner threaten you. I have witnesses in
this room who have heard every word I said to you—
Hello? Hello?" Susan stared at the receiver in disbelief, then replaced it on the cradle. "She says Ivy
enticed her son."

"What's 'enticed'?" asked Ivy.

"Led him on."

"He's such a liar!" shrieked Ivy. "I hate him. I hate
him. I hate him." Then Ivy burst into tears. "He gets
away with everything."

"What do we know about the father?" Susan asked
her brother.

"Dylan Griffiths? He's a sculptor. Been married
about six times. Twice as many children. Wives are
always suing him for child support. I believe he lives
in Amsterdam."

"Well," sighed Susan, "she's threatening court
action. But I wouldn't hold my breath waiting for a
subpoena. She's very troubled and, if I weren't in
such a foul mood, I'd probably feel sorry for her."

"Can she really put me in jail?" asked Donald.

"For being a chivalrous thug? I don't think so. But
the next time you decide to defend your cousin's
honor, please consult your father first or—" The telephone rang again. "If this is Jewel again . . ." Susan
picked up the phone and instinctively went into her
professional tones: "Given."

"Susan?"

"Yes?"

"It's Janie Moore."

"Yes, Janie," said Susan, the chill quite evident to everyone in earshot. "How are you?"

"Oh, Greenwich, defrost your voice, will ya? I'm in big trouble and you're the only person I can turn to. Please, please. You've got to meet me for a drink. I can't take much more of this."

36

ALEC GARDNER, the senior partner of Marshall,
Knowles, Ney & Hardwicke, had been on the telephone to Mitchell Levenstein for twenty minutes
advising his client to draw up a complete list of all his
visible assets.

"It's one thing for Dwight Pelham to pooh-pooh
the notion that his old friend Archie Archibald
might seriously take him to court," said Gardner.
"But that young woman of his in Asset Forfeiture—
what's her name? Given?—she'll grab everything that
isn't nailed down. Believe me, Mitch. I had clients in
the carter case. They still send me down to Centre
Street, cap in hand, every week to pry loose their living expenses from her. Now, how much is in your
name and how much is in Colette's? Mitch? Mitch?
Are you there?"

Levenstein sat behind his antique desk vaguely
aware of the lawyer's voice on the other end of the
line. But all he could think about—all he'd been
able to think about for the past week—was
Conception. She was the most beautiful woman he'd
ever met. The scent of her body haunted him. How
had it all began?

Nassim Narouz had left the table at Molnar's to

discuss business with Claxton or Crimson or whatever that big scary *shvartzer*'s name was while Levenstein had been left alone with her. After some idle chitchat—he was charmed by her West Indian accent—she went silent and stared at him for the longest time, mesmerizing him with those eyes of hers. Finally she reached her arm across the table, took his hand in her long, slender fingers, and offered to read his palm.

"You're under a great amount of stress," she purred.

"No kidding."

"But there's no need to worry. A great adventure is about to begin for you."

"Where does it say that?" asked Levenstein, loving the texture of her skin as she traced the lines in his palm.

"Here." She took his index finger, placed it in her mouth, and began to suck on it.

If he was surprised by the palpitating affect this had on his finger, he was shocked by the reaction his penis experienced a moment later. It had turned to granite.

"Did you like that?" she asked.

He nodded, started to speak, then froze abruptly as he felt her bare toe massaging his erection.

"You really liked it." She grinned. "Why don't we get out of here?"

"But what about . . . your friend?"

"What about him?" asked Conception, fixing her hypnotic gaze on him so seductively. "Edward's a very busy man. I'll have to make my way home alone. It wouldn't be the first time. Unless you'd be kind enough to escort me."

Levenstein examined his watch. Ten o'clock. He told Colette he'd be home by eleven at the latest. It was playing with fire to go anywhere near this woman. But he couldn't resist her. Not if there was the slightest chance of being with her, knowing her, touching her. And why not? Despite all her protestations and vows to the contrary, he was certain that Colette had cheated on him every time she went on location, every time he had gone out of town. But maybe she hadn't. What would Dwight Pelham have done under the circumstances? Please! The old ram would be *shtupping* her under the table by now.

So they had a few more drinks and did a few lines of blow in the taxi on the way over to her hotel. What was the name of that hotel? Somewhere on the East Side. They'd gone in a side entrance. Certainly Levenstein was feeling no pain by the time he and Conception rode up in the elevator together.

Once they were inside the suite, he hungrily took hold of her and kissed her. She slid her arms under his suit jacket and roamed over his back like so many serpents wriggling. He turned to granite once more as she led him into the bedroom where she lit a candle next to the king-sized bed and stripped off her clothes. If he had any guilty feelings about Colette, they evaporated once he was in bed with Conception. Her lovemaking was languid and sensual like the citrus-scented oil she dripped tantalizingly onto his groin. He reached up to grab her again but she gently slowed him down.

"What's your hurry?" she whispered.

Levenstein finally collapsed in exhaustion. When he came to at half past one, Conception was no longer there. The suite was deserted. No clothes, no luggage, no evidence at all that anyone had been staying there. He took a quick shower before he left to remove Conception's delicious scent from his body.

Down in the lobby Levenstein stopped at the front desk to inquire if anyone had seen Conception leave. No one knew whom he was referring to. When he recited the suite number, they informed him that it had been unoccupied for two days. What the hell was going on?

Shortly after two, he turned the key in the lock of his Trump Tower condo and discovered his wife talking on the telephone in a see-through negligee. Colette hung up the phone abruptly, rushed toward her husband in tears, then slapped his face and demanded to know where he had been all night.

"I was with Nassim. We had a lot to talk about what with the grand jury business and everything. Oh, by the way, did you ever come up with anything for Dwight regarding your friend Susan Given?"

"Don't change the subject," snapped Colette. "You were with another woman, weren't you?"

"What is this? Transference?" Levenstein laughed a little too heartily. "Who's the jealous maniac in the family? Why would I dream of cheating on you? I'm the envy of every man in America. Remember? The little Jewish guy who gets to sleep with Colette Cooke . . . when she lets him."

"Want to sleep with me, tiger?" Colette dropped the negligee from her shoulders, displaying those fabulous breasts, whose allure time and gravity had miraculously maintained in a state rivaling their centerfold celebrity years before.

Unbelievable, thought Levenstein, as his wife took him by the hand and led him into the bedroom. Two gorgeous women in one night. But, for the first time in their years together, as Colette sat astride him, riding up and down with frenetic energy, the lawyer's thoughts were of another woman. Those hypnotic eyes, that languid touch. He had to see Conception again.

The next morning Levenstein phoned Narouz's office and was informed by his secretary that the banker had returned to the Middle East. What next? There was no way he could call Crimson and ask to see his . . . what? Was she his girlfriend? Perhaps not. Maybe she was just a relative. Kid sister or cousin out for a night on the town. Certainly she'd had no qualms about going to bed with Levenstein. No fear of being discovered by the giant black man. How the hell was he going to find her again?

"Mitch? Mitch, are you all right?" Gardner was still on the telephone trying to get a response from his client.

"What? Oh, Alec. I'm sorry. I was thinking about something else."

"What could possibly be more important than this case?"

"Alec? You wouldn't have the name of a good private investigator, would you? Someone discreet."

37

BY 6:15 P.M. THE REGULARS in Sweeney Todd's on Columbus were glued to the TV screen over the bar, watching New York's latest media grotesque stumble over her own words.

"It all started with that furry guy on the *Today* show," said one myopic customer, whose foot kept slipping off the old-fashioned brass rail running around the front of the scratched and dented oak bar. "You know, the one with the frizzy hair and the bushy mustache."

"He's on *Sesame Street*," said the short, bald man standing next to him, who was wearing an Anne Rice T-shirt.

"Nah, nah, nah. Not a Muppet. This guy's a film critic. A furry film critic. That's his gimmick. That's how you get to be a film critic now. Like this one here. Two-Ton Tessie."

"Where'd they find a dame like this? Hey! Where you goin', lady?"

"Trying to get a drink," said Janie Moore, attempting to squeeze between the two men at the bar. "You got a problem with that?"

"No, lady."

"Good," said Janie, as she ordered two Bushmills

and stared up at the TV screen where an irate Marbella Morgan was huffing and puffing and taking offense at the latest "mindless, insensitive, antifeminist, racist outing" starring Felicia Silverstone.

"Alicia!" Janie shouted at the screen. "The girl's name is Alicia. Where did they find this moron?"

"It's Channel 8," The bartender bringing Janie her order shrugged. "It's like the ark. One of everything."

"They had two—God forbid! How long has she been on? Does she always stop like that? Look! She's not speaking."

"She gets upset a lot," said the bartender. "Sometimes she doesn't finish her review at all. Starts to cry. It's a real freak show. Best thing on TV since Rush Limbaugh."

"Unbelievable," said Janie as she carried the drinks across the room and set them down in front of Susan. "Have you been watching her? What is going on at Channel 8? The place has turned into a real joke."

"My niece is working there now."

"Linda's daughter? What's her name? Brandy? The Chugalug Queen of Mississippi?"

"Tennessee. She's Lisa Mercado's personal assistant."

"Gol-ly!"

"Hugh's going to be on there, too."

"Who?"

"Hugh. Carver. The father of my children. He's being billed as 'The Five-Minute Shrink.' "

"Is that a sexual reference? Someone been reading your diary?"

Susan burst out laughing, then stared fondly at her friend. "I've missed you, Mrs. Moore."

"I've missed you, too, Greenwich. But Lydia forbade me to talk to you. That was one of the clauses in our deal. Deal! White-collar blackmail."

"She found out about the thimbles, didn't she?"

"Yep. Threatened to throw the book at me if I didn't play ball with her and spill everything I know. Said us harps from the Kitchen should stick together. Said it was a tough world out there. How could we afford to send Stella to Balmoral on Kevin's paycheck alone? Especially with all the legal fees trying to get me an appeal."

"An appeal?"

"Five years. She said they could put me away for five years for suppressing evidence. The Mayor insisted on double but that's the best deal she could cut me . . . unless I played ball with her."

" 'The Mayor insisted.' She's such a liar!" snarled Susan. "I should have let her rot in jail a year ago. The woman's a monster."

"The worst part has been having lunch with her twice a week. Keeping her up to date on the investigation. I thought I could drink, Greenwich. But this dame has two hollow legs and a spare in the trunk. And the ego! She always wanted to be the next district attorney but now she's convinced herself once she cracks the Sleeping Beauty Murders she can back the U-Haul up to Gracie Mansion."

"This is frightening."

"Please, Greenwich. The woman's a psycho. Claims Cardinal Corcoran can deliver every Catholic vote in the city to her and that her megabucks boyfriend—what's his name? Marshak—will pay for the whole campaign. She's just waiting for her son to get back from diet camp this summer so the two-ton baby will look good snuggling up to his mom on the TV spots."

"This can't be happening."

"It's like the court of the Borgias, isn't it? Except there's no poison deadly enough to kill our Lucrezia. She's had me jumping through hoops for the past two weeks. Kissing her ass and walking the straight and narrow. Having to deal with Hopeless Haskell. He's a bigger liar than she is. Now this surprise birthday party at Rain with Miss Piggy. I will not be an accomplice to Lydia turning forty two years in a row! I had to draw the line somewhere. So I took my chances and called you. Lydia can't fire me for talking to you."

"I'm so glad you did, Janie. I've been desperate to talk to you. It got so bad the other night I almost poured my heart out to Hugh."

"You didn't!"

"I caught myself in time."

"What's wrong, Greenwich?"

"I don't know where to start."

"Oh, this is going to be bad. Is it medical?"

"No."

"Thank God. I don't do medical well. I'm so god-damn paranoid about my body lately. I examine my breasts with such regularity I'm getting a crush on myself. Sorry. Go ahead. I'm listening."

Susan took a deep breath then: "I met a man on St. Stephen's."

"Not another one?"

"I don't know!"

"You don't know if he's a man? Or you don't know if you—"

"Exactly."

"What? Exactly what?"

"I have difficulty discussing . . . you know, sex. I'm not like you, Janie. I believed everything my mother told me about the stork. I think she believed it, too."

"Did you have sex with this man?" asked Janie. "Let me lead you through your testimony, Ms. Given. I'm good at it, you know. I've had a lot of practice. Who was this man?"

"A policeman. A captain, actually. Captain Desmond Wilmot."

"Really? That'll be a disappointment to a lot of guys on the force. After all these years of being their secret pinup, you finally break down and screw a cop. Except he's an out-of-towner."

"I never said I screwed him!" Susan realized she had shouted the last sentence and immediately lowered her voice. "I don't know what I did with him. I had a lot to drink then I woke up on the plane to New York."

Janie held her empty glass over her head till she caught the bartender's eye, then asked Susan: "Does your Captain Wilmot know anything about homicide?"

"I doubt it. He wasn't very interested in my friend's murder. Why?"

"Because we can use some outside help with our old pal Rice Krispies. Haskell Abrams is speaking in tongues these days. He keeps lying to the media about new leads and the promise of imminent arrests. We have no prints. We have no suspects. Spring is here and women continue to jog in Central Park every day. Have *you* resumed jogging?"

"Of course."

"Of course. Silly me. Couldn't get you to stop running if I tried. Just like I can't stop a few thousand other potential victims. It's a free country. Women can run and Rice Krispies can stalk them. And the clock ticks."

"Was there a specific clock, Mrs. Moore?"

"Yeah. Rice Krispies always has a clock. He killed Mary Ellen Chernin at the beginning of March. Two weeks later he killed Natalie Margolis. It's a two-week clock, Greenwich. There's going to be a third Sleeping Beauty any day now and there's nothing we can do to prevent it."

228

38

CHUCK STURGES stared with disgust at the coffee stain on his tie. He swiveled 180 degrees in his chair, licked his index finger with his tongue, and frantically attempted to erase the offending blemish.

His coanchor, Lisa Mercado, was blowing on her newly applied nail polish when she looked up and saw Sturges with his back to her, making jabbing motions with his arm in the general direction of his crotch. "Hey, Chuck! Can't you wait till you get home to jerk off?"

Flushed with embarrassment, Sturges swiveled around in the other direction, stared up desperately toward the control booth and, in the stentorian voice that had won him three local Emmys, rumbled: "Can you guys read this?"

"What?" asked Taylor Parkhurst from the control booth at Channel 8. "Something wrong with the TelePrompTer?"

"Nooo," whined the anchorman. "My tie. I spilled coffee on my tie. I hate when I do that. People do not have faith in a messy messenger." Sturges's spiritual guide, a high-priced swami he phoned once a week on Maui, had recently stressed the concept of the newsman's historical importance to the community as its "messenger." Then he added his swami's latest words of wisdom: "Tempest tossed and tempus fugit."

Taylor groaned, turned to Hugh Carver (scratching his leg where the cast had been removed only that morning), and shrugged a mute "Now you see what I have to put up with every day?" She spoke calmly into the microphone: "No one can see it, Chuck. Trust me. We're back on the air in thirty seconds. You look great. Very much the messenger."

"Really?" Sturges's face glowed in the aftereffect of the ego balm. Then he stared into the camera and intoned in deadly earnest: "It is now almost six weeks since the killer known as The Sleeping Beauty Murderer first began his reign of terror here in Manhattan."

Hugh, who was in the control booth, observing the news team that he would soon be a part of, bent his head down and whispered to Taylor: "Isn't 'reign of terror' a bit much? Don't you think you're empowering this man by using a phrase like that to go out on the air?"

"What do you mean?" his producer-girlfriend whispered back.

"You're only feeding into this fiend's need for power and gratifying his twisted sense of omnipotence."

"Want to talk about this on camera?" asked Taylor.

"That's not my mandate," replied Hugh in his vintage, clipped Gregory Peck tones. "I'm the Five-Minute Shrink. Remember?"

"Sure. But this is an even better way to introduce

you to the audience. I love it! I love it!" The news producer pulled up a chair next to the control panel, grabbed a yellow legal pad, and began scribbling furiously. Without looking up, she called out: "Stuart!"

The skittish little Generation-Xer in question, who resembled a nervous rabbit in a black Calvin Klein suit more than a production assistant, materialized as if from nowhere and asked: "What is it?"

"Take Dr. Carver down the hall and have Margo make him up immediately. Go on, Hugh. I'll be down in a minute."

"But what am I—?" Hugh detested not being in control. It was bad enough when his leg was encased in plaster all those weeks but having this pushy anorexic tell him what to do. Beyond the pale! Still, Taylor was determined to make him a star. Hugh liked the idea of that. He'd teach Ms. Susan Given a lesson about real charisma.

"Trust me, Hugh. This'll put us both on the map."

Hugh left the dressing room and Taylor spoke to the floor manager on his headset: "Where's Brandy?"

"Who?" asked the floor manager.

"Lisa's new assistant. Find her and get her up here."

"Hi, y'all," said Brandy, sauntering into the control booth moments later as if she'd been invited to a campus keg party. "Wassup?"

"Take these pages down to Lisa," said Taylor, pausing for a moment to edit what she had just written. "Tell her to read them right after the next commercial."

Brandy's eyes scanned the handwritten text, then

her mouth dropped open: "Is this my uncle Hugh Carver?"

"Why, yes. Yes, it is."

"That's so coool!" said Brandy. "It really *is* family here. Just like Vance promised."

Marbella Morgan was wedged into the chair in front of the mirror, staring at her typed notes as Margo, the makeup artist, attempted to apply some eye shadow.

"Please, look up," said Margo, who loathed having to deal with the difficult film reviewer.

"I'm studying," grunted Marbella.

"You can always read it off the TelePrompTer."

"I don't trust the TelePrompTer."

"Siskel and Ebert do."

"Neither one is a woman."

"Oh, give it a rest, will ya."

"And what exactly does that mean?" bristled Marbella.

"It means you can go on camera tonight without makeup, for all I care."

Stuart dashed into the room and held the door open for Hugh Carver.

"Margo," said the nervous production assistant, in tones that might otherwise have indicated the studio was on fire, "Taylor says you're to put this gentleman into makeup immediately."

"No problem," said Margo, gesturing for Hugh to sit down in the chair next to the film reviewer.

"What about my eyes?" pouted Marbella. "You haven't done my eyes."

232

Taylor rushed into the room a second later and demanded to know why Doctor Carver wasn't in makeup yet.

"He just walked in," said Margo, who began to apply a base to the psychiatrist's face.

"Great," said Taylor, crouching down beside Hugh and gripping his arm. "Okay, Hugh. Here's what I want you to do. As soon as we come back from the commercial, Lisa is going to introduce you and you are going to address The Sleeping Beauty Murderer. You are going to look into the camera and—"

"Heyyy!" squeaked Marbella, as if she had seen a mouse. "That's my spot. Right after the commercial."

"I'm cutting your spot today, Marbella."

"What!? You can't do that."

"I just did. Okay? Learn to live with it. This is a news show. Not *Entertainment Tonight*. Now I want you to get tough with this Rice Krispies, Hugh. I want you to strip him of his power. I want him to know that you're not afraid of him. That you're smarter than he is. I want you to bring this vermin out from whatever damp hole he's hiding in and let him know that he can't hold sway over our—"

"You can't do this to me!" shrieked Marbella as she attempted to wriggle out of the chair her immense derriere was wedged into so solidly. "I'll talk to Dierdre about this. I know what you're up to."

"Talk to me about what?" asked Dierdre Holland, who swept into the makeup room wearing a ball gown Catherine the Great would have killed for and a diamond tiara that looked a tad ridiculous perched atop her buzz cut.

"What happened to dress-down Saturdays?" asked Taylor, staring at her boss's regal attire.

"Vance and I are on our way to the opera gala at the Plaza. But I wanted to stop in and see how everything was going. I just can't stay away from the place. Funny, isn't it? For years I couldn't give a fig about this station but now it's become the very air I breathe. So, what's the big deal, Marbella?"

The film reviewer had been hyperventilating since Dierdre had interrupted her tirade, but she now took herself off "pause" and resumed her litany of laments: "You're no different from the rest of them, Dierdre. I see that now. I'm just another quota baby to you. What do you care about my feelings, my intellect, my needs? Just get a fat woman on the air to talk about some stupid sexist movies. Well, there's a lot more to me than making witty comments about mindless drivel starring Nicolas Page and Michelle Pfeiffing. I have a masters degree from—"

"We know all about your college credits," said Dierdre. "Now, can we please—?"

"I'm not done yet!" shrieked Marbella. "I know how you've all been conspiring against me. Jealous of me. Trying to keep me down. It doesn't come as any surprise. I've been facing this sort of thing all my life. All my life!"

"What sort of thing?" Hugh Carver asked gently. He realized it was up to him to rescue all these people held hostage by the large woman's even larger ego.

"Huh?"

"What sort of thing have you been facing, Marbella? Tell me about it."

The film reviewer stared in awe at the man seated next to her. Ever since she was a little child and had seen the movie *To Kill a Mockingbird,* she had been obsessed with the notion of Atticus Finch, a decent man dedicated to the rights of people white or black or fat. Of course, when she grew older, she knew it was just a movie. But now, here, in a TV studio on Ninth Avenue, Atticus Finch—or, at least, a man who sounded exactly like him—wanted to listen to her. To hear her story. Marbella's eyes filled with tears.

"Do you really want to hear?" blubbered Marbella.

"Very much." Hugh nodded.

"Hugh, you're on in thirty seconds," Taylor hissed.

"Can you wait for me?" asked Hugh, staring into the film reviewer's eyes.

Marbella nodded. Hugh then pivoted on his crutches and made his way out of the makeup room with Taylor, Stuart, and Margo following closely behind.

"The man's a genius!" announced Dierdre as she picked up the train of her ball gown and swept out after them. "Smartest move I ever made hiring him."

When everyone had left the makeup room, Marbella Morgan stared into the wall mirror and finally spoke aloud: "Yes. Oh, yes. I'll wait for you . . . my darling."

39

SUSAN WAS STANDING inside her walk-in closet sorting through her jewelry box when Polly slid across the newly polished hardwood floor and announced: "Dad was just on TV."

"What?" asked Susan, who was clad only in her bra and panties.

"I said Dad was—Mom! Could you put some clothes on, please?"

"I will when I decide which earrings to wear to the gala tonight."

"You and Cinderella."

"Cinderella who?"

"Duh! How many Cinderellas are there, Mom?"

"A great many in England, if you must know. Most Cindys are actually—"

"I'm sorry I asked."

"Why? It's the only way you learn things." Susan found a pair of sapphire earrings she liked and affixed them to her pierced ears. "There! I think these work, don't you? And I'd rather you didn't say 'duh' all the time to critique the things you find lacking in intelligence."

"You're getting to sound more and more like Grandmother all the time."

"Duh! Just think what *your* children have to look forward to. Now, what about your father?"

"He was just on TV."

"Has his five minutes of fame begun already?"

"Dunno," shrugged Polly. "He wasn't supposed to start till next week. This was some kind of interview with Lisa Mercado."

"What was he talking about?"

"The Sleeping Beauty Murders."

"What!? Is he still on?"

"No. He was really good, too. You know that tone he uses when he thinks he knows something nobody else does?"

"You mean the one he wakes up with every morning?"

"Mom! Don't put me in the middle. I refuse to be a cliché child of divorce."

"Polly dearest, you couldn't be a cliché anything. Go on. What did your father say?"

"Basically how pathetic and impotent this Rice Krispies guy is and how he'll be forgotten as soon as some other psychotic comes along to dislodge his—"

"Your father said this on television?"

"He was ready to say a lot more but they ran out of time."

"Is he crazy?"

"Why?"

"He's just fanning the fire for this monster to strike again. Rice Krispies has a clock and your father has just—"

The telephone rang and Ivy's voice screamed out: "Mom!"

"I swear she'll give me a heart attack one of these days." Susan had her hands on her hips as she stared at Polly and asked: "Where is she?"

"In her bedroom," replied Polly. "Don't you think you should get dressed?"

"Would it be too much to ask her to walk in here and tell me that someone wants to speak to me?"

"Mommm!"

"Who is it?" Susan shouted back in kind.

"Andrea."

"Andrea who?" Oh, no. Andee Grant Carstairs. Her oldest friend from childhood, who had lately abandoned her husband, children, and Greenwich to take up residence with the lady gym teacher in Cos Cobb. Why was she phoning on a Saturday night?

"MOMMM!"

"All right, Ivy. I've got it."

Susan walked out of her closet, followed by the ever-curious Polly, and picked up the telephone: "Hi, Andee."

"Hello, Susan." A deadly pause followed.

"What's up?"

"Is this a good time?" asked Andrea.

"Hardly. I'm standing here in the altogether with a pair of sapphire earrings dangling from my lobes frantically trying to get dressed for this gala at the—"

"I need to see you, Susan."

"Want to have lunch next week?"

"How 'bout tomorrow? We could have breakfast."

"Tomorrow's no good. I have to go to church in Harlem."

"What about afterward?"

"I can do Monday after work, Andee. Can't it wait till then?"

"I guess it'll have to." Andrea followed this statement with a sigh of resignation that carried with it the weight of the world. Then she added: "Fern almost killed David this afternoon."

"Who is Fern?" asked Susan, gesturing for Polly to bring her dress over to the bed.

"My . . . friend. Did you know I'd left David?"

"Yes, I heard." Then Susan fibbed: "I can't remember where."

"I'm going out of my mind. You're my only hope."

"I'm sure it can't be that bad, Andee. We'll talk about it on Monday. Call my office in the morning. Okay?"

"Thank you."

Susan replaced the receiver on the telephone and shook her head sadly. Poor Andrea. The two women had gone to kindergarten and Ethel Walker's together. But Susan had spoken with her so infrequently in recent years that they had become almost strangers. Still they had shared so much together as children. She had played Wendy to Susan's Peter Pan.

"What's wrong with Andee?" asked Polly.

"She's going through a difficult transition. You wouldn't understand."

"Is she really a dyke?"

"Who said that?"

"It's okay, Mom. Zillions of women are coming out of the closet these days. It's not like when you were a kid."

239

"There weren't any dykes—lesbians—when I was a child. And what do you know about all this?"

"Ellen DeGeneres. K. D. Lang. Sandra Bernhard. It's an optional lifestyle, Mom. Andee just never struck me as the type."

Susan wrapped her arms around her daughter abruptly and asked: "Where has your childhood gone?"

"Mom, please don't hug me in your underwear."

"Why? You don't think I'm peculiar, do you?"

"No, but you just took a bath and you want to smell sweet for your date."

"This is not a date. It's only Mr. Archibald and it's business. Crime never sleeps."

"Why are you going to church in Harlem?"

"You don't miss a trick, do you, Polly? You'd make a great prosecutor."

"One's enough in the family. So? What's in Harlem?"

"I'm going with Cordelia. I thought it would make a change."

"From what? You never go to church."

"That's not true, Polly. Didn't we go at Christmas?"

"Like, that was two years ago, Mom. When you were doing comparative religious shopping."

"What do you mean?"

"Remember that little stretch of time when you were running all over the East Side finding a church you liked? You came home one morning all upset because the minister at Brick Church said Christ was coming back. What? Did you think he was gone for good, Mom?"

"How do you remember all these things, Polly?"

"And what about the church on Park Avenue where they wanted you to shake hands with the people beside you and the people behind you? You weren't too happy about being touchy-feely with strangers. That wasn't your idea of Christianity. You are *so* Greenwich, Mom."

"All right. All right. I can't help who I am. I envy you your flexibility, Polly. The way you just accept these things."

"Oh, yeah? I don't accept Ethan Culberg."

"Lydia's son?"

"How many other Ethan Culbergs did God inflict on the planet? It was bad enough when he played my father in *The Sound of Music* last year. Tormenting me all the time with his lies. And his creamed herring."

"That's genetic. The lies."

"Whatever. At least he wasn't making goo-goo eyes at me then and buying me Hallmark cards."

"You're joking!"

"What am I going to do, Mom? Ethan Culberg has the hots for me. He's asked me out to the movies three times."

"What did you tell him?"

"Can you have your period three times in a month? I've got to find another excuse. What's with this family? Ivy's being stalked by Gwillim Griffiths. I've got Ethan Culberg leaving mist on the back of my neck. Thank God nobody's bothering you."

"Nobody I can think of," said Susan, who immediately flashed on Desmond Wilmot, handsome and resplendent in his white uniform. "It's business. Okay?"

"What is?"

"Harlem. I just can't go up there and expect—"

"So why didn't you say so?" asked Polly. "Instead of treating me like a kid."

The telephone rang again before Susan could answer her. Polly snatched up the receiver and in her best temp voice announced: "Given-Carver residence."

Polly held the phone away from her ear as a shrill voice blasted out of the receiver: "Hi, darlin'! Where's Mom?"

"It's Aunt Linda." And Polly thrust the receiver into her mother's hand.

"Hi, Sis! Where y'all been hidin'?" Linda Given Prescott always sounded as if she were phoning from a storm cellar trying to make herself heard over the nonexistent tornado raging outside. Combined with the faux Southern accent she had acquired since moving to Tennessee, it made telephone conversation with her somewhat of a trial for her sister. "Haven't heard from you in ages. Did Brandy tell you about her job? Isn't it fabulous? Shut up, Justin!"

"Who's Justin?" asked Susan.

"A new puppy. I couldn't resist him."

"How many dogs have you got now, Linda?"

"You sound just like Phil. I think it's six. I'm just a sucker for orphans, Sis. So how's the Big Apple treatin' ya? How's the crime business? Who y'after these days? Done with those Mafia garbagemen yet?"

"Almost. I'm working on a bank case right now. OICB."

242

"You're joking!" said Linda. "Heyy! They're big time. We've even heard of them down here."

"Actually, it's a division of OICB. American Patriot."

"Dwight Pelham."

"How did you know that?" asked Susan, who was always amazed when her younger sister showed interest in anything besides dogs and golf.

"It's one of the biggest banks in Chattanooga. So you're going after old Dwight Pelham."

"Yes. As a matter of fact, I'm late for this gala at the Plaza where I'm sort of staking him out. So I really haven't got a lot of time to—"

"It's ironic, Sue. You going after Pelham."

"Why?"

"Oh, come on! Didn't Mom ever tell you that story?"

"What story? What are you talking about, Linda?"

"During World War Two. When she worked in Washington. That guy who came on to her. The one she bopped on the head with the flashlight. Didn't she ever tell you that story?"

"The date rape?"

"Is that what she's calling it now? Mom's just too au courant, isn't she?"

"The man was Dwight Pelham?"

"Yessss! I can't believe she never told you. Small world, huh? Well, Sis, have fun. And don't forget to take your flashlight."

40

ATTENDING A MAJOR social function on the arm of William Archibald was a revelation to Susan Given. Everyone who was anyone at the opera gala paused to stop and chat with the legendary crime fighter and was more than a bit curious as to the identity of the pretty blonde woman who never left his side.

"Is it always like this?" asked a wide-eyed Susan, after a gaggle of politicians, society matrons, and media moguls had paid their respects to the District Attorney and moved on.

"What?"

"Your fans. The way they treat you. I feel as if Clark Gable or Gary Cooper had invited me to the premiere of their latest film at the Chinese Theater in Hollywood."

"Is it more than a coincidence that both men are deceased?"

"I didn't mean it that way. I meant that you're very much like one of those old-fashioned movie stars. That sort of aura."

"Is it the aura or the era? I met them both, you know. Just after the war. Nice guys. A little embarrassed by what they did for a living. It's very sweet of you, Susan, to cast an elderly widower in such a romantic fantasy."

"You're not elderly. Imogen Blythe doesn't think so."

"Imogen! How on earth do you know Imogen?"

"You sent me to her. Remember?"

"Oh, of course. She's lovely, don't you think? Now then, Susan, let's not forget the object of this evening's exercise. You're here to observe Dwight Pelham. And if that 'old Hollywood' theory of yours applies to anyone, it's certainly Dwight. A veritable peacock. Always has been."

"Do you know anything about the scar on his forehead?" asked Susan, trying to sound as nonchalant as possible. She hadn't been able to think about anything else since Linda had identified the Washington Brahmin as their mother's mysterious attacker so many years before. "How did he get it?"

"A car accident, I think," replied Archibald. "During the war. Why?"

"Just curious."

"Do you know that woman?"

"Where?"

"The one with the shaved blonde hair and the tiara. She's making a beeline in our direction. Why don't I go get us something to drink? Be right back."

Before Susan could protest her boss's desertion, Dierdre Holland arrived on the scene and began to pump Susan's arm as if she expected Perrier to spurt forth from the first available orifice.

"My husband Vance and your husband Henry

have known each other for years," bubbled Dierdre, who finally stopped pumping when Susan failed to yield water.

"Actually, Henry's my brother."

"Of course, he is. Of course, he is. It's just that I've got that husband of yours on the brain."

"Estranged husband," said Susan, under her breath.

"The voice mail and e-mail we got right after his appearance this evening! I was almost late with all the ensuing tumult he aroused."

"There's still a law in New York against lynching, isn't there?"

"All positive, Susan! All positive! The viewers loved Hugh's get-tough attitude. The man is a star. I wouldn't get rid of him so fast, if I were you."

"I am rid of him. Now, Dierdre, tell me whose idea it was to have him provoke this psychotic serial murderer on the air. Didn't anyone think it might be counter-productive to all the police's best efforts to—"

"Why so formal? Lisa told me you made up the name Rice Krispies. Use it, my dear, use it! Oh, and let's not forget that niece of yours! Scarlett O'Hara's younger sister. We all just love her to bits. You must be so proud of her."

"I haven't really spoken to Brandy since she started working—"

"And I hear you run. Run! Wings on your heels, they tell me. Just started again myself after years of self-abuse. Don't get me started. Drink and drugs! The sixties lasted three decades for yours truly. Still

an addictive personality. That'll never change. But—
and we're talking a big but—the preposition, of
course—God! you have pretty eyes!—Where was I?
Running. Addiction City. Day and night. Can't stop.
Cannot stop. Why don't we run together this week?
Hmm? I'm out there at the crack of dawn."

"I'm not that early," said Susan, praying Mr.
Archibald would reappear with their drinks and rescue her. "Getting back to Hugh's TV appearance this
evening, I really think it's ill advised under the present climate to even consider continuing such bla-
tantly provocative—"

"You know, I saw you last year on Lisa's morning
show. The camera loves you, Susan. Loves you. Wait!
Wait! Major idea brewing. Looove it! What about you
and Hugh doing a *Crossfire* kind of thing? *The Ex
Factor.* Get it? We've never had a divorced couple
going at it tooth and nail on TV. Forget what I said
before. Divorce him quick. This could be a hot show.
Hot! Syndicators would eat it up. Oh! There's Ivana.
And Ivanka. Have to go talk to them. See you soon.
Think about what we said."

I didn't say a thing, thought Susan after Dierdre
had dashed across the floor of the ballroom, wondering all the while if the high-energy Mrs. Holland was
wearing Nikes under her gown. Wings on her heels,
indeed!

"Hello, Susan."

Susan spun around and was surprised to see
Imogen Blythe standing there. An alarm bell went
off abruptly in Susan's brain. Why *had* Mr. Archibald
invited her to the gala? Was it really to observe

Dwight Pelham or to act as a front, a "beard," so he could be with Imogen?

"Hello, Imogen. Are you alone?"

"No, my date's out in the lobby. So, you're here with Bill?"

"Who? Oh, Mr. Archibald. Yes. How did you know?"

"He told me. After he fixed me up with my date."

That cinched it, thought Susan. They're definitely having an affair. Why else would they both be using beards to attend?

"I'm sorry, Imogen. I'm a little confused. Why didn't he ask you himself?"

"Why would he? He asked you. Susan, what is that strange look you're giving me?"

"We're both adults, Imogen. Do we really need to go through this charade?"

"What charade?"

"You know."

"No, I don't know. Oh, Susan, you haven't fixed me up with someone else in your mind again, have you? You *are* funny. I've known Bill Archibald forever. He's my godfather."

"He is?"

"Did you think we were . . . something else?"

"Well, you call him Bill. Nobody calls him Bill."

"Except my mother, whom he almost married a long time ago. Before I was born."

"Oh, no. I feel so stupid. I was positive you and Mr. Archibald were—"

"We're not."

Archibald appeared on the scene at that moment

with a drink in each hand. His face lit up when he saw Imogen and he kissed her on the cheek. Then he stared at Susan.

"Are you all right?" asked the District Attorney. "You look a bit shaky."

"I'm fine," chirped Susan.

Archibald turned his attention back to Imogen and asked: "Where's your date?"

"Had to make a phone call. Oh, here he is."

Susan turned around and almost fainted when she saw Imogen's date walking toward her. It was Desmond Wilmot.

"Hello, Captain Wilmot," said Archibald, shaking the policeman's hand warmly. "So glad you could join us this evening. Susan, this is Desmond Wilmot."

"So nice to see you again, Miss Given," said Wilmot, taking her hand in his.

"Now how do you two know each other?" asked the District Attorney. "Oh, of course! Your vacation was on St. Stephen's. What a small world. The Captain's here assisting us with . . ."

Before Archibald could finish his sentence, a tall, imposing man with snow white hair and piercing blue eyes approached the quartet. He thrust his large liver-spotted hand out at the District Attorney and with a wide grin declared: "As always, Archie, you're a magnet for the most beautiful women in the room."

"Hello, Dwight. Have you met Captain Wilmot?"

Pelham nodded at the policeman and said: "Forgive me, Captain. I don't mean to be rude but one of the pleasures of advanced age is meeting all the beautiful girls I want to. Well, Archie, am I to stand here drooling or are you going to introduce me to these ravishing creatures?"

Susan was grateful for Pelham's appearance. It took some of the shock element away from seeing Captain Wilmot again. And it was a pleasant surprise to discover that the Brahmin wasn't as intimidating as she'd anticipated. He actually reminded her a bit of Bud Waffington and his chums back on St. Stephen's. *If yer not back in twenty minutes, I'll start without ya.*

"I'd know you anywhere, Mr. Pelham," said Susan, stepping forward and shaking his hand.

"You have the advantage of me, my dear."

"This is Susan Given from my office," said Archibald. "And this is Imogen Blythe, Harriet Reynolds' daughter."

"Harriet's daughter? She might have been your daughter, too, Archie. Once upon a time."

"Mr. Archibald is my godfather," said Imogen proudly.

"Is he indeed? Give my regards to your mother, Imogen. I remember her fondly."

And what about my mother? wondered Susan. Do you remember her at all? Perhaps not her name. But you must certainly think of her every time you brush that fine head of white hair.

"Were you staring at something, Ms. Given?" asked Pelham, catching the blond prosecutor examining the ancient scar on his forehead.

"Forgive me," replied Susan, "is that a war wound?"

"I received it during the war," said Pelham, "but not in battle. An automobile accident."

The orchestra onstage began to play a Cole Porter tune and Pelham's face lit up. "This is our vintage, eh, Archie? I am, ladies, one of the last practitioners of a long-forgotten tribal dance known as the fox trot." The old man held his arms out to Susan and asked: "Will you indulge me, Ms. Given?"

Susan's eyes met the District Attorney's for a moment. This was more than she had counted on. It was one thing to observe the enemy from a distance but quite another to be held in his arms.

Pelham's still sharp eye caught the exchange of looks and he joked: "Oh, give her permission, Archie."

"Susan's a big girl, Dwight. She can do whatever she wants."

"Well, my dear?" asked Pelham. "Who, indeed, is afraid of the big bad wolf?"

"Not I," replied Susan, allowing the Brahmin to escort her out onto the dance floor. "Actually, Mr. Pelham, if it wasn't for you, I wouldn't even be here this evening."

"Really? And what was your dear mother's name?" Pelham threw his head back and laughed raucously. "Forgive me, Ms. Given. It was Shaw's line, not mine. I've waited all my life for a chance to use it."

You don't know how close to the truth you came, thought Susan, as the old man wrapped a still powerful arm around her waist.

"I haven't been entirely honest with you," said Pelham, as he steered Susan expertly around the dance floor.

"Don't you think you should have your lawyer present before you make a confession like that?"

"You have a marvelous sense of humor," said Pelham. "I like that in a woman."

"Is that *all* you like?" asked Susan, removing the old man's right hand from the spot on her posterior where he had brought it to rest.

"I've had my eye on you for some time, Ms. Given."

"Strange, I never noticed."

"You're wasting your time in the public sector. I've seen how you handle yourself in court. Most impressive. I think we could work together."

"Are you offering me a job?"

"What does Archie pay you? Fifty thousand a year?"

"The City of New York pays me."

"I'd start you at three hundred thousand."

"Mr. Pelham—"

"You don't have to answer me right away, Susan. I can wait till after dinner."

"You'll have to wait a lot longer than that, Mr. Pelham. You and I practice two very different kinds of law."

"You're making a big mistake, Susan. I like you. I could be a very good friend to you."

"I don't think so. I think, if you knew who I really was, you wouldn't like me at all."

"Is that meant to frighten me? I don't frighten easily." Pelham drew her tighter toward him and whispered, "I find you very attractive."

"Mr. Pelham, let go of me."

"Can you feel me pressing against you?"

"Shall we add sexual harassment to the other charges you're facing?"

"I'm a man who's used to having his way, young woman."

"Really? How *did* you get that scar?"

"What is your obsession with my—"

"Our dance is over, Mr. Pelham." Susan pushed him firmly away from her. "It's been illuminating."

Imogen and Wilmot sat with Susan and Archibald making pleasant conversation throughout the dinner. If Susan was the least bit uneasy about the Captain's unexpected proximity, it took a backseat to the discomfort she felt knowing someone else's eyes were riveted on her. Angling her compact, she could see Dwight Pelham staring balefully in her direction. For someone so used to having his way, the old man was not dealing at all well with rejection.

Once dessert was over, the lights were dimmed and the evening's entertainment commenced. Eugene and Herbert Perry, the brilliant twin baritones, stepped out onto the stage and sang a duet from *Don Giovanni*.

The Perry twins took their bow to a thunderous ovation, and an enthralled Susan was clapping so loudly herself that she almost didn't hear Wilmot whisper in her ear: "I need to speak with you. Outside."

Susan turned sideways and saw that neither Archibald nor Imogen had picked up on this. By the time she turned around to face Wilmot, he was nowhere in sight. Susan got up from the table and excused herself just as the Perrys began their encore.

Out in the lobby, Desmond Wilmot waited for her with a smile on his face, as handsome and infuriating as ever.

"What is all the mystery, Captain?"

"I felt awkward discussing business in front of Miss Blythe."

"You could always come to my office on Monday."

"I told you on St. Stephen's that I suspected you did your job well, Susan. It has been corroborated. Now I need your help."

"Yes?"

"Can we meet on Monday?"

"I said you could come to my office."

"I thought, perhaps, a drink?"

"No drinks!" Susan was beginning to feel nervous and agitated.

"Dinner then?"

"Why can't we keep this on a business level, Captain? I mean, what can be so important that we can't discuss it in my office?"

"It's about Ascension. Is that important enough?"

41

AKBAR SINGH HAD been watching the short, sturdy woman on the aisle for some time now. The tiny, moon-faced Indian admired the woman's blue-black skin and the way her considerable bosom heaved when she hit the high notes in praise of the Lord. She suited his needs perfectly.

Singh twirled his handlebar mustache, plowed a hand through his thick rosewater-scented hair, and sidled along the length of the pew until he reached the far aisle of the Harlem church. Then he circled around the back and came down the center aisle, stopping at the pew where his dream girl was praying fervently.

"Excuse me," said Singh as he squeezed past the woman, interrupting her devotions. "Is this seat taken?"

"Me be savin' it," replied Cordelia Brown.

"For a friend?" asked Singh. "A man or a woman?"

"What make dat you business?" asked Cordelia, who had been aware of the Indian's intense stares for some time.

"You are from Jamaica," said Singh confidently. "I love girls from Jamaica."

"Not dis girl." Cordelia raised her prayer book up to her chin and riveted her attention on the pulpit.

"Why do you lie to me?"

"What de matter wit' you?" asked Cordelia, turning angrily on the Indian. "Comin' into de Lord's house and callin' a good Christian a liar?"

"But I know you are from Jamaica."

"Me never been to Jamaica. Go 'way."

"Are you married?"

"Dat be done a long time ago."

"Good," replied Singh. "I will marry you."

"What kind of a crazy man are you? Me don't know you from a turnip."

Three German tourists in tattered jeans and T-shirts advertising the Nuremberg Oktoberfest were seated in the row ahead of Cordelia, filming the church service with a video camera. One of them, a florid, overweight man of forty, turned around to Cordelia and said: *"Bitte!* Please to not make so much noise!"

"What you say?" asked Cordelia with undisguised annoyance. "What kind of talk is dat? Comin' in here dressed like de rag man and takin' pictures like dis some rock and roll concert. Shame on you!"

"Please," said his wife, a grim-faced creature with long, blonde braided hair down her back, who spoke in heavily accented English. "We are making here diligently the recording."

"Why you do dat?" asked Cordelia. "De minister, him ask you to do dis?"

"We love the Negro singing," replied the German woman, content that this was explanation enough. "Dieter, *schnell!*" She tapped her husband on the shoulder and pointed with excitement to the robed choir taking their places at the front of the church.

Cordelia snorted in disgust, then became aware of Singh squeezing her arm.

"Leave me be, man! What de matter wit' you?"

"I will pay you five thousand dollars," said Singh.

"What for you want to pay me all dat money?"

"Because I love you," said the mustached Indian, staring intently into her eyes. "What is your name?"

"Dat be my business."

"I am Akbar Singh. I sell dried fruit and yogurt. I make a very good living. Have you children?"

"All de chillun I need."

"Good. I can provide for them as well. Give them work in my store. One day they will own it."

"Why you gon' do dat for strangers?"

"I have a good heart."

"You got a green card?"

The pilot light of fear was ignited in Singh's eyes and he began backpedaling without missing a beat: "Why must you spoil everything by introducing bureaucracy into such an otherwise perfect arrangement?"

"Me tink you got no green card, boy, and you just lookin' for a way to stay in de country wit' you fruit and yogurt."

"Come and see my shop!"

He seized Cordelia's fingertips and kissed them just as a breathless Susan appeared on the aisle with a decidedly unhappy Ivy in tow.

"I'm sorry I'm late," said Susan. "Ivy wanted to come, then she didn't want to come. Then we couldn't find a dress for her to wear."

"I hate dresses!" said Ivy.

"Where Polly at?"

"Sleeping," said Ivy resentfully.

"Are you all right?" asked Susan, staring at her housekeeper's scowling face and wondering who this peculiar little man was hovering behind her shoulder. "Is something wrong?"

"Show de man you badge," said Cordelia, nodding her head contemptuously in Singh's direction.

"Is this man bothering you?" asked Susan.

"Him want me for de green card marriage."

"I never said that," said Singh, shuffling away toward the other end of the pew. "I don't even know this woman's name."

"Would you please to keep the voices down?" The German woman turned around once more in exasperation and was momentarily startled to see another blonde standing next to Cordelia. "You are spoiling our recording."

"Who are these hippies?" asked Susan.

"Shh, Mom!" said Ivy. "I want to hear the choir."

So did Susan. Specifically she wanted to hear and see Conception Westerfield, who, despite her heroin addiction and career in prostitution, was a devoted churchgoer and leading light of her congregation's famous choir.

Ascension's sister stood in the second row (Susan recognized her easily from the surveillance photos Tuck had taken of her the week before) and sang with fervor and commitment. Conception had a beautiful voice and performed a solo that the congregation greeted with great approbation.

Susan was baffled by this human dichotomy. How could the woman be so religious and yet lead the life she did in the company of a man as evil as Edward Claxton? When the service finally concluded and Cordelia had gone home to her family, Ivy began tugging on her mother's arm.

"Can we leave now?" asked Ivy. "*Xena* is on soon."

"You are *not* watching television this afternoon, Ivy."

"Why not? I went to church."

"One has nothing to do with the other. It's a beautiful spring day. We should go for a walk in the park."

"I'm hungry."

"That's because you didn't eat breakfast," said Susan. "I warned you you'd get hungry."

"Can we go to MacDonald's?"

"Ivy, where have I gone wrong with you? We live in New York City and yet you have the profile of some suburban mall creature."

"Mall rats!" said Ivy proudly. "Yesss! Can we go to a mall, Mom? In New Jersey?"

"This is official business," said Susan. "I need to talk with someone."

The choir, having changed out of their robes, were departing the church when Susan spotted Conception in a chic designer raincoat and called out to her: "Miss Westerfield!"

The beautiful black woman paused, stared in confusion at the blonde white woman, then called back: "Do I know you?"

"I'm a friend of Ascension's," said Susan, careful to use the present tense and not the past to speak of her brother.

Conception's face lit up with joy and she swept across the church toward Susan and Ivy.

"You have seen Ascension? When? Where?"

"I was on St. Stephen's a few weeks ago. He took me to his home several times. Betty cooked for me and—"

"Is she still big and fat?"

"She's . . . large."

"But she has a heart of gold, yes? And the children? How are the children? Oh, I'm so jealous you saw them all. I miss them so much. I haven't been home for years and years. I'm going to visit them for Christmas. But that's such a long way off, isn't it?" Then she turned to Ivy abruptly and asked: "What is your name, sweetheart?"

"Ivy Carver."

"A pretty name for a pretty girl," said Conception. "Did you go to the island as well?"

"I went skiing. In Aspen. On the baby slopes."

"I've never been skiing. I don't like the snow. It frightens me. I sit inside all winter and dream of sunny beaches. You are so lucky to have gone to St. Stephen's. How did you know where to find me, Mrs. Carver?"

"Call me Susan."

"Conception! What you doin', gal? Me got de car waitin' outside."

Crimson stood impatiently inside the entrance to the church. He was far from thrilled to see his woman chatting with Susan.

"Hello, Mr. Claxton," said Susan. "What a coincidence running into you here."

"You two know each other?" asked Conception.

"Oh, yes," confirmed Susan before Crimson could speak. "We saw each other several times on St. Stephen's."

"She's a friend of Ascension's. And Betty's. She had dinner at their house. Oh, Crimson. Must we wait until Christmas? Can't we go home before then? I miss my family so much."

"Come on, gal," snarled Crimson, grabbing Conception roughly by the wrist.

"Here," said Susan, offering the woman one of her business cards. "Call me anytime. We have so much to talk about."

The drug lord glared menacingly at Susan, then down at Ivy, at whom he smiled unexpectedly. "You be a good little girl. Don' get in no trouble. And mind how you cross dem streets. Lot of bad accidents happen all de time." Then he looked up at Susan and added the coda: "Too many accidents."

Susan was bristling with rage at this veiled threat as she stared deeply into Conception's eyes and said: "Get him to tell you about your brother."

Crimson snarled, wrapped an arm around a puzzled Conception's shoulder, and whisked her out of the church.

Ivy grabbed her mother's hand and whispered: "That guy was scary."

Susan nodded and knew she had not heard the last of Edward John Claxton.

42

RAY MURPHY WAS out of cigarettes. Not a good thing late on a Sunday night. The veteran tabloid reporter was prowling around the editorial offices, vainly seeking another human who had succumbed neither to the Surgeon General's warnings nor to the hysterical propaganda the President's wife had been fomenting since she'd gotten in over her head on health care.

"What the hell's the matter with all you guys?" growled the sixtyish, stocky, buzz-cut alcoholic old wreck, who looked and acted like a character out of *The Front Page*. A seeming anachronism in a world of laptops and sound bites, "The Murph" still had an incredible nose for news, knew everybody in the city, and managed to come up with one good scoop every month. "Smoking's in again. Brad Pitt smokes. Sharon Stone, too. It's cool to smoke. Christ on a crutch! Doesn't anyone have a cigarette for me? I need a cigarette!"

Worse, Murphy needed a lead for his column the next day. Staring at his computer screen (he'd finally agreed to work on one only after his editor informed him that no one was prepared to decipher the half-typed, half-scrawled copy he was still pounding out on his ancient Remington), he wondered where his inspiration would come from. Police brutality? How many more toilet plungers probing the depths of Haitians' backsides would the public have sympathy for and/or interest in? The Murph plowed through a hillock of notes he had scribbled on assorted bits of coffee-stained paper, bar coasters, flyers for strip joints. This looked promising. Something about the Russian Mafia holding dangerous psoltnts in Brighton Beach. What the hell were "psoltnts"? Was it a Russian word or had he been so crocked when he scribbled it originally that the note was doomed to remain permanently indecipherable?

Damn! Now it was raining outside and the nearest place to buy cigarettes on a Sunday night was a good block away. Murphy pulled open the top drawer of his desk and began sorting through the clutter and debris that had accumulated there through the years. Maybe there would be one loose cigarette. Stale, sure. But he could still light it up. How the hell could they expect him to write a decent column without a cigarette?

The telephone rang on his desk. The veteran reporter grabbed it and snarled: "Yeah?"

"Mr. Murphy?" Loud rock and roll was playing in the background and the caller's voice sounded muffled.

"Who wants him?"

"I'm a big fan of yours."

"Great. You got a cigarette?"

"I read your column regularly. You're a straight shooter. You don't kiss ass."

"Who is this?" asked Murphy, who was slightly deaf and had trouble hearing under the best of circumstances. But the heavy metal blaring away made it next to impossible.

"You've been writing about me lately. Respectfully. Not like that pompous prick on TV last night."

"I don't think I caught your name," said Murphy, taking a fresh stenographer's pad from the second drawer in his desk.

"Don't you remember, Mr. Murphy? You gave me my name last month."

"I did?" The hairs were standing up on the back of the veteran reporter's red and wrinkled neck. He had a pretty good idea who his caller was and he didn't want him to run away too soon. "Are you Snap? Crackle? Or Pop?"

"You're a smart old bastard, aren't you?" laughed the voice on the other end. "Call me Snap."

"I can't hear you too well," said Murphy. "Too much noise where you are."

"And it'll stay that way, Ray. Mind if I call you Ray?"

"Be my guest, Snap. So who's been pulling your chain the wrong way?"

"That goddam shrink on Channel 8."

"What shrink?"

"His name is Hugh Carver. Ever heard of him?"

"Not sure," replied Murphy, wondering if that was the same jerk who'd been married to Suzy Given for years. "Does he sound a little like Gregory Peck?"

"Yeah. Like a bad impersonation of Gregory Peck. I don't like the guy. I don't like what he said about me."

"I didn't see the show, Snap. So I can't really make—"

"You tell him to lay off me, Ray. You tell him to show me the proper respect. I'm not anyone he should mess with. You appreciate that, don't you, Ray?"

"Sure thing, Snap. I'm a big admirer of yours, too."

"Really?"

"Oh, absolutely. The way you've brought the city to its knees."

"You think so?"

"C'mon, Snap. Look at all the coverage you've been getting." Murphy's eyes combed the deserted City Room hoping to find someone who might be able to help him trace the call. But then he thought better of it. This could be the first of many calls if he, Murphy, played his cards right. There might be a book or even a Pulitzer to come out of this. "We don't give those column inches to a nobody."

"I like you, Ray."

"Thanks, Snap."

"You tell that Carver creep to keep his mouth shut."

"Sure thing. Now, while I got you on the phone—"

"Later, Ray."

Rice Krispies hung up. Murphy let loose a long, slow whistle. Then, hunched over his keyboard, he began tapping out a lead on his computer. Suddenly that cigarette didn't seem so important anymore.

43

...

ALAN BECKER SAT opposite his boss in her office,
staring at the awesome list of Dwight Pelham's assets.

"The man could easily refinance a bankrupt
African nation," said Susan Given. "Is this the most
current list? Alan? Alan?"

"Sorry, Susan. Did you say something?"

"Where were you?"

Becker heaved a sigh that was intended to serve as
an answer. Finally he looked up from the column of
figures and said: "My mother's in the hospital."

"What's wrong?"

"A stroke."

"Oh, Alan. I'm so sorry."

"She says it's a stroke. Who knows?"

The telephone rang on Susan's desk. She ignored
it and asked: "What do the doctors say?"

"They don't know. She's high-strung. She's got
high blood pressure. She's very high, you know. But
one thing is definite: I'm responsible. I put her
there."

The phone continued to ring but Susan still
ignored it.

"What happened?" asked the blond prosecutor.

"I finally told her about Nancy. I invited her over

266

to my place to meet Nancy and the kids. Big mistake."

"She didn't take it well."

"An understatement. Did you ever see those silent-movie clips of Sarah Bernhardt? With the fist to the forehead clutching the drapes. That was my mother. 'How could you do this to me?' 'I didn't do anything, Ma. I'm an adult.' 'Some adult! You're a monster. Only a monster would do this to me. To the Jewish people. We're a vanishing species. This *shiksa* will brainwash you. You'll forget all our customs. There'll be no one to say kaddish for me when I'm gone.'"

"What did Nancy say?"

"She was in shock. She's heard me tell stories about my mother for months but she didn't really believe them."

"Oh, I'm so sorry. What can I do?"

"Take my mother off life support. Just kidding."

A grim-faced Gretchen walked into the office and said, "That's been Lydia phoning. You better get down there."

"What now?" groaned Susan as she got up from her desk. "Try and stay focused, Alan. There's got to be an answer to all this. I'll be back in a few minutes."

Susan walked into Lydia's office and was surprised to discover Janie Moore and Haskell Abrams there as well.

"So kind of you to take the time," said the Deputy D.A., pinning and unpinning her flaming red hair. Never a good sign.

"I'm here, Lydia. What's the emergency?"

"Have you seen the *Post* this morning?" Lydia whipped the newspaper off her desk and flung it at Susan. Two crime scene photos of Mary Ellen Chernin and Natalie Margolis were on the front page with the banner headline RICE KRISPIES P***ED OFF! above them. On page 3 was a classic bit of hard-hitting Ray Murphy reportage in which the veteran newsman gave an account of his telephone call the previous night from New York's "most feared" killer at large and The Sleeping Beauty Murderer's demand that Channel 8 call off their psychiatric pit bull.

"How do we know it's real?" asked Susan.

"Ray Murphy's not going to make up a story like this," said Lydia.

"But how did Ray know this was really Rice Krispies? Anyone could call and claim to be the killer. Nothing in the story indicates proof of identity. It could all be a hoax."

Lydia and Abrams both stared at Susan as if she were speaking Swahili.

"Mr. Archibald's not happy about this," said Lydia.

"Neither's the Mayor," added Abrams.

Susan stared at the two mega-liars and wondered where the truth actually lay. She turned to Janie for a hint but her friend and colleague was busy checking the ceiling for cracks.

"This is all fascinating and will eventually make a great HBO movie," said Susan, "but what does it have to do with Asset Forfeiture?"

"What the hell are you talking about?" asked Lydia.

"I don't do homicide."

"You used to do Hugh Carver," said Lydia.

"I beg your pardon?" Susan's face reddened. "What exactly are you referring to?"

Lydia stared at Janie, who had finally stopped checking out the ceiling, and nodded for her to speak.

"We'd like you . . . to phone Hugh," Janie said gingerly.

"To what end?" asked a flabbergasted Susan.

"He's impeding a criminal investigation," said Abrams, who began to pace around the office. "I've got men in the field working day and night. Tough men. Family men. Men going without sleep to try and make this city safe again. I'm not sleeping, Susan. I'm not planning to sleep till this Rice Krispies is found. Tell your husband that."

"I don't think that'll make much of a difference to Hugh," said Susan. "He's cried for years about living in my shadow. Now he's the sun, the moon, and the stars."

"Skip the astronomy lecture," said Lydia. "Call him up and call him off. That's an order."

44

IT WAS FIVE MINUTES TO FIVE when Susan entered the tiny Bemelmans Bar through the entrance on Madison Avenue. She had spent a frustrating afternoon trying to persuade her estranged husband, his producer-girlfriend, and, finally, Dierdre Holland to abandon their sensationalistic TV confrontation with Rice Krispies. But they were all on a high from the positive reaction to Ray Murphy's column and determined to cash in on the ratings bonanza they were certain Hugh's continuing television baiting would bring.

Susan was in the midst of e-mailing a report to Lydia on her failure to rein in Hugh's incendiary diatribes when Desmond Wilmot phoned to say he'd pick her up for their dinner date at six that evening. Susan's stomach began doing flip-flops yet again. The last thing she needed to make her day complete was Andrea Grant Carstairs unburdening her soul over martinis. But it was too late to cancel now and her apartment *was* only an olive's throw away.

She entered the tiny, packed bar in the Carlyle Hotel hoping to catch a glimpse of Andrea in the crowd. She was distracted, as always, by the colorful murals that Ludwig Bemelmans, the author of the famed Madeline children's books, had executed half a century earlier in exchange for free room and board at the hotel. Susan always searched for a glimpse of Miss Clavel on the walls enjoying a day off from her charges but finally decided that Madeline's fictional teacher, though Parisian, was a confirmed teetotaler.

A woman in the corner was waving her hands over her head like a controller giving landing instructions on the deck of an aircraft carrier. Susan approached this female windmill and was shocked when she realized it was Andrea. She'd lost at least thirty pounds since Susan had seen her last. Where did those cheekbones come from? She looked ten years younger.

"Andee! I hardly recognized you."

"It's the new me." Andrea leaped up from her seat and gave Susan a ferocious hug.

"You look fabulous," said Susan, attempting to extricate herself from the embrace. "How did you lose all the weight?"

"I didn't lose it, Susan. I abandoned it. You look good, too." Andrea was studying Susan's figure as she removed her overcoat and sat down opposite her childhood friend.

"I still run every morning."

"No, no, no. There's something else. You've got someone in your life, haven't you?"

"I have my children. I have my work. There's not much room for anything else these days."

"Anything or anyone? Susan the Clam. You'll carry your secrets to the grave, won't you?"

"That's not true."

"Oh, please. In kindergarten, you'd never tell us what kind of snacks you brought from home. We had to sneak into the cloak room and watch you covertly unwrap your Kraft caramels."

"I think I'm a little better now."

"Good!" Andrea took Susan's hand and squeezed it affectionately. "We share so much history, you and I. Bridesmaids at each other's weddings. School. Summer camp. Remember that overnight when it was so cold we shared a sleeping bag? And our dreams. It was so cozy."

Is she making a pass at me? wondered Susan. After all these years? Why did she bring up that sleeping bag story? Stop being so paranoid. Andrea's just different now, that's all. Transformed. Deprogrammed. De-Greenwiched. "So . . . I gather you've lost more than weight."

"You mean my virginity?" Andrea threw her head back and howled with laughter. Susan rolled her eyes to heaven and regretted coming to meet her. "I feel so free, Susan. Fern turned a switch on in me. I still shiver thinking about it."

"How did you meet her? Fern?"

"I've known her for years. I just didn't *know* her, if you follow. She was the kids' gym teacher. I'd seen her at PTA meetings. Track and field events. Then in May I was helping decorate the auditorium for the school pageant. It was late. After ten. Everyone had left except me. I was determined to get all the balloons up. You know me. Driven!

"I was standing on a ladder wearing shorts and a

halter top—remember how hot it was in May?—
reaching up to hang this last balloon when I felt
hands on my thighs. I spun around on the ladder
and was shocked to see Fern. She was smiling at me.
Then she stepped up onto the ladder and kissed my
bare midriff. I thought I was going to faint. So tender
and erotic. I slid down the ladder and she slid with
me. Then she took my face in her hands and kissed
me. I felt like I'd never been kissed before. Have you
ever had that feeling?"

Susan nodded involuntarily. That night with
Michael in the garden behind the King David Hotel.
It all seemed like years ago now.

"I was on fire, Susan. I wanted her to take me,
touch me, kiss me everywhere. She did. And I came
over and over again." Andrea took in a deep breath,
then erupted with: "I come all the time now!"

Heads turned in the Bemelmans Bar seeking out
the author of this passionate declaration. Susan
began searching for a missing file in her red leather
briefcase.

"I don't think of myself as a hard-core lesbian,"
babbled Andrea, waving to a waiter to bring her a
refill. "I have no political agenda. I'm just a woman
who's in love with another woman."

Susan wasn't sure if she was supposed to make
some sort of editorial comment after absorbing all
this. Instead she offered: "I have to meet a visiting
police official in just a few minutes. It's in connection with a murder case and I don't want to . . ." She
attempted to rise, but Andrea pulled her back down
again.

"I'm sorry. I get carried away. This is all so new. New body, new passion. But I *do* need your help, Susan."

"What can I do?"

"It's David. He's not dealing well with this at all."

"Did you expect him to just roll over and—"

"He doesn't get it, Susan. He thinks it's a phase. He thinks I'm going to snap out of it. That is not going to happen. I'm crazy about Fern. It's not just sex. We do things together. Everything."

"I heard about the Mustang."

"What? Oh, that." Andrea giggled. "Would you believe it? I've turned into a grease monkey. I can fix anything now. Except my husband's broken heart."

"You mentioned something on the phone about Fern trying to kill him."

"David came over again Saturday afternoon. I asked him to leave. He wouldn't. We had words. Then he and Fern got into a tussle—she's very strong . . . she *is* a gym teacher—and I was certain Fern was going to kill him. With her bare hands. She could, you know." There was a blend of awe and pride in that last sentence.

"I'm still confused. Do you want a restraining order against David? What is it exactly that you want?"

"I want you to marry him."

"What?!"

"You and Hugh are getting divorced, right? Do you know what it's like out there for women starting over? Can you imagine having to date again in these times? What with AIDS and serial murderers on the loose. What could be better? You always liked David. Wasn't he Henry's best friend in high school? He's a real catch, Susan. Still good-looking. Works out regularly. Tons of money. You could quit work. The girls know my kids. They'd blend right in. Don't panic! This doesn't have to be anything immediate. I just think it's a great idea."

"That's why you wanted to see me? That's why you drove in from Connecticut? To get me to marry your husband?"

"I think the two of you are well suited. I've put some thought into this."

"Andee, you need help."

"Why?"

"Because your behavior is very . . . peculiar."

"Susan, I don't expect you to understand. You've never known passion . . ."

"Oh, yes, I have!"

"With Hugh? I doubt it. You always looked like some Hindu bride walking five paces behind him. If living as a hostage for twenty years is passion . . ."

"How do your kids feel about this?" asked Susan. "You and Fern."

"They won't talk to me anymore. Unless I come home. David's brainwashed them."

"Maybe they're just very angry with you."

"I thought your husband was the shrink," said Andrea bitterly.

"I'd better go home, Andee. I can't help you."

"Please! Don't go. Please, stay." Andrea grabbed hold of Susan's wrist and held it firmly.

"Let go of me, Andee."

A tall, striking woman with short cropped hair seemed to materialize beside the table at that moment and stared with unbridled anger at the two old friends.

"Lovers' quarrel?" asked the woman.

"I beg your pardon?" asked Susan.

"I'll bet you do. What the hell's going on here?"

"It's not what you think!" said Andrea, quickly releasing her grip on Susan's wrist.

"What does it matter what *she* thinks?" asked a very confused Susan. "Do you know this woman? Andee?"

Andrea replied meekly, "This is Fern."

45

MARGARET BARRETT and CHARLES DENNIS

NONE OF THE STAFF at Channel 8 could recall anything like it. Even at the zenith of her drinking, Dierdre Mallard Holland had never fought so publicly with her husband. But with fifteen minutes to go before the "News at Six," the Hollands were rivaling the Holyfield-Tyson debacle round for round in Vance's office.

"We finally have the chance to lift this Mickey Mouse TV station out of obscurity," shouted Dierdre. "Obscurity! And you want to blow it. What is your problem, Vance? Does the thought of success so terrify you?"

"I curse the day Chuck Sturges gave you the phone number of his swami on Maui." Then he added scornfully: " 'Tempest tossed and tempus fugit.' "

"It wouldn't hurt you to take a spiritual shower once in a while, Vance."

"Is this more wisdom of the swami? Did you know, by the way, that his real name is Lorne Lipowitz and he comes from the Bronx?"

"So the great news director finally did some legwork of his own! Too bad that energy was spent in denigrating a man whose sandals you aren't fit to fasten."

"What is this constant compulsion of yours to share our conversations with the employees?" asked Vance, who noticed his office door was ajar and went immediately to close it.

"This is their station, too," said Dierdre, gesturing grandly with one arm to indicate everyone in the building. "Don't you think all those little people have been invested with some pride in the past forty-eight hours? We're no longer the mom-and-pop channel who only show interminable reruns of *The Partridge Family*. The whole city is waiting to hear what Hugh Carver is going to say to Rice Krispies on Channel 8 this evening. We've got a media event here, Vance. I'm talking T-shirts and souvenir balloons."

"It's the height of irresponsibility. How do you expect to sleep at night?"

"Hot milk. Works wonders."

"I agree with Susan Given. What you have allowed to happen makes you an accessory before the fact. It is nothing short of criminal to continue to encourage this monster."

"The Stuyvesant Club forever. Barf! Double barf! You know, Vance, I'd have thought you'd know better than to take sides in a marital dispute."

"This is far from a domestic squabble. Susan is an assistant district attorney."

"With great legs. You've always been a leg man, Vance. I'm sure Lisa Mercado didn't make her incredible leap out of the temp pool because she sounded like Barbara Walters."

"What are you talking about?"

"Your little Evita. You think I didn't know? I was just too loaded to care. But I'm sober now and ready to keep my date with destiny. So start spreading the news, pal. Let Ted and Rupert know they've got competition. Oh, Vance! Can't you see what this could lead to?"

"Yes. Another dead woman. Why fuel the flames? This is tabloid journalism, Dierdre. This is worse than O.J. or JonBenet Ramsey. You're begging this Rice Krispies to strike again."

"Of course! Of course! So the police can catch him."

"How? Do you think they'll be hiding behind every bush in Central Park? And what if it isn't the park next time? What if it isn't a jogger?"

"That's his MO," said Dierdre haughtily.

"My God! You're really into this, aren't you? The city has two monsters on the loose now. The Sleeping Beauty Murderer and Dierdre the Yellow Journalist."

"The only one yellow, Vance, is you. Hugh Carver goes on at six forty-five."

"Are you planning to cut sports and weather?"

"Of course not."

"Oh, no. Not Marbella. We can't bump her again."

"Why not? The woman does movie reviews. And not very well."

"Well, I'm not going to be the one to tell her."

"Fine!" said Dierdre. "I'll do it."

"She's not going to take it well."

"Gee. Maybe she'll quit. I don't know why you ever hired her to begin with."

"I didn't. Your father did on one of the rare days he wasn't haunting the golf course. And, I needn't remind you, Marbella is very popular."

Two minutes later Dierdre Holland entered the makeup room and found Ms. Morgan hanging on every word Hugh Carver was saying to her.

"Self-esteem," intoned Hugh. "That must be your mantra, Marbella. It must be the very air you breathe."

"Yes." Marbella nodded. "Oh, yes."

"Sorry to interrupt you guys," said Dierdre.

"Quite all right," said Hugh, studying his face in the mirror. "Margo? Do my eyes look a little puffy to you?"

"You look great," replied the makeup woman without looking up from the latest copy of *Allure*.

"Marbella?"

"Yes, Dierdre?"

"Can I have a word with you outside?"

"Sure."

The film reviewer waddled out of the makeup room behind the station owner's daughter.

"Is something wrong?" asked Marbella.

"We may have a little time problem today. Dr. Carver's spot on Saturday was hugely successful."

"Yes. I read the *Post.*"

"We can't cut the weather, Marbella. It's . . . well, it's the weather.

"I understand." Marbella nodded solemnly.

"You do? You really do. Thank you. We'll make this up to you. I promise," said Dierdre as she danced triumphantly down the hall toward her husband's office.

"I understand," repeated Marbella. Then she turned her gaze back toward the makeup room and whispered reverently, "It's the least I can do for my husband."

46

CORDELIA BROWN OPENED the front door at six
o'clock and promptly fell in love with the handsome
man in the Savile Row suit holding a tiny blue
Tiffany's shopping bag.

"Be dis for me?" asked the housekeeper, batting
her eyes flirtatiously.

"I'm afraid not," said Desmond Wilmot, resisting
the wiles of the dreadlocked coquette and keeping a
tighter grip on the coveted Tiffany's bag. "And how
are all your people on St. Kitts?"

"How you know dat?" asked Cordelia, studying the
police captain as if he were a seasoned voodoo prac-
titioner.

"What de matter wit' you, woman? How far it am
from St. Kitts to St. Stephen's?" asked Wilmot, in perfect native patois. "Me tink you be too long in New
York."

"Ohhh, dear Lord!" squealed Cordelia. "Me tink
you be a heap of trouble to some gal. Chillun! Come
see de fancy man what come for you mama."

Seconds later Polly and Ivy appeared on the stairs
and stared in fascination at the visitor.

"I'm Captain Wilmot. It's a great pleasure to meet
you both."

"Where are you from?" asked Ivy, utterly trans-fixed by Wilmot's accent and mysterious rank.

"St. Stephen's. And you?"

"I was born in El Salvador. But my mom brought me here when I was little."

"So we were almost neighbors." Wilmot smiled. "Do you know where St. Stephen's is?"

"In the Caribbean," said Polly. "Won its independence from Great Britain in 1965. Principal exports: rum, sugar cane, and tropical fruits. Main import: tourists. Famed for its secret coves and inlets once frequented by pirates and buccaneers. And my mom went there for her vacation."

"Very impressive," said Wilmot. "Can you do that trick for every country?"

"No," said Polly. "I did a project for school on the West Indies last year. I guess it stuck. My mom's not home yet. Can I get you a drink? Would you like to sit down? Why don't you sit down first and I'll get you a drink? My sister will entertain you."

"Howww?" asked Ivy in a panic.

"Just be yourself," said Polly, gesturing for Ivy to take the captain into the living room. "Oh! What would you like to drink?"

"Some mineral water will be fine."

"With lemon or lime?"

"Lime, please," said Wilmot as he followed Ivy into the living room. "I don't believe I caught your name."

Before the younger Carver girl could reply, the front door opened and Susan made a botched attempt to sneak into the apartment and up the stairs.

"Mom!"

"Be just a second, Polly. I want to wash up."

"Captain Wilmot is here," said Polly, walking into the hallway from the kitchen carrying a tall glass of iced mineral water. Then Polly lowered her voice to a whisper: "Who is he?"

"A policeman," said Susan, who was now halfway up the stairs with her back to her daughter.

"Whoa! What's wrong, Mom?"

"Nothing, Polly," said Susan, turning halfway around to answer. "I'd just like to freshen up before—"

"Mom! Mom!" Ivy raced in from the living room. "Did you know Captain Wilmot's brother is a knight?" Ivy shrieked and pointed at her mother. "What's wrong with your eye?"

"It's nothing," said Susan, who wished she could start the whole day over again.

"It looks like a shiner," said Polly.

Cordelia, who heard Ivy's shriek, rushed in from the kitchen to investigate. "What be wrong? Oh, my Savior! What you done to you eye, gal?"

"Have you been in a brawl?" said Wilmot, entering from the living room.

"Hello, Captain," said Susan, trying to keep her cool under the circumstances. But it was no use. She buried her face in her hands and said: "I'm so humiliated."

Without blinking, Wilmot turned to Cordelia and asked: "Is there a steak in the refrigerator?"

"I thought we were going out to dinner," said Susan.

"For your eye," Wilmot replied gently. "We must attend to it immediately."

Polly stepped forward and handed him his glass of mineral water.

"Thank you. Your children are delightful." Wilmot then took Susan's hand and led her into the living room. "I trust you left the other chap for dead. At least, gave as good as you got."

"I can never show my face in the Carlyle again," said Susan, settling down onto the chintz sofa.

"Tell us what happened," said Wilmot. "Here." Cordelia had arrived with a porterhouse steak, which the captain applied gingerly to Susan's black eye.

"I went to meet my friend Andee. We're old, old friends. But Andee didn't tell Fern about coming to meet me. I'm not sure where Fern thought Andee was supposed to be. But apparently she found Andee's Filofax and saw 'Drinks at the Carlyle. 5 P.M.' in bold letters. I'm sure it was the bold letters that triggered Fern off. Triggered? Detonated! Of course, they were both shouting at each other by this time. Everyone in the bar was staring at them."

"Your friend Andy sounds a trifle daft," said Wilmot. "Leaving his Filofax around for his wife to find."

"Fern's not his wife. Her wife. Andee's a woman." Then she turned to a confused Ivy and added: "Andrea Grant. Mrs. Carstairs."

"Poor you!" said Wilmot. "Getting caught in the crossfire of a lesbian quarrel."

"Andee's gay?" gasped Ivy. "Sookie Carstairs' mother? Polly, did you hear this?"

Polly shrugged. "I knew. What happened, Mom? Why did Andee slug you?"

"You knew?" asked Ivy. "When did you know? How did you know? Nobody told me."

"Be quiet, Ivy. Go ahead, Mom."

"It wasn't intentional," said Susan. "Things just escalated. Stuff that had obviously been festering under the surface. Fern insulted Andee. Andee slapped her. Fern hauled off to slug her back. I stepped between them to try and stop them."

"Oh, you didn't!" said Wilmot.

"Was I wrong to try to stop them?"

"You got Andee's black eye," laughed Wilmot. "How much more wrong did you want to be?"

"I don't think it's funny, Captain."

"Please, call me Desmond."

"I can't go out to dinner like this, Desmond."

"Then I'll cook that steak for you once you're done with it."

"What were they fighting about?" asked Ivy, still fascinated by the row at the Carlyle.

"Andee's friend thought I was . . . someone else."

"Who?" asked Ivy. "Who did she think you were?"

"Ivy, don't act so dumb," said Polly. "You know."

"Ohhhhh!" Then Ivy turned to her mother and asked, "Are you gay, too?"

"Good one, Ivy," snorted Polly.

"Well, I don't know," said Ivy. "Dad said Mom never liked sex."

"Your father said that?" Susan was horrified. "When did he say that?" Then she remembered Wilmot listening to the conversation with rapt atten-

286

tion. "You know, Desmond, I think we *should* go out to dinner. Don't you?"

"But your eye."

"A little makeup will do wonders. Girls, come upstairs with me. Say good-bye to Captain Wilmot."

Ten minutes later Susan and Wilmot (still carrying the blue Tiffany's bag) were strolling up Madison Avenue en route to the captain's favorite French restaurant on Eighty-sixth Street. They were making idle conversation until Wilmot announced, "I want you to come back to St. Stephen's."

"You do?" Susan noticed the Tiffany's bag for the first time. What was the man thinking of? They hardly knew each other. Or did they? Had they? The butterflies were all but crashing into the walls of her stomach now. "Don't you think we should talk about it first, Desmond? My recollection of what happened is a bit shaky, to say the least."

"I have witnesses now."

"You do?" Someone had seen them together? This was something Susan had never dreamed of. "Can't this wait till we get to De Marchelier? I think I need a drink."

"I thought you weren't drinking."

"No rum."

"Ah! You remember the rum?"

"I remember forgetting the rum. I mean I forgot what happened after the rum."

"You danced."

"I did?"

"Yes." Wilmot's smile lit up his face. "Not easy to do with a sprained ankle. You know, you *are* a trifle accident prone, aren't you?"

"Captain, I don't know what it is you have in mind. But whatever happened that evening, I mustn't—I mean I can't go back to St. Stephen's with you."

"But I have Percy and Cecil in protective custody now. Combined with your testimony, we can convict Crimson of Ascension's murder."

"What!? That's why you want me to go back?"

"Of course. What did you think?"

"I thought—I mean after that night—at the restaurant—I don't know why I—"

"Oh, before I forget," said Wilmot. "I believe this is yours." He held the blue Tiffany's bag up to her.

Susan put her hand inside the bag and withdrew a neatly folded Ace bandage. She stared at it with a mix of relief and apprehension. Finally she cleared her throat and asked: "Did I . . . lose anything else that night?"

"No," smiled Wilmot, offering her his arm. "One of us was a perfect gentleman."

47

LISA MERCADO STARED into the camera at 6:45 P.M. and announced: "Here, once again, is Channel 8's own Doctor Hugh Carver."

"Thank you, Lisa." Hugh cleared his throat, arched one eyebrow, and spoke in his most solemn Gregory Peck tones: "I am addressing that pathetic creature who calls himself The Sleeping Beauty Murderer. What's wrong, little boy? Did I upset you so badly the other night you went crying to the newspaper for help? What did they say to calm and balm your bruised ego? Whatever it was will only be temporary. You need help. You're not well. Let me help you. I understand your pain. I am available to you on a twenty-four-hour basis. Here is a number to call— day or night."

Crimson groaned and switched off the television in his Harlem apartment. Where the hell was Marbella Morgan and her movie review? She was the only reason the drug lord ever bothered to watch Channel 8. He picked up the telephone to dial directory inquiry for the station's phone number when Conception staggered out of the bedroom in a slip and began weaving unsteadily toward him.

"I want to talk to you, Mr. Claxton."

"Me don't talk to no junkie."

"Ha! You think you can dismiss me that easily?"

"Go back to bed, woman."

"I've been thinking, Crimson."

"Leave me be."

"What are you afraid of? I haven't said anything to you yet."

"Dat be a good ting for you."

"You're hiding something from me," said Conception, wagging a long finger in the drug lord's face. "I know you too well, Edward Claxton. I know all your moods. You're hiding something, aren't you? Huh? What did that woman mean the other day?"

"What woman?" Crimson picked up the remote once more, clicked the TV on, and began surfing through the channels to try to drown out Conception's insistent voice. Finally settling on MTV, he turned up the volume on an old Tupac Shakur video. "Dat boy had talent. Too bad him gone and took a bullet."

"The woman in the church on Sunday. Ascension's friend. Why did she tell me to ask you about my brother?"

"Stop dis now," growled Crimson. "Dis ain't no good."

"What does she know about Ascension? Why did you tear up her card?"

"Go back to bed, woman."

"Why did you tear up her card?" repeated Conception, crossing her arms across her chest.

Crimson leaped at her like a panther, grabbed her hair in his powerful fist, and jerked her head backward till she cried out in pain.

290

"Didn't me warn you, bitch? Why for you want to make Crimson angry? Don't you want no more Aitch? You ain' gonna get none if you act dis way."

"What are you afraid of?" gasped Conception. "What does that woman know?"

"Her don't know nothin'. You don't know nothin'. Now, get back in de bedroom and don' come out till me call you."

"Let me go!"

"Say please to me, gal. Say 'Please, Crimson. Me been a bad girl. Me so sorry.' "

"What happened to Ascension?"

Crimson slapped her across the face ferociously. A thin trickle of blood began to run down a corner of her mouth.

"Don' you hear me good, gal? Go back in de bedroom or you don' get no mo' Aitch. You ain' no good witout you Aitch. And you ain' gon' get it from nobody but Crimson."

Conception paused for a moment then whispered: "Please, Crimson."

"Please what, bitch?"

"Please, let go of my hair."

"What else?"

"I don't understand."

"What else you got to say to Crimson? You gon' tell he how sorry you am, aintcha?"

"Yes."

"Go 'head."

"I'm sorry."

"You gon' be a good gal, aintcha?"

"Yes. Please, let me go."

"You ain' gon' give Crimson no mo' trouble?"

"I promise."

"Cuz me gon' hurt you real bad. Me hurt you so bad no man gon' want you no mo'."

"Please, Crimson!"

"Y'ain't gon' ask no mo' questions?"

"None."

Crimson grunted and released his grip on her hair. Then he turned around and began surfing through the channels once again. This gave Conception just enough time to pick up a large cobalt blue ashtray from the coffee table and crash it down on the back of the drug lord's head. Emitting a guttural groan, he dropped to his knees, then collapsed unconscious onto the carpet.

Conception couldn't tell if her lover was dead or not. But she knew enough not to wait around to find out. He *would* kill her for certain when he came to. What should she do? Pack a suitcase? No. He might wake up any second. She snatched her bag from the hall table, grabbed her fur coat from the front closet, and put it on over her slip. What about some Aitch? She'd need some Aitch soon.

Crimson groaned and stirred on the carpet.

He was still alive. She'd worry about a fix later.

She ran down the hall and pressed the button for the elevator. Come on! Come on! He'll strangle me right here in the hallway. He doesn't care and no one will dare stop him. Where is the elevator? Why doesn't it come? She stared back down the hallway toward the apartment in terror. Then she saw the door leading to the fire stairs and raced toward it.

Down, down, down the stairs. Out onto the street. Where would she go? Where could she hide that Crimson wouldn't find her?

She looked up and down the street for a cab. Where was he now? Maybe he was coming down the stairs. Please, God! Save me. Help me to get away from him.

"Conception!"

Who was that? Someone across the street. In a limo.

The man got out of the back of the limousine. A white man. He looked vaguely familiar. Now he was running across the street toward her.

"I don't mean to scare you," said Mitch Levenstein. "You probably think I'm crazy. I hired a detective to find you. I've been sitting in the car here for two hours. Afraid to ring your bell. I can't get you out of my mind. Please, don't run away. I just want to talk to you."

"Get me out of here!"

Conception took his hand, squeezed it, then started dragging a mystified Levenstein back across the street toward the waiting limousine seconds before a bloodied Crimson stumbled out of the building.

48

"SO? DID YOU have any trouble recognizing me?"

"Not really."

"Why?" asked Brandy. "Cuz I'm so tall?"

"You're exactly as I imagined you'd be," smiled her date.

"That can work both ways, can't it?"

"What would you like to drink?"

"Sorry?"

"Is that the name of a drink?"

"What?"

"Nothing. It's awfully loud in here. Don't you think?"

"It's my favorite bar. People here are so cool."

"And they're all deaf!"

"I like your tie. Hermès?"

"My name is Drayton. Remember?"

"I know you're being funny cuz you get a dimple in your cheek when you talk but I can't hear a darned thing you're saying."

"Would you rather go somewhere else?"

"This is my favorite bar."

"What would you like to drink?"

"Uh-huh."

294

The conversation had transpired in this fractured vein for the first ten minutes Brandy Prescott and Drayton Simms III were together in the crowded Second Avenue bar near Seventy-ninth Street. She was wearing an orange dress and he was wearing a three-piece Brooks Brothers suit. They both found each other attractive but weren't gleaning much mutual information due to the deafening noise level.

"How are you enjoying Channel 8?" shouted Simms, one word at a time.

"I'm having a ball," replied Brandy. "They're just the nicest people. Real family. I'm Lisa Mercado's assistant. Do you know her?"

"Not in person. What's she like?"

"A real pistol. Never stops. Refuses to take no for an answer. Tries to learn something new every day. I think that's real important, don't you?"

"I wouldn't be a good reporter otherwise."

"Are you covering the Rice Krispies story?"

"No. I'm doing the Dwight Pelham case. That's how I met your aunt."

"Who's Dwight Pelham?"

"Sorry?"

"I'd like a beer."

Simms turned to the wild-eyed girl with the nose ring vainly trying to cope with the drink orders behind the bar. By the time he turned around again with two glasses of draft beer, Brandy was chatting animatedly with two other men, who split as soon as the reporter handed her a drink.

"Friends of yours?" asked Simms.

"They're the nicest guys. I see them here all the time." She clinked her glass against his then swallowed half the contents in one go. "Scuse my chugalugging. I was thirsty. Sorry I was late getting here, Draycott."

"Call me Dray."

"It just got a little crazy at the station tonight. My uncle Hugh—well, he was my uncle. My aunt Susan's ex-husband-to-be. Anyhow, he's been treating this Rice Krispies guy on the air."

"What do you mean?"

"He's a psychiatrist. There was a big write-up on him in the paper today. Don't you read the *Post*?"

"Not very often."

"Oh, you should, Dray. They've got the best stories. And big pictures. I don't read the *Times* very much. It's way too serious. And it's real hard to hold on to in the subway. Have you ever noticed that?"

"I tend to do most of my reading at the office," said Simms, wondering if the tall Southern girl was putting him on or if Susan Given had fixed him up with her as a practical joke.

"I think it's neat how we're both in the news business. I guess that's why Susan wanted us to meet. Networking. That's the key to success, don't you think?"

"I suppose."

"Is there a lot of adultery in your office?"

"What!"

"I don't like telling tales out of school but our station is just one big sexual merry-go-round. Could I have another beer?"

Simms ordered her another beer and then another.

"My ex-uncle is having an affair with the woman who produces the news," said Brandy, abandoning all discretion after her third beer. "Skinny little thing from Boston. Must be like having sex with dental floss. Do you like skinny women, Dray? I *do* like that tie. My daddy says a tie is a man's signature. You got nice handwriting. What are your honest feelings about a woman using her body horizontally to rise vertically? I so admire Lisa's drive but I question her methods. Maybe if I was Hispanic, I could empathize more. I'm all for flirting. That's cuz I'm Southern. As long as no one gets hurt. I hate to hurt anyone's feelings. Do you think I'm too sensitive for the news business? I think Diane Sawyer's tough but sensitive. She is my absolute god. Do you know her? I'll bet she never did the weather. No one's gonna believe me talking about clouds and inversions. I'm too smart to do the weather. Don't you think?"

Simms looked at his watch. It was eight-thirty and he was starving. How much more of Brandy Prescott was he going to be able to take? Could he remember a previous dinner date and escape from this inebriated girl?

"Something wrong?" asked Brandy.

"I'd completely forgotten—"

"You're not gonna ditch me, are you, Dray? You're awfully nice and I know I'm a bit drunk."

"Of course not, Brandy," said Simms, feeling the cad of the world for thinking of abandoning her. "I just realized I haven't eaten anything all day and wondered if you'd care to join me for dinner."

"Aren't you sweet! Why don't I just go powder my nose first? Promise you won't go anywhere."

"I promise."

Brandy took his face in her hands and kissed him on the lips. "I like you so much. You're a real gentleman."

She wandered through the crush of people toward the alcove that housed the telephone and rest rooms. Her hand was on the knob when an arm snaked around her waist and pulled her away from the door.

"Where's my baby been hiding?"

Brandy was startled and in her present condition had trouble focusing on the tall, muscular man clutching her so tightly. Then she spotted the three hoop earrings in his right lobe and a smile crossed her face.

"Russ!"

"Been a long time, babe."

"Where have you been?" She threw her arms around his neck and tried to kiss him but he pushed her away. "What's wrong? Aren't you glad to see me?"

"Just remembering how that bitch aunt of yours threw me out of the house."

"Forget her. She's just a little uptight. Ohhh! I'm so glad to see you. So much has happened since I saw you last. I'm working for a TV station."

"Where you living?"

"With my grandmother in Greenwich."

"Bummer."

"But I'm looking for a place in town. Over on the West Side. Near work."

"ABC?"

"I only wish! No, it's just little old Channel 8."

"Cool."

"Maybe you'll come and visit me there. I'll give you a tour. You can meet Lisa Mercado. She's hot. You'll like her."

"As much as I like you?" Russ pulled her back into him and began nibbling on her ear.

"Stop!"

"Wassup?"

"I've got a date."

"Get rid of him."

"I can't. My aunt set me up with him."

"That's a good reason to dump him. Come on, babe! I've been waiting for you for a long time."

"I can't, Russ."

"Don't piss me off, Brandy."

"Don't talk to me like that, Russ. I don't appreciate it."

"You appreciated me enough the last time. You couldn't get enough. Remember?"

"Let go of my arm, Russ."

He shoved her up against the wall and forced his tongue inside her mouth. She tried to get loose but he was too strong for her.

"What's going on here?" asked a man trying to get to the men's room.

"You got a problem?" asked Russ.

"Yeah. I gotta pee."

Brandy took advantage of this momentary diversion to break loose from Russ and dart back into the crowded bar area. She looked around for Dray but couldn't see him anywhere. She was scared. She hadn't been this scared since she'd come to New York.

49

"IS THAT HER FINGER?"

"I don't know."

"Susan, you should be able to recognize your own niece's finger."

"Not when it isn't attached to her body."

"No problem."

Lydia Culberg left Susan alone to stare at the tagged, severed finger lying atop a glistening aluminum table in the morgue. Seconds later the volcanic redhead reappeared through the swing doors pushing a gurney and whistling "All the Things You Are."

"Let's see if we can get the little sucker to fit," said Lydia, as she lifted the sheet covering the body atop the gurney. "Course it's going to be a real bitch if rigor mortis has set in. She was awfully tall, wasn't she? Something wrong, Susan?"

"This is all my fault," sobbed Susan, staring down at her niece's corpse. "What'll I tell my sister?"

"Do you have to tell her anything?" murmured Lydia. "Lie. I always do."

"How could I lie about this?"

"Don't identify her. We can tag her as a Jane Doe and dump her in the Bronx."

"Does it have to be the Bronx?"

"Hell, no. There's a nice landfill in Queens."

"I'm not sure, Lydia."

"Susan, believe me: the first time is always difficult. After that it's like falling out of bed."

Falling out of bed. Falling out of bed. Falling out of bed. The telephone rang and Susan woke abruptly from her nightmare. She squinted at the Sony Dream Machine, then grabbed her glasses. Six-thirty. Sleep had been fitful since Brandy had phoned her aunt the night before, scared out of her mind and asking if she could come over. She never turned up. The girl sounded as if she'd had a few so Susan wasn't sure how seriously to take her.

A guilt-ridden Susan grabbed the telephone and all but croaked: "Brandy?"

"Oh, Brandy. Thank goodness. I was hoping you'd be there."

"Mother, it's Susan."

"Oh, hello, dear. I was just talking to little Brandy."

"No, you weren't, Mother. That was me. Isn't Brandy with you?"

"No, she didn't come back here last night," said Marian. "I was hoping she'd spent the night with you. It's not very safe with that maniac murdering all the female joggers in New York."

"I think there are a few of us left," said Susan, staring at the chair where she had placed her jersey and running shorts the night before. "I wouldn't be too concerned," said Susan, not wanting to cause her mother needless anxiety by telling her about Brandy's phone call the previous night. "She probably stayed with a girlfriend from work."

"Or some boy she picked up in a bar," said Marian. "I'm beginning to think that child's a bit reckless when it comes to social skills. I should loan her my flashlight."

"Speaking of which, I finally met Dwight Pelham."

"Who?"

"Dwight Pelham."

"What about him?"

"Isn't he the man you bonked on the head with a flashlight all those years ago?"

"Who told you that?"

"Linda."

"Why would your sister tell you something like that?"

"Isn't it true?"

"It's not a question of truth, Susan. It's simply not the sort of thing one discusses on the telephone."

"So you're not denying it."

"I think you've been a prosecutor too long, dear. It's had an adverse affect on *your* social skills."

"Perhaps. But it *is* a beauty of a scar, Mother. You should be proud."

"I don't want you sharing this story with your intimate circle."

"I didn't know I had an intimate circle."

"Your fellow lawyers or whomever you let your hair down with."

"I don't let my hair down much these days."

"What about last night?" asked Marian. "I phoned your house and Ivy told me you were out to dinner with a handsome black man."

"That was business. I'm assisting Captain Wilmot

with an investigation. Now, Mother, I don't want to sound abrupt or lacking in social skills but I've got to get going on my run."

"All right. Call me when you hear from little Brandy."

"And vice versa, Mother."

No sooner had she replaced the receiver when the phone rang again. Susan crossed her fingers and prayed it would be her niece.

"Hello?"

"Susan? It's Imogen. Did I wake you?"

"No. I'm just on my way out the door."

"Running?"

"Yes."

"Oh, good. I'm sorry about yesterday morning."

"What happened?" asked Susan.

"Nothing. We had a date to run together but I got an emergency call from Bellevue. One of my patients attempted suicide."

"Oh, that's okay. I mean it's dreadful but I'd completely forgotten about it as well. Is your patient . . . ?"

"She's under heavy sedation. Anyhow, can I meet you this morning? I'm just leaving myself."

"Great! I have so much to tell you."

Imogen lived on the West Side and they agreed on a spot near the north end of the park where they could meet in twenty minutes.

Susan did have a lot to tell her former therapist. She'd finally reveal her absurd fear of Desmond Wilmot and how he had gallantly returned her Ace bandage to her. She would share the news of the Captain's investigation and how he had managed to locate Betty and the little children, who had been spirited off by Ulysses and Randall in the middle of the night and taken by boat to a neighboring island where they would be safe from Crimson's wrath. Once the drug lord had left for New York, Wilmot had clamped down on Percy and Cecil and played the two hapless thugs off against each other. Now, with Susan's corroborative testimony, Crimson could finally be brought to justice.

All this was running through Susan's mind as she entered the park at Seventy-ninth Street and began jogging toward the Jacqueline Onassis Reservoir. Minutes later she was on her familiar circuit around the circumference of Central Park. She was nearing the Warriors Gate when she spotted the police. Dozens of them.

Susan felt physically ill. Rice Krispies was right on schedule. Every two weeks. Like clockwork. Somewhere beyond that familiar yellow tape a blond female jogger would be lying dead—brutally murdered with the top two joints of her fourth finger missing and capped by a thimble.

Then Susan saw Janie and called out to her.

Janie looked up sadly and gestured for Susan to stay back from the crime scene.

All Susan could think of was Brandy. No! Not Brandy. Please, God! Don't let it be Brandy.

50

THE FRANK E. CAMPBELL Funeral Chapel was on Madison Avenue right around the corner from Susan's apartment. The Channel 8 news truck was parked on Eighty-first Street and there were various TV and print reporters hovering around outside on the sidewalk. By the time Susan arrived inside the chapel the place was packed.

Susan slipped into a pew at the back next to Janie.

"What are you doing here?" whispered Susan.

"Working. Always a chance the perp might turn up."

"I can't believe she's dead. I just saw her the other night."

"When was that?"

"Saturday. The opera gala. She wanted to go running with me. This is so bizarre. I can't believe I'm not in bed dreaming all this."

"Wouldn't that be fun, Greenwich? I'd like a piece of that dream, too. Then I could dump Lydia, Archie, the Mayor, and the Lieutenant Governor in the Twilight Zone while I hop in the shower. Unfortunately we're not dreaming. And they all want to know when we're going to catch him. Whoever he is. Have they forgotten it's the police who catch the bad guys? We just prosecute. . . . How well did you know this Dierdre Holland?"

"Not very. I only met her on Saturday night. And her husband gave Brandy that job at the station."

"Think she had a screw loose?"

"Why do you say that?"

"Here's a woman whose TV station is waving a red condom in the face of this psycho. They've got your husband baiting him on the air. And at the same time, they're warning women not to go jogging in the early hours or after dark. So what does this broad do? She goes jogging at dawn. Dawn! Didn't the woman have a sex life? Her husband certainly did."

"Vance?"

"Busy boy, our Mr. Holland. Seems to have screwed every female who worked at the station. Except the big fat girl who does the movie reviews."

"Think there's a chance it wasn't Rice Krispies?"

"What? The tabloids are lying? How could such a thing be possible? Next you'll be telling me the earth isn't flat. Oh, no. We had the whole scenario. Severed finger. Capped by a thimble. She was a Sleeping Beauty, all right."

"Then you don't think Vance Holland's a potential suspect?"

"Nah! I'm just at a loss with the whole thing. Haskell came up with a theory straight out of Agatha Christie about the thimbles. He was certain they were the answer. He had Lydia believing the thimbles were custom made for Harry Winston. Doesn't Ralph Lauren make straitjackets for morons like him? A two-dollar magnifying glass held up to the light clearly revealed People's Republic of China. Rice Krispies probably bought 'em at Woolworth's liquidation sale. Of course, this won't stop Haskell from flying over to Beijing to check out all the thimble factories. Tell you one thing about this Rice Krispies creep: he leaves a fuckin' mess behind."

"He's going to slip up somewhere, Janie. There's got to be a blood trail. Prints."

"Not unless the guy has a white Bronco to leave them in. God, this case depresses me! . . . Think those are Dierdre's parents up there? The front row?"

Susan stood on tiptoe and stared toward the front row where Harry and Eunice Mallard sat on one side of their two teenage granddaughters with the girls' father, Vance Holland, sitting on the other side. Seated directly behind Holland were Taylor Parkhurst, Lisa Mercado, and Brandy Prescott, who finally checked in with her aunt the morning after her date to report she hadn't become Rice Krispies's latest victim, having passed out on Draycott Simms III's sofa in Tudor City.

"Don't look now, Greenwich, but here comes your husband."

Susan turned her head and caught Hugh Carver making his way down the aisle toward the front of the chapel. But instead of sitting in the pew next to his mistress, he chose the one opposite her where his new colleague Chuck Sturges made room for him.

"Did you see Hugh's broadcast last night?" asked Janie. "He was really over the top."

"No. I went out to dinner."

"A date?"

"Janie, can we stick to the subject at hand?"

"You went on a date? Not Captain Wilmot!"

"It was strictly business."

"Greenwich, you are blushing."

"Only because this conversation is inappropriate to the surroundings."

"Tell me something. His equipment? Was it mythic?"

A familiar racking cough rescued Susan from this carnal cross-examination and the two A.D.A.s inhaled the all too familiar blend of nicotine and scotch on the backs of their necks.

"My two favorite dolls," cooed Ray Murphy in his rough sandpaper voice, followed by one of the veteran reporter's monumental coughing fits.

"Well, if you have to croak," whispered Janie, "you certainly picked the perfect place."

"That's the Irish sense of humor for you," said Murphy, poking Susan in the back with his index finger, once he'd recovered from his attack. "So? Got any leads?"

"What? Hasn't your boyfriend Rice Krispies checked in with you yet to crow about his latest atrocity?" asked Janie. "Honest to God, Murph! Haven't you any sense of responsibility? Giving that monster so much attention."

"I'm trying to steer him toward you, Janie."

"Pull the other leg, Ray. It's got bells on it. How the hell did you get in here anyhow?" Janie turned around to stare at the stocky, buzz-cut wreck wearing a wrinkled dark suit that undoubtedly doubled for his pajamas.

"I'm a mourner. Didn't you see my black arm-band? Hey, Suzy! Didja see my piece on Dwight Pelham yesterday? I quoted you."

"Accurately, I trust?"

"Christ on a crutch! You're not talking to some rinky-dink pinhead straight out of journalism school. When did I ever get a word wrong? Burp once, I put it in italics." Murphy then shifted the subject abruptly while studying the crowd of upscale mourn-ers. "Think your man is here?"

"Over there," replied Janie, nodding toward the second row. "Sitting next to Chuck Sturges."

"You're kidding!" Murphy wiped his spectacles with a filthy handkerchief, squinted through the lenses and recognized Hugh Carver listening with rapt attention to the minister recounting Dierdre Mallard Holland's struggle and inevitable triumph over drug addiction. "Very funny. Well, I guess I'll be shufflin' along," said Murphy rising from his seat behind the two women. "Nothing earth shattering going on here. But I'd watch my step if I were you, Suzy."

"Me? What disinformation has Lydia been passing on to you now?"

"Forget Lydia. We got ourselves a serial murderer on the loose," said the old crime reporter earnestly. "The guy stalks blond women who jog in Central Park. Attractive blond women. You fit the pattern. Hate to see anything happen to you. Take my advice: join a gym for a while. That's what I'd do."

"I don't think I'm in any danger, Ray."

"Bet she didn't either," said Murphy, nodding in

the direction of Dierdre's body on display in the casket. Then he leaned into Janie's ear and asked, "Think you'll catch him soon?"

"I'm the second step in the food chain, Murph. I just prosecute."

"Don't forget your old friends if anything good comes your way."

"I heard about a case of hijacked Irish. Still in bond. That good enough?"

"You're your father's daughter," said Murphy, giving Janie's cheek a pinch before he left the funeral chapel.

"I'm my father's son and that's the fucking problem," said Janie, once the reporter had left. "Hormones in a state of chaos in my formative years. You were always girlie, weren't you, Greenwich? Dolls, right? Never a baseball bat."

"Is there anything wrong with that?"

"Honey, honey. The defense rests. You're strictly a female female. One only need look at you. Actually, you're looking particularly female today. The first flush of blush. Must have been your man from the islands."

"Would you just drop it once and for all?" Susan stole a look at her watch. 10:45. "I've got to get downtown."

"Me, too. Rice Krispies is definitely not here."

Life's passing parade continued to troop endlessly down Madison Avenue as the two A.D.A.s emerged from Campbell's funeral chapel. The piercing cry of "Girlfriends!" froze their hearts on the spot. Lisa Mercado rushed out of the mortuary to greet them like long-lost relatives coming through customs at JFK. Then she gestured for her crew parked on Eighty-first Street to move their asses pronto.

"How *are* you?" gushed Lisa, giving the women huge hugs and kisses on both cheeks, while someone thrust a microphone into her hand.

"Isn't this a bit insensitive?" asked Susan.

"Hardly," said Lisa, affectionately mimicking the blond prosecutor. Then she added hastily: "Dierdre wouldn't have wanted it any other way. I just know she'd want me—all of us—to find her killer." Then she leaned into Janie's face, lowered her voice and asked: "Got any dirt?"

"I just prosecute," said Janie, who had decided the phrase would be her new mantra. "Check with the police."

"Oh, that Haskell's such a stinker. Promises, promises." Everyone knew that La Mercado and Haskell Abrams were having an affair but Lisa still pretended in public that their relationship was strictly business. "It's getting serious now, isn't it?"

"Murder is always serious, Lisa."

"Yeah, but . . . you know what I mean, Janie. This is like Jack the Ripper time. Women are getting scared."

"You don't have anything to worry about—unless you decide to dye your hair."

"Sleeping Beauty can't be Puerto Rican?" asked Lisa defensively. "Is that what you mean?"

"I think Janie means he's going for WASP blondes," interjected Susan hastily, hoping to avoid a PC arm wrestle. "That's what you meant, right?"

Janie nodded at Susan, then lit a cigarette. She held one out to Lisa as a conciliatory gesture. The newsperson shook her head and Janie finally spoke: "I don't think there's a man that could handle any one of our jobs any differently. But when they hit the walls that we do, they punch holes in those walls—knuckles dripping blood—and people are impressed. We're not supposed to punch holes—that's not girlie—and, if we cry, we're not fit for the job. So what the fuck do we do?"

"She's deep," said Lisa, nodding her hair-sprayed head appreciatively.

"Bottomless," said Susan. "Celtic blood. Centuries of brooding and plotting have genetically led her to the woman you see before you. No murder will go unsolved on Janie Moore's watch."

"Now, that's what I call a sound bite," said Lisa, signaling to her cameraman to cut.

51

HUGH CARVER HAD been avidly looking forward to Dierdre Holland's funeral. Not that he'd been overly fond of her but because of the good PR his appearance would engender. Plus the numerous compliments that would undoubtedly arise over his recent TV appearances. Personally the Holland woman had been far too pushy for his tastes. He liked his females docile. Not that Taylor Parkhurst fit that category either but the anorexic producer had "discovered" him and paved the way for his new-found stardom. Hugh would always be grateful to her for that and would let her know when the time came to dump her—which would be sooner rather than later. He had his sexual sights set on the voluptuous Lisa Mercado. Good career move, good bed move.

The last person he needed to see as he headed down the center aisle of the Frank E. Campbell Funeral Chapel that morning was his estranged wife. Ironically, Susan was the *first* person he saw sitting on the aisle next to that big-mouthed Janie Moore. Hugh had always loathed her. An unrelenting man hater if there ever was one. What the hell were those two harpies doing at the funeral?

An hour later, racing into the foyer of the town house on East Sixty-third Street, Hugh was in a foul mood as he collided with his lawyer Ralph Kregar, who had his own office on the third floor of the same building.

"This must be how you've lost all that weight," said Kregar, a large, florid man with blond hair, bulbous nose, and beady eyes. "Dashing hither and yon. Caught you on television again last night."

"And?"

"You're a powerful presence, Hugh. Charismatic."

"What's wrong, Ralph?"

"Nothing."

"I'm your therapist, Ralph. I know when you're hiding things."

"Joyce got upset." Joyce was Kregar's wife and a highly successful interior decorator in the city.

"About what?"

"She watched the news this morning. Dierdre Holland's murder."

"A tragedy to the community. I didn't know her well but she *was* my employer. Bundle of energy. I've just come from her funeral. Very touching service. Did you know the woman was on the 1976 Olympic water polo team?"

"Joyce thinks that possibly your TV appearance incited this Rice Krispies character."

"Really, Ralph! Can I stop the sun from rising every morning? Can I stop it setting at night? This pathetic Rice Krispies creature can't control himself. There is an inevitability about his actions. He would have killed no matter what. Your wife is frightened and feeling powerless about a situation she can't control. She has to lash out at someone. Why not me? A lifelong, devoted family friend. I'm not offended, Ralph. Your wife has an ingenuous, childlike quality that is both seductive and engaging. It certainly serves her well in her profession. But when that child is threatened in the adult world . . . Oh, brother! Need we discuss your extended periods of involuntary sexual abstinence when 'Baby Joycie' isn't happy?" Hugh clamped a comradely hand down on Kregar's shoulder. "That's a freebie, Ralph. Cherish it. Now, I really must be racing. I've got a twelve o'clock patient."

Hugh felt a surge of power as he took the stairs two at a time. He had just reached the sixth step when Kregar called out to him: "Neil Stern phoned."

"What does that weasel want?" asked Hugh, contemptuous of his wife's divorce lawyer.

"Wants to set a court date."

"Fuck him! And fuck her!"

Hugh entered the second-floor suite he shared with two other psychiatrists and moved briskly toward his private entrance when he was stopped by Nora, a white-haired woman in her mid-sixties, who served as the communal receptionist.

"Dr. Carver."

"Is Mrs. Schrank here?"

"Yes, doctor, but—"

"What is it, Nora?"

The receptionist beckoned him closer to her desk. "I didn't want anyone else to hear."

"Is something wrong?"

"The police phoned," replied Nora in a hushed voice.

"What about?"

"Mrs. Carver has been arrested."

"Why are they phoning me?" Hugh had resisted every impulse to shout "Good!" at this bit of news. What escapade had Susan been caught out in after leaving the funeral? It had to be something extraordinary for her pals the police to be holding her. He'd get custody of his girls yet.

"She's making a terrible fuss at the station and is threatening a civil suit if you don't come and get her. That doesn't sound like Mrs. Carver to me."

"It's not my problem," said Hugh, who walked into his office ready to listen to Sylvia Schrank's endless litany of complaints and petty abuses heaped on her by (in no particular order) a far from grateful world, husband, and charity committee she chaired.

"I'll tell you what it comes down to, Dr. Carver. Plain and simple. Appreciation. Know what I mean? What would it take for any of these people—not just that putz husband of mine—to show me a little appreciation? I'm not asking them to kiss my ass. I hate that. But someone, anyone, to say: 'Sylvia, you're fabulous. What would we do without you? You're a bright ray of sunshine in our nuclear winter.' Not a bad image, huh? See? I could say something like that and no one would comment. No one would say: 'That's so clever. How did you think of that?' You know why they don't? Cuz they're jealous. It's always been this way. I'm threatening. Nuts, huh?

A little woman like me. But I have a big mind. That's the difference."

Hugh had been half listening for over twenty minutes to the tiny, pug-faced, jewel-encrusted old woman when he leaned forward, tapped her knee, and asked if she wouldn't mind returning to the waiting room for a second.

"But I'm talking! I have the floor!"

"Mrs. Schrank, I wouldn't do this if it wasn't an emergency."

"What kind of emergency? We've been sitting here alone for twenty minutes. Nobody buzzed. This isn't professional. I pay for you to listen."

"Is this about the money, Mrs. Schrank?"

"Did I say that?"

"You intimated. I know you're a wealthy woman . . ."

"Not so wealthy. Comfortable. Are you holding that against me?"

"We're wasting time."

"What is so important it can't wait until—"

"It's none of your business."

"You sound like my husband."

"Please, Mrs. Schrank. I'll only be a second."

"For the record: I don't like this."

Sylvia Schrank left the office. Hugh dialed Susan's office number and asked to speak to Mrs. Carver. Gretchen informed him that Ms. Given was not in.

"Do you have any reason to suspect she might be . . . in custody?" asked Hugh.

"None whatsoever," replied Gretchen and hung up.

Hugh began to tap out a military rhythm on his desk, then dialed another number. Cordelia Brown would know. The phone rang but it wasn't the St. Kitts housekeeper who answered.

"Given."

"Susan? What are you doing there?"

"I live here, Hugh. Remember?"

"Have you been . . . released?"

"Not till you give me a divorce. How'd you like the funeral?"

"Susan, have you been in jail this morning?"

"Have you started pouring vodka on your Wheaties?"

"The police just phoned here and . . ."

"Yes?"

"Nothing."

Hugh hung up abruptly and buzzed Nora, who gave him the contact number at the police station. He reached the desk sergeant, who transferred him to the appropriate department, run by one Sergeant Ernest Brauer.

"This is Hugh Carver." His Gregory Peck out-pecked Peck himself. "I believe you were trying to reach me."

"Oh, yeah," replied Brauer. "Your wife's making a helluva racket down here."

"I think there's been some mistake."

"I don't think so. You're Dr. Hugh Carver? The TV shrink, right? We just arrested Mrs. Hugh Carver on charges of shoplifting. In Bergdorf's. She had over five thousand dollars' worth of men's jewelry on her. Said they were gifts for you."

"But that's impossible. I just spoke to . . . What does this Mrs. Carver look like?"

"Five three. Fat. Maybe two hundred pounds."

"What?!"

"I beg your pardon," said Sergent Brauer, not wishing to sound insensitive. "Amply proportioned. You coming down here or what?"

52

SUSAN HUNG UP the wall telephone in the kitchen and stared curiously at Janie. The two women had popped into Susan's apartment after leaving Campbell's to pick up Susan's briefcase and were about to leave when the telephone rang.

"What is it?" asked Janie.

"Granted, Hugh is a bit odd . . ."

"That's generous."

"But why would he phone here in the middle of the day and ask me if I'd been in jail this morning? If I'd been 'released'?" When Janie did not reply, Susan picked up the phone and dialed her office. Gretchen confirmed that Hugh had just phoned there as well and inquired if Susan was "in custody."

"He's playing mind games," said Janie, after Susan hung up the phone again. "Now that he's a TV personality, he's power mad."

"He was always power mad," said Susan. "No. There's something else going on here." Susan checked her briefcase to make sure all the files she'd need were there before venturing downtown again. Her office was planning to freeze Dwight Pelham and Mitchell Levenstein's assets that day and she wanted to be certain there was no mistake on the paperwork.

"Maybe you could get Lisa to investigate him."

"Why would she investigate a colleague?"

"Heyy! She's our new best friend all over again. We bonded out there on the street, Greenwich. Didn't you see how she bought that bullshit speech of mine?"

" 'Punching holes in the walls'? 'Knuckles dripping blood'? I thought it was very moving. Didn't you mean it?"

"Nah. I think I stole it from some old Steve McQueen movie. But Lisa bought it. Lisa loves our ass and we can tuck her away in our back pockets till we need her again."

"That is so cynical, Janie."

"Come on, Greenwich. Grow up. We're not exactly in a white-gloves business. We get shit dumped on us every day and we've got to dig through the mess any way we can. That's why Archie turns a deaf ear to any complaints about Lydia's bad behavior."

"When did you join the diplomatic corps, Janie? I can think of a lot better words to describe Mrs. Culberg."

"What good would it do? We all know Lydia's a drunken, egomaniacal nympho, who fucked her way up every rung of the ladder. But bottom line: she's the buffer. She's the champion shit shoveler. She's the signpost leading to the only result Archie cares about: more convictions. It's what keeps us in business. The office had a sixty-three percent conviction rate last year. Not bad, huh?"

"Except for the thirty-seven percent that *did* get

off. We don't bring people to trial unless we're convinced they're guilty. That's one-third of our prose-
cutions down the drain."

"That's the game, Greenwich. Know how we lose
that one-third? Combination of brilliant defense
lawyers, bad judges, and overworked, understaffed,
and—don't quote me on this—sometimes inept
prosecutors, who couldn't survive for one day on the
other side of the courtroom. Come on. Let's go fight
crime."

They were about to step outside to buzz the elevator when a more hyper than usual Brandy
Prescott arrived at the front door and began babbling away immediately: "Lisa told me you guys
were at the service but you disappeared before I
could even . . . Wasn't that just the saddest thing?
Of all people! So vital! So much to offer! So much
to live for! They've got to get that Rice Krispies bastard, Susan. They've just got to! Oh, hi, Janie. You
look nice. Do you think my dress was somber
enough? I haven't been to a funeral since my grandfather died. But I was still a teenager then. I just
cried and cried all morning. Dierdre was an incredible woman. All that energy. She was such an inspiration to me. The way she pulled her life together
again. She was going to take me to AA meetings
with her. I think I'll still go. Did you meet her
daughters? Aren't they great? Am I talking too
much? I'm so excited! Vance has asked me to
become his personal assistant. He says, with Dierdre
gone now, he's going to need a really good first
mate. Isn't that just the coolest thing?"

"I only hope you're up to the job," said a deadpan Janie, staring at Brandy's incredibly long legs.

"I think I am." Brandy nodded bravely.

"What happened to you the other night?" asked Susan.

"I told you. I stayed on Draycott Simms' foldout sofa. He was a perfect gentleman."

"I'm sure he was. But what was that phone call about? You sounded positively terrified."

"I had a few too many to drink, Aunt Susan. Then I couldn't find Dray. The bar was so crowded. I was real disoriented. That's all."

"What else?"

"Why are you cross-examining me?"

"Occupational hazard," said Janie, tugging on her colleague's arm. "Come on. Let's go to work."

Susan held her ground and asked: "Did something else happen, Brandy?"

"I ran into Russ again."

"Russ?"

"You remember Russ? With the earrings?"

"I certainly do." How could Susan forget the image of the buff young man standing naked in her kitchen that night? "What happened?"

"He got a little out of hand. Scared me. But I'm okay now. Hell! I just got a fabulous job."

The telephone rang and Cordelia Brown's voice boomed down from upstairs.

"Miss Given!"

"I just left!" Susan shouted back.

"Her say it very important."

"Who?" Susan groaned, walked into the living

324

room, and picked up the telephone. "Given."

"Susan? It's Colette. I need to speak to you."

"If it's about freezing your husband's assets, I really can't discuss it with you."

"What assets? What are you talking about? I need your help. Mitch has vanished."

53

HUGH CARVER SAT drumming his fingers on the battered wooden desk in the waiting room of the Seventeenth Precinct on East Fifty-first Street. He had no desire to be there but Taylor had insisted he deal with the situation for the good of the station and his own future in broadcasting. The last thing they (Channel 8) needed in light of Dierdre's tragic death was an even more bizarre scandal involving two of their most popular commentators.

The door opened a few seconds later and a chunky woman in her early forties wearing a too tight gray suit entered the room with a fake alligator zipper binder wedged under her arm.

"You the husband? I'm Ophelia Feldman. With the Public Defender's Office. You don't exactly look like a charity case."

"I beg your pardon? I'm not her—"

"What's the matter? Too cheap to lay out some cash for your wife's defense? Maybe we can use that. Driven to the brink by your miserly . . . How long you been married?"

"She's not my wife."

"Who isn't?"

"The woman in custody."

"She says she is."

"That's a delusion. She's in love with me. Rather, she thinks she's in love with me."

"What's your secret?"

"I beg your pardon?"

"The secret of your charm." Ophelia unzipped her binder and removed a file folder. "It certainly escapes me."

"Is it absolutely necessary that you be present?"

"Why? You going to knock her around a little more?"

"What on earth are you talking about?"

"It's all here in black and white, Petraczek. You have a record of aggravated assault, battery, intent to—"

"My name is Hugh Carver."

"What?"

"My name is Hugh Carver."

"You're not Auguste Petraczek?"

"No."

"Oh, Jesus!" Ophelia plopped down in the chair next to Hugh's, put her head down on the battered wooden table, and began to sob. "I can't take this fucking job anymore. I've been at it for five years. Every fucking loser in the world gets dropped on my desk. I went to night school for eight years to get a goddamn law degree and this is how I end up. No decent firm wants me. I tried to get into the District Attorney's Office. They didn't want to know. This is all I could get and I can't even do this right. What is wrong with me? Why am I such a goddamn loser?"

The public defender clutched the psychiatrist's lapels and began sobbing on his shirtfront just as the door opened once more and a policewoman led Marbella Morgan inside.

"Hello, darling. I'm so glad you could come. I knew you would." Then Marbella noticed Ophelia clinging to Hugh's lapels and trembling with emotion. "Who is this woman?"

"What the hell's going on here?" asked the policewoman.

"She's overwrought," said Hugh, trying to disengage himself. "I think you should send for her supervisor."

"Don't try and brush me off," said Ophelia, pushing herself away from his chest and wiping the tears from her pudgy cheeks. "I'm fine now." She shuffled through her files, then looked up at Marbella. "Mrs. Carver? Mrs. Hugh Carver?"

"Yes," replied Marbella, beaming at Hugh proudly. "I never get tired of hearing that name."

"Wait a minute," said Hugh, turning in exasperation to the public defender. "You thought I was Adolf Petraczek."

"Auguste," said Ophelia, correcting his error. "Haven't *you* ever made a mistake? Please, sit down, Mrs. Carver. We'll try and get through this as quickly as possible."

The policewoman gestured for Marbella to sit. She squeezed into the wooden chair on the opposite side of the table from Hugh, then stretched her arms across, took Hugh's hand in her porcine fingers, and kissed it. He pulled his hand away immediately.

"He says he's not your husband," said Ophelia with disdain as she studied the police report.

"I don't mind," said Marbella, with the patience of a saint. "We're all entitled to our little quirks."

"How long have you two been married?"

"Little quirks!" Hugh was on the verge of apoplexy. "Why don't you phone the District Attorney's Office and ask for Susan Given Carver? She'll put an end to this farce."

Ophelia ignored Hugh's outburst and asked Marbella: "Mrs. Carver, why did you steal the watch and cufflinks?"

"For him." Marbella nodded toward Hugh. "I wanted him to know how much I care. I just didn't have the money."

"You don't work?"

"Of course, she works. Don't you have a television?"

"Please, let your wife answer the question."

"She's not my wife!"

"What is it? A weight thing?" asked Ophelia. "Afraid to be seen in public with her?"

"This is Marbella Morgan!" shouted Hugh, as he leaped to his feet and pointed a finger at the demented woman with the beatific smile. "The movie critic."

"Anybody have a pen?" asked Ophelia, shaking her ballpoint violently. "These things always go dead on me."

Hugh reached inside his suit jacket and removed his prized Mont Blanc fountain pen. He handed it over to Ophelia then turned his attention back to Marbella.

329

"I can help you," said Hugh gently.

"We can help each other. That's what a good marriage is all about."

"Yes. That's true. Except we are not married, Marbella. We hardly know each other. I met you twice at the television station. You're not Mrs. Carver."

"Oh, I know that, Atticus."

"Did she just call you Atticus?" asked Ophelia, putting down the pen and looking up from her file. "What is that? Like a nickname?"

"She thinks I'm Gregory Peck," said Hugh in hushed tones. "Rather, a character he played in—"

"What are you whispering to her?" asked Marbella. "What are you and this woman up to?"

"Take it easy," said the policewoman, stepping forward to restrain the movie critic if necessary.

"How long has this been going on?" asked Marbella, now quivering with rage. "How long have you two been playing fast and loose? Answer me! Answer me!"

"Take it easy, honey," said the policewoman, grabbing Marbella's beefy arm.

"Lemme go!" roared Marbella, wrenching herself loose from the policewoman's grip, grabbing the Mont Blanc pen from the desk, and driving it deep into Hugh Carver's chest.

54

LYDIA CULBERG WAS clearly out for blood as she paced up and down her office the next morning. Finally she froze, thrust a finger in Susan Given's face, and quoted from the previous evening's "News at Six" broadcast: " 'No murder will go unsolved on Janie Moore's watch'?"

Susan shut her eyes and sighed deeply. Then she said: "I was being facetious."

"Now my feelings are hurt," said Janie, sitting next to her on the hot seat in the Deputy D.A.'s office. "I was planning to put that on my résumé."

"It's not funny" growled Lydia. "Who do you two think you are? Starsky and Hutch?"

"Cagney and Lacey would be more apropos."

"I'm warning you, Janie. One more crack and—"

"Lisa caught us at a vulnerable moment," said Susan. "I didn't realize the camera was rolling. There was quite a lot said prior to the clip you actually saw."

"Oh, I suspected that. I've asked for a copy of the entire interview," said Lydia.

"It wasn't an interview!" protested Janie. "We went to the funeral to see if Rice Krispies might turn up. And Lisa thrust a microphone in our faces. She caught us off guard. We assumed it was deep background."

"The deepest," added Susan.

"Oh! Are you working homicide now, Ms. Given?" asked Lydia in mock fascination. "Not enough on your plate in Asset Forfeiture? Hmm? Have you already settled the American Patriot case without my being informed?"

Susan wondered how Lydia would feel if she knew that one of the plaintiffs in that case—Mitchell Levenstein—had been missing for the past three days. Susan had spent the previous evening with a forlorn Colette Cooke, who had paced her luxurious Trump Tower co-op chain-smoking and wishing aloud that she'd been a better wife. Colette was certain Mitch had run off with another woman. Dwight Pelham had been phoning frantically day and night for word of his missing partner and swearing the former Playmate of the Year to secrecy about her husband's unexplained absence.

Colette then recounted her tale of Pelham's sexual advance years before in East Hampton. Susan, in turn, told Colette how she'd been groped by the Brahmin on the dance floor at the gala much more recently. After a few more drinks, she even told the actress the truth about Pelham's scar.

But under the present circumstances, Susan decided it was unwise to tell Lydia about Levenstein's disappearance. Not until the possibility of interstate flight became more of a reality. Instead, she replied: "I knew the dead woman and I was paying my respects."

"And getting more media coverage for your hidden agenda at the same time," said Lydia, pinning and unpinning her hair.

"I have no 'hidden agenda,' Lydia, and I resent your insinuation."

"And what about this?" Lydia held up that morning's *Post* and displayed a front-page photograph of Hugh Carver being wheeled out of the Seventeenth Precinct on a stretcher to a waiting ambulance. The headline read: MOVIE CRITIC GIVES THUMBS DOWN TO TV SHRINK.

"You and your husband are bigger news than Kathy Lee and Frank Gifford. Did you read what Ray Murphy wrote?"

"No, I've had more important things to attend to. My daughters have been in considerable shock since the incident."

"Oh, then let me read it to you," said Lydia, turning to the double spread on pages 4 and 5. "I had no idea your husband was a chubby chaser."

"We are legally separated, Lydia."

"Funny. I always thought the guy was a bit of a stuffed shirt. Ah! Here we are. Ray was really in top form with this column:

Who says the pen is no longer mightier than the sword? Not movie critic Marbella Morgan, who drove an expensive Mont Blanc fountain pen deep into the chest of her Channel 8 colleague, Dr. Hugh Carver, yesterday afternoon.

This shocking act of *amour fou* occurred to the great embarrassment of the NYPD in an interview room at the Seventeenth Precinct on East Fifty-first Street, where Ms. Morgan was taken after allegedly stealing a diamond-encrusted wristwatch and a pair of gold cufflinks from the men's jewelry department of Bergdorf-Goodman's.

Security officials at the fashionable East Side store said that when apprehended, the hefty movie critic identified herself as "Mrs. Hugh Carver." This must have come as a surprise to the real Mrs. Hugh Carver, Assistant District Attorney Susan Given (who was not available for comment).

So what's the true story? Nobody in the know seems to be talking. Marbella Morgan is presently under psychiatric observation by a team of the state's top shrinks. Dr. Carver is under guard and under wraps at Mount Sinai Hospital. The usually loquacious Susan Given certainly isn't talking. And witness Ophelia Feldman has taken an abrupt leave of absence from Legal Aid. To be continued.

"Well," said Lydia, putting the newspaper down and pausing for breath. "What do we think about that?"

"Ray Murphy has hired a ghostwriter," said Janie. "No way he'd ever come up with 'amour fou' on his own."

"I resent being called 'loquacious,'" said Susan. "I pride myself on being discreet and—"

"Strange isn't it?" asked Lydia. "That so much of Ray's column relies on interviews with people from

Channel 8. Doesn't your niece work there, Susan? Is it a coincidence she was just promoted assistant to the News Director, whose late wife happens to be Rice Krispies' most recent victim?"

"Your thinking process is all too labyrinthine for me, Lydia. But I am impressed by your penetrating investigative powers. If only you could use them to solve crimes that don't involve your ego."

"I'm warning you, Susan. Watch it!"

"Watch what, Lydia? I'm only doing my job. Something that continually seems to drive you crazy."

"Doing your job, huh?"

"Yes!"

"Roasting Dwight Pelham over the flames, are you?"

"We've frozen his assets. He's coming in to see me the day after tomorrow."

"And what about his partner? I hear you're friends with Levenstein's wife."

"I met Colette on my vacation."

"Uh-huh. No conflict of interests there, right?"

"What possible—"

"I just wondered why you haven't told anyone in this office that your girlfriend's husband took a powder three days ago. Isn't that something we should know? Or are you giving your Hollywood friends preferential treatment these days?"

"I only learned about it last night, Lydia. I have no reason to suspect Levenstein is attempting to flee this jurisdiction. It sounds like a domestic dispute to me and, frankly, none of our business."

"Anything that affects this office, Ms. Given, is *my* business. You don't make any more decisions without clearing them with me. Got it? You don't make a lunch date before checking with me. This is going to be another one of your goddamn messes and I'm sick of cleaning up after you."

"May I leave now?" asked Susan, who feared she might hurl herself on top of the Deputy District Attorney and tear out her red hairs by the roots.

"Not yet." Lydia turned her gaze on Janie and said, "I have had the Mayor on the phone to me all morning. When the hell are we going to do something about Rice Krispies?"

"Ask Haskell Abrams. He's got to arrest someone first. Remember?"

Lydia stuck a finger in Janie's face and snarled, "You are on suspension."

"Teacher's pet," said Susan mockingly. "No preferential treatment, Lydia. Remember? You'd better make it both of us."

"You got it, sweetie." Lydia pinned up her hair once more and returned triumphantly to her desk. "Now, go home, both of you. Ponder your sins. Find out how much they're paying checkout girls at the Food Emporium these days. Then come crawling back to me."

55

"SO, HOW'S THE *SHIKSA*?"

"Do you care?"

"Why shouldn't I care? She seemed like a nice woman."

Alan Becker stared in disbelief at his mother sipping a glass of iced tea while propped up in her semi-private room at Mount Sinai Hospital. Finally he asked: "Do you want me to call a doctor? Or a rabbi?"

"Why?"

"You've obviously taken a turn for the worst."

"Don't mention wurst," said Rose Becker, making a horrible grimace. "You know how it gives me gas. My father, *oliva shalom*, loved wurst. On rye. With Gulden's mustard. You only knew him when he was old and frail. Young, he looked like Warren William. I'll bet you don't remember him, do you?"

"Grandpa? Sure, I do."

"No, no, no. Warren William."

"No. Who was he?"

"Shame on you! The original Perry Mason. Long before TV. Back in the thirties. In the movies. Later he played the Lone Wolf, too. Oy, was he gorgeous! Tall with a long face, a thin mustache, and a voice that growled. Too bad you didn't inherit any Warren

William genes. You'd be beating the girls off with a stick."

"Thanks a lot, Mom," said the short, stocky Becker, self-consciously plowing a hand through his thinning hair.

"He made movies with Bette Davis and Joan Blondell," said Mrs. Becker, oblivious to the wound she had inflicted on her son's ego. "I used to cut his picture out of movie magazines and make believe he was really my father. I'd tell myself he only pretended to work in a dress factory so the neighbors wouldn't be jealous if they found out he was really Warren William. He died young. Fifty-three. He loved wurst and eggs, too."

"Warren William?"

"No. Your grandfather. Remember the picnics we'd all take in Uncle Benny's car up the Hudson? What kind of a car did Benny drive? Remember that Chinese girl he dated?"

Becker turned his head to the window and wondered how much more of his malingering mother's mental meandering he could take. How much longer would the doctors allow her to remain in the hospital? Hadn't they caught on to her yet? Unless there *was* something truly wrong with her.

"I don't think so," was Becker's eventual reply.

"Of course not," replied Mrs. Becker. "You weren't even born then. My grandmother was still alive. "

"Warren William's mother?"

"Exactly. Didn't speak a word of English. She walked into the parlor one night and found Benny necking with the Chinese girl. Imagine! My father put an end to the romance. Benny was heartbroken. He was so crazy about her. Grandma wasn't surprised. 'I knew it would never work,' she said in Yiddish. 'I took one look at her eyes. A Galitzianer! Not for us.' Oh, how we laughed for years. Everyone except Benny. . . . You still haven't answered me."

"What was the question, Mom?"

"How's Nancy? How are her kids?"

"Is this a trick question?"

"Is this how you talk to a mother?"

"I know how your mind works, Mom. The little traps you set for me."

"I've had a lot of time to think, Alan. I'd forgotten how little there is to do in a hospital. Remember Uncle Nachum? Spent half his life in the hospital. Life's not long enough for that. You were a little boy yesterday. Now I'm an old woman. Go know! The world has changed since I used to cut out Warren William's picture. She was nice, that Chinese girl. Benny never forgot her. Would she let you raise the kids Jewish?"

"Who?"

"Nancy. Is she religious?"

"We've never discussed it."

"You should. And, if she won't, she should still respect your faith."

"Is this vaguely like your blessing, Mom? Or am I dreaming this?"

"I'm tired, Alan. Let me shut my eyes a minute."

Becker wandered outside to the corridor. It had been an exhausting day for him. First, Lydia Culberg had burst into his office at 9:30 A.M. demanding to know where Susan Given was. When Becker reminded the Deputy D.A. that she suspended Susan the day before, the volcanic redhead erupted and insisted she had done no such thing.

Then Lydia insisted Becker get Susan on the phone and have her turn up for work ASAP before she really did suspend her.

Two hours later a beaming Susan waltzed into the office assuming damage control yet again for one of Lydia's screw-ups. Apparently the deal Lydia cut with The Matador's lawyer weeks earlier had been thrown out of court by the appeals judge. They were back to square one again and only Susan could bail them out. Susan agreed to come back only if Janie's suspension was lifted as well.

Susan gave the Matador paperwork to Becker while she prepared for her meeting with Dwight Pelham the next day. Becker had been hard at it until five o'clock when he took the subway uptown to visit his mother in the hospital.

Becker was hungry when he left his mother's room and, when he couldn't find a vending machine on the floor, went downstairs to the gift shop in search of a snack. He was pleasantly surprised to see a familiar face pausing in front of the candy counter.

"Ivy?"

"Oh hi, Alan."

"What are you doing here?"

"I can't make up my mind between the Skittles or the Sour Power."

"No, no. Why are you here at the hospital?"

"Visiting my dad." Then Ivy added breathlessly, "He was stabbed."

"Yes, I know. Is he okay now?"

"Uh-huh. The pen still works. Isn't that amazing?"

"I beg your pardon?"

"The pen Marbella stabbed him with. It still writes. Wouldn't that make a great commercial?"

"Are you here with your mother?" Becker's eyes scanned the gift shop for a glimpse of his boss.

"No. My sister and Cordelia. They're upstairs. Dad's on the phone with his new girlfriend. Why are you here?"

"Visiting my mom."

"What's wrong with her?"

"I'm not sure."

"Oh. Are you going to buy something?"

"Maybe some trail mix," said Alan. "I don't want to spoil my appetite before dinner. Nancy's such a good cook and . . . what're you staring at?"

"That woman over there," whispered Ivy. "I know her from somewhere. What's wrong with her?"

Becker gazed at the magazine rack, where a beautiful light-skinned African-American woman was scratching her arms in an agitated fashion and shifting her weight from one leg to another.

"She's not well," said Becker, who suspected the woman was a junkie in desperate need of a fix.

"Oh, I remember now," said Ivy, who promptly skipped toward the magazine rack and planted herself in front of the woman, who stared down at the child in astonishment as though a fairy had just emerged from under a lilac bush.

"Hi. I met you in church. I'm Ivy Carver. You said it was a pretty name."

"Ohhh, yes," replied Conception, whose strung-out state had affected her memory. "I remember now. Weren't you with your mother? She gave me her card. I was supposed to phone her. How have you been?"

"Fine, thanks. My dad was stabbed by a coworker. He's upstairs recuperating."

Ivy then went on at great length about Marbella's fragile emotional state and her lengthy history of mental illness, which the movie critic had failed to disclose to the station's human resources officer when she first went to work there. Conception did not absorb a word of this as she gazed anxiously through the glass window toward the lobby where she waited for her knight errant to reappear successfully from his mission.

Becker had to go back upstairs to his mother and held his hand out to say good-bye to Ivy. Just as Ivy thrust her hand out to shake his, Conception burst between them and dashed out of the gift shop.

"Where do you know that woman from?" asked Becker, as he watched Conception race across the foyer.

"She's a witness," said Ivy.

"To what?"

"My mom didn't say. But she lives with a really scary guy."

"That one there?" asked Becker, nodding toward an unshaven man in faded jeans, Nikes, and a cashmere overcoat.

"Nope. The scary guy was black with a bald head."

Then who's this? Becker asked himself. Why does he look so familiar?

Becker stepped outside the gift shop to try to hear what the two were saying to each other.

"You lied to me," cried Conception.

"I tried," said the man. "The doctor I know isn't here. Please, keep your voice down."

"I was better off with Crimson!"

"You'd be dead by now. Where are you going?"

"I've got to get out of here. I'm going crazy."

"Wait! Wait!"

The man disappeared through the great glass doors just as Becker realized who he was. . . . Mitch Levenstein.

56

SUSAN SAT BEHIND her desk, staring at the white carnation in Dwight Pelham's lapel. The fresh cut flower, combined with the Brahmin's elegant gray pin-striped suit, gave him the unintended appearance of the head floorwalker in the glory days of Bonwit Teller.

"Thank you for coming in this afternoon," said Susan, nodding at Pelham and his celebrated lawyer, Raymond Cordell Northridge. "You've caused quite a sensation around the office. Several secretaries asked if I could get them your autograph."

"Didn't I tell you she was a charmer, Ray?"

"Ms. Given, I'd like to make this visit as brief as possible," said Northridge, clearing his throat, ignoring his client, and getting right down to business. As this was his first meeting with Susan, he was on his best behavior and spoke more like an admiral than a common sailor.

"I'm in no rush, Mr. Northridge." Susan was determined not to let the legendary trial lawyer intimidate her in any way. "We'll stay here all afternoon, if we need to. Please, proceed. Oh, by the way, where is Mr. Levenstein?"

"I don't represent him," said Northridge, shifting his large bulk in the chair. "He has his own attorney."

"Have you spoken to him recently?" Susan stared into Pelham's blue eyes.

"I speak to the dear boy every day," replied Pelham, without blinking. "He's presently in Washington. On business."

That's a lie, thought Susan. Or does he know where his protégé and Conception are hiding out together? Becker had phoned Susan the night before and reported seeing the odd couple together at Mount Sinai Hospital. She was tempted to call Colette and give her an update but decided it best not to get the actress's Cherokee up.

"Will he be back soon?" asked Susan.

"By the end of the week, I believe."

"May I continue?" asked Northridge. And without waiting for an answer, he resumed. "There are many who feel your office behaves in an unconstitutional manner. . . ."

"Are you saying the District Attorney's Office is unconstitutional?"

"You won't trap her that easily, Ray. Isn't she marvelous?" Pelham blew a kiss in Susan's direction. "I offered the girl a job but she brazenly refused me."

"I was referring to the notion of asset forfeiture," said Northridge. "One appreciates the lack of funds that law enforcement suffers from and one certainly does not bemoan the fate of the drug dealers' whose ill-gotten gains you have—"

"Let's take our gloves off, Mr. Northridge."

"Fine. I'll take my fucking gloves off. You seized eighteen million dollars of my client's money."

"It was closer to nineteen," said Susan, trying not to appear startled by Northridge's salty language.

"You've inflicted immediate and unjustified hardship on him. You've deprived him of the basic funds with which to purchase food."

Susan turned to Pelham and asked: "Did you eat lunch today?" He nodded. "Where?"

"21."

"Who paid?"

"I have an account there."

"Where are you going for dinner?"

"Is that an invitation?" Pelham sniffed his carnation and flashed his teeth at her.

"He's not starving," said Susan in dismissive tones.

"Yet. Dwight is a proud man," said Northridge. "He'd never tell you this but he's supporting his goddamn children and grandchildren. To the tune of three hundred fifty thousand a year."

"Why?"

"Private reasons," said Pelham.

"Don't they have jobs?" asked Susan. "Don't they have husbands? Or wives?"

" 'Are there no prisons?' " asked Pelham. " 'Are there no workhouses?' "

"Are you comparing me to Scrooge, Mr. Pelham?"

"I have responsibilities to my family," said Pelham. "Your case against me is an inconvenience, if not a joke. You will end up costing the taxpayers millions in pursuing it and your own reputation will be ruined."

"Is that a threat?" asked Susan.

"Call it a prediction."

"Hey, guys. Why don't we put our gloves on again?" asked Northridge, trying to steer the conversation back on course. "My client may not be starving at the moment but it's only a matter of days before he will be subsisting purely on credit. Due to your misguided zeal, Ms. Given. He has several homes of his own to support—in Manhattan, East Hampton, Washington, and Palm Beach—in addition to the aforementioned assistance he gives his children and their—"

"We only seized Mr. Pelham's assets in New York," said Susan, flipping through the file on her desk. "That's all we're allowed to. There are still two million dollars in various securities that he owns back in Washington. Correct? I would think they'd take care of any short-term cash-flow problems he might have."

"I am emotionally attached to those shares," said Pelham without blinking, "and wouldn't feel comfortable disturbing them at the present time."

Susan burst out laughing and the two men stared at her in shock.

"I'm sorry, gentlemen. People come in here begging me to release millions of dollars for housekeeping, children's tuition, therapy for their Great Danes. But emotional attachment to stocks and bonds? That's a first."

"I either served on the boards of those companies," explained Pelham loftily, "or they were clients."

"Use the shares as collateral," said Susan. "Anything else?"

There was a knock at the door. Tuck poked his head round the corner.

"Sorry to interrupt," said Tuck, "but we got a situation out here."

Susan excused herself and followed Tuck into the outer office, where she was surprised to discover Desmond Wilmot and Alan Becker waiting for her.

"What's going on?"

"Crimson has found Conception," said Wilmot. "He's on his way to her as we speak."

"How do you know?"

"We've had a tap on his phone for a week now," said Tuck. "Crimson's been tearin' the town apart tryin' to find her and she finally phoned him. Real strung out and needing a fix bad."

"Where are they?"

"Out on Long Island."

"Where?"

Tuck stared down at the floor in embarrassment, then murmured: "There was a fuck-up with the eavesdropping equipment. We ain't got the exact address but we know it's one of them Hamptons."

"Of course it is!" said Susan, flashing back to Colette's ribald tale of Pelham's invading the cabana years before and what Ray Northfield had just said in her office. Levenstein was hiding out with Conception at his boss's summer house. "East Hampton. I can get the address."

"Your Mr. Becker tells me that Conception is probably with another man," said Wilmot. "A man you are prosecuting. Is this case important to you?"

"Very important."

"Then we'd better find out the address immediately. If Crimson finds Conception with another man, he'll kill them both."

57

COLETTE COOKE WAS doing about ninety on the outskirts of East Hampton when she heard the police siren growing louder behind her. Perfect! She'd driven all the way from Manhattan in less than two hours only to get busted at the finish line. Did she have her license and registration? Whoops! Don't open the glove compartment.

The siren was deafening now and Colette pulled the BMW over to the soft shoulder. What if he looked in the glove compartment? As the uniformed policeman strode toward her, her brain continued to replay the telephone conversation she'd had three hours earlier with her husband.

"Hi."

"Mitch! Where are you?"

"I've done something stupid."

"You sound exhausted. Where are you?"

"I haven't slept for three days."

"Is it the case?"

"What are you talking about?"

"The bank. They've frozen all your assets in New York. Haven't you read the paper?"

"No. I've been too busy making a fool of myself."

"What have you done, Mitch?"

"I just want you to know, Colette, you're the only woman I've ever loved."

"You must really be in trouble, tiger. Have you killed someone?"

"No. But I need you to do something for me."

"Where are you?"

"I did something weird. Not sure why but I'm paying the price now."

"Are you alone?"

"No."

"Are you with . . . a man?"

"Of course not. What the hell do you think I am? My God, Colette! After all I've been through, you think I'm a fag?"

"Dwight's been phoning here twice a day. He's freaking out cuz you haven't phoned him."

"I haven't even phoned the guru!"

"That *is* serious," said Colette. And she heard her husband giggle slightly. "Are you with a woman?"

"Will that affect your decision?"

"Do I know her?"

"I doubt it very much. I don't know how to explain. It was like an obsession. I was possessed. Couldn't get her out of my mind. Even hired a detective to find her."

"Correct me if I'm wrong, but didn't I star in this with Bruce Greenwood and Bryan Cranston on USA last year?"

"Someone's trying to kill her, Colette."

"No, no. That's the movie I just did."

"It's not funny."

"Believe me, Mitchell, I know it isn't."

There was a long pause before Levenstein asked his wife, "Can you get some smack?"

"Are you hungry?"

"Not snack. Smack. Aitch."

"Heroin? You want me to get you heroin?"

"It's not for me, baby. I swear."

"Mitch? What the hell is going on?"

"Trust me."

"What are you? Crazy? You vanish for three days in the middle of a criminal investigation. Dwight is driving me nuts trying to find you. You're shacked up with some woman. And you ask me to trust you?"

"She's going to die, Colette."

"What the hell do I care?"

"Please, baby."

"Don't 'baby' me, Mitchell. And how the hell do you expect me to score heroin anyhow?"

"Scott. Your agent. He can get it for you."

"It's not quite the same as asking for theater tickets."

"Pleeease!"

Colette finally gave in and called her agent. She blurted out her need for the heroin and, without blinking, Scott gave her the number of a dealer in TriBeCa, who sent a bag up to her by messenger. Then she got the BMW from the garage and drove east on Fifty-seventh toward the FDR Drive. Once she crossed the Triborough Bridge she put her foot to the floor and zipped along the Long Island Expressway in record time. Until . . .

"Any idea how fast you were going?" The policeman, a big, beefy, blond hulk in his late twenties, opened his citation book without bothering to peek through the window. "Could I see your license, please?"

"What seems to be the problem, officer?" Colette was busy undoing two more buttons on her navy blue silk blouse.

"Are you aware that this car's registration has lapsed?" asked the cop, refusing to look at Colette as he jerked his thumb at the sticker in the lower left-hand side of the windshield.

"No," replied Colette, who was now convinced the hulk had to be gay. Or a Mormon. Men had swooned for a brief glimpse at what she was all but shoving in the guy's face. "I never drive the car. It's leased."

"Why are you driving it now?"

"What's your name?" Colette was determined to make eye contact with this tight-ass.

"Can I see your license, please?"

"It's at the house."

"You're driving without a license? No registration? And speeding? This is *not* your lucky day. Do you have any identification?"

"Do you watch TV?"

"Beg pardon?"

"Have you ever read *Playboy*?"

The policeman finally bent down, stared through the window, blushed, and finally asked: "You aren't Colette Cooke, are you?"

"Why, yes," replied the actress, taking a deep breath, which levitated her cleavage up to his eye level. "How did you know?"

"I used to have your picture taped to my locker."

"Aren't you sweet! What did you say your name was?"

"Merle. Merle Grandowsky."

"Mmm. That's a strong name. Polish?"

"My father's family. My mother's French Canadian. Got some Mohawk blood."

"Really? I'm part Cherokee."

"I know," nodded Grandowsky. "I remember from *Playboy*. Favorite movie: *Ryan's Daughter*. Favorite book: *The Diaries of Anaïs Nin*. Loved waterskiing. And you were a Scorpio."

"Still am. That's quite a memory, Merle."

"I'm a Cancer."

"Which makes us compatible. Well, what are we two Indians going do about all this?"

"I'd love to let you go, Miss Cooke . . ."

"Call me Colette."

"But I'd be in big trouble with my sergeant. If you only had your license."

Colette stared at Grandowsky and decided he was the answer to all her problems. She wasn't going to deliver the smack to her "possessed" husband. No. Mitch needed to have the shit scared out of him. Bring him to his senses once and for all. Turning up with a cop would do the trick. And get rid of the mysterious bimbo at the same time.

"Could you follow me home, Merle? I've got my license there. Would you mind? It's just in East Hampton."

"I *do* need to see your license, Colette."

"Of course you do."

Colette led the way into East Hampton and

Grandowsky followed closely behind. In a few months the town's streets would be choked with traffic and tourists, but midweek in April it was all but deserted.

Dwight Pelham's two-story Colonial house was palatial and commanded a beautiful view of the Sound. Colette steered the BMW up the long, winding driveway and the police car was right behind her.

"Wow!" said Grandowsky, as he got out of his car and followed her up the front steps. "This is some—"

Grandowsky never finished his sentence. A gun was fired from inside the house. The bullet entered the cop's chest and he crumbled to the ground. Colette screamed. This was no TV movie.

58

THE SUN WAS BEGINNING to sink as the trio crept around the perimeter of Dwight Pelham's property, doing their best to avoid detection by the occupants.

Tuck was the first to spot the body lying in the drive. Tapping Wilmot's shoulder, he pointed to Grandowsky and said in a low voice: "Crimson must be here."

The St. Stephen's police captain nodded, then turned to Susan and gestured for her to return to their car parked a quarter of a mile back down the road. Susan shook her head in defiance, then said in a low voice, "This isn't your jurisdiction."

"Is she always like this?" Wilmot asked Tuck.

"She's got her own mind," said the undercover cop fondly.

"Is he alive?" asked Susan, nodding toward the fallen policeman.

"I pray he is. But we can't do nothin' for him till we get some backup," replied Tuck. He turned his gaze to the four cars parked in the driveway. "The Seville is Crimson's. The rental car must be Levenstein's. Black-and-white belongs to the poor guy in the driveway. So where does the BMW fit in?" He removed his gun from his ankle holster, checked

356

the safety, and passed his cell phone to Susan. "Get a make on it, Ms. Gee, and call the locals for that backup. Tell 'em one of their boys is down. That should get 'em moving. Cap'n, you got a gun?"

"Yes, thank you, Mr. Maxwell."

"Where are you going?" whispered Susan.

"Check out the firepower inside. See where the switch box is. It's gonna be dark real soon and Crimson ain't gonna like bein' at a disadvantage."

"A remarkable chap," said Wilmot after Tuck had sneaked off toward the back of the house. "I wish I had him working for me."

"Make him an offer. He loves deep-sea fishing."

"Ah! That's most unfortunate. When would the man do any police work? St. Stephen's is a very seductive place."

"You don't have to remind me," said Susan.

"I do hope you'll come back and visit us soon."

"Very soon. As a witness. Remember?"

"I meant as my guest."

"What happens to all those nieces you have lunch with?"

"They would make superb baby-sitters for your daughters."

"Desmond, you are incorrigible."

"Is that a yes?"

Susan put a finger to her lips, dialed her police contact, and gave them the license number of the BMW in the driveway.

Inside the house Mitch Levenstein watched with a mix of fear and fascination as his wife fastened a rubber cord around a frail and semicomatose Conception's upper arm.

"Tighter," said Crimson, training his gun on both Colette and her husband.

"You want to come do this?" asked the actress, staring at the drug lord without blinking. Then she picked up the hypo, stared in dismay at Conception's arm riddled with track marks, and asked Levenstein: "This was your obsession? How could you have thrown away your career and our marriage for this junkie?"

"Tell you woman to keep she mouth shut," Crimson warned Levenstein.

"Honey, do as he tells you."

"I wasn't nuts about this asshole the first time I met him," said Colette, trying to find a vein.

"Me don't know you."

"Oh, yes, you do, pal. The casino at the Henry Morgan. The night you had Ascension killed. Or killed him yourself."

"Shut you mouth!" warned Crimson.

"Who's Ascension?" asked Levenstein.

"Ascension," moaned Conception. "Is Ascension here?"

"Ascension's dead," said Colette.

"Is that true, Crimson?"

"Give she de fix!" ordered Crimson. "Now!"

"Why don't you tell her the truth?" asked Colette.

"Me gon' kill you!" roared Crimson, leaping across the room and grabbing hold of the actress's hair.

"You *did* kill him, didn't you?"

"Shut up, Colette. He means it."

"What a tower of Jell-O you turned out to be, Mitch! Here. Do the honors." Colette tossed the hypodermic to her husband just as the lights went out everywhere.

"What goin' on?" shouted Crimson. "Who fuck wit' dem lights?"

"Maybe it's voodoo," snarled Colette, who had moved to the furthest corner of the room.

"Where you am?" asked an enraged Crimson, grasping at the air where the actress had been a second before. "You get you ass back here."

"What's the matter? 'Fraid of the dark? A great, big—"

Colette never finished her sentence as a large, hand covered her mouth and she heard a voice whisper in her ear: "It's okay. I'm a police officer. Keep crawling backward toward the kitchen. Nod if you understand." Colette bobbed her head up and down. "Good. Get movin'."

"What goin' on?" demanded Crimson when he heard the sounds from the other side of the room. Then he fired a shot in the direction of the room.

Tuck raised his gun and fired at the light from the gun blast. Crimson cursed and ran toward the hallway.

The front door burst open and Wilmot rushed in with his gun drawn. Crimson saw the Captain's silhouette illuminated by the moonlight and fired. Wilmot fell forward. Crimson stepped over his body and rushed out of the house.

Seconds later Tuck had restored the electricity to the house and was standing in the hallway as a disheveled Susan stumbled inside, breathing heavily. "I tried to stop Crimson but he slapped me and took off in the Seville."

She saw Wilmot lying on the floor and dropped to her knees beside him.

"Desmond! Are you—"

"It's just my shoulder. How is Conception?"

Susan walked into the living room as a shaken Colette entered from the kitchen.

"Should have known you'd be here, Susan. I've been to some wild parties but they were strictly B-list compared to yours."

"Are you okay, Colette?"

"Oh, sure. Just like one of my movies."

Wilmot made his way across the living room, attempting to disguise his pain, knelt down beside Conception, and took her hand. "Hello, child. Do you remember me?"

Conception opened her eyes, stared up at him, and managed a smile. "Captain Wilmot. What are you doing here?"

"Shh. Shh. Rest, child. You're safe now."

A tear rolled down Conception's face and she whispered faintly, "Ascension."

"Just relax," said Wilmot, stroking her brow gently.

"He is dead, isn't he, Captain? My brother's dead."

Wilmot nodded.

"And Crimson killed him." She clutched Wilmot's hand. "Get him, Captain."

"I will," replied Wilmot. "Then you will come back to St. Stephen's and watch him stand trial for the murder of your brother."

"You won't catch him," said Conception, trying to sit up but collapsing from lack of strength. "He's the Devil. He always wins."

An ambulance siren could be heard in the distance.

"Hey!" said Colette, looking around the room. "Anybody know where that husband of mine is?"

Colette cried out when she saw the body on the floor beside the sofa. The bullet Tuck fired at Crimson in the darkness had hit Mitch Levenstein instead.

59

LEVENSTEIN AND GRANDOWSKY were both alive but in critical condition when the ambulance arrived at Pelham's house. They were rushed to the hospital in East Hampton along with Wilmot and Conception.

Susan stayed at the hospital for an hour chain-smoking with Colette. Once she learned Captain Wilmot was out of danger, she hugged Colette, then went back to the city with Tuck.

They drove in silence for the first hour until Tuck tried to find a good jazz station on the radio. That's when they heard: ". . . a distinguished career in public service for almost half a century under six different presidents. Mr. Pelham was eighty-four years old."

Susan thought she was dreaming, then she began twisting the radio dial and tried to find another news station. Finally she picked up the cell phone and dialed Ned Jordan's office.

"Mr. Jordan isn't here at the present time, Ms. Given," replied the Federal Prosecutor's secretary. "Is there any message?"

"Do you happen to know if Dwight Pelham died?"

"Yes. A heart attack. About two hours ago. Mr.

Jordan was very annoyed. Oops. Don't tell him I said that."

Susan hung up the phone.

Four days later Susan sat in her office reading the account of Dwight Pelham's funeral as reported by Draycott Simms III in the *New York Times*. Three ex-presidents had attended the service in Washington as well as Mr. Archibald. The article chronicled the high spots in Pelham's years of public service, quoted President Clinton's eulogy at length, and made only passing and cursory reference at the end of the piece to the specter of "unproven" scandal that had hung over the late Brahmin's last days.

"Unproven!" said Susan aloud in disgust. She was certainly glad her niece was no longer keeping company with the news-fickle Dray-Three (although she was more than a bit concerned where Brandy's devotion to the much older Vance Holland might lead the Southern Amazon).

Mitch Levenstein did not attend the funeral (his wife, Colette, stood in for him and was prominently featured in all media coverage) as he continued to remain in critical condition in East Hampton. The forfeiture procedure against American Patriot was put on hold pending an improvement in the surviving partner's condition.

Desmond Wilmot was back on his feet two days after the shooting and had spirited Conception Westerfield off to a detox clinic in another state where, hopefully, the fugitive Edward Claxton would not be able to find her.

"Unproven," repeated Susan as she tossed the *Times* into the wastepaper basket beside her desk.

"What's unproven?" asked Becker, walking into the office with a huge grin on his face.

"What are you smiling at?" asked Susan.

"Your goddaughter Susan Gerhardt is about to get a stepfather."

"You and Nancy are getting married?! What happened? Did your mother die? I'm sorry, Alan. I didn't mean—"

"It's okay. And so's my mom. But her near-death experience or whatever it was she had has changed her—"

The phone rang on Susan's desk and she held a finger up for Becker to hold his thought.

"Given."

"Susan? It's Neil. Remember when I phoned three days ago and asked you to keep tomorrow at ten open?"

"Did you? I'm sorry, Neil. My life has been a little crazed." Susan flipped through her appointment book. "Yes. Here it is. 'Ten A.M., Neil Stern's office.' "

"I lied," said Stern. "It's not in my office. It's in court."

"What! What's in court?"

"Your husband's near-death experience has made him a changed man. He wants to give you your freedom."

"You're joking!"

"See you in court, Ms. D.A."

Susan hung up the phone in a state of elation,

rose from behind her desk and, uncharacteristically, hugged an astonished Becker.

"There is a God, Alan."

"I've never doubted it."

"And He or She loves me."

"Careful, Susan."

"What? You're enjoying the benefit of a near-death experience as well. I'm going to be free at last. Free, free!"

"It ain't over till it's over, Susan. Don't put a curse on yourself."

"It's my lucky day, Alan. Nothing bad can happen to me."

"Don't you believe in hubris?"

"Is that Jewish?"

"Greek."

"Mediterranean." Susan shrugged playfully. "Doesn't apply to me. I'm a cold, clinical WASP. And I'm on a roll. I am invincible."

Susan returned home on a cloud of invincibility. Hubris be damned! She wanted to celebrate. She'd take the girls to dinner at Petaluma, their favorite restaurant. Then she thought about it and decided it might be in bad taste. After all, Hugh *was* their father. As it turned out, both girls were swamped with homework and couldn't go anywhere. What to do? What to do? Susan turned on the TV and turned it off immediately. Too passive. She craved activity. What? What? She began pacing the apartment like a caged animal. Tomorrow she would be divorced. Tonight she was going crazy. Antsy. Desperate to jump out of her skin. What about a shower? No.

What she wanted—really wanted—was a run. But it was already dark and she had promised her daughters she would never, *never* run after dark. But just this once. Susan walked over to the bedroom window and stared out at Central Park. Maybe a little run. Not the whole circuit. Just the reservoir. It was well lit. She'd do it in twenty minutes. Less. She'd feel better. Then she could help the girls with their homework.

Feels good already, she thought as she laced up her running shoes. She was pulling her hair back into a ponytail when Polly wandered into the bedroom.

"Mom, have you got an eraser?"

"Somewhere," said Susan, rising and pulling her shoulders back. "Try my desk."

"Like, where are you going, Mom?"

"Quick run."

"It's after seven. It's dark. And Rice Krispies is still on the loose."

"Oh, Polly, don't be so melodramatic. I'm just going for a quick spin around the reservoir. Nothing can happen to me. I'm invincible. I am woman."

"You are nuts. And I don't have a black dress to wear to your funeral."

"I'll be back in a flash. Then we can order dinner from Viand." Susan kissed her frowning daughter on the forehead, went down the stairs, and rang for the elevator.

"You goin' for a run at this hour?" asked the night doorman. "That such a good idea, Ms. Given?"

"It's a great idea, Luigi. If I'm not back in half an hour, have them flash the Bat signal."

Luigi was holding the front door open just as her niece Brandy appeared in an emotional state.

"Oh, Susan, I'm so glad you're home. I just had the worst fight with Mom on the phone."

"Can't this wait?"

"She said the worst things to me about Vance. She doesn't even know him. What does it matter if he's old enough to be my father? I'm not sleeping with him—although Lord knows I find him attractive as hell. The poor man just lost his wife. All I'm trying to do is be kind to him and the girls."

"Brandy, please! I'm going for a run. I'll be back in twenty minutes. The girls are upstairs. Go wait with them and we'll order some food when I get back."

The pavement felt good under Susan's feet as she made her way down Eightieth toward Fifth Avenue. She hadn't run at night in years. She'd forgotten how crisp the air was. Entering the park at the Miners' Gate on Seventy-ninth, she waved a jaunty salute to the gold bear standing on perpetual guard. Before she knew it, she was on the East Drive, then going up the stairs to the jogging track around the Jackie O. Reservoir. Oxygen. Beautiful, life-giving oxygen swelling her lungs. Hardly anyone was running at that hour. She was glad of the solitude.

The moon was reflected in the water and the distant honking of car horns was the only reminder that the time was the present and not some long-ago New York. Susan thought of Jack Finney's novel about the Manhattan time traveler. Wouldn't it be funny if she, too, had gone back in time that evening? What if

when she emerged from the park in her jogging out-
fit it was New York in 1958? Or 1938? Or 1898? What
would people make of a woman dressed as she was?
No, she couldn't go back in time that night. She was
getting a divorce the next day. Nothing must stand in
the way of that historic event.

Curious how silent it had become, thought Susan.
Where had everyone else disappeared to? She was
alone on the jogging path.

Then she heard the footfalls. Ever so faint. Then
louder and louder. Someone was coming up the path
behind her. She wanted to turn her head, glance
over her shoulder, and be relieved to see a familiar
face. But she was suddenly afraid. What if it was Rice
Krispies? How ironic. After all the warnings—Ray
Murphy at Dierdre's funeral service, Alan Becker
only that afternoon—she was next on his list. The
serial killer was long overdue on his timetable and, as
everyone had said, she fitted his MO perfectly.

No! No way. She hadn't lived this long to end up
in a pool of blood in Central Park with a thimble
capping her amputated finger.

"Not this girl!" she shouted into the air as she
began to speed up her pace. "I'm getting a divorce
tomorrow."

But the faster she ran, the faster her pursuer's
pace became. Damn! He was fit. Her eyes darted
about, looking for the next exit from the park. She
had to get off the path. She must get away from him.
She didn't want to die!

The she felt a hand clamp down on her shoulder.
Huge and black. She wrenched her arm forward a_.d

was loose from the man's grasp. She had to get off the path. Immediately. She would hide in the park. She'd have a chance that way.

"Damn you, bitch!" growled the man behind her. There was something familiar about his voice. She knew him. She turned her face sideways and saw him coming up beside her now like a champion race-horse heading toward an unseen finish line. It was Crimson.

Thank God! she thought. It's not Rice Krispies. It's Crimson. But what did he want with her in the middle of Central Park?

Just then Crimson rammed her with a powerful thigh and she went flying off the jogging path, trip-ping over her own feet and tumbling down the bluff into the shrubbery.

Seconds later the drug lord was towering above her with an evil glint in his eye. "Me gon' kill you now."

Well, that certainly answered Susan's question.

Five minutes earlier Desmond Wilmot emerged from a taxi in front of Susan's building and caught sight of a familiar figure rushing along Eightieth Street toward Fifth Avenue.

What was Crimson doing so close to Susan's build-ing? If, indeed, it was Crimson. Wilmot had come straight from LaGuardia to tell Susan about Conception's improved condition and to take her and the children out to dinner.

Wilmot sounded agitated as he asked Luigi to announce him to Ms. Given.

"She's not in," said the doorman.

"Do you know where she went?"

"You a friend of hers?"

"Yes. And a policeman."

"She went for a run. Just a quick one she said."

"God in heaven! Are the children at home?"

"Sure. Miss Given's niece is up there with them."

"Connect me with her, please."

A second later Brandy picked up the phone and listened intently as Desmond Wilmot instructed her to call Tuck and have him send a squad of police to meet him in Central Park near the jogging path.

"Is it Rice Krispies?" asked Brandy breathlessly.

"I don't know what you're talking about, young woman. But your aunt's life is in danger. Please, do as I say."

Brandy hung up the telephone, called the police department, and then phoned Channel 8 to give them the exclusive.

Fifteen minutes later Tuck found himself moving stealthily in a crouching position through the shrubbery north of Ninety-fifth Street and gesturing to the uniformed police who had accompanied him to fan out farther.

One of the cops groaned.

"What happened?" whispered Tuck.

"Fuckin' rock. I stubbed my—"

"Shh! Didja hear that?"

"What?"

"A scream. A woman's scream."

"I didn't hear anything."

It was a woman's scream. And this time it was ear piercing.

"Let's go!" said Tuck, drawing his gun and rising to his feet. Seconds later he and the police were moving swiftly through the park in the direction of the woman's screams.

They found her on her bloodied knees. Her satin jogging shorts were torn and her blond hair was obscuring her face.

"You okay?" asked Tuck, crouching down beside her. "Damn, Ms. Gee. What the hell were you doing out here at night? Good thing Captain Wilmot stopped by or—"

"Who's Captain Wilmot? Who are you?"

Tuck lifted her chin and realized this wasn't Susan. She was a girl barely out of her teens.

"Who are you?" asked Tuck.

"Christine Lord."

"What happened, Christine?"

"I was doing the circuit when this guy started jogging beside me. Really cute. Wanted to know if I was an actress. I told him I'd done a few commercials back in L.A. Just local, nothing national. Then he pushed me off the path. Next thing I knew he was on top of me, tearing off my shorts and unzipping his fanny pack. Then I remembered my pepper Mace. That's one of the commercials I did. See? You wear it around your neck like a whistle. I sprayed it right in his eyes and he stumbled away howling. Then I freaked out and started screaming."

"Hey, Tuck!" said one of the cops searching the bushes nearby. "Take a look at his."

The cop came over to Tuck holding something in his palm.

Tuck murmured something under his breath then showed the object to the girl. "You don't know how lucky you are, Christine."

"What is that?"

"A thimble."

"Oh, my God! That was him? The Rice Krispies guy? Oh, my God!" She began sobbing.

Tuck wrapped the thimble in his handkerchief, then rose to his feet once more.

"Is it really Rice Krispies?" asked one of the cops.

"Yeah. And he can't have gone far. Brody, you get Christine out of here and get a full statement. Then call headquarters and tell 'em to send us as much backup as they can. ASAP. The rest of you . . . fan out. We're lookin' for two men now. And Susan Given."

Five minutes earlier Susan Given found herself lying on the ground staring up at a grim-faced, drug-fueled Edward Claxton.

"You ain' been nothin' but trouble since me meet you. Why you make so much trouble for Crimson? Hmm?" And the drug lord kicked her fiercely in the side. "What me ever done to you?"

Susan rolled away to avoid another kick and scrambled to her feet.

"Why don't we just call it bad timing?" asked Susan, stalling for time while her eyes darted about looking for the best way to run for it.

"Where be Conception?"

"I don't know."

"You boyfriend Captain Wilmot, him know."

"He's not my boyfriend."

"You make me mad, woman."

"Believe me, it's not my intention. I think we got off on the wrong foot, Mr. Claxton. We needn't be enemies, you know."

"Where be Conception? Where you hidin' me woman?"

"I'm not hiding her anywhere."

Crimson pulled a gun out of his trousers and aimed it straight at Susan's head.

"No more talk, bitch. You gonna die now."

"Kill me, you'll never find Conception."

"Shut up!"

Some instinct told Susan that there would be no more talking. He was going to fire the gun at her. Point blank. And she would die. Unless . . . Her mind flashed back to Priam and Orestes and all those cockatrice lessons. She had nothing to lose and it was the last thing Crimson would be expecting.

She let loose a rooster crow as Ascension's sons had taught her and sent her right leg flying up in the air, connecting with Crimson's wrist. The move caught him by surprise and in that moment she spun around and kicked him in the face. He went stumbling backward and Susan went running like the wind through the park.

There was no rhyme or reason in her movement. Sheer panic was propelling her and the frustrated cries of rage from Crimson, who was somewhere behind her. Where was Fifth Avenue? Or Central

Park West? She had no idea where she was. All she could think of was distancing herself from the furious roars behind her.

Then she saw a man stumbling toward her.

"Help me! Help me!" she gasped.

But, she realized as he drew nearer, the man was in need of help himself as he groped about blindly. He was a young man and there was something familiar about him. What was it? Where did she know him from? Then she saw the three tiny hoop earrings in his right earlobe.

"Russ! Is it you?"

"Who's that?"

"Susan Given. Brandy's aunt. What's wrong, Russ?"

"Can you help me, Aunt Susan? I can't see very well."

Susan looked around desperately. How far behind was Crimson? How could she help this poor half-blind boy and still save herself?

"Please, help me, Susan."

"Russ, listen to me. We've got to get away from here before—"

She was now close enough to Russ for him to grab her by the arm, twist it behind her back, and hold a knife up to her throat.

"You're my ticket out of here, Aunt Susan. Nobody's going to do anything to me as long as I've got you. Right? Right?" He jerked Susan's arm further up her back.

"Let go of she!" roared Crimson, coming upon the scene.

"Who the hell is that?" asked Russ.

"Let me go, Russ. He's got a gun."

"Bullshit. Listen, pal, get outta my way or I'll slit her throat. I mean it."

"Her be my kill, boy. Let she be."

Haskell Abrams was in the midst of a heated argument with Lisa Mercado.

"I am ordering you and your crew to get the hell out of here, Ms. Mercado."

"I got every right to be here, Lieutenant. This is my exclusive."

"See those sawhorses? This is a crime scene. I am sealing it off. And you are on the wrong side of the barrier."

"Listen, my burro," said Lisa, lowering her voice to a whisper, "if you ever hope to sleep with me again, you'd better drop this—"

Lisa stopped talking when she heard the gunshot.

"What the hell was that?" asked Abrams, rushing over to where Tuck was standing.

"A gunshot."

"I know that, Maxwell. Whose gunshot, that's the big question."

Two more gunshots were heard, then the sound of someone rushing through the park.

"Get ready to fire, men," said Abrams grimly.

"Have them hold their fire, sir," suggested Tuck, "till we see who it is."

"Right, right. Hold your fire, men. Let's try and identify them first."

Seconds later Susan Given came into sight, running for her life with Crimson behind her firing his gun.

"Fire now!" ordered Abrams.

"Not yet!" shouted Tuck, who ran toward Susan and tackled her to the ground before the hail of bullets riddled Crimson's body.

60

LISA MERCADO'S TAPE was confiscated and Channel 8 went to court demanding the public's right to view the death of Edward Claxton and/or Haskell Abrams's attempt to have Susan Given assasinated (depending on whose version of the story one was listening to). As of this writing, the tape has never been broadcast.

The young man found dead in Central Park was identified as Russell Fairchild Jr. He was twenty-eight and had come to New York from Nebraska ten years earlier. He'd survived as a bouncer and bartender but, when asked, always told people he was an actor. (Although Fairchild never actually had an acting job, he'd auditioned for *Rent* no less than six times.)

Janie Moore was certain the Rice Krispies killing spree had finally come to an end until Christine Lord's parents arrived in New York from Pasadena. Things then became a little less certain. Ms. Lord, who narrowly avoided being Rice Krispies' final victim, was reluctant to view the body and, when she finally did ("Under coercion," said her fat-cat Republican father), she was unable to make a positive identification of Fairchild as the man who attacked her.

It was only when the police searched his squalid one-room apartment on Eleventh Avenue two days later that they discovered the severed fingers of Dierdre Holland, Natalie Margolis, and Mary Ellen Chernin frozen solid in the ice tray of his ancient refrigerator—each one with a brightly colored bit of ribbon tied around it. Neighbors described Fairchild as a pleasant enough solitary sort of fellow, who liked to jog. No one seemed to remember him ever having a steady girlfriend.

Ironically, Edward Claxton died a hero (despite his being brought down by a hail of police bullets in Central Park). Because he was never brought to trial and convicted for drug trafficking, Crimson would enter his island's mythology and inspire several ballads as a martyr, who traveled to distant New York and gave his life ridding the big city of an evil monster.

Susan Given's nightmares returned with a vengeance following her brush with death that night in Central Park. Now she had the formidable trio of Edward Claxton, Russell Fairchild, and Junior Tesla all trying to kill her. Phoning Imogen Blythe at two in the morning to make an appointment, she discovered the smoky-voiced psychiatrist had gone on vacation to, of all places, St. Stephen's.

The sleepless Susan managed to elude the media hordes (including her own niece Brandy) camped outside her building the next morning. Taking the service elevator on Madison, Susan slipped out onto the street undetected where her faithful brother Henry was waiting for her in his Range Rover.

Arriving at the courthouse she discovered her lawyer, Neil Stern, pacing up and down in the corridor muttering to himself.

"Are you okay?" asked Stern, as she walked toward him. "I saw the *Post* this morning. My God! That was a close call."

"What's wrong, Neil?"

"What do you mean?"

"I saw you pacing up and down."

"You know, you're lucky to be alive, Susan. This sort of thing is getting to be a habit with you. I'm amazed you even turned up this morning. If it was me—"

"What's wrong, Neil? You are avoiding something."

"Vance Holland fired Taylor Parkhurst yesterday. Which meant the end of Hugh's career in broadcasting. Taylor apparently ran back to her old job and old boyfriend in Boston. So Doctor Carver is brooding and Ralph Kregar got him another adjournment to ease his pain."

"What!?"

"There'll be no divorce today, Susan."

"Where is Edward Claxton when I *really* need him?" muttered the blond prosecutor. "Hugh did this on purpose, didn't he? After all I've been through—not just last night—I deserve this divorce."

"God knows."

"I begin to wonder if He does. Or maybe I'm a victim of my own hubris. Or maybe God's a patient of Hugh's, too."

Susan Given (and still) Carver heaved a deep sigh,

picked up her red leather briefcase, and started to walk away. "Call me when we get a new date."

"Where are you going?" asked Stern.

"In the best of all possible worlds, I'd go home to sleep. Or take Captain Wilmot up on his offer and return to St. Stephen's. Maybe I will someday and take the girls with with me. But right now, I'm going back to Centre Street. I don't know if I've mentioned this to you before, Neil, but crime never sleeps."

About the Authors

MARGARET BARRETT is an attorney and writer who lives in New York City.

CHARLES DENNIS is a writer and actor. His play *Going On* has been produced in New York, London, and Los Angeles; his novel *The Next-to-Last Train Ride* was filmed as *Finders Keepers*. He appeared as Sunad from Zalkon on *Star Trek: The Next Generation*®.

ANNA SALTER

"Dr. Michael Stone is sure to take her place
beside the major characters in crime fiction."
—Andrew Vachss

SHINY WATER

"A jolting debut."
—*The New York Times Book Review*

FAULT LINES

"An absorbing thriller."
—Amazon.com

Available from Pocket Books

POCKET
BOOKS

2065

Author of the *New York Times*
bestsellers *Harvest* and *Life Support*

TESS GERRITSEN

BLOODSTREAM

A NOVEL OF MEDICAL SUSPENSE

Woven with the kind of action and detail
only a doctor could deliver, and propelled by
an expert sense of small-town terror,
Bloodstream is Tess Gerritsen's most unforget-
able thriller yet.

**Now available in hardcover
from Pocket Books**

POCKET BOOKS

2040

False Accusations

ALAN JACOBSON

Alan Jacobson has created the year's most
gripping page-turner, a suspense masterpiece
powered by stunning twists. With intensely real
characters and details drawn from Jacobson's
first-hand medical and legal expertise, *False
Accusations* is a tale of deadly revenge—where
the assurance of "innocent until proven guilty" is
not what it seems.

**Now available in Hardcover
from Pocket Books**

POCKET
BOOKS

2064